WILD FIRE

THE FIRE SERIES

D1075768

ALSO BY ANNE STUART

ROMANTIC SUSPENSE

ROMANCE

One More Valentine
Rafe's Revenge
Heat Lightning
Chasing Trouble
Night of the Phantom
Lazarus Rising
Angel's Wings
Rancho Diablo
Crazy Like a Fox
Glass Houses
Cry for the Moon
Partners in Crime
Blue Sage
Bewitching Hour
Rocky Road
Made in America #19
Banish Misfortune
Housebound

Museum Piece
Heart's Ease
Chain of Love
The Fall of Maggie Brown
Winter's Edge
Catspaw II
Hand in Glove
Catspaw
Tangled Lies
Now You See Him
Special Gifts
Break the Night
Against the Wind

NOVELLAS

Married to It (prequel to
Fire and Ice)
Risk the Night

HISTORICALS

SCANDAL AT THE HOUSE
OF RUSSELL

Never Kiss a Rake
Never Trust a Pirate
Never Marry a Viscount

THE HOUSE OF ROHAN

The Wicked House of Rohan
Shameless
Breathless
Reckless
Ruthless

STAND-ALONE TITLES

The Devil's Waltz
Hidden Honor
Lady Fortune
Prince of Magic
Lord of Danger
Prince of Swords
To Love a Dark Lord
Shadow Dance
A Rose at Midnight
The Houseparty
The Spinster and the Rake
Lord Satan's Bride

WILD FIRE

THE FIRE SERIES

ANNE STUART

 Montlake
Romance

This is a work of fiction. Names, characters, organizations, places, events, and incidents are either products of the author's imagination or are used fictitiously.

Text copyright © 2017 Anne Kristine Stuart Ohlrogge
All rights reserved.

No part of this book may be reproduced, or stored in a retrieval system, or transmitted in any form or by any means, electronic, mechanical, photocopying, recording, or otherwise, without express written permission of the publisher.

Published by Montlake Romance, Seattle

www.apub.com

Amazon, the Amazon logo, and Montlake Romance are trademarks of Amazon.com, Inc., or its affiliates.

ISBN-13: 9781503941724
ISBN-10: 1503941728

Cover design by Jason Blackburn

Printed in the United States of America

For Jo Beverley—you'd argue that my hero wasn't heroic enough, and I'd argue back, and we would have had a great time. I miss you. Have fun with all the noble heroes in heaven.

Chapter One

Sophie Jordan lay utterly still in the inky darkness, the cool tile floor beneath her sweating body, as she checked her heart rate. Steady and solid after she'd done two dozen reps in perfect silence. She'd been working herself up slowly over the months—as soon as she started breathing heavily she had to stop. There were no cameras or microphones in her huge bathroom, but she wasn't sure how sensitive the bugging devices in her bedroom were. For all she knew, they could pick up the sound of her increased respiration.

It was good practice anyway. When you were a prisoner in an armed fortress, silence was your friend. Sophie sat up quickly, fluidly, then rose to her feet once more, going through the training moves she remembered from what seemed like so long ago. She could feel the strength flowing through her, the pleasant pull of her muscles, the ease of her body. She would have given ten years off her life to be able to run outside, beneath the sun or the stars, breathing in fresh air. Instead, she ran in place, her bare feet silent, energy pumping through her body, the walls of the bathroom cool around her in the night air. She was sweating, but she never dared to take a shower afterward—it would raise too many questions. She finished up her workout, going through her cool-down stretches, shoved her sweat-damp hair away from her face, and silently opened the door to her bedroom.

She kept it inky black, no trace of moonlight filtering in. She had no guarantee that Archer's cameras weren't temperature sensitive—he could very well be watching the heat signature of her body as she moved back to the big bed. It would be just like her psychotic husband to let her think she was fooling him, fooling everyone, when he knew her secrets all along. After all, he'd done it once before.

She couldn't let that fear stop her. She had no choice but to put her head down and plow ahead, building strength, biding her time. If it was all another trap, then so be it. He might be able to see her outline, but there was no way he could know how strong she was. Even she wasn't sure if she was back to her full strength yet—she could only keep training and hope for the best.

Sooner or later, Archer would tire of his cat-and-mouse game. He'd either kill her or let her go, though she wouldn't place any money on the latter. Archer liked power too much, and he took pleasure in other people's pain.

She'd done her best to give him his money's worth.

The sheets were cool as she slid beneath them, and she shivered slightly in the air-conditioning. It kept the room a little too cold, but she had no choice—she couldn't have any windows open if she wanted to keep what little privacy she could get away with, and she'd suffocate without the air.

Her only bit of luck was Archer's general squeamishness when it came to bathroom matters. Not only did he not want to see her on the toilet—he didn't want anyone else to either. So at least the bathroom was sacrosanct, and she could move around there all she wanted.

She lay back in the bed, closing her eyes, listening to her heartbeat slowly return to a resting rate. *Two more weeks at the most*, Sophie thought. Two more weeks and she'd be ready to go. For now she had no choice but to continue her charade.

She'd trained herself to fall asleep instantly, and the next thing she knew someone was drawing aside the curtains, letting the bright, tropical sunshine flood the room. She opened her eyes, watching as the woman moved to the bedside.

"Did you sleep well, Mrs. MacDonald?" Rachel asked, the woman's classically beautiful face set in unemotional lines as she flipped back the covers to expose Sophie's motionless legs. Archer liked to surround himself with feminine beauty, and even her de facto nurse could have had a modeling contract. Rachel was close to six feet tall, with endless legs and the best boobs man could buy. Archer had always had a weakness for Barbies.

"The pain kept me awake for a while," Sophie said in the soft, faintly plaintive voice she'd perfected.

"Did you take your pills?"

"Of course." The stash of Vicodin was hidden in a hollowed-out section of her mattress. She had learned from her early training to hold on to whatever might make a weapon, and besides that, drugs were always an easy currency.

"I'll talk to Dr. Corbin—perhaps we might switch you to Percocet if you aren't getting relief." Rachel slid her arms beneath Sophie's limp body and pulled her into a sitting position, managing to twist her back painfully. Rachel was very strong, and she topped Sophie's height by a good three inches. Sophie had no idea who would win in a fight— Rachel was bigger, but Sophie had the advantage of having been trained. Like Archer, Rachel enjoyed hurting her a little too much when given the chance, and the long-absent Dr. Corbin gave Rachel more than enough opportunity.

At least Sophie didn't have to worry about the old mob doctor showing up and calling her out. No one cared if she lived or died, and Corbin wasn't going to fly to Isla Mordita again to see a patient who didn't matter, whose condition he'd decreed was permanent. Rachel had some sort of medical training—enough to be able to give clumsy injections and painful massages that left Sophie a mass of bruises—but she didn't know enough to recognize muscle power, particularly since Sophie managed to cover her legs as best she could.

She couldn't wear long sleeves in such a hot climate, but the muscles in her arms were easily explained away as the result of using a wheelchair, and Archer seemed to accept them as the natural outcome of her condition. Maybe.

There was also a pair of pathetic, bright-pink one-pound weights she'd been allowed, but Sophie ignored them in favor of the heavy tomes provided for her library. The muscles she'd developed were a little too impressive if someone looked closely, but fortunately nobody did.

"It's a beautiful day, Mrs. MacDonald. Will you be wearing the usual?"

The "usual" was a long, loose-fitting sundress, something that required little effort to put on and covered up any number of secrets. "That would be fine. Just leave everything in the bathroom and I'll manage myself."

Rachel let out an annoyed huff. "I don't know why you refuse to let me help you dress. That's what I'm here for—to make your life easier."

Sure you are. Sophie kept a sweet, frail expression plastered to her face. *You're a jailor and a spy, nothing more.* "And you're doing a wonderful job. But I've told you—I'm not comfortable with nudity, especially since the . . . accident, and dressing myself is good for me."

"And I suppose you don't want help with the shower either? What if you slipped?"

"I haven't yet."

With silent disapproval Rachel pulled a deep turquoise sundress out of her closet, along with the expensive underwear Archer had bought for her. There were matching sandals for every dress—the room-sized closet off the bedroom was color-coordinated and packed full. Rachel dumped the clothing in the bathroom, then came back to the bed, sliding her strong arms around Sophie's limp body and pulling her onto the wheelchair, slamming her against its metal arms as she did so. Sophie didn't flinch, smiling gratefully as Rachel placed her immobile legs on the footrest. After all these months she still wasn't sure what would incite Rachel to hurt her. She might like the sound of Sophie's pain, want more of it. Or she might simply want to break her.

Either way, Sophie wasn't going to give in to Rachel's physical taunts. It was one thing to complain about the pain of her nonexistent condition, another to let Rachel win. Besides, Rachel thought she held all the cards and that poor little Sophie was at her mercy. With any luck Sophie would have a chance to show her otherwise before she escaped.

Sophie began rolling toward the huge, specially equipped bathroom and Rachel spoke up. "Your husband is expecting a business acquaintance tonight," she said. "He said to tell you he hopes you'll feel well enough to join him for dinner."

That was something new. The only time she saw her husband was when he made one of his rare visits, and he spent all his time on the first floor of the partially remodeled plantation house. Those expensive changes hadn't included an elevator, and presumably Sophie was trapped on the second floor, with only the wide, sweeping staircase between her and any kind of freedom. One of the other bedrooms had been finished, and there used to be the constant sound of hammering, the smell of freshly sawed wood filling the air. That noise had stopped recently, but Sophie had no illusions that the remodeling project was finished. The terrace outside her locked French doors was still littered with construction debris, and the last time she'd been taken down to the pool, the cabana had been in the midst of being torn down. There hadn't been time to fix it.

At least Archer's grand master suite, the one she'd once shared with him, was on the first floor. She could only hope that at times he forgot about her completely—it would give her an advantage when she was finally ready to make her move. She knew it was a foolish hope on her part—Archer never forgot an injury, never forgot anything, and he had a particular fondness for brutal, complicated revenge.

"Who's coming?" she asked.

Rachel shrugged. "You know Archer doesn't volunteer information. Should I tell him you don't feel up to it?"

Sophie was tempted. The less she saw of Archer, the greater advantage she would have. But Archer didn't do anything without a good reason, and this mysterious stranger must be someone important if he wanted to show off his handicapped wife. "I can do it," she said in a wan voice. "I wouldn't want to let him down."

It wasn't the answer Rachel wanted, but she had no excuse to put her hands on her, and retribution would have to come later. "I'll tell him you said yes, then," she said. She let her cold eyes run over Sophie's body in the wheelchair. "If you won't let me help you, then I'll go order your breakfast. Unless there's something else?"

Sophie smiled sweetly, a look that always seemed to leave Rachel unmoved. "I'll be fine. You do so much for me anyway."

"It's my job."

Sophie didn't even blink. Rachel's job was to spy on her and probably fuck her husband. "And you do it so well."

Rachel cast her a suspicious glance, but Sophie's face was absolutely innocent. She'd been working on her expression in the mirror of the bathroom, where no cameras could catch her, and she knew she was damned good. All that training had stayed with her, and she'd always been a terrific liar.

"Archer wants you downstairs by six for drinks. I'll come up earlier and help you dress . . ."

"I'll be dressed."

Rachel let out a little noise of irritation. "And I'll bring Joe to carry you."

"Poor Joe," Sophie said softly. In fact, Joe was one of the few men on Isla Mordita she trusted. He was huge, bald, immensely strong, and genuinely sweet. She'd once seen him kill a man by breaking his neck with his knees, and she knew he was responsible for many more of Archer's murders. But Joe was always careful and considerate with her, and he disapproved of the way Archer kept her shut away. He wouldn't actually be an ally when she got out of there, but she hoped he wouldn't get in her way. She wouldn't want to kill him. "Tell Archer I'm looking forward to it."

She didn't miss Rachel's expression. Rachel believed Sophie was desperately in love with Archer MacDonald, longing for any sign of attention, and jealous of Rachel's obvious closeness to him. Sophie had done everything she could to foster that impression.

In fact, last she'd figured out, Archer was sleeping with three different women on his small, private island off the coast of Florida. As far she could tell, though, Rachel reserved her jealousy for Sophie, which was interesting. She must think Sophie was a greater threat than she actually was.

Sophie could have told her the only reason Archer kept her around was to play cat-and-mouse games with her. That, and simple revenge. When he tired of it, he was going to kill her, or send someone to do it. She expected it would be the latter—Archer never wanted to get his hands dirty, and while he took pleasure in his small cruelties, so far he hadn't cared enough about her to bother himself with her execution. Archer was too fastidious, and blood was so messy. She was just an afterthought, one he'd deal with sooner or later, if she didn't get out first.

But that didn't explain why he'd want her downstairs to entertain his mysterious guest. And there was no question that the guest would be mysterious—very few people were allowed on the island—and when they came, she seldom saw them. Archer kept his business dealings away from here, in Miami, in New York, in New Orleans. This was his fortress, his safe house, and he'd managed to keep it a better secret than most nowadays, when information was only a click away, on the darknet, if not through the usual channels.

Isla Mordita had once been the property of a Cuban plantation owner, and the ruins of the old sugar mill stood on one end of the island. She and Archer had sex inside the mill when she'd been stupidly, blindly in love with him. She was past berating herself for her gullible idiocy. That had filled the first year after the so-called accident, when she was confined to the bed, unable to move. By the second year, when she started to get some feeling back in her legs, she'd moved past that, into a plan for escape.

So why the hell was she supposed to make an appearance this evening? Archer liked to pretend theirs was a normal marriage, that he was a doting, devoted husband immensely proud of his courageous, beautiful wife. And she'd make herself pretty—she had learned long ago how to transform her ordinary features into the illusion of beauty, how to move, how to convince anyone that she was exquisite. She could do the opposite just as easily, and for a moment she was tempted. How would Archer respond to an aging troll who presented herself as his wife?

He wouldn't like it, and she was smart enough not to pull the lion's tail, not when escape was so close. He could make her life very unpleasant if she displeased him. He'd hurt her before, and she still bore the scars. She imagined he probably did research on his ever-present tablet, looking for the most painful treatments for someone with a devastating spinal injury, and a thorough businessman like Archer MacDonald was very good at research.

In the meantime, she was going to take a shower in her unobserved bathroom, and she was going to use all the customized adjustments as if she needed them. There was no lock on the door, and Rachel had burst in on her a number of times, running her cool, dismissive eyes over Sophie's body and smirking.

Sophie wasn't built like Rachel and the women Archer usually slept with. Even at her thinnest, her most fit, she'd still had real boobs and hips. She was simply shaped that way, and the first year, when she lay in bed and could do nothing but eat and watch old movies on TV, she'd gained a good twenty pounds.

Some of that weight was still on her, she suspected, but now it was muscle. Rachel might make the mistake in thinking her curves denoted weakness, but Sophie knew better.

She took her time in the shower. It was going to be a long day, longer now that she knew someone was waiting for her. Hell, it might be her executioner—it wouldn't be past Archer to import someone from the mainland just to finish her off in style. Joe would do it if Archer gave him the order, but he wouldn't like it, and Archer liked to keep his employees happy.

She didn't think that was it. She knew Archer better than he realized, and even though she didn't see much of him, she could read his moods. He wasn't ready to close that chapter of his life. He was having too much fun keeping her a prisoner, by both the isolation and the supposed weakness of her body.

She had managed to fool him when they'd met, and he held a grudge—Archer believed in retribution, not forgiveness. She still had a little time left, though there was no way to be certain how much. This was all going to come to a head before long. If Archer started bringing her downstairs more often, she could firm up her plans. Being a prisoner on an island, even one relatively close to the coast, made escape difficult, and she was no Diana Nyad to swim that distance. There was always the chance she could make it, but she was going to exhaust every other possibility before taking that rash step.

There had to be someone to bribe, some escape route that Archer hadn't blocked.

In the meantime, she would spend the day as she always did, seemingly serene and content to the ever-present cameras, sitting in her wheelchair, reading. No one could tell she was doing isometric exercises as she made her way through dense Russian novels, another form of Archer's torment. When the time came, she would be ready. Would it be tonight?

Chapter Two

He sat in the bow of the boat as it sliced through the open water, feeling the salt spray on his face. The night was calm, the cabin on the boat was warm and stocked with a bar, but he stayed where he was, perfectly still, staring out into the night sky.

It was late autumn, and even in the Gulf of Mexico the nights were cool, the sun setting early. In the gathering darkness Malcolm Gunnison wasn't worried he'd reach Isla Mordita on time. Archer MacDonald's men would be responsible, and he didn't think they were likely to take any chances with their mercurial boss.

He laughed to himself without real humor. *Mercurial* was a good word. *Sociopath*, *psychopath*, *monster* were just as fitting. Archer MacDonald, Princeton graduate, son of old money, had aristocratic good looks and charm that dazzled enough people that he'd managed to build an impressive power base. The man was brilliant, with ceaseless energy and ambition, from his starting point as a dot-com millionaire through his interest in highly illegal arms deals and drug exports, up to and including the creation of a mysterious new biological weapon, and he was a force to be reckoned with. It was no wonder he'd retreated to his private island where he could control his empire without interference.

Not that Malcolm cared. He worked for the Committee, a covert, international organization that paid no attention to legal or moral implications in its quest to make the world a safer place. He'd spent the past two years in England, but now he was working out of the new American branch in New Orleans, disingenuously titled the American Committee for the Preservation of Democracy, and facing a whole new world of problems.

The Committee wasn't an entity that ignored flagrant danger, nor were the powers that be troubled by due process. Mal's job was to charm Archer MacDonald right back, find out who his sources were for the biological weapon he was planning to distribute, and then kill the man.

Escaping the island with his life after the deed was done was a given, of course. Whether he chose to save Archer's wife was entirely up to him.

He had no plans to have anything to do with her. He knew he might have to kill her if she got in his way. Intel about what actually went on at Isla Mordita was sketchy, but word was that things were not going well between Archer and his wife. From his research Mal knew that Sophie Jordan MacDonald was a smart woman—even if she'd been blinded by Archer in the first place she'd probably seen through him by now, almost three years after their hasty marriage. There was always the possibility she could be an ally to Mal, but he wasn't going to count on that. She'd made a massive error in judgment by marrying Archer, believing in the charming front he presented to the world. If she had been too stupid to see through that front, then she was unlikely to provide much help. And she'd screwed the pooch three years ago, so no one really gave a damn about her.

Including him. He could probably avoid killing her, and once Archer MacDonald was dead and the source of the weapon neutralized, the danger would be past. He'd make his getaway before any of MacDonald's thugs could stop him, and the wife could figure her own way off the island, if she survived.

He'd never known Sophie Jordan back when she'd first started working for the Committee—he'd been stationed in Africa—but he'd seen pictures of her, ordinary ones from her childhood in Virginia, photos after she'd gone through her training with the Committee. She'd been striking—even in the black-and-white photo he could see that her dark eyes were mesmerizing. They should have known better than to send a new trainee to Archer MacDonald, but back then his boss had his own agenda as far as the Committee was concerned.

Mal preferred the new American branch. He'd spent the past four weeks at the old house in the Garden District in New Orleans, absorbing intel, training, letting his hair grow too long as he slowly became another person, and he wondered how Sophie Jordan had transitioned. After her time in the State Department and later under the shady auspices of the Committee in London, she could have been so used to acting a part that she might not have even known who she really was underneath. That was always a danger in this business.

He was prepared for anything. He hadn't gotten to where he was, survived as long as he had, without being able to handle the unexpected. The fact that he was tired, burned out, and edgy would make no difference, not in this operation. He'd deal with all that when he got back to New Orleans—assuming he did.

He'd be a fool not to realize that any job might kill him. Hell, a taxicab coming around a corner might mow him down—there were no guarantees in life and particularly not in his. All he could do was look straight ahead to the job he was doing and ignore the rest. The past was done—nothing he could do to change it. Maybe the future would be better. Maybe not.

He thought back to Sophie Jordan. She might have thought she was getting out of the game when she fell in love with Archer MacDonald and married him. So she wasn't entirely to blame for her stupidity. So many years ago she'd been sent with a small team for initial surveillance, her very first mission, and her job had been to watch and learn. Instead, she'd caught the eye of their target, and Archer's sudden interest had been too good of a chance to let slip by. She'd been given the job to kill him, and instead she'd turned her back on the Committee and the world, believing him to be innocent. Malcolm doubted she was still as naïve, although how someone could have been that gullible in the first place, after all her training, eluded him. Only what passed for true love could cause someone to make such a fatal mistake. It was a damned good thing he knew true love was a myth.

He leaned forward in the boat, staring into the darkness. He hadn't been given a particular timeline for this job—it depended more on outside influences and how completely MacDonald believed him. Like how long it took him to discover where MacDonald was sourcing the potentially devastating new biological weapon that the Committee had picked up on its radar, and when he could neutralize that source. It was interesting that it had taken his supposed former involvement with the Committee to make Archer drop his guard enough to invite Mal to his island fortress. Most people didn't even know the Committee existed, even those with the power and resources that Archer had. But then, it would never do to underestimate MacDonald. If he knew about the Committee, did that mean he knew about his wife having been sent to kill him? Most likely—three years was too long to live a lie, even the best of them. For all he knew, Sophie Jordan might be long gone. He didn't think so.

Archer didn't do anything without a reason, and Mal was ready to move at the first hint of something off. He only hoped the mission wouldn't take too long. Playing a part was something he did automatically, but he didn't like it.

I'm a machine, he told himself wryly, staring out into the darkening sky. He could see the distant outlines of the island up ahead, and he straightened, narrowing his eyes. For however long it took, he could be a machine—humanity was waiting for him back in New Orleans when he finished the job.

He just wasn't sure he was looking forward to it.

Joe carried Sophie as carefully as he always did. She was wearing a long dress, one that covered her legs, and sandals on her feet. One of Archer's servants had even appeared earlier and given her a pedicure, so that her toenails were a bright copper that matched the color of the dress. It had been hard as hell to remain limp and unmoving as Elena had manipulated her feet, but Sophie had practice from the hours of massage and rehabilitation she'd been put through, and she'd been motionless, listening to Elena's chatter.

She was sitting in her wheelchair now, in the huge living room of the old colonial mansion, one of the rooms that Archer had almost finished. The ceilings were twenty feet high, fans spinning lazily overhead, the walls painted a creamy coral, the furniture large and overstuffed. Not that she would know—she stayed in the wheelchair on the few occasions she'd been allowed down there. There was a new painting on top of the unnecessary fireplace—it looked like a French master and she had little doubt it was real. Archer liked the finer things in life, and he didn't stint himself.

"Darling!" her husband said, coming in one of the far doors, and she slapped a smile on her face, putting just the right amount of longing in her eyes. She would never give up trying to fool him, and she knew there was always just a drop of uncertainty in his hatred for her, the possibility that he might be wrong about her treachery.

But Archer MacDonald was not a man who spent much time considering his own fallibility. He came over and embraced Sophie's sitting body with careful enthusiasm, kissing her freshly painted mouth. "You look magnificent!"

"So do you, Archer," she said, trying to sound shy. It was nothing but the truth. Archer MacDonald was gorgeous. He'd been on *People* magazine's list of sexiest men several times, as sexiest dot-com millionaire and then sexiest entrepreneur. Sophie had laughed at that term when she'd been doing her research before she'd met the man, thinking it was a naïve euphemism. And then she'd met him and drunk the Kool-Aid and everything had gone bad.

"I won't have you sitting in that fucking thing," he said, swooping her into his arms and carrying her to the sofa. "We don't need to be reminded that you're a cripple."

She looked at him with composure. He always used the words to wound, but she was made of Teflon nowadays. Nothing could stick to her. "Thank you, Archer," she murmured.

He grinned at her. "Always happy to oblige," he said, the smile never reaching his eyes. "Joe, make me a scotch on the rocks and a gin and tonic for my wife."

"Yes, sir." The big man moved to the bar that was set up discreetly in one corner.

To Sophie's quickly masked horror Archer dropped down beside her, draping an arm on the sofa behind her back, casually domestic. "Any sign of our guest?"

"Boat's just docked," Joe said. "I can keep Miss Sophie company if you want to go greet him."

Wrong thing to say, Joe, she thought. While Joe's loyalties were firmly with Archer and always would be, he was fond of her. And Archer wouldn't like that.

"I think I know what I'm doing, Joe," Archer said affably, his grin still in place. This time it even reached his eyes, Sophie thought with distant admiration. It was no wonder she'd been fooled.

Archer moved a little closer to her, and she could smell his expensive cologne, feel his body heat, and the memory of sex came rushing back. She'd been celibate for more than two years now, and with Archer her only possibility, she intended to remain so. The thought of him touching her made her sick.

Every now and then some new, good-looking man would show up on the island on some sort of business, and Archer would make certain Sophie got to meet him. She knew their practiced attempts at flirtation were on her husband's orders, but too bad for Archer. She had no idea why he played that particular game—when he'd been in love with her he'd been uncomfortably possessive. Maybe he simply wanted to watch as someone else fucked her limp body—he was perverse enough. Maybe he wanted to watch as they blew her brains out.

But all those handsome men left her cold. She'd learned her lesson: never again would she trust in some man, particularly in the high-stakes world she'd chosen for herself.

Archer was watching her with seemingly tender amusement. No, the amusement was real, but the tenderness was not. She knew Archer had discovered what had first brought her into his orbit, though he'd never admitted it, never questioned her directly. He'd simply ordered one of his men to shoot her.

She'd managed to survive, and instead of ordering a second attempt, Archer played the brokenhearted husband. For the first six or seven months she'd expected him to finish the job, but she'd been in too much pain to care. After that, once she started getting feeling back in her legs, she began to work on a way to stop him and his destructive plans.

He was her husband, and at first she'd had enthusiastic sex with him, thought she was in love with him—until she'd slowly begun to realize what a colossal idiot she'd been. In the beginning she'd berated herself, hated herself. Not any longer. She was going to finish her mission.

She wasn't troubled by any qualms now. She'd shoot him and happily watch him die. She still hadn't decided whether she'd make him suffer or not. She supposed it depended on the situation. If time was short, she'd shoot him in the head and have done with it. If she was alone with no imminent threat, then she might take her time, not just for her own sake but for the sake of all the people he'd destroyed over the years.

Joe handed them their glasses, and she raised hers, clinking against her husband's shorter one. "Cheers."

"Here's to good health," Archer responded, moving closer, the smell of the scotch outweighing the smell of his cologne. "And a long life."

She noticed he didn't say whom he wanted to have good health and a long life. She smiled sweetly. "Amen," she murmured.

"Mr. Gunnison," Elena announced from the doorway, and Sophie turned her head at the same time Archer did, prepared to see another pretty boy offered up for her frustration. Suddenly, unbidden, came words from her favorite poet, Dorothy Parker. "What fresh hell is this?"

Chapter Three

He was a dangerous man. Sophie recognized it immediately, from his cool green eyes to the way he carried himself. He was tall, lean, with too-long dark hair brushing his shoulders, a narrow, clever face, and the sexiest mouth she'd ever seen. He wasn't perfect—he had an imposing nose along with his high cheekbones, but overall he was mesmerizing, a far cry from the male catnip Archer usually dangled in front of her. She looked the stranger over, the black suit so well tailored that there was no way it could hide the bulge of a pistol, so he must be unarmed. That should have set her mind at ease, just a little bit, but her inner alarm kept blaring. Here was a man who was so dangerous he didn't need a gun. Archer surrounded himself with lethal men, but this one was on a whole new level.

Archer rose, setting his drink on the table beside his laptop, and moved forward, offering his hand in greeting. "Malcolm Gunnison! I never thought this day would come!"

Sophie saw the tiniest hesitation before the man put his hand in Archer's—not long enough for Archer to feel insulted, but just long enough to make it clear he wasn't Archer's patsy. Interesting, she thought, her wariness amping up.

"MacDonald," he said in greeting, and another shiver ripped down her body. He had a faint British accent, an upper-class one, something she recognized from her training in London. For a moment it brought that time back, and she felt a stab of pain over everything she'd thrown away.

"Call me Archer," her husband said jovially. "Joe, get a drink for our guest. He prefers his single-malt scotch straight up, no ice, no chaser."

There was a glint in Gunnison's green eyes. "You've done your homework, I see."

"I have people who take care of that, and they don't make mistakes," Archer said. "It's rare that I even let anyone on the island. This is my sanctuary, my sacred space, and I hate to let business intrude. You're a special case, Malcolm."

There was no missing the guest's sardonic expression. "I'm honored."

Archer was in a good mood and not easily offended. "You should be. Let me introduce you to my wife. Sophie, this is Malcolm Gunnison, from England in case you can't tell. He's here as a consultant."

Consultant, Sophie thought derisively. *That's what he calls all of them.* She smiled obediently as she raised her hand, but to her shock he took it and brought it to his mouth, brushing his lips against the back. She yanked it away before she could stop herself, then managed a shaky laugh.

Archer had a smug expression on his face. "Old-fashioned, are you, Malcolm? You know here in the colonies we don't go around kissing hands anymore. In fact, I'm not very fond of anyone kissing my wife."

"I can see why," Mal said, his eyes still on her for a moment, and for the third time a shiver ran down her spine. Then he turned his attention to Archer. "As for the colonies, we lost them long ago. However, I wasn't aware that this island is part of the United States. I'm afraid that might cause some legal problems for me . . ."

"It's not," Archer said. "It's mine."

"Some government must lay claim to it. You can't have your own kingdom anymore."

"You underestimate me," Archer said pleasantly. "I can do anything I please. It's all about exploiting weaknesses. As for governments laying claim, the problem and the blessing is that too many governments think it belongs to them, in particular Cuba and the United States. No one wants to make things difficult just as international relations between the two countries are getting back to normal, so they leave me completely alone, and Mexico has enough problems on its own without bothering about one tiny island." He smiled at his guest, charming as always. "So you see, it works out very well."

Malcolm nodded, accepting the drink Joe brought him. Sophie thought she could feel his eyes on her, but when she looked at him she found all his attention on Archer. "Are we going to talk business?" he said.

"There's no hurry. Have a seat. No one takes their time anymore," Archer lamented. "Let's be civilized. My cook has outdone herself tonight, the air is cool, and we have the company of a beautiful woman. We'll have plenty of time for business."

Malcolm nodded again, and this time his eyes didn't brush hers. "I hadn't realized you were married," he said slowly.

"I try to keep my personal life private," Archer said, dropping back down beside her. His weight on the feather cushion made her tilt toward him, but she wasn't about to put her hands on him to stop herself. He caught her arms with casual possessiveness. "Darling, are you all right?"

Sophie withheld her instinctive growl. So Archer wanted an ornamental idiot for a wife. Why had he brought her downstairs to play this charade in front of the newcomer? Gunnison wasn't his usual man bait.

But she knew the answer was breathtakingly simple and nothing new: Archer liked games.

"I'm fine," she said, gazing up at him adoringly. If he wanted a bimbo, she could play one.

Archer slid his arm around her, and she hoped to God he couldn't feel her skin crawl at his nearness. He nuzzled her neck, and his teeth grazed her carotid artery, an act that years ago had driven her mad with excitement when they'd fucked.

Now she wanted to throw up. She held very still, and then, unbidden, her eyes met Malcolm's.

He was watching the two of them with an enigmatic expression on his face, and all her Spidey senses went into overdrive. Not from the psychopath nuzzling her neck, but from the elegant stranger. She knew she should turn into Archer's embrace, but there were limits to her own endurance, so determined to be stoic, she let him kiss her neck and tried to turn her gaze away from the stranger.

She couldn't. She was caught by his face, mesmerized, though she couldn't begin to read his thoughts. She had been so good at that in the past, recognizing tells, intuiting people's thoughts beneath their surface demeanor. For a moment she wondered whether she'd lost that ability during her years of captivity or if this man was particularly opaque. But since she was having no trouble with other people, she decided this man had defenses so powerful even she couldn't get through them. That meant his training was better than hers.

No wonder she felt the danger. She stopped trying to look away, meeting his gaze steadily as Archer slobbered on her neck. She shivered, which Archer took for encouragement and sexual excitement, and his hand reached down the low front of her dress for her breast, squeezing painfully.

Malcolm's eyes dropped to that hand, and Sophie pulled back, the strange tie broken. She caught Archer's delving hand with hers, pulling at it with gentle pressure. "Archer, we have company," she said plaintively.

He leaned back, and she saw he had a noticeable erection beneath his expensive trousers, and the nausea came back again. She'd assumed he'd never touch her again, at least not sexually, preferring more nubile partners for his particular brand of kink. If he came to her room later she wasn't sure what she would do.

Archer grinned, his long teeth flashing. "Oh, I think Malcolm recognizes how irresistible you are."

Malcolm said nothing, and Sophie's eyes met his for a moment. There was nothing there. "I wouldn't want to intrude," he said in that polite British voice.

To Sophie's relief Archer pushed off the overstuffed sofa, stretching. He had bulked up, she noticed, with wider shoulders and arms. He looked a little top heavy, but still traditionally gorgeous, far more so than Malcolm Gunnison. So what was it about him that made her want to stare at the newcomer?

"Oh, we're a long-married couple, aren't we, baby?" Archer said with his winning smile. "Plenty of time for that. I think dinner should be ready." He glanced down at her. "Sophie, are you joining us?"

What the hell game was he playing? She was sitting on the sofa, her wheelchair out of sight. Did he expect her to flop on the floor and crawl into the vast dining room? Or was Archer expecting her to decline the invitation? But why?

Who knew why Archer did anything? She smiled up at him. "I'm famished," she said.

A brief expression danced across his guileless blue eyes, and she wondered if he didn't want Gunnison to know she was crippled. Too bad for Archer's plans, though she would probably pay for it later.

"Joe," Archer called, not hesitating, and a moment later Joe appeared, pushing the wheelchair.

Gunnison's expression didn't change—he was that good. Any normal human being would have reacted, which told Sophie that their newcomer was far from an average human being, and despite her misgivings she felt a grudging admiration for him. But then, what use would Archer have for someone with normal reactions, like empathy?

Archer put his arm around Gunnison's shoulder in a friendly gesture. "I think you'll like what I've planned. Once we finish dinner Sophie will go to bed—she tires easily, as you can imagine."

Joe scooped her up carefully and set her in the chair, and she redistributed her long skirts over her legs before pulling up the neckline that

Archer had been pawing at. Her husband watched Gunnison carefully. At least that answered one question: He'd wanted to see Gunnison's reaction to her condition. His lack thereof had established him as someone cold-blooded enough to work with.

Which didn't mean that Archer was happy with her, but that was no particular problem. She'd learned to disassociate from pain in the first year, when relief was doled out sparingly as part of Archer's torment. She could take anything he could do to her.

She rolled herself into the dining room. Archer and Malcolm were already seated, talking in low voices when she came in, and Archer lifted his head to give her his deceptively welcoming smile. "There you are, darling! What took you so long?"

She wanted to snap, "What do you think?" but good sense kept her silent. To her surprise Malcolm immediately rose to his feet when she entered the room.

"Oh, Lord, you Brits have such good manners," Archer complained good-naturedly, following suit. "I promise you, Sophie doesn't give a damn if you stand up when she rolls into a room. Do you, darling?"

Sophie maneuvered herself to the remaining place at the table, on Archer's left, directly across from Malcolm. "It's very nice," she murmured, earning herself another bit of displeasure. She lifted her head to look at Malcolm, smiling at him.

No reaction as he reseated himself. *Well, screw him*, she thought. It wasn't as if good manners meant he was on her side. He'd probably be just as happy to slip a knife between her ribs as Archer. No, scratch that. Archer would do it with pleasure—Malcolm simply wouldn't care. He was a man with no emotions, no feelings, as far as she could see.

His advent on the island was still a good thing. Anything that distracted Archer and kept him busy was a benefit. "How long are you staying with us, Mr. Gunnison?" she inquired, reaching for her glass of wine.

Before she realized it Archer had snatched the wineglass from her hand, just as she inhaled the bouquet from a very fine cabernet. "Oh, no, my darling!" he chided, clearly ignoring the fact that he'd ordered her a gin and tonic earlier. "You know you shouldn't combine the wine with all those painkillers you take. I'll have to talk to the servants—there shouldn't have been a wineglass at your place setting, and they should know that by now."

Hardly, Sophie thought testily, since she hadn't been at the table for God knew how long. Before she could respond, Malcolm answered her question.

"I expect to be here a week or so," he said.

Excellent! She couldn't have asked for better timing. "How lovely," she said in her breathiest voice, batting her eyes at him. If Archer wanted games, then she could play them.

To her shock she thought she saw a flicker of reaction in those very green eyes of his, one of amusement. A moment later it was gone, and she knew she'd imagined it. Malcolm Gunnison didn't give a damn what she said or what she did, and he presumably had no sense of humor at all. Few of Archer's confederates did.

Gunnison's good manners didn't extend to dinnertime conversation. He and Archer spent the entire time conferring, leaving Sophie to concentrate on the first steak dinner she'd had in recent memory. It was absolutely worth it—Archer always had the best. The wine would have been lovely with it, but she let go of that particular injury. There were fresh asparagus, crusty rolls, new potatoes, and a lemon tart of such lightness that Sophie could have devoured the entire thing. Her midnight workouts left her with a strong appetite, one she couldn't assuage with the bland garbage Rachel brought to her. When she got off this fucking island, she was going to eat like a pig.

So she ate slowly, cherishing every bite, pushing the sound of their voices—Archer's upper-class, Eastern Seaboard drawl mixed with Malcolm's cool, British accent—into the distance. She was half-aware of the stranger's voice—there was something inherently delicious about it, the depth and timbre of it, as well as the accent. Too bad he was clearly a cold-blooded criminal, probably a sociopath like her husband.

Then again, he was very good-looking, with those piercing green eyes. It explained the odd pull she felt, the fascination. That, or she'd developed a taste for murderous psychopaths. The thought was depressing.

Not that he was paying any attention to her. She might as well be invisible, though she had little doubt he'd instantly rise when she left the table.

"Are you ready for bed, darling?" Archer interrupted her confusing thoughts. "I know how it tires you to come downstairs, and I wouldn't want you to overdo."

So they were ready to get down to the nitty-gritty and didn't want her around to hear. Fine with her. She'd go upstairs and watch *The Walking Dead* again, knowing full well that the man—the men—downstairs were a hell of a lot scarier than phony zombies.

She set her face in an expression of weary gratitude. As usual, energy was pumping through her, and she could have stayed up for hours, but she knew the role she had to play. "I hate to admit it," she said faintly, "but I really do need to retire. I'm sorry to leave you two on your own, but I'm certain you have a lot to talk about." She began to roll back from the table, wishing she'd thought to tuck some rolls beside her, but then they'd fall out when Joe carried her upstairs. Maybe next time, if there was a next time, she'd wear something with an empire waist so she could tuck extra food inside her bra.

Malcolm rose, and this time Archer joined him, moving to give her a chaste kiss on the forehead. "I won't join you tonight then," he said regretfully, and relief flooded her. Not that she had expected him to come up that night—she'd sometimes gone months without seeing him—but sooner or later she was going to pay for her subtle misbehavior with pain, not with sex. Chances were that he'd wait until his guest had left, but she'd already be long gone.

Her room was hot, stuffy, when Joe deposited her back inside, and he went and started the air-conditioning before turning back to her. "Anything I can do for you, missus?" He insisted on calling her that, much as she hated it.

Sophie laughed wryly. "Bring me some more of the lemon tart," she said, "and maybe a pint of Ben and Jerry's Phish Food to go with it."

At least Joe wasn't a man to hide his thoughts or feelings. His mouth widened in a conspiratorial grin. "I can do that. You wouldn't be able to finish the whole pint of ice cream, though, and the rest would melt."

"Wanna bet?"

"I'll send Elena up. Mr. Archer will be too busy with his guest to notice."

So Joe knew she was under restricted rations too, and he didn't mind breaking the rules in small ways. It didn't mean he wouldn't kill her if he was ordered to, but he'd be very sad about it for a few days.

Elena arrived by the time she'd stripped off her clothes and pulled her nightgown around her, zombies already streaming. Elena didn't make the mistake of questioning Sophie's ability to devour an entire pint of ice cream—after all, she was a woman. And she'd brought up at least half the torte.

Sophie was the prisoner of a psychopath, trapped on an island, in a wheelchair, with criminals and killers all around her. But right now she had zombies and ice cream, and she intended to enjoy every minute of it.

Chapter Four

Mal looked at the man he was going to kill and smiled pleasantly. "She's quite lovely."

"My wife?" Archer MacDonald said disingenuously, looking after her departing figure. "She is, isn't she? She's had a hard time the last few years since the . . . accident, but she never complains."

"Accident?" All this was news to Mal, and he cursed the faulty intel that had sent him into this situation half-blind, though it was no one's fault but his own. It had been up to him to make sure all the information he had was up to date and correct, and he'd spent the past month in New Orleans working on it. Clearly he hadn't spent long enough, but he'd been itching to get to work.

For a moment he wondered whether Archer would change the subject, but eventually the man grimaced, poured a little more scotch into his own glass and into Mal's, and set the bottle back on the table. "She was shot by accident. Someone was trying to kill me," he said.

Mal raised his eyebrows. He didn't bother asking why—both of them were aware of Archer's true nature and his business interests. He had enemies by the score. "How did they get so close?"

"I'd overestimated how safe I was here on the island. It hasn't happened again."

"On the island?" Mal asked. "How could someone get here without you knowing?"

"Oh, he was someone I knew. One of my bodyguards, if you must know; a man I trusted with my life and my wife. Fortunately he was a piss-poor shot when rattled, and his bullet hit Sophie. Or unfortunately," he added quickly.

Archer's honesty would go only so far. The devoted husband act was just that, an act, and Mal wondered if Sophie realized it. She'd seemed so taken with Archer, as most women were, dazzled by his good looks and easy charm. Though there was that brief look in her dark brown eyes while Archer was chewing on her neck that suggested something more than tacit acceptance, and Malcolm was a man who never accepted anything on face value.

"What happened to the shooter?" Mal said.

"What do you think?"

Mal didn't bother to consider it. Given what he knew of Archer, he decided there was a good chance the bullet had always been meant for the bride, probably to kill her. Archer would have gotten rid of the shooter because he bungled the job.

But if he wanted her dead, why was she still here, albeit in a wheelchair? Maybe Archer liked having her under his thumb.

"Is she going to recover?" Mal kept his voice casual. In truth, he didn't care, he just needed to have as much information as possible. She'd looked healthy enough as she snuggled on the sofa with her husband, but looks could be deceiving. He needed to identify and catalog everyone on the island if he was going to do his job and get away safely.

As for Sophie, he had three choices. He could kill her, leave her on the island to fend for herself, or take her with him when he left. She'd lost any claim to the protection of the Committee when she'd betrayed them all by falling in love with Archer MacDonald, and his bosses were agreed that the choice was up to him. There were mitigating circumstances, of course. She'd been too green to be entrusted with a mission like that, but the Committee had a history of harsh retribution. The fact that he hadn't been ordered to kill her was as close as they came to mercy.

He didn't give a damn one way or the other. He could wait to see how things unfolded. If she was still in love with MacDonald then he'd leave her if he could, kill her if he had to. If he found she could help him, if she was willing, then he'd consider getting her off the island. She had a certain skill set—or she had at one point—and those didn't come easily. She'd hardly be welcomed back into the fold of the Committee, but there was always the possibility that the American branch might be willing to give her a chance.

"Recover?" Archer echoed absently, and then he quickly plastered a sorrowful expression on his too-handsome face. "Tragically, she won't. She'll never walk again. I brought in the best specialists, but they all said it was hopeless."

Mal didn't bother trying to look mournful. "It must be difficult," he said in a bored voice. "Why don't you just get rid of her?"

Archer didn't pretend to look shocked. They both knew who they were, what they were capable of. "Oh, I couldn't do that. In sickness and in health and all that."

Mal had no trouble hiding the disgust he felt for the lying hypocrite. He was a professional. "Very noble."

"Oh, she can be quite entertaining. She does everything I tell her to. She's quite desperate to please me." Archer leaned forward. "As a matter of fact, you and she share something in common."

"Do we?"

"My wife was once a member of the same organization you used to belong to," Archer said casually, his blue eyes guileless as he dropped his bombshell.

It took all Mal's skill not to react. "Really? It's not very many people who leave the Committee and survive. I never heard of her while I was there."

"No, you probably didn't. They sent her to kill me and instead we fell in love."

"Are you sure she was Committee? How did you find out?" Mal asked, wary. Everything Archer said to him was probably some sort of test.

Archer shrugged. "I have my methods."

"And how did she get past those methods?" he said casually.

"We were in love," Archer said simply, a bright smile on his face. "It makes even a genius stupid. You can't imagine what it was like to have those gorgeous brown eyes shining up at you, full of love."

For a moment Mal pictured it, and he felt an uncomfortable hitch inside. He didn't want anyone staring up at him with love—he didn't believe in it. But Sophie's brown eyes could test even the most stalwart resolution.

"We *were* in love." Mal didn't miss the past tense. Clearly Archer included himself in the category of genius, and Mal wasn't about to dispute it. Archer was shallow, venal, obsessed with himself, but it took a fair amount of brains to commit atrocities on an international scale and never get caught.

He said nothing. Archer was telling him all this for a reason, but he couldn't be certain why. Maybe he didn't swallow the story that Malcolm was former Committee. "Interesting," he said mildly enough. "How long ago did she work for my previous employers?"

"Three years, give or take."

"After my time. I got out long ago," he said. "So why is she still here?"

"I told you. I enjoy keeping her around."

He wasn't going to say anything more, so Mal changed the subject. "In the meantime, I'm here to talk about . . ."

"Not tonight," Archer protested. "I hate doing business in the evening. Why don't we just relax, play some pool, enjoy ourselves? I don't think I have to tell you that Sophie isn't the only woman in the house, and the others are fully functional."

For some reason that pissed him off. First he cripples his wife, and then he mocks her? Mal didn't have any illusions about what a monster Archer MacDonald was. "Not interested." Any woman Archer offered would be there to spy on him. "Pool sounds good."

He rose, stretching, and Archer rose too. They were about the same height, Mal noticed. Six foot two or thereabouts, though Archer outweighed him by a good thirty pounds, all in his heavily muscled shoulders, none of which would slow Mal down when the time came. He fought dirty.

Archer probably did as well, but not as dirty as Mal. He had no compunction, and most civilians, even psychos like Archer, were a little squeamish.

It wasn't going to come to that unless he made a mistake. He planned to take Archer out with a simple double tap to the back of the head: no muss, no fuss. But first he had to find out exactly who was supplying Archer with his biological weapons, in particular RU48, the ridiculously named Pixiedust. After that, the man would be toast.

What was going to happen to the woman upstairs was another matter. Once she'd thrown over her mission, she lost all hope of protection. She deserved everything she got.

He glanced at Archer. He had to be careful not to beat him at pool—that would put him in a bad mood, and Mal needed him feeling unthreatened for the time being. He grabbed his whiskey glass. "You in the mood for a little wager?"

Archer's eyes lit up. "My kind of man. I knew we'd get along the moment I saw you."

Mal said nothing, just smiled. Being chosen for this particular mission was no accident—Archer MacDonald was an Anglophile, a gambler, someone who had a bad habit of taking people at face value. All Mal had to do was show up, well dressed and suave, use a British accent, and Archer would be drawn to him. Not that the accent was entirely fake—Mal's father was British, and after his parents separated, he'd gone to school in England, spending his vacations in the U.S. with his mother. He could slip between accents easily; he was fluent in French, Italian, and Spanish; he could be anyone he needed to be. Malcolm Gunnison was a convenient creation, close enough to who he really was to make the performance almost automatic. He'd used him a couple of times during the past few years when he'd been in the employ of the Committee—it was probably time to retire him. It was never a good idea to become too comfortable with an identity, particularly one that was so close to his real name.

He didn't make it to his bed until after three in the morning. Archer had been too drunk to notice that Mal wasn't keeping up with him, though Mal did his best to slur his words slightly, just in case Archer cared. Archer's performance as a devoted husband vanished as several beautiful young women joined them in the pool room: Rachel, Amy, and he forgot the other one's name. Archer had seen to his own comfort quite nicely.

Rachel had been the one to show Mal to the bedroom on the second floor, and she made it clear she would be more than happy to demonstrate the use of the heavy linen sheets, but he ignored the offer. "Where does Archer sleep?"

Rachel lifted her brows. "Archer's not usually into men," she said cautiously.

He controlled his instinctive irritation. It was little wonder she'd jump to that conclusion after his rejection of her truly spectacular body. She looked like a Barbie doll—tall, endless legs, big tits. He could say she wasn't his type, but hell, she was anyone's type. He didn't bother to deny her suggestion. "I don't want to wake anyone up. I don't need much sleep—I tend to get up early, and I wouldn't want to be a bother."

She gave him a long, measuring look. "Archer's rooms are on the first floor. This floor is only half-renovated—be careful not to wander

33

off from this area. There's another bedroom that's been redone, but the rest of the place is still under construction. It's dangerous."

"So I'm alone up here?" That would be excellent—the last thing he needed was someone watching him, listening to him as he moved around the room, setting up his equipment.

"Sophie's rooms are next door. She sleeps very heavily, though—she takes enough Vicodin to knock out a horse," Rachel said with a laugh.

Good to know. "Why is she up here when she's in a wheelchair? Is there an elevator?"

"Why do you think Archer put her up here? This way she can't show up where she's not wanted. Months go by without Archer seeing her—out of sight, out of mind."

"Must be hard on her," he said in a noncommittal voice.

Rachel shrugged. "She knows better than to complain. There's not much she can do about it. As long as she gets her Vicodin she's happy."

So Sophie Jordan was hooked on pain pills. No wonder he hadn't heard anything about her—she'd simply disappeared into a cloudy world of drugs. It was good news. As he'd suspected, she wasn't going to be any problem; she wouldn't even guess why he was there. She wouldn't interfere, and he wouldn't have to kill her. He'd be more than ready to do so if necessary—he didn't let anything get in the way of a job—but he preferred to keep the body count as low as possible. He could just leave her behind and someone else could clean up the mess.

Rachel was lingering by the door, clearly wanting to stay, so he yawned extravagantly. She took the hint. "Good night, then. Maybe you'll have more energy tomorrow."

He glanced at the Patek Philippe that was part of his cover. In fact, it was his own watch—it had been a very small part of his first sanctioned assignment for the Committee, and Peter Madsen, the current head, had told him to keep it. He seldom wore it—it would be too easy to identify him if he had some signature piece of clothing or jewelry—but for Malcolm Gunnison, so close to his own persona, it had felt right. "It already is tomorrow," he pointed out easily.

"You'll find out that hours mean nothing here on the island. The day is when you get up, whether it's six a.m. or six p.m., and it goes until you're in bed." She rose up and kissed him on his cheek, and she smelled like Poison. It was an excellent choice in perfume for her. "Maybe you'll feel more welcoming tomorrow."

He said nothing, watching her go. She closed the door behind her, and the first thing he noticed was the lack of a key. *What the hell did I expect?* he thought. The only kind of lock Archer MacDonald would have was one that locked him in.

He turned around and surveyed his room. It was cold from the air-conditioning—the faint hum would cover his movements if anyone happened to be listening, but he preferred fresh air, even tropical air. He turned it off, then pushed open the French doors to the inky dark night.

There was a covered balcony running the entire side of the house, and the walkway was littered with boxes and wood scraps and the detritus of carpentry work. To the right there was one set of doors before the end of the building, and he looked at it through narrowed eyes. He hadn't expected them to give him such unfettered access to a former Committee agent. They must know she was harmless—there was nothing she could do or say that would get in the way of Archer's agenda. That, or all this was another test.

He looked out into the night sky. There was a soft breeze, and he could smell the salt of the ocean not far away, the rich scent of the tropical foliage. He glanced down to the grounds, just in time to see someone with a gun turn the corner of the building. *At least one outside guard then, possibly more.* He turned back, his eye catching a quick glimpse of a nearly unnoticeable camera in the roof of the balcony. He didn't pause or focus on it but strode back into his room, leaving the doors open to the night air.

He was going to have to rethink his plans, he thought, pulling off his already-loosened tie. If there was a camera outside his room, then he could be damned sure there were some inside, and while the thought was tempting, he didn't think it would be a good idea to train his own surveillance device on Archer's. Not that he'd worry if he were caught—a man in his position, the position Archer believed was his, wouldn't take any chances. Without moving he could see three cameras in the room, as well as two bugging devices, and there were doubtless more. He went to his case, slid his hands under his perfectly packed clothes, and released the latch on the false bottom. He found the bug detector by feel alone and drew it out, turning it on. Archer, or a minion, would be following his every move, and he had a part to play. The handheld machine began to screech, and he traced the noise to the bugs, each one in turn, yanking out the tiny cameras, pulling the microphones from the leads and crushing them beneath his foot. The cameras joined them, and he scooped up the shattered electronics, opened his door, and left them in a little pile outside, a message for Archer MacDonald. If Malcolm was who he was pretending to be, then he wouldn't put up with being spied on. If Archer wasn't smart enough to realize it before, he would now.

According to the state-of-the-art bug zapper, there was no more sur-veillance, and so Mal undressed lazily, tossing his clothes on the nearby chair before pulling on some sleep pants. He was tired and he was restless. It was a good thing he didn't need much sleep at night—he had trained himself to go for days without any sleep at all, and he'd had a positively decadent six hours the night before, tuning out the New Orleans street noise as well as the creaks and groans of the refurbished nineteenth-century mansion that was now the headquarters of the American branch of the Committee. Archer would sleep late, and Mal could make do with an hour or two after he finished a little reconnaissance. What better place to start than Sophie MacDonald, wife, operative, gullible traitor, drug addict?

She'd be so out of it she wouldn't even notice that she had a nighttime intruder.

He was smart enough not to try the hallway—there would be more surveillance out there, and dismantling it might be considered overkill. No, he'd use the balcony—if he kept to the wall he could avoid the camera. Chances were she couldn't lock her doors either, at least not from the inside, and he was more than adept at picking any lock he'd come across so far.

He paid no attention to the cold tile beneath his bare feet. The noise of the air-conditioning would drown out any sound he might make, and Archer's wife would be too doped up to hear him. He reached out and turned the handle on the door. Locked, but it only took a moment to fix that.

The door opened silently, and the still body in the bed didn't move. Stepping inside, he closed the door behind him, plunging the room into darkness again. He could see the pinpricks of a blinking red light in the vase of fresh flowers, see another in one corner of the room, a third beside the huge television screen. At least Archer had given her that much to fill her empty days, though he hoped to hell he'd let Sophie choose what she wanted to watch rather than stick her with football highlights. Those cameras wouldn't pick up his movement in the midnight-dark room—there hadn't been a camera invented that would pick up on him, not with the jammer clipped onto his sleep pants. He moved closer to Sleeping Beauty, looking down at her.

No, she wasn't conventionally pretty. Asleep, her muscles relaxed, her face scrubbed clean of makeup, she looked surprisingly ordinary, just a young American woman who was in the wrong place at the wrong time. She had shoulder-length brownish-blond hair in need of shaping, dark eyebrows, and he remembered her eyes as a deep chocolate brown. He looked for signs of pain marking her face, but it was smooth. Either Archer had paid for plastic surgery or Sophie was relatively pain-free.

In his experience Vicodin didn't do shit, but he was usually bleeding to death from some attack or another before he tried it, and there wasn't much that would help that. Someone half his weight would be much more susceptible—maybe her liberal use of the drug kept the pain at bay. If so, he couldn't blame her. If she took it simply to forget she was married to Archer MacDonald, he wouldn't blame her either. She'd screwed the pooch when she'd ditched the Committee for a psychopath. She even seemed to believe the man still loved her. Maybe she just zoned out because being bound to a wheelchair was too depressing.

Whatever the cause, it was his good luck, and he leaned over her, looking at her exposed arms for track marks. She looked in better shape than he would have thought, given her circumstances. Then again, she had to convey herself in a wheelchair—it would be logical for her arm muscles to start building. At this point she could give Michelle Obama a run for her money.

He reached for the covers, ready to pull them down and finish his inspection when he changed his mind. He could do that later—for now he needed to check out the lay of the land, look for an easy escape. There was a phone beside her bed, but he was willing to bet it wouldn't ring anywhere but on this island. At least it meant help was only a phone call away. So was disaster for him.

He stared at her closely, leaning down. She was breathing easily, deep and solid, and if she wasn't sound asleep, then she was a better operative than he was, and that was a stone-cold impossibility. He stepped back, moving around the room, cataloging its contents. There wasn't much that could end up helping him. Not that he'd expected she'd have a handgun beside the bed, and besides, he was well armed beneath that secret panel in his suitcase. She wasn't going to provide any particular help for him during this job, but she probably wasn't going to be a hindrance either. He'd get away with ignoring her just the way her husband did, unless the bastard came by for his occasional conjugal visit.

That bothered the hell out of him, and he wasn't sure why. If she was still in love with Archer, she was probably pathetically grateful for any attention he gave her.

He backed away from her slowly, his eyes running over her. She looked just the slightest bit fragile, vulnerable, exactly the kind of woman he found annoying. He had no savior complex—he liked women who could take care of themselves and didn't need rescuing.

Still, there was something about her, something sensual in her smooth, pain-free face, her soft, generous mouth, her tousled hair as it spread out over the pillow behind her, and for a moment he fantasized about having her beneath him, that tawny hair spread out on his pillow. And then he made an almost silent sound of disgust. What the hell was wrong with him? He never had sex when he was on assignment, not unless it was part of his cover, part of his job. Fucking Archer's crippled wife was in no way part of the plan.

So why was he thinking about it? She certainly hadn't been sending out signals—she'd seemed barely aware of him that night, all her attention focused on her husband. She was still just as deluded as she'd always been, which meant she was the enemy.

Not that he'd counted on her being an asset. He didn't tend to work well with others. For now she could sleep the drugged sleep she deserved. He'd figure out what to do with her later.

Archer MacDonald stretched out on one of the lounges by the side of the pool, cradling a whiskey in one hand, and considered the day. His treacherous wife amused him—he knew women well enough to recognize that she still wanted him. She was probably smart enough to know he was behind the bullet that had crippled her, and she'd been smart enough to fool him in the first place. He'd been in such a rage when he found out the Committee had managed to infiltrate his life that without thinking he'd given the order to terminate her. First, though, he'd put a hit out on his lawyer, who'd taken so damned long to find out the truth about his doting wife. Then it was Sophie's turn, but that idiot hadn't managed a good shot—she'd moved at the last minute—and it had given him enough time to rethink the situation. She was in love with him; he'd never had the tiniest bit of doubt, and she took pleasure in anything he doled out to her. He loved that she was now entirely under his control. She'd had a powerful sexual appetite—that was one of the things he'd liked most about her, and of course he wasn't going to fuck a cripple, but he'd enjoyed tempting her, bringing in good-looking men when she couldn't do anything about it, couldn't move, couldn't feel anything. She hadn't been interested—again, she was still too in love with him, he knew—and he'd given up on the idea. It was the advent of Malcolm Gunnison that had made him decide to drag her out, like an old, abandoned toy. Gunnison was a different sort of man—there was a chance he'd be more to Sophie's tastes than the pretty boys he'd brought to the island. Throwing the two of them together could be vastly entertaining. Sophie would be wracked with guilt, and Gunnison would most likely do what Archer wanted him to.

Archer believed Gunnison's story—he'd had him checked so thoroughly he even knew what the man liked in bed. Still, it didn't hurt to test Malcolm, and videos of his wife having sex with another man could brighten a boring night. He could even make her watch them, long after Gunnison left.

In the end he never trusted anything or anyone, not even his own knowledge and his instincts. Malcolm Gunnison was a former Committee operative who'd left to become a middleman for a half dozen of the most notorious regimes in the world. He was here at the behest of an Eastern European despot, thinking he could work a deal for Archer's newest creation. Pixiedust was his baby, the groundbreaking chemical that could wipe out one hundred thousand people in twenty-four hours, with an exponentially expanding death toll in the following days. Such a weapon was a little too dangerous even for Archer—he had no particular desire to see the majority of the earth's population wiped out. There would be no challenge left. But that was what made Pixiedust so groundbreaking. There was an antidote for it, and a vaccine, which would make anyone exposed to it invulnerable. As long as the antidote was administered by vaccine within twelve hours of exposure, it would work, but it took weeks for the victims to get back on their feet.

That part suited him just fine. If one planned to subdue a rebellious population or conquer a neighboring country, having the majority of the survivors out of commission long enough to install a new infrastructure seemed an excellent plan.

There was a small glitch, but he had every confidence that Chekowsky would take care of it. A twenty-four-hour lead time would enable a man to solidify his power—twelve was a little rushed for effective extortion. Chekowsky could get around this—he was the genius who first invented the stuff, locked away in Archer's underground laboratories in Texas, and Archer paid him what he was worth. It never did to cheap out when you demanded the best. He could easily have Chekowsky terminated once the Pixiedust formula was perfected, but there was the strong possibility that Chekowsky could come up with something even more valuable. With a mind like Chekowsky's and the advantages of Archer's money, there were simply no limits.

Archer had done his best to convince Malcolm Gunnison that he was negotiating with him alone, but it wouldn't do to underestimate the man. Gunnison was ruthless, deadly, and he was no fool. He had to know Archer was considering other offers.

They would acknowledge that particular problem when they came to it. It was unreasonable to assume that it could be limited to one person, that if someone like Putin bought it in Russia, it couldn't also be used in the Middle East or in some of the less stable countries of South

America. There would be enough to go around for anyone willing to pay Archer's price.

And a weapon like that could generate income for the buyer as well. Infect the people and then demand an astronomical sum from them for the antidote. Archer would hardly be fool enough to limit such an asset to one buyer, no matter how high the price.

But Archer was a patient man. He could use this delay with Chekowsky to his advantage. While his research and his instincts told him that Malcolm Gunnison was as mercenary and as soulless as he needed to be, Archer was too smart a man not to be aware that things could change.

And there were endless possibilities for amusement. Yes, his treacherous Sophie was still pining for him. But he saw the way she glanced at Malcolm, with dislike and unwilling fascination. He could have a very good time throwing the two of them together, watching the sparks fly. He had cameras everywhere.

No, he was willing to wait. Things happened when they were meant to. He could wait.

Chapter Five

Sophie heard the quiet click of the door as Malcolm Gunnison left her room, and she let out a deep breath. What the hell was that man up to? Didn't he know Archer had every room bugged, and he'd have no trouble observing his guest prowling around his wife's bedroom?

She was the only one who knew that. And Gunnison wouldn't be seen. The inky darkness she'd insisted on made movement indiscernible, but there was always a chance Archer was using some kind of infrared technology, one that picked up on body heat. Not that he had any particular reason to bother with that kind of surveillance for his pathetic, crippled wife, but underestimating Archer was never a good idea.

Her unwanted guest hadn't made a sound—in fact, she'd been lying there, awake after her series of exercises, and she hadn't even heard him open the locked door, an impressive feat. There was nothing particularly suspicious about his ability to pick a lock—anyone who came out to Isla Mordita would come from the darker side of society. Mr. Gunnison, if that was even his name, was doubtless a liar, a thief, and a murderer. Archer wouldn't care—in fact, he'd be more likely to trust him if he came with a suitably criminal pedigree. She wouldn't put it past Archer to challenge Gunnison to break into her room and leave without waking her up. Of course, Archer thought she was strung out on Vicodin and slept like the dead, and she was happy to foster that impression. She didn't need anyone to suspect she could get around just fine.

She lay without moving; listening, but she heard nothing, not the sound of his own balcony door closing, not the quiet sound of his movement in the room on the other side of the wall. That was no surprise—the walls were plaster, built for a time without air-conditioning or even electricity, and the thick whitewashed walls muffled everything. There was no way she could be certain he'd returned to his room, no way she could even know whether the opening and closing of the door was a trap.

It didn't matter. She was stiff from holding herself so still, and besides, what would one of Archer's criminal associates want from her? If he thought he could use her as leverage, he was going to be disappointed. She didn't have the faintest idea why Archer was keeping her alive. She'd been living on borrowed time and she knew it. He could have her taken out on a whim, and sooner or later he would, unless she finished him and got the hell out of Dodge. There was nothing Malcolm Gunnison could do that would make her position any more dangerous.

She pushed herself to a sitting position, making sure she kept her legs still and lifeless beneath the heavy sheets. She leaned back against her headboard, and the wood made a soft creak, so slight that most people wouldn't notice, but Sophie froze. Archer would have only the best, most precise microphones—they would have picked up that thump, isolate it as coming from her room. That thump was an anomaly, and she knew better than to hope Archer would ignore it.

She switched on the light beside the bed, dragging her body over, and blinked against the blinding brightness. With a sigh of resignation she pulled herself into the wheelchair that had been left beside her bed and slowly rolled it toward the big bathroom. Archer might question why she hadn't slept through the night like she usually did, but he could hardly argue with her plainly biological excuse. She pushed the door shut and leaned her head against it, taking deep breaths. This wasn't what she wanted—drawing attention to herself would be the kind of mistake that could end up with her being dead and buried in a shallow grave somewhere on this island. She wondered exactly how many corpses littered the five square miles. Emilio, the man who had "accidentally" shot her, was one of them. So was Emilio's girlfriend. Over the last two years people had come and gone, come and not gone. As long as Archer was convinced she still adored him, he'd be content to keep her around for amusement's sake. If he found out she just didn't give a damn, he'd have her killed without hesitation.

She stayed in the bathroom for as long as she could manage, pacing back and forth in complete silence as she considered her next-door neighbor. Exactly who was Malcolm Gunnison, and why had he risked discovery to sneak into her room in the middle of the night? Had Archer hired him? Maybe he was outsourcing her execution, but if so, why the delay? Killing someone was easy work—no one would know that better than Archer.

She rolled the chair back to the bed, maneuvering herself onto the mattress awkwardly. She'd originally thought the arrival of a guest on Isla Mordita would be a benefit—someone to take Archer's mind off of her. Not that Archer usually wasted a second thought about her—if he didn't have such a razor-sharp intellect, she'd think he'd forgotten all about her. But Archer didn't forget anything. Malcolm Gunnison was probably here for something that had nothing to do with her, but then, why had he come into her room? Was it on Archer's orders? And what about Archer—did he have a specific reason, or was it simply to fuck with her?

She couldn't afford to panic. Her escape plan was simple—she knew the highly regimented schedule of the guards, knew who would be on duty and when. Marco took guard duty on weekends; during the week he was Joe's second-in-command. Marco was the one who carried her places when Joe was busy, who brought her chair. Marco was the one who watched her when she swam in the warm, beautiful pool, her legs trailing uselessly as her arms sliced through the water. Marco was the one who told her about his love life and his mother and grandfather in Cuba, struggling to get by. Marco who was a stoner.

Archer didn't give a damn about Marco's affection for weed, and he even tolerated the garden where he cultivated it. He didn't know that Marco liked more than weed, and that she'd been passing her Vicodin on to him, just enough to whet his appetite.

She really didn't understand his affection for the stuff. She'd taken it during the first year and half after she'd been injured, and while it had put a dent in her pain, it never removed it completely—and as far as she could tell, it provided no pleasant feeling whatsoever. The most she felt was a little sleepy. But Marco seemed to love the stuff, as much as he could get. She was counting on his greediness—he went through the drugs like a gluttonous child. Once she handed over the stash hidden in her bed, he would devour them and be out of commission. Getting away from the house would be relatively easy. Using the boat Marco had boasted about might be more of a challenge.

He wasn't supposed to have one, of course. It was nothing more than a glorified rowboat, one Marco used for his occasional attempts at fishing, which were really no more than an excuse to get stoned away from everyone else. She would have been surprised that Archer put up with him if Joe hadn't divulged some of his past. If it weren't for Marco's impressive marksmanship, Archer wouldn't be where he was today. She wouldn't have thought Archer was one for loyalty, but apparently she was wrong, because Marco was given a huge amount of leeway.

She figured she had a fifty-fifty chance of getting away from there, odds that went way down if she finally finished her assignment and put a bullet in Archer's brain. Her best chance would be to sneak off when no one was looking, when Archer was otherwise occupied, and get the hell out of there. If she wasted time killing him, she would probably be signing her own death warrant.

Hell, she'd probably drown in that stupid small boat anyway. If she managed to get off the island, she simply had to keep heading west to the closest solid land, Mexico, and then go from there.

As a plan it relied too much on luck and circumstances, and on her faulty judgment of character. She might think Marco was easily seduced by a handful of pills, but she'd been convinced Archer was a good man, not the monster the Committee had painted him. She'd been convinced they were in love. She'd been convinced he'd never hurt her.

She hunched down in the bed again, pulling the covers around her body and turning off the light, and she allowed herself a grimace of pain in the unseeing darkness. It still hurt when she twisted a certain way, and it probably always would. It made no difference. In fact, she almost welcomed the pain. It reminded her that she was alive, not in one of those shallow graves on the edge of the island. At least, not yet.

It was late when she finally woke, jerked into alertness by some dream she refused to let herself remember. Her heavy curtains had been pulled open, and a tray of congealed scrambled eggs and cold coffee sat on the table beside her bed. Rachel must have come and gone, not bothering to wake her. Making a face, she pulled herself into a sitting position, glancing out at the tropical sunshine. It was after eleven—she usually woke up at six and then waited hours for Rachel to make her appearance. She cursed silently. Another change from routine that Archer would notice. If she was going to get out of here, then she had to make sure nothing else out of the ordinary drew his attention.

She heard the soft knock at her door, and she called out, "Come in," before she could think twice. Rachel never knocked—she just barged in.

The man calling himself Malcolm Gunnison stood in the doorway, his face the same blank expression she was getting used to. He'd dumped his bespoke suit, trading it in for jeans and a long-sleeved shirt rolled up at the elbows. He really did have endless legs, she thought, momentarily distracted. Or maybe it was simply that he wasn't as top heavy as the men she was used to on the island. Everyone there had pumped iron to the max, so at times she felt like she was living in a land of thick-muscled mutants. Even she had done some weights, supposedly to enable her to haul her inert body around. In truth, she simply wanted all the strength she could get, and an excuse for her impressive guns.

Which meant that she, or any man on the island, could probably flatten the elegant Mr. Gunnison. Good to know.

She looked at him warily. "Yes?"

He didn't smile—she wondered if he was capable of it. "Your husband would like you to join us for lunch," he said, and the English accent slid down her spine.

She mentally shook it off. "I haven't had breakfast yet."

He glanced at her untouched tray. "I wouldn't if I were you. Joe will come fetch you in half an hour."

Fetch? Did people really say fetch? It would be a waste of time to argue, to plead a sleepless night—Archer always got his way, sometimes by charm, sometimes by force. She managed to put a pleased smile on her face. She had no idea who this man was, whether he was the obscurely titled "consultant" or something else entirely, but he was here at Archer's behest, which meant he was the enemy. "I'll be ready," she said, using her arms to pull herself to the side of the bed.

He stepped inside her door, into her room, an act that would have shocked her if he hadn't already been prowling around. "Do you need some help getting dressed?"

There were limits to how pleasant she could be. "From you? I don't think so," she said, and then immediately regretted it. Most people wouldn't have seen that interested light flash in his clear green eyes, so fast did it come and go, but she wasn't most people. That had been some kind of test, and she'd failed it. Or passed it, depending what outcome he'd been hoping for. He'd paid very little outward attention to her the night before, apart from his random courtesies, but now he was directing his focus at her, and she'd been a fool not to be more careful. She quickly moved to make up lost ground. "But if you could send Rachel or Amy up I'd be very grateful." She gave him the winsome smile she'd been practicing, the one that would melt Archer's most ruthless employees.

Malcolm didn't even blink. "Certainly," he said politely, moving back into the hallway. A moment later she could hear his footsteps on the stairs, could hear them quite clearly because he'd left her door open, the son of a bitch. But why?

Had Archer begun to suspect her? Had he really brought Malcolm to the island to unmask her? That would explain everything, including the man's late-night wanderings. When it came right down to it, nobody set foot on Isla Mordita without Archer knowing exactly who and what they were. Malcolm would be no threat to Archer, and therefore no help to her. She was going to have to watch herself for the next few days.

That is, when she wasn't watching Malcolm Gunnison.

Malcolm joined Archer MacDonald on the shady terrace that ran along one side of the house. The water in the swimming pool was sparkling in the sunlight, and the one called Rachel was tanning herself, topless, on the side. She really did have the most impressive pair of man-made tits, Malcolm noticed, unmoved. He had never been fond of plastic in bed.

"Is my wife joining us?" Archer demanded lazily, taking a sip of the drink he'd been nursing.

"She said she'd be delighted." It was a lie, of course. Sophie had looked at him like he was a snake who'd slithered into her room before she remembered she was supposed to be sweet and frail. For some reason he didn't feel like complicating her life by passing on her lack of enthusiasm for today's outing. Not without a reason.

Archer looked smug. "She still adores me," he said, running an admiring eye over Rachel's deeply bronzed body. "I try to give her the attention she craves, but there's only so much I can do."

She hadn't looked like she was craving attention, but Malcolm didn't point that out either. This mission depended on Archer believing him—there was no other way he'd survive long enough for Archer's pet scientist to arrive, but he was going to enjoy killing Archer MacDonald. That in itself was unusual—he didn't tend to care one way or another about the people he'd been ordered to terminate. For some reason he really hated Sophie MacDonald's husband.

Mal made a noncommittal sound, reaching for his own drink. It was surprisingly good, but then, it was to be expected with Archer's lavish tastes. The blend of fresh tropical fruit and the bite of rum were perfect for a hot midday in the tropics, although he had to watch himself. His host had tried to drink him under the table last night, and failed. He was going to have to decide which would fit his operation better—sobriety or a carefully orchestrated drunk.

"You know, you could do me a favor," Archer said slowly, his eyes never leaving Rachel's distant, perfect body.

"Could I?"

"You must be bored to death. Chekowsky's hit a complication and is running a few days behind, and it's too much trouble to send you back to the mainland. Once I allow someone on Isla Mordita, I don't let him leave until our business is finished, and we've only just begun."

As a threat it was unnecessary—anybody fool enough to arrive on this island would have no illusions about how dangerous the man was, and Mal wasn't going to leave until he'd finished his business—all of it. "I'm not easily bored," he said. "What is it you want?"

Archer turned to him, that charming, well-bred smile on his face. "I'd like you to pay attention to my wife. She hasn't much of a life, poor darling, and I think having a handsome man flirt with her would cheer her up enormously. I wouldn't have to spend so much time worrying about her."

If Archer spent even five seconds thinking about the woman, Mal would be surprised. He kept his face impassive. "What does this paying attention involve?"

"She's quite pretty, don't you think?" Archer said.

"Not bad."

Archer chuckled. "You don't like to give anything away, do you?"

Mal let out a deliberate, long-suffering sigh. "Tell me what it is you want me to do, Archer, and I'll be happy to help you out. You want me to fuck your wife?"

Archer didn't even blink. He simply shrugged. "If you want to go there, yes. She needs distraction. She has no feeling below the waist, and I was never into necrophilia, but if you want to have a go at it, feel free. She'll do anything I ask her to, and she's certainly not getting any from me."

Mal said nothing. For a moment he remembered the scene from *Raiders of the Lost Ark* where Indiana Jones, when faced with an ominous, sword-wielding giant, simply shrugs and shoots him. Mal would have given anything to be able to just reach over and snap Archer's neck.

He couldn't. He had to wait for Archer's fucking Pixiedust and its inventor.

"Unless you're not interested in women," Archer added in a faintly taunting voice. "I had you thoroughly vetted before you got here, but we might have overlooked something. Rachel told me you sent her away."

"Rachel's not my type."

"What about Sophie?"

He thought back to her, to the dark brown eyes that gave away nothing, the mouth that looked soft and tempting. He was a professional—he'd fuck anything he had to in order to complete a mission, and he'd do it well. He could give her what she clearly hadn't had in years, apparently with her asshole husband's approval. There was just one little problem. He wanted to.

Taking another sip of his drink, he glanced at his host. What possible benefit could the man find in whoring out his wife? Simply to demean her? Mal would have thought a man like Archer would be possessive to the point of murderous, yet instead he was serving up Sophie as a perk for his guest. Why? Did he expect to watch? And what would that deceptively docile woman do when she heard about her husband's plans? "So when is it we can expect your pet scientist?"

Archer shrugged. "Delays in science are simply part of the price of admission. Trust me. It'll be worth it when the compound is finished."

"So that's time I spend on this island with nothing to do?"

Archer grinned. "You can always do Rachel. Or Amy for that matter."

Mal looked at his host for a long moment, then spoke. "I think I'll do your wife," he drawled.

Archer's grin widened, and Mal knew, just knew, that he was thinking of the cameras and microphones he'd seeded throughout the house. Archer had every intention of watching, and probably wanking off to the sight of his wife having sex with someone else.

He really, really wanted to shoot the man. Instead, he smiled faintly, the most Malcolm Gunnison could offer.

"It's a deal then," Archer said. "I'm counting on it."

"What is?" came Sophie MacDonald's voice from the doorway. *She knows how to make an entrance, even in a wheelchair*, Mal thought. She would have been taught that when she worked for the Committee, even if her training had been incomplete.

"We're just making a small wager on when Chekowsky will show up," Archer said without hesitation. "It might not be till next week."

Her eyes met his, warm-brown and steady, and Mal breathed a sigh of relief. Obviously she hadn't heard their discussion. Not even the best operative could cover up a reaction to something like that, and this was the husband she seemed to adore, the man she'd thrown away her career and the trust of her friends for. "And what did you guess, Mr. Gunnison?"

"Mal," he corrected. "I said in the next couple of days."

She tossed back her hair and he watched her, allowing himself to observe her in full daylight. Last evening he'd been circumspect, and during his late-night reconnaissance there hadn't been enough light to see clearly, but now that he seemed to have promised his host that he'd bang his wife, he figured he could look at her all he wanted. She was prettier than he'd realized, even with shapeless hair, and that wide mouth of hers gave him all sorts of nasty thoughts. She was wearing a flowing sundress, the skirt covering her body. "For your sake I hope he's here sooner," she said, not meeting his gaze.

"Chekowsky has his own timetable," Archer advised Mal. "He'll show up when he's ready. Sorry for the wait."

Mal allowed himself a small, feral smile, just for Archer's sake. "Then I'd better find something to keep me busy," he said softly.

Archer's conspiratorial grin was answer enough.

Chapter Six

Sophie was so furious she wanted to throw up. She kept her hands in her lap to disguise their shaking. Eavesdropping was one of the few weapons she had at her disposal, and she used it at every possible moment. So the elegant Malcolm Gunnison thought he was going to do everyone a favor and fuck her, did he? At least it was good to know that Archer still thought she adored him. Keeping that sweet, slightly stupid smile on her face took tremendous effort, but she managed as she rolled up to the table, taking the cup of coffee Mal handed her.

She took a sip, and the blessed bite of Sumatran caffeine almost softened her rage. She wasn't particularly worried—if she was going to play that she was still in love with her husband, then she wouldn't be interested in sleeping with someone else, particularly if she had no feeling below the waist.

Sex hadn't even been an issue up to that point. For the first year she'd been in too much pain, and after that she'd lost interest entirely, despite Archer's malicious temptations. The longer she was celibate the easier it was, and right then she'd rather screw a warthog than any of the damned men on this island.

"Can I get you something to eat?" Mal asked in an offhand voice, but Sophie wasn't fooled. As a seductive overture it was fairly bland, but he hadn't offered to do anything for her before, aside from helping her dress. At least his attempts to be charming could be a distraction, and she'd be long gone before push came to shove. There was no way she would go to bed with him, doubtless with Archer watching, just to shore up her cover. The Committee had insisted the operatives be above such qualms, but that was where she'd failed. She'd thought herself in love with Archer, that he loved her in return, and she'd been beating up on herself ever since she realized the truth about him.

She looked up at Mal through her eyelashes. "That's very thought-ful of you," she said in a deliberately dulcet voice. "Just some toast and orange juice."

His mouth tilted in a faint smile. "You really ought to try some of this fruit creation Archer ordered."

"Yes, darling," Archer chimed in. "It's so good you'll feel like danc-ing. If it weren't for that damned chair, of course."

Just one of Archer's usual barbs—he seldom let a conversation pass without reminding her that she was a cripple. She arranged her features into a doleful expression. "Remember I'm not supposed to drink, not on top of all the pain meds I take."

"What do you take?" Malcolm asked.

She glanced back at Mal. If only he weren't so different from Archer's generic handsomeness. In another life, another world, she might even be tempted by Malcolm Gunnison. His green eyes were almost iridescent—she'd never actually seen that color in real life, and his mouth was wickedly distracting. She had no idea why she was so fascinated by him—he wasn't the most lethal, the most charming, or the most beautiful man that Archer had brought to the island, trotting them in front of her to see if she'd bite.

She'd never been tempted before. But the inescapable and unpleas-ant fact was that ever since she'd heard her husband solicit Malcolm's services, a small part of her brain had been trying to come up with an excuse to let it happen.

She was going stir-crazy, and the only surprise was that it hadn't hit her sooner. She'd never been at the mercy of her hormones in the past—while her sex drive had been healthy, her passion for Archer had been as emotional as it had been physical, blinded as she'd been to Archer's true nature. She'd seen him as she wanted him to be, not as he was.

Maybe she simply needed to get laid. If she had any sense, the first thing she would do once she got away from here would be to go to a bar and pick up the most gorgeous man she could find to work off the years of frustration. Maybe not conventionally gorgeous, though. Maybe someone who looked a little like Gunnison.

"I don't have any pills to spare," she said shortly, reminding herself that Malcolm wasn't going to be that man.

"I wasn't asking," he replied lazily, his green eyes drifting over her. They gave absolutely nothing away. "I'm just curious what kind of pain you're in."

"Why?"

"I wouldn't want to tire you out."

That was enough to shock her. Surely he wasn't going to come right out and tell her what Archer had suggested?

Apparently not, if Archer's choking sound was anything to go by. "How do you think you're likely to do that?" she said in an arch voice, ignoring her husband. "I'm not about to go hiking around the island with you, no matter how bored you are waiting for Archer's other guests. I take Vicodin and occasionally Percocet. They control the pain and I sleep very well." Might as well make it clear that she had no idea he'd been scouting her room last night.

"I'm delighted to hear it," Mal said.

Archer rose, his iron chair scraping on the stone surface. "I'll leave you two to entertain each other," he said easily. "I've got too much work to do to sit around in this hot sun."

"I thought you wanted to see me, Archer." She put a plaintive note in her voice, aware that Malcolm was watching her.

"I wanted you to keep our guest occupied, angel," he murmured, coming toward her, and she did her absolute best not to stiffen. He sometimes gave her a paternal kiss on the forehead when he was playing games, but if he tried it this time, she was afraid her skin might crawl and give her away.

It was far worse. He put one of his hamlike hands under her chin, tilting up her face, and set his mouth on hers, wet and open, his tongue seeking entrance.

She wanted to bite him. She wanted to throw up in his mouth, and for a moment she was afraid that was exactly what she'd do. She clenched her fists together, hiding them in her skirts, and kissed him back, putting all the enthusiasm she could feign into it.

Archer drew back, his mouth wet, a smug expression on his face. He really did believe she still loved him, still wanted him. He had an impressive brain—there was no denying that—but for some reason he had no trouble accepting the sudden absence of at least thirty points from her IQ. She looked up at him hopefully, knowing her eyes were shining with unshed tears. Tears of rage, but he'd assume it was longing.

"Ah, darling, I miss you in my bed," he said in a low, suggestive voice.

"I can still take care of you," she purred, calling his bluff. The only times he'd come to her room were to pick a fight and then take out his frustration, and given her supposed weakness, there was nothing she could do but take the vicious abuse. He'd probably started it in an attempt to find out whether she really was helpless, and quickly discovered he got off on hurting her. She pushed past memories from her mind with an ill-concealed shudder, but with Archer's ego he probably assumed it was sexual excitement. If he tried, she might just kill him with her bare hands. She could, too. Enough of her training with the Committee remained that killing him would be a simple matter, despite his size and strength.

"Hush," Archer said. "Malcolm's been asking all about you. Why don't you let him say marvelous things to you that will put a smile back on that pretty face?"

Malcolm had said barely anything about her except to question Archer's plan, but his face was inscrutable. "Go away, Archer," he said pleasantly. "Sophie and I will have a very good time without you."

Sophie managed not to snort.

Archer's bright smile had once dazzled her. "C'mon, Rachel. Let's leave these two alone to get to know each other."

With feline grace Rachel rose to her feet, and a moment later they were gone, leaving the terrace empty, silent, awkward. Sophie shifted in the wheelchair as much as she dared, and then her eyes met Mal's oblique look. "So?" She didn't bother to hide the challenge in her voice.

"So," he said, his voice deep, almost erotic. It made no sense that a man who seemed determined not to show any reaction or emotion would have such a sexual voice. In fact, it wasn't just the voice that was sexy, it was the way he moved, the way he looked at her. Hell, if she thought she could get away with it, she'd damned well let him seduce her. She tried to pull her gaze away, to look at him dispassionately, but at that moment *passion* was the key word. There was no way she would be able to lie motionless beneath him.

Thank God she didn't blush. She could play this any number of ways, but she had the impression that Malcolm Gunnison wasn't as gullible as the psychopath she'd married. The more she tried to play a role the more closely Malcolm watched her. It was time to try a variant of the truth.

She leaned back, her fingers toying with the long skirt. "So," she said again. "I assume you're simply placating my husband's deranged ideas."

Her change of tone didn't surprise him. She doubted anything would. "Which deranged ideas?"

She took a deep, imperceptible breath, then smiled at him. "I love my husband very much, and I'd do anything to make him happy, but I am not going to bed with you. Why he would think I would want to is beyond me."

Malcolm didn't even blink. "I thought you were eavesdropping," he said. "Don't you know that's a dangerous thing to do? You tend to hear things you don't want to."

She shrugged, reaching for her coffee. It was cool now, and she hated her coffee lukewarm, but she needed something to do with her hands. "I wouldn't say it was something I didn't want to hear. I heard that my husband loves me and is willing to do anything to make me happy, and he doesn't usually like to share. And I learned that you think I'm attractive enough to take to bed, even if only half of me is in working order. Very flattering. Needless to say, I have absolutely no interest in screwing you, no matter how sexy you are."

"You think I'm sexy?" There was real amusement in his voice. "I thought you kept all that adoration for your husband."

"I love my husband, Mr. Gunnison," she said sternly.

"I didn't say you didn't." He rose, moving around the table toward her, and she remained perfectly still. The absolutely worst part of being in the damned wheelchair was having people loom over her. She'd thought she'd gotten used to it, but Malcolm Gunnison was another matter. Without her husband's bulk he seemed taller, more dangerous, which was absurd. She knew, to her regret, that no one was more dangerous than Archer MacDonald. "You don't want that coffee, do you?"

"It's cold," she agreed. So were the jellied scrambled eggs and damp toast. She'd pretty much lost her appetite anyway.

"Let's go for a walk instead."

She eyed him coolly. Was there any way he could suspect? No, she was too good at covering up. If she could manage to fool everyone around her for so long she could certainly fool a stranger. "In case you hadn't noticed, I can't walk."

"I noticed." He moved behind her, reached down, and unlocked the wheels. "That doesn't mean you have to stay in one place." He turned her, quite deftly, and in the next moment he was wheeling her away from the house. She arched her neck to look back at him, but his expression was entirely unreadable. She needed to get used to that—he wasn't giving anything away.

"Where are you taking me?"

"Out of range of the house."

So he knew there were cameras and microphones? Of course he did. Archer didn't bring innocents to the island, and there was nothing naïve about Mal's clear green eyes. "Turn left," she said abruptly as he reached the corner of the terrace.

"I'd planned to turn right."

She shook her head. "Turn left," she repeated. "There's a fairly level path down to a small hidden cove, and you shouldn't have any trouble pushing me. It's very peaceful." There was also a long stretch with no surveillance at all. If for some indiscernible reason Mal had come to the island to kill her, then she'd just played into his hands, and she couldn't rule that out. Then again, the only person who'd want her dead would be Archer, and he'd want to watch.

Maybe the Committee was tying up loose ends and had decided to punish her for ignoring her mission and running off with Archer, which had to be the stupidest thing she'd ever done in her life. It didn't matter that she'd been thrown into the mission before she was ready—there was still no excuse.

But Malcolm wasn't a member of the Committee—she knew that without any shadow of a doubt. The Committee members she'd known had essentially been soldiers, and Malcolm was too elegant, too self-contained to be an efficient soldier. He was someone who would work alone.

No, he was a far cry from the Committee, and besides, they'd written her off years ago. She'd made her bed and now she had to fester in it. They weren't going to rescue her, but they wouldn't waste manpower getting rid of her. Malcolm Gunnison was no threat to her, even if it felt like he was the most dangerous man in the world.

He turned left, pushing her over the closely cropped grass, and in moments they were on the narrow path that led down to the beach. She didn't like having him behind her, pushing the chair, but she didn't have much choice in the matter. It had been so long since she'd been down to the small cove that she was willing to do anything to get there, even allow the enemy to transport her.

Of course, it remained to be seen whether or not he was the enemy. He might be the only person on the island to have no agenda of hurting her. His late-night foray into her room could have been simple reconnaissance by a wary criminal. It seemed that he was either there to kill her, in which case she'd already be dead, or he was just one of her husband's cronies. Corrupt, evil, and soulless, as all of them were, but no more threat to her than Elena, the cook, although Sophie wasn't even certain about her. Archer had ways of getting people to do what he wanted, including bribery, threats, and extortion.

Mal didn't seem like someone who'd be coerced into doing anything. Indeed, whoever sent him here would have had to believe he could stand up to Archer. Which meant he was probably no threat to her.

So why did she feel hyperalert around him, restless and churned up? It was either the stomach flu or lust, she told herself with latent amusement. Not that he wasn't lustworthy, with that long, lean body, but she'd much prefer stomach flu. She allowed herself a furtive glance over her shoulder, but he had the same enigmatic expression on his face that he'd had before, giving nothing away, and she told herself that after the past few years, the last thing she was interested in was sex.

The thick foliage began to disperse, and suddenly they reached the small crescent of sand leading down to the deep blue-green water, her own particular place to think, to dream. She'd considered asking Archer to put a pathway to the spot so her wheelchair could reach it, but in the end she'd changed her mind. Archer had never known about it, and this place was hers and hers alone. She had no intention of sharing it.

So why was she sharing it now, with this enigmatic stranger? She'd have to figure that out later.

It didn't look as if anyone else had been there in her absence. The wooden bench where she used to lie, reading her novels, was now over-grown with weeds, the paint peeling off from the constant exposure to sun and rain. The formerly clear water was full of seaweed as it lapped against the shore, but she didn't care. Without realizing it, she let out a sigh of contentment.

"You like this spot better than the wide beach I came in on?" Malcolm said, and Sophie jerked in surprise. For a brief, dangerous moment she'd forgotten all about him, awash in the joy of returning to her favorite place.

He parked her wheelchair at the edge of the sand, locked the wheels, and moved around her to stand by the water. He was wearing sunglasses, though she couldn't remember when he'd put them on, and it almost seemed as if he'd dismissed her from his mind.

She knew better than that. "This is my own secret place," she said finally. "I used to come down here and stay for hours, and no one would ever bother me."

He didn't look back at her. "Used to?"

"You know better than anyone how difficult it is to push a wheel-chair down that path," she said sharply.

He turned then, his sunglasses in place, shielding his eyes and his expression. "You appear to have a household ready to wait on you," he said lightly. "Why didn't you simply ask for someone to bring you down?"

"Appearances can be deceiving," she said. It wasn't a smart thing to do. Malcolm Gunnison needed to think she was deeply in love with her husband, content as a pampered cat.

But why? If Malcolm had come to hurt Archer, then she could help him in return for an escape from this golden prison. But if he'd come to hurt her, to do Archer's bidding and report back to him, then she was better keeping her thoughts and her feelings to herself, as she'd done so well for the past few years. She'd let her instincts betray her once, when she'd fallen for Archer, and she was still paying the price. It would be a cold day in hell before she trusted this man.

She gave a small, self-deprecating laugh. "Don't pay any attention to me, Mr. Gunnison. Every now and then I feel a little bit sorry for myself. Of course you're right—Archer would do anything for me. All I have to do is ask. I just feel that my demands are so many and I give so little back that I don't want to be any more trouble than I have to be. Besides, I kind of like keeping this place a secret, just for me." She knew she was selling it, with a wistful smile and the faintest fluttering of her hand that disguised the muscle and made her seem frail and weak.

She just wished she could see his eyes to make sure. He stared at her for a long, thoughtful minute, saying nothing, and then he moved closer. "Then why did you bring me here?"

The simple question shouldn't have shocked her. Why in God's name *had* she brought him here, to the one place that felt safe? Now it would feel contaminated, ruined.

Oddly enough, though, it didn't. She floundered for an answer and came up with a logical one. "It was the only way I could get here," she said. "And you'll be gone soon enough and no one else will know about it."

He said nothing, and she couldn't tell whether he bought it or not. In fact, she'd been an idiot to direct him down here. The fewer people who knew about this place, the better.

"Do you want to get out of that damned chair?" he said after a moment, his voice casual.

She looked up at him in alarm. "And do what?"

He shrugged. "I don't know. Sit in the sand, put your toes in the water, make sand castles."

"Sand castles are a waste of time. The moment you build them, the tide rolls in and washes them away." Shit, why did she say that? He seemed to have the ability to draw the most revealing things from her. She laughed again. "You see, I warned you I was feeling sorry for myself today."

He dropped down on the wooden bench, ignoring the peeling paint as he watched her. "You know what you do then, Mrs. MacDonald?" he said softly.

She hated that name with a fierce passion, so fierce that she couldn't let it pass. "Call me Sophie," she said abruptly. "And don't tell me you come back and build another sand castle the next day, only to have it wash away again. I'm not that naïve."

He pushed his dark glasses up onto his forehead, and she could see that sharp green gaze of his, uncomfortably intimate. "I don't think you're naïve at all, Sophie." His voice caressed her name, and for a moment she wondered whether "Mrs. MacDonald" might have been preferable after all. He was a cool, distant, dangerous man, and yet somehow he was getting too close. "And I think you're far too practical to keep building castles in the sand, or in the clouds, for that matter. I think you know as well as I do that you find a good, solid surface and build your defenses there."

For some reason the thought of her huge bathroom, the one place where she could move and train her body back into obedience, came into her mind. "Who said anything about defenses? I thought we were talking about castles."

"All good castles need defenses, Sophie. You should know that."

It was almost as if he thought there were some reason she should be conversant with castles and defenses. "I never put much thought into it," she said airily. "And I hardly need any defenses here on Isla Mordita, when I have my husband and so many people looking out for my welfare. In fact, the only unknown potential source of danger is you, Malcolm." There, she said it, she thought, waiting for his reaction.

He dropped his glasses back down on his nose. "Whatever gets you through the night." He leaned back, tilting his face up to the sun, and she said nothing, watching him, the long lines of his body, his dark hair falling away from a face that was almost ascetic. He was wearing jeans today, and for a moment she decided he couldn't be British. All British men wore socks with their sandals.

His blue linen shirt was rolled up at the sleeves, and his forearms looked strong, his hands beautiful. Jesus, even his toes were beautiful. Maybe she had overestimated her own abilities. Even with the element of surprise she had some question whether she'd be able to best him or not if he were the enemy.

She needed a gun. She'd known that all along—a simple firearm for one added bit of protection when she was finally able to make her escape. She'd been an excellent shot, had been even better with a knife, but she preferred hand-to-hand combat. Years ago she could take down a man twice her size in less than a minute.

She didn't think Malcolm Gunnison would be quite that simple to vanquish. A handgun could stop anything short of a stampeding elephant, and there were no elephants on Isla Mordita.

She tilted her own head back to look up into the bright blue sky. The soft breeze across the water made her think of freedom, and if she'd been in any less control of herself, she would have wept. She never cried, not after the first year of her imprisonment. Instead, she let the tension drain from her body as the sun beat down on her, the wind ruffling the trees all around, and she sank back, soaking up the warmth and beauty of the day. There was no guarantee that Malcolm wasn't here to harm her, but she was relatively certain she wasn't in danger at that particular moment. No one was watching. No one would expect anything from her. She closed her eyes and breathed in the day.

Malcolm knew the moment she relaxed, drifted into a light sleep. It surprised him—she'd been sleeping like a rock the night before when he'd gone into her room, and with all the pain meds she was on, she probably got more than her share of rest. It could have been the Vicodin that made her drift off now, but it didn't seem a drugged sleep to him.

He opened his eyes to watch her. Her pale face was tilted back toward the sun, her eyes were closed, and he could see a fresh tracing of freckles across her cheekbones.

She was in her early thirties, seven years younger than he was. He'd heard about her when he was in Africa—not that many women worked for the Committee, and she'd showed enormous promise. They'd been grooming her for great things, but fate had intervened in the form of Archer MacDonald. He'd taken one look at a junior operative who'd simply been there to observe, and apparently the man had fallen in love. It was totally out of character for a sociopath like MacDonald, but if a man was going to fall in love, then Sophie would be the woman to tempt him, he thought lazily. It was a good thing he had no such weakness. Given Archer's unexpected infatuation, no one in the London office could let such an opportunity pass them by, so they'd let Sophie go into the fray when she was unprepared, and disaster had followed.

He wondered what he would have thought of her had he met her back then. Probably not much—the woman was as dumb as a rock to have fallen for Archer MacDonald under any circumstances.

Too bad he found her attractive, with her dark eyebrows beneath the tousle of unshaped, tawny hair. He'd like to pretend it wasn't so, but he was always honest with himself, and he knew there was something about her that drew him. He had absolutely no idea what it was. He could barely see most of her body beneath those long flowing things she wore, and to put it crudely, only half of it worked. He was broad-minded, but that was an unlikely turn-on. Whenever she was around Archer, her intellect seemed to drop, and the rest of the time she seemed faintly crabby, particularly with Mal. That in itself was also interesting—while he hadn't bothered to hit her with his well-practiced charm, she had no reason for her hostility. Unless she suspected he might be a danger to her darling Archer, but that option seemed unlikely, given her lack of mental acuity.

She was probably nothing more than she seemed on the surface: a fretful, spoiled wife who'd outlived her usefulness and had spent the past few years trapped on an island with nowhere to go.

Maybe.

But you didn't survive long in the life they'd chosen if you went with the obvious, and he was taking nothing at face value. She'd been smart enough to have gotten through the rigorous Committee training. Before that she'd worked for the CIA and the State Department, and she'd graduated from Sarah Lawrence summa cum laude. Her dossier had been thorough—including the death of her diplomat parents in a plane crash when she was thirteen, her upbringing with her rigidly conservative aunt. Little wonder she'd gone into government work; less obvious was why she turned to the Committee. It wasn't the place for conservatives who followed rules.

After three years of marriage, two of them bedridden and as a virtual prisoner, wasn't she likely to have seen through Archer's amiable exterior? Or had being so dependent made her cling to him? He glanced down at her motionless legs beneath the flowing skirt. *Nothing at face value*, he reminded himself.

He heard the sound from a distance, someone moving down the path to the small clearing, the footsteps practically inaudible, the rustle of the shrubbery no more than the sound of the breeze. Archer was trying to sneak up on them, and with anyone else he might have gotten away with it. He underestimated Malcolm, which was fine with him, and Mal didn't move from his spot on the bench, seemingly oblivious. Archer wanted to surprise them, not kill them, but Mal moved his hand to the front pocket of his jeans, to the outline of the zip knife he kept there. Whether he could throw it faster than Archer could fire was uncertain, but he was counting on Archer's motives being relatively innocuous, at least for now.

Archer was almost there when Malcolm saw Sophie's eyelids flicker for the briefest instant. *So even in her sleep she had heard him*, he thought. She was stretched in her chair, every muscle relaxed in feigned sleep, but if Archer opened fire he had little doubt her old training would take hold and she'd dive for the sand. Not that it would save her—she would be an easy target if and when Archer was ready to get rid of her. But that wasn't going to be today.

"I thought I'd find you here!" Archer announced as he appeared at the end of the pathway. Mal looked up at him from behind his mirrored sunglasses, not even pretending to be surprised. It was Sophie's behavior that interested him. The moment Archer spoke she jumped, as if startled into wakefulness. She didn't overdo it—just the slightest jerk, and she turned her head back and greeted him with a sleepy smile. This—his first bit of proof that Archer's wife wasn't the docile victim she appeared to be.

"You surprised us," she said in a slightly husky voice that was entirely fake. She'd known perfectly well he was coming. This was getting interesting.

Archer towered over her, leaning down to give her a kiss on her pale mouth, and Mal watched her body rise toward his, instinctively moving into the kiss. Or that was what she wanted it to look like. He was beginning to question all his assumptions about the former Committee member.

When Archer moved back she looked up at her husband adoringly, her rich brown eyes warm with love, but he'd already dismissed her, turning his back on her to look at Malcolm. "You've made quite a hit with my wife," Archer said cheerfully. "As far as I know she's never let anyone bring her down here to her special place. Even I've been off-limits."

"I didn't know you even knew where it was," Sophie said softly.

"Of course I did, baby," Archer said smugly. "I know everything that goes on at Isla Mordita, especially when it concerns my sweet wife." He glanced up at the gathering clouds. "I think you two picked the wrong time for your walk—we're about to get one of our usual late-morning rain showers. Malcolm, come back with me and we'll play a game of pool. I'll send Joe down to fetch Sophie."

Mal didn't rise from the bench. "I wouldn't think of leaving her," he said, managing to sound almost indifferent. "I'll bring her back up to the house and meet you in the pool room."

Archer snorted but didn't look displeased. "That wheelchair is just about solid gold, but it doesn't go up the path nearly as well as it goes down, and she's going to be bumped all to hell if you try it. Joe's a bull—he won't have any trouble, and I wouldn't want my baby to be in any more pain than she's already in."

Only the slightest twitch below her left eye showed she didn't like being called "baby," another fascinating bit of information that Archer missed entirely. "Not a problem," Mal said, rising. "I'll carry her and Joe can bring up the wheelchair."

Archer stared at him for a long moment, considering. And then he grinned, flashing his big, perfect teeth in a blinding smile. "You're a better man than I am. She's put on a few pounds while she's been bedridden, and she's no featherweight."

Mal checked her out of the corner of his eye, but she didn't react to that jab at all. "I'm stronger than I look," he said mildly. In fact, despite Archer's bulked-up shoulders, Malcolm thought he could probably take Archer easily enough. He was naturally built along lean lines, but that didn't mean he didn't possess a deceptive amount of power.

Archer smiled at the two of them impartially. "I'll tell Joe to take his time," he said, and disappeared back up the path.

More of his twisted matchmaking, Mal thought, still clueless to the reasoning behind it. He rose, moving toward the chair.

"I don't mind a few bumps . . ." Sophie began, but Mal simply lifted her up in his arms, holding her against him. Archer was right—she was no sylph, but it felt like muscle beneath the flowing sundress, another interesting observation.

"It's starting to rain"—he cut her off—"and I'm not in the mood to get drenched."

She looked at him, her eyes at his level now, though his were still covered by mirrored sunglasses. "Then put me down and run back to the house. I'm waterproof."

"So am I," he said, and started up the slope.

Chapter Seven

Malcolm moved up the path without the slightest effort, when the burly Joe would have been panting heavily, and Sophie tried to keep still. The rain had begun to fall in earnest, plastering them both, so that their damp bodies and wet clothes clung together as he strolled toward the house, and she did her best to hold herself stiff in his arms. For some idiotic reason she was tempted to press her head against his shoulder. There was something disturbing about being held tucked against him, his warmth flowing into hers.

She was a tall, strong woman, but he was a tall, much stronger man, and everywhere her body touched he seemed hard as iron. She knew she should push him away, but she couldn't. There would be no way to break free of his arms, not unless she had the chance to fight dirty, and even then he might be invulnerable. She couldn't even begin to guess what he was thinking.

He looked down at her. "Relax. I'm not about to carry you off and have my wicked way with you. You're acting like my body is poison. It's not."

"I'm not used to having men cart me around." She tried to relax a little bit against him. The more she reacted to him, the weaker her position. She needed to be immune to the effect he had on her, or at least appear to be.

"No? I thought you couldn't walk."

She looked into the dark glasses, feeling her self-assurance come back. Here, at least, she could be truthful. "I spend most of the time in my room. When I leave it's usually Joe who carries me."

There was the slightest hint of a smile on his mouth. "Joe's not a man?"

"Of course he is. I mean . . . that is . . ." She couldn't think her way out of the mess she'd gotten into. She could hardly tell him that he was the only man she'd found attractive in years.

He probably knew, but thank God he changed the subject. "You've got freckles," he said. "Don't you ever get out in the sun?"

She considered not answering. "Not much. I burn easily." A lie, but she'd already slipped up. He didn't need to know that she hated her husband—it would put her in too much jeopardy. "The balcony off my bedroom is in such rough shape they keep the door locked so I don't accidentally hurt myself." Of course they did it to keep her imprisoned, but she was talking too much and couldn't help herself. Breathing fresh air, today and yesterday, was its own painful pleasure. She'd grown so sick of the artificial, regurgitated air of her bedroom that she'd almost forgotten what the sea breeze felt like, tasted like. Maybe that was why she suddenly felt she couldn't wait any longer to leave.

He said nothing, not even a noncommittal sound, and when they crested the hill, Joe was waiting for them, an unhappy expression on his broad face. He reached for her and for a moment it seemed as if Mal's arms tightened around her.

Mal let her go without a word. For a moment their clothes stuck together, her sundress against his soaked linen shirt, and then Joe pulled her back, carting her off before she could control her rattled brain enough to utter a polite thank-you. When she glanced back over Joe's shoulder, Mal was already gone.

Half an hour later she lay stretched across her bed, her eyes drifting closed. It had to be midafternoon, and the rain hadn't stopped. In the semitropical climate of Isla Mordita the daily rains usually lasted for no more than half an hour, filling the cisterns and leaving everything sunny and bright and newly washed. It was rare when the weather settled in for the entire day, turning the island into a veritable steam bath once the sun came out again.

Today was one of those days when the sun seemed to have disappeared, plunging her large, sparsely furnished room into darkness. She should turn on the light to banish the shadows, but she couldn't bring herself to move.

Sophie shivered slightly in the cool air. She hadn't bothered to change out of her wet dress once Joe had taken her from Malcolm's arms and returned her to her prison, and she knew she ought to find the remote control on her bedside table and at least turn down the air-conditioning, but she was feeling too indolent.

She'd had the oddest feeling that Malcolm hadn't wanted to relinquish her to Joe, which was, of course, ridiculous. They didn't trust each other, though she had no idea what exactly he might suspect her of. In fact, any guest of Archer's would be wise to suspect everyone, and Malcolm Gunnison was no fool.

Neither was she. Archer surrounded himself with criminals, thieves, and murderers, and even the best of the bunch, like Joe and Marco, couldn't be counted on. If Archer decided he'd had enough of her, she'd have no recourse. Marco liked his pills, but he liked being alive more, and disobeying Archer would put a swift end to it. Joe might be fond of her, but there wasn't much room for sentiment in his tough old body. He'd spent a lifetime breaking the law, and if he had any softer feelings, they would have disappeared long ago.

Maybe she should think about leaving sooner rather than later and forget about her plan to kill Archer. Someone else would have to take care of it, but she had little doubt it would happen eventually. She shouldn't risk her sketchy escape plan just for the pleasure of putting a bullet between those baby blues. Even if it seemed to be Malcolm's brilliant green eyes that kept haunting her.

She rolled over onto her back, shivering slightly, careful to keep her legs limp and unresponsive. She knew where the cameras were, and while it was always possible Archer no longer had anyone watching her, she couldn't afford to take a chance.

Things had been the status quo for so long she'd thought she could afford to spend two more weeks in endurance training. It was early November—she'd randomly chosen the fifteenth as a good day to escape. In the past Archer had always returned to the mainland around that time, which coincided with his birthday. His elderly father was still alive, though with borderline dementia, and Archer made it a habit to visit him. The elder MacDonald probably didn't recognize his son anymore. With a certain amount of glee Archer had informed her that the old man had forgotten her existence years ago, and the one time she'd met him, he hadn't had much use for Archer. It had been startling, after watching everyone fawn over her husband, to see someone who didn't seem to adore him, but later she decided that Armstrong MacDonald probably knew far too well exactly who and what her husband was. He'd reacted to her with a slightly impatient pity, which had disturbed Sophie even more at the time.

Now she knew why.

Joe always accompanied Archer when he left the island, but there would still be more than a handful of people watching her, people with strict orders to keep her in line. It was possible everyone on the island would be more alert when Archer was gone. It was just as possible they'd slack off, particularly if she did nothing to draw attention.

Time was running out—she knew that as surely as she knew her own name. She could double her middle-of-the-night training efforts. She could fool anyone in the world, including Archer, that she was content in her confinement. At least she thought she could. With someone like Mal Gunnison she wasn't quite so certain—if anyone could see through her charade, he would be the one.

But why would he bother? He was probably no better than Archer, and she would fall very low on his radar. She just wished he hadn't carried her through the rain, his hard, hard body holding hers. It had been so long since she'd been aware of any man—maybe her libido wasn't dead after all. She had to put that out of her mind—she'd have more than enough time to explore her libido once she got off the island.

She closed her eyes. It was late. She'd had Joe draw the room-darkening shades over the window, telling him she planned to nap, but even in the murky darkness sleep was the furthest thing from her mind.

She couldn't stop thinking about Mal. *Who is he? Why is he here?*

She closed her eyes. She wasn't interested in watching movies, reading turgid Russian prose, or listening to the audiobooks that Emilia, one of the maids, would lend her when no one was looking. If she thought she had a chance in hell of getting away with it, she would have found a way to sneak into the room next door and see if she could find out any answers about Malcolm Gunnison, but the cameras would pick up her movements, and given her luck, Mal could return just as she was in the middle of it. She had no choice but to stay where she was.

She was weary, confused, with too many things batting at her. The likelihood of Archer summoning her down to dinner again was low. She closed her eyes, listening to the steady beat of the rain against the terra-cotta tiles on the roof, and drifted off.

She heard him come into the room. She'd always been a light sleeper, and after the Committee she'd trained herself to wake at even the slightest unexpected breath. Someone was there, and she had absolutely no idea who it was.

Common sense told her it was Rachel, snooping again, but even the practically silent tread sounded as if belonged to a male. Not Joe's shuffle, and no other male servants would come upstairs. It had to be Archer, or Mal.

She wanted it to be Mal, and that truth was such a shock that her eyes opened, when normally she would have feigned sleep. The man was sitting in the darkness, watching her, and she could barely see his silhouette. *It's all right*, she told herself hurriedly. Of course she wanted it to be Malcolm. Malcolm had no reason to hurt her. Neither did Archer, but that had never stopped him before.

"There you are, sleepyhead," Archer cooed in a soft voice. "I wondered when you were going to wake up."

She lifted her head, summoning a sleepy smile. He wanted her to show fear, and that was the one thing she refused to do. "Have you been here long?"

"A while," he said. "I wanted to talk to you about Mal."

"It's probably not a good idea," she said in a low voice. "These walls aren't that thick. He could hear you." *Please leave*, she thought desperately, showing none of it. *Please, please leave.*

Archer leaned forward, and she could see the gleam of his oversized white teeth in the murky light. "That's why I chose now. Your friend Malcolm has gone for a walk, and he's halfway out to the sugar mill, according to my men. He won't be back for at least an hour."

"But it's raining," she said. Archer could be lying, just trying to spook her. Tormenting her was one of his favorite pastimes, but he enjoyed psychological torture as much as he enjoyed hurting her.

"You've been asleep. It stopped half an hour ago." He rose, slowly approaching the bed. "I'm not happy about the way you look at my guest."

How do I look at his guest? Sophie thought in confusion. She'd done everything she could to appear unaffected by his presence. And hadn't he wanted Malcolm to seduce her?

She knew what was coming then. Archer never needed an excuse—he used whatever popped into his head. Malcolm was far away from any noise she or Archer might make, and her stomach was a knot.

She pushed her body up into a sitting position, smiling at him hopefully. The first blow across her face almost threw her off the bed.

———

Sophie lay on her stomach, fighting the need to curl up in the fetal position and hold her arms against herself. She sucked in her breath, listening to her body, trying to catalog what he'd done to her. She'd always been good with pain, and as far as she could tell he'd done nothing that would interfere with her escape. He hadn't bothered hitting her legs—he believed she had no feeling in them and that wasn't any fun for him. As long as she could run, she was in good shape.

Her arm hurt—he'd wrenched it. That could a problem if she had to row, but she'd deal with that later. Right then all she wanted to do was lie still and regain some equilibrium.

She heard the scratching noise from a distance, and she lifted her head. It was so quiet she thought she might have imagined it, but she had never been prey to her imagination. Were there mice on Isla Mordita? Even worse, were there snakes?

She pushed herself up slowly, remembering to keep her legs still. She hated snakes with a fiery passion—a silly weakness that she hadn't managed to overcome. She'd used her mental training to survive the endless days in the bedroom, the removal of any meaningful human interaction, Archer's occasional temper tantrums like the one today, fits of rage that never had any rhyme or reason, and she figured she'd done a decent job of it. Once she got free she wasn't going to curl up in a weeping bundle of PTSD.

But she hadn't been able to meditate away her fear of snakes.

She heard the sound again, coming from the deck outside the door, and she froze, as the knob turned and the door was slowly pushed open.

Malcolm stood there, silhouetted against the setting sun, and for a moment her breath caught, before she regained control of her common sense. With almost superhuman effort she managed to pull herself into a sitting position, ignoring the pain in her wrenched arm, the dull throb in her ribs. If he'd broken them she would have to find something to tape them with—otherwise they could slow her down if she had to make a run for it.

"What are you doing here?" she demanded, furious that her voice came out a little shaky. She should have gotten used to Archer's occasional attentions by now—there was no need for her to feel sorry for herself. He hadn't had time to get properly worked up, and the bruises would fade quickly.

"Archer said you fell down the stairs," he said, and he sounded almost annoyed. "Why did you do a stupid thing like that?"

"Why would you care?" she shot back without thinking. He'd sounded different in his irritation, and then she realized what it was. His English accent had faded.

"I don't, particularly," he said, his anger vanishing as if it had never been there, and he stepped into the shadowy room. It was a lie, and she wondered why. Why he would care one way or another if she'd been hurt?

"Then why are you here?"

He hesitated for a moment. "The rain's stopped," he said, "and the sun is starting to come out."

"It usually does," she said caustically. "You still haven't told me why you're here, and for that matter, where did you get the key for that door?" She knew perfectly well he'd picked it, just as he had last night. She even knew he'd deliberately made more noise this afternoon, just to alert her. Whoever he was, he was good. The fresh air drifted in, and she felt cool, healing energy begin to surge through her bruised body.

His mouth curled, just slightly. "I decided you shouldn't be kept a prisoner in this room. You should at least have the run of the balcony."

"It's covered with wood and construction debris," she protested, stalling for time. She needed to get herself into the bathroom and assess the damages. Archer had come up with the perfect explanation for any bruises, but she wanted to see for herself how bad they were.

"I cleared it. Hop into your chair and I'll show you."

"I don't hop anywhere," she said severely.

His smile was wider now, startling her. He'd been so dark and unreadable that seeing him actually smile was unsettling. It was a charming smile, hinting that there was more beneath his cool, distant exterior. "Of course you don't," he said soothingly. "My bad. I forget you're paralyzed."

She should believe him, but she didn't. She'd given him absolutely no reason to suspect her, but there was something going on behind those green eyes, and she hadn't the faintest idea what it was. She knew one thing—she should never underestimate Malcolm Gunnison.

She pushed her legs over to the side of the bed, not bothering to hide her grimace of pain. The ribs felt bruised, not broken, and the side of her face throbbed, but it was her right arm and shoulder that hurt the most, that had taken the brunt of his punishment, and using them to lever her body into the chair made her want to whimper. Nothing that a little ibuprofen, ice, and sheer will wouldn't bring under control, but she wasn't about to show weakness in front of Mal. She landed in the chair a little less gracefully than usual, and her limp legs hit against the footrests with a clanging sound. She needed to be left alone to lick her wounds. He wasn't getting the message.

She picked up her legs and placed her supposedly useless feet on the footrests before she unlocked the wheels. At least she didn't need to pretend about the pain, and she slowly wheeled herself around the big bed to stop in front of him as he filled the French doors. She could see the sun behind him, sparkling off the rain-damp palm trees, and she could smell the hypnotic ambrosia of the ocean and wet earth. Pain was the least of her problems, and she knew with sudden certainty that nothing could keep her locked in her bedroom anymore, not common sense, not her sadistic husband, not the danger that Malcolm Gunnison represented, not even the risk of her escape. He was gilded by the sunlight, but he was no angel—of that she was sure. But the question still remained—was he a devil?

She looked up at him, her face still in the shadows. He hadn't changed either, and his linen shirt was still damp, clinging to his chest, revealing more muscle than she would have thought for such a lean body.

"Are you going to just stand there?" she said, not bothering to hide her impatience. "Or are you some troll guarding the entrance, and you want me to pay my way?"

She caught him off guard. His slow smile widened, and she felt a sudden tightening in her stomach. This dangerous, dangerous man shouldn't have a smile like that, one that was absolutely breathtaking. "Depends on what you have to offer," he said.

She didn't smile back—she couldn't afford to—but resisting that smile was ridiculously difficult. "Not much that you would want."

"I don't know about that," he said, and she held her breath as he moved, knowing he was going to touch her.

Instead, he stepped back, holding the wide door open for her to roll the chair through, and her sense of relief was so strong she almost missed her own thread of regret. Yes, he was a danger. But she didn't frighten easily.

The moment she reached the rain-washed flagstones of the balcony, she forgot all about him. She could see the ocean from up here, the sun as it was dipping lower and lower in the west—the scents of the island were almost overwhelming. Even after all this time she felt herself seduced by the beauty of the place, the feel of the hot, lush air on her skin, the soft breeze ruffling her hair, the sinking sun warming her face.

"Isn't this better?" He was right behind her, too close, and once more she had the odd sense that he was going to touch her.

He didn't.

"Much better," she said, unable to keep the note of longing from her voice as she looked out over the sandy beach where she used to run, the riot of flowers in the garden she'd once planned and tended.

She felt him step back. "I'll leave you to enjoy yourself," he said.

This time she did turn, moving her chair to look up at him. "Why did you do this?"

His expression had frozen, and she realized belatedly that he hadn't had a good look at her yet. "What the fuck did you do to yourself?"

She was tempted to wheel away from him, but that would be even more awkward. She could feel heat flame her face, but she did her best to look calm. "Archer told you," she reminded him. "I fell down the stairs."

"How?"

"What do you mean, how? How does anyone fall down the stairs?"

His green eyes were eagle-sharp, all charm vanishing. "You look beat to shit," he said, "but a fall down those stairs, with the wheelchair on top of you, could have killed you, or at least broken a few bones. Yet you look like you took a tumble in your bathroom, not defied death. I'm still asking you. What happened?"

She could tell him none of his goddamned business, but that might seem defensive. The last thing she wanted him or anyone else to know was that she had to put up with Archer's sadistic abuse. It shamed her.

She had no choice but to compound the lie. "I didn't fall all the way down the stairs," she said. "It was just partway, and I fell out of the wheelchair without bringing it with me. In fact, there's nothing to make such a fuss over. I felt dizzy, came out of my room to call for Joe, and the next thing I knew I was halfway down the stairs, hurting like hell."

He looked at her for a long moment, his eyes running down her body, from her bare feet peeping from beneath the sundress to her bare arms. "And you'd have no reason to lie," he said eventually.

"Of course not!" she said, surprised enough to sound believable. "Why would I?"

"You tell me." He leaned over, placing his hands on the arms of the wheelchair, trapping her. *But then, supposedly I am already trapped*, she reminded herself.

"Look," she said in a reasonable voice. "My husband loves me, and even if he didn't, he's very careful about his possessions. He wouldn't let anyone get away with hurting me."

"I'm sure he wouldn't," Mal said. He leaned forward and his fingers brushed against her upper arm with exquisite tenderness. "You just happened to land on something that left a bruise with a remarkable resemblance to a hand."

She looked down. It was there on her arm, the outline of Archer's hand where he'd gripped her so tightly it still ached. She met Mal's calm gaze. There was no pity, no emotion at all. "So it does," she said, shrugging, able to stop her wince in time. "Do I strike you as the kind of woman who would allow herself to be manhandled?" She almost didn't want him to answer.

"It depends who and what you really are," he said. "And whether you really belong in that wheelchair."

The words were like a punch in the stomach, but she managed not to react. "Oh, actually I'm just fine. I spend all the time in my room tap-dancing—I hope the noise hasn't bothered you."

There was the faintest hint of a smile on his mouth, but he didn't say anything, just started for his open door. He paused at the entrance. "I'll leave you to enjoy some time to yourself. Feel free to tap-dance if the mood strikes you."

"Why did you unlock the door?" she said suddenly, unwilling to let him leave. "I don't think my husband will approve."

"No, I suppose he won't," Malcolm replied. "He likes to keep you like a rare specimen, a butterfly under glass. That way he can take you out any time he wants and pull your wings off."

He knew. Of course he did—Mal wasn't a man who missed anything, and adding two and two wasn't rocket science. She wasn't going to bother denying it.

"But they always grow back," she said. She tried for an easy laugh, knowing it was unconvincing. "I'll just enjoy the terrace while it lasts."

"Oh, it will last," he said smoothly. "Your husband will do it if I ask him."

"My husband doesn't do anything he doesn't want to do. That's the advantage of being a billionaire. Why should it be any different with you?"

"Leave that up to me," Malcolm said.

Before she could ask another question he was gone, and she breathed a reluctant sigh of relief. She'd said more to him in the last five minutes than she'd said to anyone else in the years since she'd been shot. Those were dangerous waters.

She rolled the chair back to the edge so she could look at the sea, all the time conscious of the camera on the overhanging roof trained on her. At least the cameras were stationary, and it was easy enough to figure out the trajectory of its view—where she'd be safe to move, where she wouldn't be watched.

Would Malcolm really be able to convince Archer to leave the door unlocked, the stretch of balcony cleared? Archer wouldn't have much excuse not to, but that wouldn't faze her husband. If he wanted her locked up, he would do so.

And what kind of leverage did Malcolm have? Archer could buy anything he wanted, steal it, murder to get it. He had all the money he could ever need, enough power—personal, financial, and political—to keep him happy. What could someone like Malcolm Gunnison possibly have to offer that would compete with that?

As if summoned by her thoughts, Archer strode out onto the beach, wearing his swim trunks, one of the women on his arm like a trophy. From that distance Sophie couldn't quite tell which one it was—the three of them looked alike, but from the immovable plastic boobs she guessed it was Rachel who was dressed in the monokini. They were at the water's edge when Malcolm joined them, and for a moment Sophie's breath caught. He'd changed too, in record time, and for a moment she couldn't pull her eyes from him.

He should have looked thin and weak next to Archer's bulked-up physique, but Sophie wasn't fooled. Beneath the smoothly tanned skin were taut muscles, possibly even a match for Archer's brute strength.

Malcolm said something and Archer threw back his head and laughed. He glanced up at the balcony, and if she hadn't been shielded by the half wall he would have seen her there, watching. In fact, he gave a little wave in her approximate direction anyway, seemingly light-hearted, as if he hadn't used his fists on her less than an hour ago.

So Malcolm must have told him he'd unlocked the door, and Archer wasn't objecting. What kind of hold did Mal have over her husband?

She glanced over at his door. He'd left it open, but there was no way she was going to risk searching his room in broad daylight. For all she knew it could be a trap—she didn't trust Mal any more than she trusted Archer. In fact, she trusted him less. With Archer she knew what she was facing. Malcolm Gunnison was an enigma, and she wasn't about to risk anything, ever again, on some damned man.

Chapter Eight

Malcolm took his time getting back to his room. If there was any trace of the operative Sophie had once been, she would have used that time to search his room, and he'd left an almost imperceptible thread across the threshold of the French doors leading out onto the balcony. It was still in place. His own room was three steps down, and she wouldn't be able to manage it in her wheelchair, but he'd wondered. Either she'd gotten rusty, or she really did belong in that wheelchair.

There was no sign that she was faking—he was simply trained to question everything. He'd checked the soles of her shoes and the bottoms of her feet—always a simple tell if someone actually walked. None of the countless pairs of sandals had ever touched the ground, and her perfectly manicured feet looked soft and useless. He'd put a bug in her room, one she hadn't found, but he'd heard nothing unusual during the night—when she got up to go to the bathroom the sounds were clearly that of someone using a wheelchair. Then again, she still had all her cameras in place and a former operative would know that. She wouldn't dare slip up.

He could always go in and pull out her cameras as well. Archer had accepted Malcolm's own debugging, but he might not be so sanguine about the surveillance on his wife, particularly when he got off on hitting her. He probably kept the surveillance tapes and watched them late at night, jacking off, the asshole. Then again, he'd suggested that

Malcolm fuck her, and Malcolm could make it clear he never enjoyed an audience. It would be a good enough reason.

Except that if he were really going to screw her he wasn't going to take any chance that Archer could watch.

He still couldn't figure out why the hell Archer wanted him to bone his wife. It had to be some kind of test, or even a punishment for his bride. He'd known Sophie had come from the Committee—otherwise there'd have been no need to try to kill her, and then keep her prisoner on this island. Whatever game he was playing, Mal had to make sure he wasn't going to end up on the losing side. Sophie's place there was a foregone conclusion, and he couldn't jeopardize his own position in trying to protect her.

He showered off the salt water, pulled on boxer briefs, and headed into the closet. They'd said her fate was up to him. He could kill her if he needed to, leave her, or bring her out. She'd committed an unpardonable act, and he'd had every intention of letting her fend for herself. That was before he'd seen her, though.

She wasn't his responsibility, he reminded himself. He was there because she'd failed, and it had taken this long to build up the intel, the infrastructure, to get close to Archer again. She deserved nothing.

He rose, glancing out the open French doors to the sunset streaking the sky. He didn't have to decide yet. Not until Archer's fucking scientist showed up with the RU48. Until then he'd take it one step at a time. In the meantime he was going to head downstairs and see if he could catch her in some microscopic move that would prove whether she really couldn't walk. If she was faking it, then she had to slip up sooner or later. If she wasn't faking, if she really was stuck in that wheelchair, he didn't know if he still had enough of a conscience that he could live with leaving her behind. Not that he owed her anything—he'd killed for less of a reason than her mistakes.

He should be thinking about his mission, not wasting his time on an extraneous detail like Sophie. He dressed and was headed for the door when something stopped him; that damned, illogical voice that had been interfering more and more with his life. He glanced out at the balcony—no sign, no sound. He should simply go down to dinner, but he knew he wasn't going to.

Sophie was sitting in her chair, just inside her open door, reading a massive book. She knew he was there—he could read it in the slight twitch in her bare shoulders above the sundress, but she deliberately didn't look up. All right, he could go with that. He stood there and watched her with interest.

The bruises on her arms could have been worse, he supposed. The imprint of a handgrip was clear, and there were other marks as well. He couldn't see the pattern of old breaks, so at least Archer had stopped before he reached that point. She was holding a pack of ice to her face, the darkening bruise on her jaw clashing with the flush of pink on her cheeks, and the spattering of freckles was still there from her time in the sun, an oddly lighthearted counterpoint to the signs of abuse. Her shoulders had a touch of color as well, and he noticed that the golden freckles had traveled there too.

Her brown eyes were expressionless as they took him in, and she dropped the ice pack on the table and closed the book, not bothering to hold her place. Momentary insanity, he told himself, strolling through the door to her side. He'd always been a sucker for vulnerable women. Madsen told him it was his knight-in-shining-armor complex. "That doesn't look like much of a page-turner," he said in a cool voice that gave nothing away.

She handed it to him, and the damned thing must have weighed five pounds. "*War and Peace?*" he said in surprise. "You strike me more as the bodice-ripper type."

She scowled at him, then winced as the expression must have tugged at her bruised cheek. "This was Archer's idea. He thought, since I had so much time on my hands, that I should improve my mind. He sometimes forgets that I'm not another Rachel."

"Which one is Rachel?" He knew perfectly well who she was—he knew everyone on the island—but he wanted to see her reaction.

"She's the one with the plastic boobs."

He nodded, hiding a smile. Sophie was probably a respectable 34B, if he knew women, and he did, but when it came to boobs and thighs, American women were notoriously insecure. Most women who worked for the Committee didn't bother with such shallow concerns, but Sophie had been out of the game for a long time.

He was watching her legs covertly, careful to make sure she didn't realize what he was doing. Not a twitch. Had Archer hit her there as well? He shrugged. "I hadn't noticed."

She gave him a disbelieving look. "Don't be ridiculous. She shoves them in everyone's face."

He hid his amusement. "Maybe she's not my type."

"She's every man's type."

"Maybe I don't like women?" he suggested.

She didn't even pause. "I'd have a hard time believing that," she said flatly.

That was enough to startle him again. "What makes you say that?" He'd never had any problem convincing people he was gay if his role called for it.

She tilted her head back, examining him slowly, as if considering. "Instinct," she said finally.

"You have such infallible instincts when it comes to judging men?" It was a low blow, and cruel, but he said it anyway.

Her expression was stony. "No. Just when it comes to you."

"I'm flattered." In fact, he was wary. She was more observant than he wanted her to be, a needless complication. He should never have cleared off the balcony for her, never have taken her down to that small crescent of beach. Not that he didn't have the perfect excuse—Archer had asked him to screw her. But since he had every intention of resisting temptation he should have just kept his distance.

It was definitely odd—usually he was either attracted to a woman or not, and there was nothing more likely to make him lose interest than complications. Sophie MacDonald was beyond complicated—she was a Gordian knot of epic proportions. The last thing he needed to be doing was thinking about what she might like in bed. What would please her. How much she could feel.

A soft breeze came up, blowing her skirt against her motionless legs. "May I help you downstairs?" he said, seemingly the perfect gentleman, when in fact he wanted to hold her again, see if he could figure out exactly what was wrong with her lower limbs.

She shook her head. "I'm not invited down tonight. Archer decided I've had too much stimulation and need a quiet night in my room." Her words were calm, her face expressionless, and yet he could practically feel the rage vibrating through her. Her mask was slipping, at least when he was around. Did she have any idea how dangerous that was?

"Nonsense." Before she could realize what he was doing, he'd scooped her up out of the wheelchair. She resisted for a moment, but her legs were motionless.

"Archer isn't going to like this," she warned him.

He shifted her a little higher. "Put your arms around my neck so I don't drop you," he said, and he half-expected her to hit him. She hesitated, and then to his surprise did as she was told, her body relaxing against his just slightly. Just enough.

He looked down at her, and then he did one of the stupidest things he'd ever done in his entire life. He dropped his head down and brushed his mouth across hers, lightly.

Her shocked intake of breath was amusing. "Why did you do that?" she demanded, sounding angry and confused.

He shrugged, shifting her closer against his chest. "I wanted to see if I liked it."

She was struggling under some strong emotion, but he couldn't quite tell what it was. Fury? Longing? A combination of both? "And did you?"

She really had the most beautiful warm, brown eyes. No wonder a psychopath like Archer had fallen for her—who wouldn't? "I don't know yet," he said lightly. "I'll have to try it again when someone hasn't slammed a fist into your mouth." He waited for her to deny it. Kissing her had been a very bad idea, because he wanted more, and even if he ignored common sense and his mission, he couldn't ignore the very real pain she must be feeling.

Her expression darkened. "No one slammed a fist into my mouth," she snapped. "And if you try it again, that's exactly what I'll do to you."

"Of course you will, Sophie," he said dryly. "Ready for dinner, or should I see if there are other, less damaged parts of you I could kiss?"

She actually did try to hit him then—a lost cause when she was trapped in his arms. "No?" he said. "I'm willing to wait." He started toward the door, opening it with ease and carrying her through it. "And don't worry that your husband might object to your presence tonight— he wants to placate me while I sit around on this damned island wait- ing. Besides, I think he needs to look at your face."

There was still tension in her body, but she said nothing as they started down the stairs. They met the burly guard halfway down, a pugnacious look on the man's face. "Boss said you were to stay upstairs, missus," he said, and made as if to take her from Malcolm's arms.

Stupid move on his part. "She's coming down for dinner," Mal said flatly, considering his options. Normally in a situation like this he wouldn't rock the boat. If the man, Joe, tried to take her away from him, he could disable him with a kick that he wouldn't see coming, but he hoped he wouldn't have to go that far. A bull like Joe wouldn't be disabled long, even with a kick to the groin, and Mal didn't want to be grappling on the stairs with Sophie in the way.

"Could you get my chair, Joe?" Sophie said.

Her request distracted the bodyguard long enough to let Mal think about what he was doing. Archer wouldn't like a confrontation at this point any more than Mal did, and it could backfire on Joe.

Finally the man stepped back with a brief nod. "If you want to go downstairs, I'll carry you," he said finally, not giving up. "You know Mr. MacDonald doesn't like other men touching you."

"He'll tolerate me," Mal said, pushing past him. "And don't bother with the wheelchair—I can take care of her." He continued down the stairs, holding her carefully, not looking back.

"Now that you two dogs are finished fighting over me," Sophie said in a caustic voice, "maybe you should just take me back . . ."

"Maybe you should stop letting men bully you," Mal said.

He would have found her tart expression comical if it weren't for the bruises. "That's exactly what I'm trying to do. Take me back upstairs."

"I'm talking about men who would hurt you."

She laughed out loud, the sound bitter. "And you're exempt from that list?"

It shouldn't have bothered him, but he did. Score one for Mrs. MacDonald. Maybe all her training hadn't disappeared. He might even have to go as far as killing her—he was hardly a safe haven. If he knew anything about women, he knew that ones who have been abused tend to have a love-hate relationship with their abuser. She might want Archer dead, but she could just as easily hate whoever did the deed.

Archer was waiting for them by the time they reached the bottom of the stairs, his usual affable smile on his face, but Mal could see in his eyes that he'd done exactly what Archer wanted him to do. *Tant pis.* If Archer thought Mal was playing into his hands, so much the better.

"You changed your mind about coming down, darling!" Archer cooed. "I'm so glad. After that wicked fall I thought you might not feel able to join us. So clumsy of you. How many times have I told you to be careful?"

Damn. She's good, thought Mal. There wasn't a trace of tension in her body as she smiled at the bastard. "I'm sorry, Archer. I should have waited for Joe."

He leaned forward and gave her an affectionate tap on the chin. "My naughty girl," he said with such rich indulgence that Mal was impressed. Did these two play out these games without an audience, or was their mutual hatred out in the open? Did he smile as he hit her? Archer held out his arms. "I'll take my wife. After all, she's my burden, not yours."

Mal wasn't about to relinquish her. "Not tonight," he said evenly.

There was a sudden stillness in the room, as if time had stopped. Mal had thrown down a challenge, and a man like Archer would never let someone dictate to him. Maybe he was going to flip out, and this whole debacle would be over.

He wanted it all to be over. He wanted to kill Archer MacDonald, and he had ever since he'd seen the bruises on Sophie's face. *What the hell is wrong with me?* he thought. He had a mission to complete, and RU48 was an important part of it. If he killed Archer now, it would set them back months, something the world couldn't afford. But he wasn't about to step back. Archer had started this game, with Sophie as the prize. Mal played to win.

After a frozen moment Archer raised a patrician eyebrow, and the tension drained from the room. "Oh ho! It seems you've got a conquest, my little Sophie. Not that I blame him. You're still one hell of a woman." He turned. "We're having drinks by the pool. Join us out there."

He drifted off, but Mal made no effort to follow him. He was aware of Sophie's dark eyes staring up at him. "Are you out of your fucking mind?" she demanded. "What are you doing?" For once her voice was devoid of all of the roles she'd been playing—it was flat, even business-like. But she was no longer a professional.

He looked down at her, the bruised cheek, the wash of freckles, the rich brown eyes, and the mouth he'd kissed . . . he shouldn't be thinking about her mouth. He was a man known to be the consummate professional, a killer with ice in his veins. Could he actually kill her if the time came? "What do I think I'm doing?" Mal echoed lightly. "Putting the cat among the pigeons." Keeping a firm hold on her, he strode out to the veranda.

Sophie had had more comfortable meals in her life. The barbs between Archer and Mal were flying fast and furious, making her acutely uncomfortable, even more so because she couldn't read the level of true animosity between the thinly veiled insults and suggestions. She only knew that Archer was enjoying himself immensely—nothing made him happier than sparring with an equal partner. She'd decided long ago that that was one reason he hit her—he wanted an adversary, and she refused to give him one, no matter how he attacked. He'd never said a word about what he'd discovered about her true identity, and she'd never hinted that she knew he was behind her almost murder. She just smiled sweetly at him, her only form of revenge.

Her jaw hurt when she chewed, but she gave no sign of it. The two men were deep in their contest, and it seemed as if no one were paying attention to her, but she knew otherwise. Both of them were watching her and pretending they weren't, and she was pissed off, restless, annoyed. She wasn't sure who she was angrier with—her murderous husband who had used his fists on her just a few hours earlier or the man who had seemed to help her.

Why the hell had he kissed her? Despite outward appearances she wasn't stupid enough to think he didn't have some complicated, probably lethal, motive behind it. People in Malcolm Gunnison's world—that world inhabited by the Archers and the various other soulless people she'd met along the way—didn't kiss like that, they fucked. If they kissed at all, it was simply as foreplay, a far cry from the brush of his lips against hers. She'd never been kissed like that—all gentleness from a man who probably didn't have a gentle bone in his body. She wanted to throw her wineglass at him.

She wasn't going to do that, of course. She was going to sit there and smile airily and not give anything away, not her hatred of Archer and his vicious hands, not her confusion over Mal. In fact, she wasn't going to think about that kiss at all—it was an aberration, done to set her off balance. Or maybe he just felt sorry for the beaten wife. Except you didn't put your mouth against someone's if you were feeling sympathetic.

No, she wasn't going to think about it.

Problem was, she didn't trust Mal any more than she trusted her husband. No one on this island was innocent, not even her, and enough of her training remained that she recognized Mal as very dangerous indeed. Possibly more so than Archer. Archer was prey to his own mega-lomania, his inflated sense of self and privilege. She didn't think Mal had any weaknesses at all. Whatever game he was playing with her had to have some sinister motive. Maybe it was simply to fuck with Archer's mind, maybe it was more complicated. After all, Archer wouldn't know he'd kissed her—they'd been out of the range of the cameras, and she suspected Mal knew exactly where all the cameras were, just as she did. He'd done nothing else to suggest he had any real interest in her—she was a pawn between two treacherous men. When she left, she ought to put a bullet in his brain as well as Archer's.

Could she do it? She couldn't figure out what the kiss was, but of one thing she was certain—it was a lie. Gentleness and tenderness had fled her life long ago, and she recognized a wolf when she saw one. Beneath his elegant clothes and his British accent Malcolm Gunnison was a feral, treacherous creature, and he was here for prey. It was logical to assume that whatever Mal was hunting was under Archer's direction.

But Mal didn't act as if he answered to anyone, in particular her husband. Supposedly Archer wanted him to go to bed with her, though she couldn't imagine why. Maybe simply as a test of loyalty—if you screw my crippled wife, then you must *really* be willing to do what I want.

If the man was in business with Archer, then he had to have done any number of things that were worthy of a death penalty. Shooting him would make her life simpler.

She'd never killed anyone in her life—Archer would have been her first—and she never thought she'd hesitate. She wouldn't now, when she found her chance.

Maybe she'd let Mal live, just for the sake of that lying kiss that had felt so good. She could always shoot him in the knee before she left. In the kind of life he had to live, in order to be among Archer's people, no one survived long. But she didn't have to be judge, jury, and executioner. She might as well face the ugly, unpalatable truth. She was attracted to him, when she thought she was too smart to be tempted by anyone.

Three years ago she'd destroyed her life by falling in love with a liar and a criminal and a psychopath. As far as she knew, if she didn't keep a tight rein on her thoughts and feelings, she could do it again. In which case she might as well turn the gun on herself.

There had to be something deeply wrong with her that she kept looking for signs of redemption in the dangerous man who'd come to the island. She hadn't really found any, but that didn't mean she wouldn't keep trying. She wondered if it was for the simple reason that he'd actually been kind to her in his own way, taking her down to the beach, clearing off the balcony for her . . . kissing her. She must be so starved for any sign of decency that she was willing to start building fantasies about a man as tender as a feral wolf. She had to stop it.

But next time he decided to scoop her up and take her somewhere, she was going to fight tooth and nail. Or she might just have to kill him after all.

Archer MacDonald leaned back on the chaise, surveying the sky dreamily as Rachel worked him with her mouth. He put out his hand to push her downward, then frowned as he saw the bruising on his knuckles. He'd accidentally hurt himself while he was teaching his errant wife a lesson. He seldom made mistakes—he knew the soft, painful parts of a body, knew just where to hit, to twist, to apply pressure without making marks. Unfortunately he got overexcited this afternoon. It was the bitch's fault—he saw the way she looked at Malcolm Gunnison, and it fired his blood. If she thought Malcolm was going to be her knight in shining armor, her noble rescuer, then she would suffer a painful disappointment. Never again would someone be able to sneak into his life beneath his radar—Gunnison had been vetted by some of the most powerful people in the world, including his current employer. He was responsible for a truly impressive amount of transactions in the third world, and he had even less of a conscience than Archer did, which was high praise indeed. No, the man was enjoying the game as much as Archer was, and poor little Sophie was stuck in the middle.

It had come to him out of the blue, the thought of putting Sophie in Malcolm's bed. She really had been a bit of a puritan—it was that innocence that had first drawn him. Her sexual experience had been limited, for all that she tried to appear like a woman of the world, and that disparity between her cool sophistication and her uncertainty in bed had excited him.

She was still a prude, maybe she'd become even more of one. He'd thought it would be interesting to see what she could do in bed. He certainly wasn't going to try it—he didn't like broken things, deformities, dysfunction. The thought of fucking a woman with no feeling below her waist made him a little sick.

It also excited some dark part inside him. She'd always been a good fuck, but he knew a lot of that was because she'd been so in love with him. She still was—no matter what he did, she still loved him. He was completely sure of that. Getting her in bed, making her do what he wanted, could keep him entertained for weeks, but he wasn't about to touch her until he knew what he was getting into, literally. Would she be all nasty and dried out?

Sophie hadn't been interested in any of the young men he'd brought to the island, and Archer had grown bored with the game. But now she was looking at Malcolm Gunnison with more interest than she'd shown since the accident, and the answer was quite simple. Mal could go first, lighting the way, so to speak.

He'd even allowed Mal to dictate his access to his own wife. Archer hadn't minded—it would make the reunion that much sweeter. He'd learned long ago that greedily grabbing for everything, be it money, power, or sex, could backfire, and he still owed Sophie a great deal of payback.

He slapped Rachel's head, urging her to go faster. Odd, but he was a little miffed at first when Sophie seemed to weaken toward Malcolm. She'd resisted everyone else. He understood her very well after all these years. She still loved him, longed for his touch, and even welcomed his abuse—since he would give her nothing else. Her immediate reaction to Malcolm had been hostile, but he'd caught her looking at the man, and he would bet his life that she wanted him.

He'd planned to have Malcolm use Sophie while he watched, just to liven things up a bit while he waited for Chekowsky to arrive. He hadn't counted on Malcolm destroying his surveillance equipment, but he wasn't disappointed. Just more proof that Malcolm was as high on the food chain as he presented himself. Archer couldn't imagine why he'd want a broken toy like Sophie, but he must be bored as well, and women like Rachel grew boring very quickly.

Archer leaned back as Rachel hunched over him, sweat dripping off her face, onto his belly. He should punish her for that, but it didn't seem worth the effort. No, he was more interested in the thought of seeing exactly what Gunnison would do with Sophie. His Sophie. She would need to be punished for it, of course. He could feel the anticipation rush through him.

It was on ongoing conundrum. He wanted Sophie gone, but if anyone was going to kill her, he reserved the right to do it.

The answer appeared in front of him like a divine vision. He could have Gunnison kill her. The man was a machine—killing would be child's play. He'd probably get off on the idea of finishing Sophie. Most of the men he knew liked killing women—he, for one, preferred them to men. You got more bang for your buck: tears, pleas, panic. It was no fun to kill operatives—they were stoic, giving him nothing. No, he didn't think Gunnison would give him an argument if he asked him to fuck and then kill Sophie. The only question was whether he would let Archer watch.

He'd insist on it. After all, it wasn't often that a host provided such singular entertainment. He wanted, needed, to see the light in her eyes fade as she knew she was dying. He needed to watch her struggle. He shoved Rachel away from him, standing up abruptly. Gunnison wouldn't deny him, not if he wanted a deal for the Pixiedust.

It all depended on whether Mal was someone who took pleasure in his work or simply, coldly, did what needed to be done. The latter kind of people were easier to trust—they didn't allow anything to distract them from getting the job done with robotlike efficiency.

Archer was having his doubts. Mal was interested in Sophie, though Archer couldn't understand why. She was nowhere near as beautiful as the other women on the island, and she was stuck in a wheelchair. Hardly the stuff of erotic dreams.

But there was something about Sophie, and always had been, even when she'd been lying through her teeth and setting him up. Something that he'd never been able to put his finger on had drawn him to her, and in the past few years he still hadn't managed to figure it out. If he could pinpoint it, he could get rid of it, as brutally as possible.

It wasn't her strength—he'd rendered her as weak as possible. It wasn't her sense of humor—he'd managed to strip that away as well. Maybe it was the fact that she adored him, no matter what he did to her . . . but he was used to adoration. It bored him.

No, there was something indefinable about Sophie, and what he didn't understand he destroyed. He'd been doing it in stages, but it was time to finish it.

Archer smiled expansively. Malcolm Gunnison had come with the highest recommendations. It would be ridiculously simple to get rid of one extraneous, traitorous bitch of a wife. Really, it was all working out beautifully.

Chapter Nine

In the end it was surprisingly easy. Sophie had more than enough time to lay out her plan during dinner, the men's voices a backdrop in her head. There was something off about Malcolm Gunnison. Something that didn't compute. He wasn't one of the pretty boys Archer had brought in to test her—despite that brief kiss, he'd done no overt flirting. She had the sense that he watched her, but he was watching Archer even more closely. Like most of Archer's associates, he was clearly a man who trusted nothing and no one, and that should have been standard operating procedure.

So why was she so obsessed with him? There was something beneath his enigmatic exterior that nagged at her. It wasn't the threat of violence—that was all around her, in the air she breathed, in the life she'd chosen years ago when she'd been young and smart and invulnerable. It wasn't the unexpected moments of gentleness. No one in Archer's life was who they presented themselves to be to the world, and she'd grown used to that, having played her own role for so long. But Mal was different. She knew it instinctively, and she intended to find out why.

The smart thing to do would be to ignore him, just as she'd ignored Archer's earlier imports. She had no illusions that Archer had brought Mal here simply to mess with her—Archer didn't care that much. Archer and Mal had some nefarious business going on, probably

Archer's hideous biological weapon she wasn't supposed to know anything about. The question was, did Mal have his own agenda as well?

If he did, it would have nothing to do with her. No one even remembered she was alive, or if they did, they didn't care. Her parents had died in a plane crash when she was in her teens, and Aunt Sylvia, who'd looked after her, died of emphysema not long after Sophie graduated from Sarah Lawrence. She'd had friends in college, friends in the State Department, but they'd gone on to have their own lives, and she'd been ordered to lose touch with them once she joined the Committee.

The Committee would have purged her from its records. No one gave a damn whether she lived or died, and she knew Mal's occasional glances had less to do with her and more to do with what his real plan was.

It wouldn't be easy. He had to have known Archer's men would search his luggage and his room at regular intervals, and she'd have a hard time finding out anything about him. But that didn't mean she wasn't going to try.

He was matching Archer drink for drink, and the more he imbibed the more scrupulously polite he became, while Archer just got sloppy. She knew Archer well enough to know he wasn't as drunk as he appeared to be, and she would have been willing to bet ten years of her life that neither was Mal. Then again, the way things were going, she wouldn't have another ten years, so that would be an easy bet.

But no one had a hollow leg, and there had to be some effect from the amount of rum he was tossing back. All she had to do was get some of her pain meds into him and he'd be out like a light, giving her the chance to search Mal's rooms with him none the wiser.

She had some with her—when she'd discovered Marco's affection for Vicodin she'd made it a habit to tuck some of them into a wad of tissue and keep it in her bra in case she had a sudden need to barter. How to get it to Mal was the problem. The men were ignoring her, but she could hardly reach over for his glass and toss a handful in.

But in the end it had come together with such ease that it was almost laughable. A trip to the bathroom, a sullen Rachel pushing her, gave her enough time and privacy to crush the handful of pills she had into a fine powder. She scooped every trace back into the tissue, keeping it in her hand as Rachel took her back, the wheelchair bumping over the thresholds and the slate flooring. When she returned to the dining room, Archer and Mal were out on the terrace, watching the dark, roiling clouds of the approaching storm.

Rachel, of course, sailed right past her, out to the men, her sullenness vanishing in a cloud of vivacity like strong, cheap perfume, and Sophie didn't hesitate. Mal's glass of fruity liquid was still mostly full, and she tipped the powder into it before heading back to the opposite side of the table, just before the men came back in. She was relatively certain she had blocked the security camera trained on the table, but in the end she was just going to have to risk it.

Most of life was a matter of luck and timing. Mal and Archer could have moved out onto the sand, finished with dinner and finished with her. They could have come back and switched to brandy or coffee, or Mal could have sensibly declared he'd had his limit of the sweet, fruity drink Elena had come up with at Archer's behest.

But Mal had come back in, as Archer's nonstop banter accompanied him, and when he took his seat, the first thing he did was pick up his frosty glass. And then his eyes met hers over the rim.

Sophie felt an unexpected stab in her stomach. Could that huge amount of painkillers prove lethal on top of all the alcohol he'd consumed? Or more likely the amount of acetaminophen in the Vicodin could destroy his liver or his kidneys or whatever dire thing too much of the drug did. She couldn't let herself worry about it. She was in a fight for her life, and she had to use whatever weapons she had.

"Sophie, baby!" Archer said in a booming, slightly slurred voice, catching her attention, and she gave him her best smile, taking a masochistic pleasure in the pain it caused her jaw.

"Yes, my love?" she answered, all dewy sweetness.

"I think you should spend the night down here for a change. It's been so long since we've shared a bed." Most people wouldn't see the malice in his eyes—but Sophie couldn't miss it.

She released a loud, breathy sigh, focusing all her attention on him, vaguely aware that Mal was observing all this. "Oh, could I?" she said. He was most likely calling her bluff, but she couldn't afford to risk it. She could put up a convincing front for short periods of time, but trapped with him in a bedroom would end with one of them dead, and even if it was Archer, as she assumed it would be, her own death would follow shortly if she hadn't had time to firm up her escape. "I would love it so much, but I would need some help."

Archer waved that away with an airy hand. "Joe can carry you anywhere you need to go," he said.

She could feel Mal's eyes boring into her, but she kept her eyes focused on Archer. "I have my period, and I can't really take care of things . . ." She let herself trail off, loving the shade of green that Archer turned.

Mal made a choking sound that could have been surprise. It might even have been laughter. She turned to him, but his face gave nothing away. "I'm sorry to be indelicate at the dinner table," she said, "but these are things you simply have to deal with when you're confined to a wheelchair."

It *had* been laughter. She didn't know how she knew it—he gave no outward sign, but she was sure of it. If she had any doubt, his lift of his almost-empty glass in a small salute confirmed it. He drained the last few drops, and ignoring her misgivings, she felt satisfaction move through her.

"Perhaps you'd better be in your own room tonight, where you'll be more comfortable," Archer said hastily.

Squeamish bastard, she thought with mild triumph. It would serve him right if his prudish tendencies brought him down.

She arranged her face in lines of stricken disappointment. "You're probably right," she said reluctantly. She dared another glance at Mal, wondering how long it would take for the pills to start working. "In fact, I should probably go up now. Could you call Joe?"

She expected Mal to jump to his feet, countermand the request, and swoop her up in his arms. He didn't move, thank God. She didn't like being held by him. She didn't like his strong body, his arms, touching her, the feel of his heart beating against her skin.

"Joe!" Archer bellowed, startling Sophie, and a moment later the big man appeared. "My wife is ready for bed. Take her upstairs and see that one of the women . . . er . . . takes care of her. Send Rachel," he added with a trace of malice.

Sophie wasn't sure who the malice was intended for—her or Rachel—and she didn't much care. "You're very sweet," she said, then allowed herself one last glance at Mal as Joe picked her up.

Always the gentleman, Mal rose, and Archer followed suit, grumbling as he threw his napkin on the table. Mal was looking a little glassy-eyed, she thought happily. The pills were already working. Maybe, for once, things would really go her way and he'd pass out downstairs, sleeping it off on one of the big sofas. It didn't matter—either way she could easily search his room without him being the wiser, maybe finding a clue as to who and what he was. She'd kept enough of her training to know how to successfully toss a room, and if there was anything there to find, she'd find it.

At least she could try. "Good night, gentlemen," she said. "Thank you for the dinner and conversation."

Archer nodded, not seeing through her veiled barb, but Mal didn't miss it. "I'm afraid we ignored you," he said in an attempt at smoothness that came out slightly slurred.

"Nonsense," she said. "I loved the company."

Archer came over toward her, planting a kiss on her forehead. "Always a delight, baby. Sweet dreams."

Malcolm Gunnison said nothing, blinking at her, and Sophie let Joe carry her up the stairs like a dog who'd retrieved a pilfered bone.

Mal didn't come up to bed for more than two hours. Sophie had done her exercises, and then lay on the smooth bathroom floor, waiting for the sound of his footsteps. If he wasn't up by four, she was going to risk it and go in there on her own. She kept drifting off, then jerking awake in sudden terror, and she was about to give in when she heard him stumbling up the broad, curving stairs, mumbling to himself. No, singing to himself in a sort of monotone. She tried to make out the words. She almost hoped it would be "If I Only Had a Brain" but instead it was an off-key rendition of . . . good God, it was a Springsteen song that took her a moment to recognize, particularly with his slurred lack of melody. "Tougher Than the Rest." Is that what he thought? She was about to prove him otherwise.

She levered herself into bed. No one had come to help her with her nonexistent menstrual needs, and indeed, the women on the island knew she managed to take care of them herself, but no one would dare discuss such things with Archer. It was a very dark night—a storm was coming in, obscuring moon and stars, and the wind whipped through the palm trees, shaking them to their foundations. She'd left the door to the balcony open—the sounds of the weather would keep her movements unnoticeable.

In fact, the power was likely to go out, and when it did even the million-dollar generator Archer had installed was unlikely to kick in without someone, probably Marco, trudging through the rain and wrestling with it. It never worked well with a high wind—an ongoing problem that she only hoped would happen tonight. Her night vision was like a cat's, whereas anyone else might be at a complete disadvantage. She wouldn't need a flashlight, though with the amount of drugs she'd given Mal, she could probably shine one directly in his eyes and he wouldn't notice.

She lay perfectly still. She could hear him stumble around the room, swear, then stumble again—followed by an ominous crash. She held her breath, wondering if he'd passed out, but a moment later she heard him again, sounding like some kind of drunken bear, thrashing and cursing.

Eventually all was silence. The wind made listening problematic, but she could tell he was definitely passed out. Whether he'd made it as far as the bed or was stretched out on the floor, he was definitely gone. She counted to a hundred, in Spanish and then in French, just to give herself enough time, and then slid out of the bed. Everything was coming together perfectly—the approaching storm would cover anything she did.

She moved across the floor like a ghost, her bare feet silent. She was wearing a T-shirt and boxers—she'd left behind the flowing negligees Archer had insisted on. She planned to change before Rachel came in the morning, but in the meantime she could move freely, and it was glorious.

It was almost cold out on the balcony, but Sophie ignored it. She'd been fully prepared to pick the lock to his door, but he'd left it open, and even in the darkness she could see his shape stretched across the bed, unconscious.

One chair was overturned, a small side table broken and splintered, and pieces of clothing lay strewn across the floor. She took another fast glance at him, then sucked in her breath. He was wearing boxer briefs, nothing more, and she should probably count her blessings. He'd likely been in the midst of stripping completely when he passed out, and no matter how much of her training she clung to, it would have been distracting. It was already bad enough.

She'd seen him in the ocean from a distance, but as her eyes grew accustomed to the shadows in his room she could see him quite clearly. He had the kind of body that hid its strength—his muscles were lean and tight, his skin smooth. He had the body of a dancer, not a weight lifter, someone with power and grace that was both gorgeous and lethal. She stood in the doorway, looking at him, watching his chest rise and fall, cataloging the scars. He'd lived a violent life—that was no surprise. She knew the starlike scars a bullet left, she recognized the healing pink line from knife slashes, and she recognized the even patterning of torture. Who the fuck was he? And whose side was he on?

She needed to find out, and soon. He'd removed all his surveillance equipment—Joe had told her that with a kind of wonder that Archer let him get away with it—and once she stepped into the room she was off the radar. She took a step down.

His breathing was slow, deep, drugged. She moved over toward him, silent as a ghost, and watched him, barely breathing herself. His face gave away no secrets, even in his sleep. His too-long hair had fallen across his eyes, and she wanted to reach out and brush it away. She did no such thing. She was a statue, watching, looking for any sign.

And then she let out a slightly audible sigh of relief, and he still didn't move. Even if the worst happened and he came to, he'd be so drugged he wouldn't remember. But she might have given him enough to kill a horse. She just hoped it wasn't enough to kill him.

She started with the drawers, going through them carefully. Nothing but soft fabric, nothing but the very best, she thought. His boxer briefs and T-shirts felt like silk, and she wondered how they would feel against a body. His body. He'd brought two suits, both tailored, and handmade shirts with no identifying tags on anything—he could have bought them in London, Hong Kong, or Paris. There were even handmade leather shoes on the floor of the closet along with his suitcase. She reached for it, feeling the weight. It felt heavier than an empty suitcase ought to be, and she wondered if she had the time to take it into her room and examine it. Covering the latch with her hand to muffle the sound, she tried to open it. Nothing, of course. The damned thing was locked.

The sudden silence hit her like an explosion, and she froze in place. The wind had finally done its damage—the power was out. No one had ever bothered to check on her in the past when the generator went down, and she doubted they would this time, but the sudden pitch black startled her and she lost her balance, landing on her knees at the edge of the closet.

To her absolute horror she heard sounds from the bed. The faintest of noises as the mattress shifted, the rustle of covers, the sound of a body moving against the five-hundred-thread-count linen sheets. Was he awake, or just thrashing in his drug-induced stupor? In a panic she pulled herself into the almost-empty closet, curling up in a tiny ball behind one of the louvered doors and burying her head against her knees, holding her breath. Nothing. Just a silence and a blackness so thick she wanted to choke on it, she who was never prey to weakness like claustrophobia or heights or blood.

She barely made it. She heard the noise of the mattress, the sound of bare feet hitting the floor, and all she could think was *Oh shit, oh shit, oh shit*, while the man who was supposed to be unconscious rose from the bed. She couldn't see him, but she figured he must be swaying, trying to regain his equilibrium, and maybe he'd simply pitch forward and black out again. *Please, please, please*, she implored a God who had so far managed to ignore absolutely everything she'd asked of him, be it sparing her parents' lives or warning her that she'd been wrong about Archer. Silence had answered the first request, a bullet in the back the second. *Don't let him find me*, she found herself begging, hating herself for her weakness.

He didn't do a face-plant beside his bed. Instead he walked slowly from the alcove where the bed was, moving toward the bank of closets, but this time he didn't stumble, this time he didn't smash anything or knock it over. Had he recovered that quickly? Impossible. On the rare occasion she took one Vicodin, it made her groggy as hell the next day, all without putting a dent in her pain. He couldn't be resistant to the amount she'd fed him.

He was coming closer to the closet, and she shut her eyes tightly, stupidly, feeling that if she couldn't see him, then he couldn't see her. He was humming again, and then the door to the closet was shoved closed, squeaking noisily, shutting her inside.

He moved on, and she heard him in the bathroom, the sound of running water, still with that damned singing under his breath. And this time he didn't sound the slightest bit out of it.

She found she was biting her lower lip so hard she was drawing blood, and she forced herself to stop, to take a deep, silent breath. He'd get back in bed, and when he fell asleep the drugs would take over again, and she'd be able to sneak out. Maybe even take the mysterious suitcase with her—she could put it back before he woke up. He'd be none the wiser.

For a long time she heard absolutely nothing, cocooned in her darkness. Had he fallen asleep in the bathroom? Had he left the room? She couldn't hear anything at all, not the sound of his footsteps, not the quiet suspiration of breath. He might as well be dead.

Mal had to be as much of a soulless monster as Archer, or close to it. He would be no loss. But if she killed him, it would have to be hand-to-hand, and despite her justified confidence in her own skills, a man with the body like that could best her. Not only because he was taller and heavier, but also because, clearly, he could withstand far more pain than she'd ever had to bear, even with her gunshot wound. Hand-to-hand and she'd be dead.

She needed a gun, though she had no idea where she was going to get one. No matter how many pills she dangled in front of Marco, he wouldn't swallow any kind of an excuse to get her a gun, and she hadn't run across anything in this room.

Though there was always the suspiciously heavy suitcase.

There was still no sound from the room beyond. She couldn't stay in the closet forever—it would get light sooner rather than later, which would make getting back to her own bed even more difficult. Rachel would check on her, and if she found the bed empty and the wheelchair abandoned, all hell would break loose. She moved, slowly, silently, trying to peer beyond the louvered doors, and felt the first trickling of relief. He was back in bed—she could see the shape of his body through the slats of wood. He was unmoving, dead to the world, and all she could hope was that the last little bit of crushed drug had finally reached his system.

There was nothing in the closet she could use as a weapon if she were wrong. An Italian leather shoe wouldn't do much damage no matter how hard she hit with it. She could throw the suitcase at him, but that wouldn't buy her anything more than a few seconds. With someone as drugged as he should be, a few seconds might even be enough, though she'd rather not count on it. If she had to run for it right then, there were way too many obstacles. The island was small, and unless the wind had died down the seas would be too rough for her to even attempt to cross them.

Her muscles were cramping—she hadn't given herself enough time to cool down properly after her training—and when she tried a small, surreptitious stretch her hand knocked against the wall. It was a very quiet thud, but she froze. This was the test. If he was out of it, he wouldn't have heard her. *Please God, let him be out of it.*

The figure on the bed didn't move. Instead, there was a choking noise and then a very loud snore, and Sophie sank back in relief. For once it appeared that God was listening.

She slid onto her knees, staring at the shadowy outlines of the suitcase in frustration. In daylight she could pick the lock, see what was inside, read any papers that might identify him. In the smothering darkness, though, there was nothing she could do but get the hell out of there as quickly and quietly as humanly possible. There would always be another time.

Her cramped limbs gave a silent protest as she rose to her feet, still hunched over in the closet. She pushed one of the doors open just a crack—thank God Archer insisted on everything being in top-notch condition. There was no betraying creak of the hinges. Mal lay still on the bed, and she pushed the door wider.

Still no movement. The door to the terrace was open, though the strong night winds were stirring the curtains, providing a blessed bit of noise to cover her. She pushed the door the rest of the way, and stepped out onto the cool tile floor.

The arms that came from behind her clamped around her like iron bars, slamming her back against a hard body, and she exploded like a crazy woman, fighting, kicking, using every dirty trick she could think of. She wrapped her leg behind him, pulling them both down, and they were rolling on the floor, thrashing, struggling in the inky darkness, all in a desperate silence where the only sound was her heartbeat and tightly controlled breath. He made no noise at all, not when her knee missed his balls but landed hard in his stomach, not when she bit his arm to make him release her, bit so hard she could taste blood, but his hold didn't weaken. She was strong, she was fighting for her life, but he was bigger, stronger, and she knew—she'd already known—that Malcolm Gunnison was too powerful for her. In frustrated fury she sank back against the floor, her nemesis straddling her, holding her down, and she stared up into his eyes, wishing she could rip her hands free so she could claw at him.

They had ended up over by the French doors, and the faintest light was coming in, heralding the approach of dawn. She was panting silently, her heart racing. He was totally relaxed, his head tilted to one side as if examining some exotic species. "Why, Mrs. MacDonald," he said, his mocking voice a mere thread of sound. "Holy Mary, it's a miracle."

Chapter Ten

Sophie stilled the last of her struggles, sinking back against the hard-tiled floor in defeat. "Get the hell off me," she whispered furiously.

He pressed in harder, holding her down with his hips, his shoulders, his legs keeping hers still. "I don't think so." His voice was a breath of sound. "I'm comfortable enough."

"I'm not."

"Tough. I want answers."

"Go to hell."

"Yup," he said succinctly, and for a moment she was silenced.

He wasn't that heavy. She was completely immobilized, his hand was holding her arms over her head, and she considered slamming her forehead against his, but he stayed far enough out of reach that it wouldn't be that effective. She wanted to growl in frustration. "What do you want?" she finally demanded.

He looked down at her, considering. "I have to say I'm impressed. For a woman trapped in a wheelchair you have surprising skills."

"Don't play games with me!" she snapped.

"Why not? It's fun."

Her eyes flew wide. "Fun?" she echoed in a rage. "You rat bastard sadist! Get the fuck off of me."

Of course he didn't move. She was slowly becoming aware of the heat of his body—he was wearing only boxers, and she could feel his skin everywhere against hers. It was unsettling.

"What were you looking for? Maybe your husband is in on this whole charade and he sent you to spy on me."

Her laugh was bitter. "Yes, and he hits me for encouragement."

He shrugged without loosening his hold on her. "Okay, so he doesn't know. That doesn't answer my question. Why are you risking what I assume is a careful charade by coming into my room? Unless you find me irresistible, in which case you should have just joined me on the bed instead of hiding in my closet. Then again, you thought I'd been fool enough to drink that little cocktail bonus of yours tonight, so I wouldn't have been much fun."

"You didn't drink it." It wasn't a question—of course he didn't. "Why not?"

His eyelids lowered contemplatively. "You have a tell. When you're lying, or playing a game, or up to something, you play with your hair. I would have thought Peter Madsen would have trained you better. You're still surprisingly good for someone so long out of the game."

She froze, no longer thinking about the hard, warm body pressing into hers. "You're Committee," she said flatly. Why hadn't she guessed it?

"You should have asked your husband. He probably would have told you."

"He knows?" she said, aghast. "Why are you still alive?"

"Because I'm good at what I do. And because he thinks I'm a former operative, working on my own. I think my connection with the Committee was partly how I got in. He's still holding a grudge about you."

She'd managed to rein in her emotions. "We've never talked about the Committee."

He raised an eyebrow. "Never?"

"We pretend I'm a loving wife and he's a devoted husband. It's an unspoken contract." Her voice was bitter. "Why are you here? Is it to rescue me?" The moment the words were out of her mouth she realized how ridiculous they were. She'd betrayed the Committee on every level with her mindless infatuation. "Or to kill me?" she added, a sop to her pride.

"I'm not here for you at all," he said, dismissing her. "There's a little task you left unfinished, and it's taken us this long to get back in. As for you, no one gives a shit what happens to you. It's been left up to my discretion. I haven't decided whether to kill you or just leave you here with whomever I leave alive."

She was cold. The tiles were hard and icy beneath her, the tropical wind swept the sweat from her body, and even the warmth of his skin against her didn't penetrate. "Why don't you get the fuck off me and off this island? I have every intention of finishing what I started."

"Before you fell madly in love?" he said, his voice an annoying coo. "What's taken you so long? As far as I can tell, you blew your cover two years ago when he shot you."

"He didn't shoot me—one of his men did. And I don't know how long he knew who I was—Archer is someone who likes to play with his food. He could have known when he married me." She didn't think so, but then she didn't like to think back to those first few weeks when she was so blinded by love and sex.

"And in all this time you haven't figured out the answers? Who did train you? Madsen is better than that."

"I was trained by the Ice Queen, and I was trained well."

"Then you're just incredibly stupid."

She couldn't deny it. "I've basically been held a prisoner in my room for the last two years, and for the first year I really couldn't walk. I haven't been given a whole lot of chances, and I would have to rely on surprise and talents, since I no longer have any access to a weapon. If we're going to have a rational discussion, do you suppose you might get off me? I'm not particularly comfortable."

"I don't give a damn whether you're comfortable or not," he said. "And I haven't decided whether I'm going to kill you."

This time she didn't let his cool words get to her. "If you're going to kill me, now isn't a particularly good time, unless you're ready to finish the mission. For one thing you'd have a hard time getting off the island—the sea is very rough from all the wind and the storm, and I doubt a helicopter could land, if you've got that in the offing. Plus, I suspect you're here for Archer's beloved Pixiedust as well, and until that old fart Chekowsky shows up, you're stuck. A dead woman next door or in your bedroom might complicate things needlessly, and I know Committee members are all about getting the job done with the least amount of fuss."

He looked down at her for a long, silent moment, and then he moved off her, fast and graceful, reaching for her hand and hauling her to her feet. It was a very strange sensation. She hadn't stood next to anyone in more than two years, and she hadn't realized quite how tall he was. She could only hope her expression gave nothing away. For some reason she suddenly felt more vulnerable than she had when she was lying beneath him, or looking up at him from her wheelchair.

"Good point," he said. He glanced out at the slowly lightening sky. "Okay, we'll talk. You take the bed, I'll take the chair."

She glanced over at it. He'd piled pillows in the middle of the mattress so that it would look like he was still asleep, and she'd fallen for it. She couldn't even think of how and when he could have managed it. "Nice trick."

"An old one. I can't imagine why you're still alive when you're so gullible."

"Maybe I'm better than you think."

"Since my opinion is low, that wouldn't be too hard." He dropped down into the chair beside the bed, watching her. "Well?"

She had the entirely juvenile desire to flip him off, but she simply stalked past him and climbed onto the bed. She wanted to shove the pillows off, or throw them at him, but instead she simply arranged them behind her and leaned back, crossing her legs in an attitude of complete relaxation. "I have every intention of taking care of Archer myself."

"In which decade?"

She controlled her instinctive snarl. "In the next two weeks, if you must know. I'll figure out a way. I could probably break his neck in hand-to-hand if I'm focused enough."

"The way you immobilized me?" he said.

"Archer doesn't have your training." *Or grace*, she added silently, refusing to give him that much.

"You could use a knife," he suggested. "The kitchen must be loaded with them."

He was probably being facetious, but she took him at his word. "I've considered it. I'm good with a knife, but it's more problematic. I know how to kill people quickly, where to strike, but you have to have perfect aim, and I don't think Archer is going to stand still and let me practice."

"There's a place on the back of the neck that causes instant paralysis," he offered in the same tone as if he were suggesting they have fish for dinner. "Do that first and you could take your time killing him."

"The thought is appealing," she said, slightly horrified, "but again, it requires either perfect aim or the ability to sneak up on him. I've been able to train my body, but I really haven't had the opportunity to practice my throwing skills." She kept her voice flat and unemotional.

"I don't think you could take him in hand-to-hand combat. He's huge."

"He's clumsy," she shot back. "And I'll use whatever I have at the time."

"No, you won't, because I will have taken care of him first."

"No! He owes me. If anyone kills him, it's going to be me," she said fiercely.

He laughed at her, and somehow the barely audible tone infuriated her. "Because you've proved to be so reliable in the past, haven't you?

Don't get in my way. I have no particular interest in killing you, but I wouldn't hesitate if I think you're a liability."

She glared at him. "You stay out of my way and I won't have to kill you."

His faint smile was even more annoying. "You can try."

Sophie Jordan MacDonald had long, shapely legs that he could see quite clearly beneath that oversized T-shirt she was wearing. He'd been able to see her feet and ankles, felt the muscles and resilience in her body when he carried her—he wondered what had kept him from figuring out the truth for so long.

There was a simple answer—she was good, despite her flawed record. She'd had some of the best recommendations during her time in London, and even though she'd originally been sent as a part of a team, simply as backup, they wouldn't have sent anyone they weren't sure was capable of killing Archer MacDonald if it came to that.

But she'd been thrown in the deep end before she could really swim, and she was lucky she'd survived, though he guessed it was more than luck. The bullet that had originally crippled her hadn't been a fatal one, and since then, she'd not only survived but thrived, though he doubted she'd call it that. She was looking at him like he was the enemy, and that suited him just fine. He was the enemy—if she did anything, anything at all, it could end in disaster. If he were as cold-blooded as he should be, he'd figure out a way to kill her, swiftly and efficiently, making it look like an accident. Most operatives wouldn't hesitate.

"Why are you looking at me like that?" she demanded in an angry whisper.

He shrugged. He ought to put on some clothes—sitting there in nothing but his boxers made the proximity of all her skin more disturbing, and it brought back the feel of her body beneath his, the soft swell of her breasts pressing against her worn T-shirt, against his chest, her long legs entwining with his as she did her best to fight him. He still had a pain in his right kidney from her knee, but it could have been a lot worse, and the bite on his upper arm was oozing blood. "I was thinking about ways I could kill you and get away with it. You're already too much of a complication and I prefer to keep things simple."

She had to know he was partly serious, but she didn't even flinch. "What did you come up with? I could try it out on you."

"We're not the same, sweetheart," he said dryly. "I was considering breaking your neck and placing your body artistically at the bottom of the stairs. After all, you've supposedly fallen once today. Or I could toss you off the balcony and they could go with accident or suicide, which Archer might find more believable."

"Accident," she said calmly. "He still thinks I'm in love with him."

"That's what it looks like. Does he think you don't know he was behind the shooting?"

"We've never discussed it, but I don't think he'd underestimate me that badly. He believes I married him because I loved him . . ."

"Which you did," Mal pointed out.

She didn't react. "He knew I was infatuated with him, and he's such an egomaniac that he easily believes I still adore him no matter what he does. It's one of his few weaknesses."

"So why did he marry you? He doesn't strike me as the kind of man to fall madly in love."

"I have no idea. Maybe he liked the idea of being in love, and I was infatuated enough for both of us."

"Does he fuck you?" He was trying to make her uncomfortable, but she gave no sign.

"No," she said coolly. "He doesn't like illness, or deformity, or anything less than physical perfection. It's part of his OCD tendencies. He hasn't even demanded a blow job." She said the words deliberately, giving away her discomfort. Otherwise she wouldn't have needed to prove how unmoved she was.

"Too bad. You could have bitten off his dick."

"Not tempting," she said.

"I could also drown you." He continued their earlier conversation, preferring not to think of Sophie and fucking in the same scenario. "Either the pool or the ocean."

"You'd have to figure out how I managed to get downstairs when I'm supposedly in a wheelchair," she pointed out. "You could say I asked you to bring me down for a swim but then you fell asleep and I disappeared. It's a little lame, but it might do." She gave him a dulcet smile. "Just trying to be helpful."

He wasn't going to give her a reaction either. "Very thoughtful. I could say you crept in here for sex and I thought you were an intruder and shot you."

She considered it, then shook her head. "Weak," she judged it. "For one thing this room is two steps lower than the balcony, and the wheelchair wouldn't make it down. I suppose I could have flopped on my belly and crawled over to you like some Persian mistress, but then you wouldn't have shot me."

"I could shoot you in the doorway."

"You wouldn't mistake me for anyone else when I'm in my wheelchair. Besides, Archer wouldn't have let you on the island with a gun."

"And you think Archer always gets what he wants?" he countered softly.

He saw the slight flicker in her eyes as she digested the fact that he was armed. She pretended to ignore it. "You could strangle me and say it was rough sex. Archer would love that."

"But then I'd have to fuck you."

The words were out in the room like a physical thing between them, and he could feel his dick getting hard. Death had never been a turn-on for him, but the thought of screwing Sophie Jordan was enough to overshadow the discussion of murder.

She wrinkled her nose in disdain. "On second thought I'd rather drown."

"I don't know that I'm giving you a choice in the matter."

She was looking at him out of those warm, dark eyes. That was another tell of hers, one he didn't bother to point out to her. Those pansy-brown eyes beneath the dark, arched brows gave a lot away, and that was always the hardest thing to control. He was doing his best to keep the barriers of distrust and contempt a powerful wall between them, but if she stopped thinking about herself and the mess she'd made—if she really looked at him closely—she'd probably realize she was safe. He didn't kill for pleasure, and he avoided collateral damage whenever he possibly could. Not that she *was* collateral damage, he reminded himself as his eyes drifted over her. She was a traitor, a royal fuck-up, and by the standards of the Committee she deserved everything she got.

He shrugged. "I think I'll let you live for the time being."

Her face showed no reaction. "Are you sure that's wise? After all, maybe I really am still desperately in love with Archer. If I told him about you, it could get me back in his good graces."

"You trying to talk me into it?"

He could see the way her mind was working. She was considering whether she should egg him on into trying, evaluating her chances of success. Since he'd just taken her down in hand-to-hand, and she had no other weapons at the moment, it would be a waste of time. Apparently she realized it too, so she shook her head. "I wouldn't want you to jeopardize your redundant mission by having to explain my dead body."

"Redundant?" he echoed.

"You're not going to kill him. I am. Then, if you're really butt-hurt about the whole thing, you can always kill me and take the credit."

He wanted to smile. She didn't give an inch. "It's a thought."

"We'll see who gets to him first." She slid off the bed, her body strong, fluid, moving past him, almost daring him to touch her. And he wanted to, so damn badly.

But he didn't. He watched her as she strolled toward the French doors, silhouetted against the coming dawn. The power was still off, so she could make it back to her room without being observed, but it could come back on at any time, and he didn't want her caught walking out of his bedroom. That wouldn't be good for either of them. She paused, looking back over her shoulder, and her smile was deliberately seductive. "May the best man win."

She was gone.

He was hard. It was as if his body had been given permission to react to her once she was out of reach, and he gave a silent laugh. He didn't like complications, but he had the suspicion he was going to enjoy this one. There was even a good chance she'd get to MacDonald before he did—she fought hard and didn't give in.

He'd have a bruise on his side from her knee, and he glanced down at the bite mark on his upper arm. Shit. It looked like just what it was, and he'd already gone into the ocean with Archer and his bimbo without a shirt on. The sudden appearance of a bite on his body would require explanation, and he could think of no simple answer. It could easily pass for the aftermath of rough sex, but Archer would know if anyone on the island had been in Mal's bed. He could throw Sophie under the bus, say he'd done what Archer, the sick bastard, had asked, but he needed time to decide how he was going to handle that, how he was going to turn it to his advantage.

When he'd come upstairs he was playing the full drunk, both to fool Archer and to convince Sophie he'd finished her doctored drink instead of silently pouring it into his linen napkin and dropping it under the table while Archer distracted her. He'd bumped around in the room, broken things in his subterfuge, which would easily explain any bruises. It wouldn't explain a bite mark.

He rose and went to the closet, a grin on his face as he remembered her hiding there, foolish enough to think she could get away with it. Hauling out his suitcase, he dumped it on the rumpled bed, unlocked it, and reached into the hidden compartment for the zip knife. He knew how to use it—he'd dug bullets out of his own flesh with it, cut throats, done worse with such a small blade. He knew how to transform a wound. Without any artificial light he was going to have to go by instinct, but he was good at what he did, and he cut into his bicep without blinking, watching the blood slide down his arm. The artwork required patience, a steady hand, and precision, and by the time he was done, the early dawn light was streaming into the bedroom, and he was satisfied with the results. Folding up the knife, he put it back, then climbed into his bed, making sure he smeared his blood on the sheets. He needed an hour of sleep, maybe two, and then he'd be good to go. He closed his eyes, then opened them again with a groan.

The sheets smelled like Sophie. Like she'd smelled when he carried her—gardenias. It was just the faintest hint of the flower, probably in her shampoo, and it was only a trace that lingered in his bed. Hell, it might even be his imagination. His own blood should have overpowered the scent of her.

It didn't matter—all he could think about was Sophie in his bed.

He should have cut her throat.

Chapter Eleven

Sophie slipped into bed, closing her eyes. She was exhausted, but her adrenaline was pumping, her heart was racing, and she wanted to go and shut herself in the bathroom so that she could pace and think about all this, but Rachel would be up soon, and she had to make everything appear normal. She wasn't afraid Mal would give her away—he had too much to lose. He wouldn't know that she would never give him away. Archer's death was more important to her than her own life, although she wasn't into noble self-sacrifice, thank you very much. She wanted to dance on that bastard's grave and then go out and celebrate every damned thing she could—food, sex, freedom.

There was only one problem—sex involved men, and she really didn't want to get close enough to one to be vulnerable again.

Of course, sex didn't have to involve men. She'd been adventurous in college, and she was open-minded, but she'd come to the unhappy realization that she just happened to like cock, and substitutes wouldn't do.

She'd worry about that once she got off the island—there was no one here, absolutely no one she'd let touch her with a ten-foot pole. Particularly not the man next door, who for some goddamned reason had kissed her, though an errant glance at Mal in his snug underwear made her consider that particular measurement. Had he suspected she could walk when he'd done it, or had he been sorry for the poor little crippled girl? Or even worse, was he turned on by the thought of a paraplegic in bed?

She wasn't going to think about Malcolm Gunnison. He'd do what he was going to do, and she'd make her own plans. Between the two of them, Archer would die, and for now that was good enough.

⎯⎯⎯⎯⎯

By the time she woke up it had to be close to noon. The power had come back on sometime while she slept, but the clock by her bed was flashing twelve with annoying regularity. The day was overcast again—unusual past prime hurricane season. She lay perfectly still as she slowly came awake, and then the happenings of the night before hit her with a vengeance, and without realizing it, she said, "Oh, shit!" out loud and very distinctly.

Archer would have someone listening, of course. Or maybe he sat around at night and played the recordings made earlier. Or hell, maybe he just had the surveillance on but no longer bothered to check. After all, she hadn't done much that was interesting in a long time but roll around her bedroom.

Whatever it was, in the long run it hardly mattered. She'd been terrified of showing any anomalies, but the very normalcy of her life would appear suspicious. And Archer knew perfectly well that Mal's entrance into their lives had changed things.

She pulled herself out of the bed and into her wheelchair, wincing slightly. Enduring Archer yesterday afternoon had been bad enough—her wild tussle with Mal left her aching all over. She was going to need a hot shower and a couple of Tylenol.

She started toward the bathroom, then caught a glimpse of herself with sudden horror. She looked dusty, disheveled, and her feet were dirty. Holy Christ, she was lucky Rachel hadn't come traipsing in. Although if she had, she wouldn't have been able to see much beneath the sheet, thank God. Sophie needed to scrub herself from head to foot, cover up, and get her ass downstairs by hook or by crook. The one thing she wasn't going to do was stay locked in her room, wondering what Mal was saying or doing.

She didn't trust him for one moment. Oh, he was Committee, all right—even though she'd been so sure he wasn't—and he was good. Impressively so, if she had to admit it. He was utterly ruthless, charming, and completely devious, and she didn't doubt he'd out her to Archer if he thought it would be to his advantage. She needed to keep an eye on him—she couldn't afford to be blindsided. Things were moving too quickly now—after years of almost stultifying boredom everything had switched to overdrive. And if she didn't adjust, she'd go down as surely as Archer would.

The hot shower went a long way toward improving her equilibrium. She was washing away Archer's abuse. She was washing away the feel of Mal's body as it covered hers, the grip of his arms around her, the touch of his mouth against hers. She needed to be baptized by her own determination, letting nothing get to her.

She dressed, ignoring her bruises, then rolled over to the French doors, taking a deep breath before she pushed them open. For all she knew, Mal would be there, waiting for her, and she hadn't decided exactly how she was going to deal with him.

It was going to be tricky. It had to be handled like two porcupines making love—very carefully. Not that she wanted to think of Mal in terms of sex, but it was pretty much impossible not to. He wasn't her type—too lean, too elegant, too subversive. She had always preferred men with broad shoulders and a rough-hewn edge. But type no longer seemed to matter, and if she tried to ignore the fact that her body seemed to respond to his, it would only complicate matters. She'd learned denial was a waste of time—you had to accept the facts, no matter how unpleasant, and get on with it.

The simple fact was that she was attracted to Malcolm Gunnison, whether she liked it or not. Attracted sexually, when she thought that part of her was dead, and attracted to his abilities. After all, he was everything she'd been training to be, and she found his talents slightly dazzling. Admitting it was the first step; knowing she wasn't going to do a fucking thing about it was the second, more important step. She couldn't afford to show any vulnerability right now. She couldn't afford to ever again.

The balcony was empty, the doors to the adjoining room flung open. She listened, but there was no sound of movement from beyond. The camera would be on her until she moved past the outer edge of her door—she'd calculated that years ago—so she moved to the balustrade, looking out over the roiling sea. She saw, to her horror, that most of the household was out on the beach in that storm-tossed mess. One of Archer's smaller boats must have come loose from its mooring—it was bobbing about in the waves, and they were trying to steady it and drag it onto the sand before it bashed against the rocks at the edge of the long, curving beach.

Bellowing orders, Archer wrestled with one of the ropes, and Mal was by his side, dressed only in rolled-up jeans, a wide white bandage around his bicep. What had he done to himself? And then she remembered the resilience of his skin beneath her teeth as she fought him, and she gave in to an entirely evil laugh. He was going to have a hard time explaining that to Archer.

No one was left in the house. She rolled farther down the balcony, out of range, and stopped by the doorway of his empty room. She was going to have to wash her feet again, but she couldn't miss this chance. She couldn't be sure she'd have enough time to get downstairs and reconnoiter, and the beach was too close to the house, but she could certainly finish what she started last night, secure that Mal wouldn't be lying in wait.

In the light of day she could see where the cameras had been dismantled, roughly—the wiring still sticking from the ceiling and the wall. Why had Archer let him get away with that? It wasn't as if other people wouldn't be interested in his pet project. Malcolm might be there to set a trap for Archer—maybe Archer was setting a trap for him. She glanced back at the ocean, but they were still struggling with the boat, the prisoner on the second floor forgotten.

She slipped from the chair, moving into Malcolm's shaded room like a shadow. He knew she could walk, and he'd left his door open. Of course, he must realize that someone who'd trained with the Committee could easily pick any lock, but the open door seemed almost too good to be true.

She moved quickly and carefully, going through the drawers again, this time with the benefit of sight, searching between the mattress and box spring of the king-size bed, then underneath it. He'd left nothing incriminating behind, but she hadn't expected he would, at least not in an obvious place. If he had, she would have to assume it was planted. She knew how to search a room swiftly and efficiently, and the last thing she reached for was the suitcase in the back of the closet, hauling it out in triumph.

It was too heavy to be empty, and he'd left it unlocked this time, though when she opened it the expanse of gray fabric revealed nothing. It took her only a moment to find the fake bottom, and she sat back on her heels and stared at the cache of weapons with awe. There were a total of seven handguns of varying brands and sizes. How often would he check his stash? He'd have no reason to—if she took one, there was always the chance he wouldn't notice. And if he did, what could he do about it?

She took the smallest, a Beretta Bobcat .22 that was a newer model than the one she'd trained with. She didn't know if a .22 bullet would stop Archer if he were in a rage, but an elephant gun probably wouldn't either. She was an excellent shot, or she had been, and a .22 between the eyes was just as effective as a .45 Magnum.

There were even extra bullets for the gun, though none for the larger handguns, which surprised her enough to wonder if this cache was actually a trap. It didn't matter—she needed any kind of help she could get. He couldn't be sure she was the one who'd taken it—by the time he discovered the gun was missing, there could be any number of people in the household who could have helped themselves to his cache of weapons. She shoved the small gun into one pocket, the extra bullets in the other, looking to see if she might find anything else useful.

The small knife could come in handy, and it would be easily hidden, but she'd didn't like the intimacy of using a knife on someone, despite her talent for it. She opened the knife anyway. Funny—it looked like the blade was rusty, or no . . . that was more like blood. Mal was not the kind of man who wouldn't take care of his weapons, and she stared down at the knife curiously. He must have cut someone, and since there was no current uproar, he had to have killed whoever's blood was on that blade, and recently, before he had time to clean it. She dropped the knife back into the case, closed it, and put it back in the closet where she'd found it, controlling her instinctive shiver. He was most likely to have taken down one of the outside crew, probably when he was prowling around. If he'd killed Marco, her one chance at an ally, she was going to have to kill Malcolm.

She bounded up the two steps and slipped back into her wheelchair, pausing long enough at the edge to look down at the sea. The boat had been beached, though it looked a bit battered, and everyone was standing around talking. She saw with relief that Marco was out there. In fact, everyone she remembered on the island was out there. So who had Malcolm stabbed?

Malcolm and Archer were off to one side, talking, and Rachel was flashing her magnificent tits around, Sophie thought with a curl of her lips. They seemed to be deep in conversation. About her? Or had they moved on to more interesting topics?

It didn't matter. Before she left, she was going to kill Archer MacDonald, and she wasn't going to let Malcolm Gunnison get in her way. She had to figure out where to shoot Archer, so he'd die slowly and painfully but be unable to come after her. She had enough time to consider her options. She took a deep breath, looking out toward the dark, angry sea and the world that lay beyond it: freedom, and a world without Archer MacDonald.

She headed back into her room. It would be a waste of time to call downstairs when everyone was out on the beach, but sooner or later someone would bring her some food, and she could get Joe to carry her back down. That, or she'd sit at the top of the stairs and yell until someone came to get her.

Until then, there was always *War and Peace*.

Malcolm resisted the temptation to open Sophie's door, going straight to his own. He had no idea how she was going to manage the truth that was now uncomfortably between them, and he was looking forward to finding out. Her training, if it had come from Isobel Lambert, the Ice Queen, had to be some of the best, but she'd been under a form of solitary confinement for years. She could still fight—his bruised kidney could attest to that, and she seemed more than capable of carrying off a long-term deception, which impressed him, though he was reluctant to admit it. Would she be able to be around him and not give anything away? The only way for two people to keep a secret was if one of them was dead, and he intended to be very cautious in the following twenty-four hours until he was certain she could handle things.

His grim laugh was silent. As if he wasn't very cautious when he was on a mission, cautious until it was time to move. Nothing had changed as far as he was concerned. If she couldn't handle it, if she started acting suspiciously, then he'd have to take her out, and that would probably precipitate everything else. He didn't have a clear sense of which was more important—killing MacDonald or destroying access to RU48, and his boss Madsen had been similarly vague. He'd do what he could do, as quickly and neatly as possible. In the meantime, he would simply have to watch.

Mal toweled off when he came out of the shower and headed to the closet. The suitcase was two inches off the imperceptible mark he'd left that morning, and he nodded in satisfaction as he dragged it out. She'd taken the Beretta and the bullets, just as he'd intended. Did she think he wouldn't notice? She probably didn't give a damn. Some nearly forgotten sense of fairness told him she needed at least a fighting chance in this volatile situation. That didn't mean she could be trusted—leaving that handgun for her might backfire, and she was probably already considering taking him out as well.

Serves me right, he thought, shoving the suitcase back. Leaving a gun for her had been quixotic at best, more likely bone-stupid, and if he ended up with one of those tiny bullets in his brain, he could at least be sure she'd finish Archer as well. Mission accomplished, and he really didn't give a shit about anything else. He was burned out and everyone knew it, but there'd been no one else to send, no one with the right qualifications.

There was, of course, always the remote possibility that someone else might stop him as well. He was going to have to make sure she knew everything, and he hated that. He didn't like working with partners, and when he did, it was at least someone he'd known for years and could trust.

He wouldn't trust Sophie farther than he could throw her, and she was a more solidly muscled handful than she had seemed. He had to consider that her entire wheelchair act might be a conceit of

Archer's—they could both be playing him. She certainly made it convincing, though, when she looked up at Archer with melting adoration.

He needed to remember that, in case she ever turned those pansy-brown eyes up to his with similar passion, unlikely though the thought seemed. She'd betrayed the Committee; she seemed ready to betray Archer. She'd probably do anything to stay alive, including selling him out at the first chance she got.

He was going to have to be very, very careful.

Chapter Twelve

"I hope you're enjoying yourself," Archer MacDonald said to Mal with one of his affable grins. "It's a cloudy day, but the weather never stays bad for long, and you look to me like a man who needs a vacation."

Mal stretched back in the wicker chair in Archer's office, letting the glass of iced tea warm in his hands. He made it a habit to avoid drinking things that were handed to him whenever he could get away with it, and Archer wasn't paying attention, clearly focused on other matters entirely. Mal waited patiently for Archer to come to the point.

"I don't need vacations," he said in the bored voice he used for this incarnation of Malcolm Gunnison.

Archer looked shocked. "Everyone needs vacations! You aren't a machine."

"I try," he said, as low affect as he could manage. "I will admit it's been very pleasant here, whether I needed it or not."

Archer's grin widened, and Mal gazed limpidly at his long, aristocratic teeth. *Had the upper classes once been crossbred with their horses* he thought absently. Almost everyone of the so-called upper crust seemed to have large, slightly protruding teeth. "I knew you liked it!" Archer crowed. "If I really thought you weren't having a good time, I would have had to do something about it."

"Like what?"

Archer shrugged. "Have you killed," he said affably.

"I doubt that would improve my enjoyment of Isla Mordita."

"Just kidding, old man," Archer said airily. *Did men really call each other "old man" nowadays?* Mal asked himself. It seemed to him that Archer was playing some sort of role too. "I would have found another way to make you like it here. I don't give up once I set my mind on something."

Mal looked at him. It sounded like a tossed-off sentiment, but Mal wasn't fooled. Archer would do anything to get his way, and beneath that upper-class, Ivy League charm, he could be absolutely ruthless. "Neither do I," Mal said.

Their eyes met for a moment, predator to predator, and there was a moment of stillness. Then Archer spoke. "I would have expected nothing less from a man in your position." He lifted his head, and all seriousness vanished. "I think my wife has decided to join us."

Mal had heard it too—Joe's heavy breathing on the winding steps, the hush of wheels against the tiled floor. Sophie was bringing the battle to them. He gave a half smile. "Good. No offense, old man," he used Archer's archaic term deliberately, "but I'd rather look at her face than yours."

"There *is* something about her," Archer admitted. "You should see her when she's dressed up—she can be quite stunning. A far cry from the slightly bedraggled and worn-out invalid she is now."

Mal couldn't imagine someone looking less bedraggled or worn out. He surreptitiously touched his bruised side, remembering her knee. "I thought you were trying to talk me into fucking her."

Archer's grin widened. "Are you interested?"

"I might be." Mal's voice was flat, giving nothing away.

Archer was almost gleeful. "Actually that's what I wanted to talk to you about. I'm going to need you to take care of that today."

Mal raised an eyebrow, keeping his expression unruffled. "Why?" he said calmly.

"I'm worried about her," Archer said mournfully. "You saw her bruises. I hate to tell you, but those were self-inflicted. I caught her just in time. She's so anxious and depressed about being in the wheel-chair that she's about reached her limit. I need you to screw the shit out of her."

That was a pathetically weak reason, and Mal wasn't about to hop to it. The man Archer knew didn't take orders. "I don't have a magic dick, Archer. She's your wife—why don't you fuck her into a good mood?"

"Oh, I would. But I have this little problem." He made a face. "I was less than careful during a recent business trip, and I'm afraid I'm a bit under the weather, so to speak. Nothing antibiotics won't cure, but Sophie's immune system is compromised because of her condition, and even with a condom I couldn't take the risk."

Jesus, Mal thought. "What makes you think I don't have similar or even worse problems?" he drawled.

"Do you?"

"No." He was tempted to lie and say he had herpes, but that prob-ably wouldn't make any difference. Archer wasn't going to be taking Sophie to bed again—Mal could read the signs. Sophie was on bor-rowed time, and only his arrival had stopped her eventual execution. "What makes you think she'll even have me?"

"Oh, I've seen the way she looks at you. We agreed after the acci-dent that that part of our marriage was over, but she still has needs. She'd have you if you aren't too squeamish."

"Squeamish?" he echoed, then realized Archer was referring to Sophie's supposed disability.

But Archer wasn't. "A tiny show of force might be necessary."

"You want me to rape your wife?" Mal was good at hiding his reac-tions, but this time it was called for.

"Oh, it wouldn't go that far. I told you, she wants you. You're the only thing she's shown the slightest bit of interest in for years. I think that's what brought her to . . . hurt herself. Your arrival made her realize everything that she was missing . . ." Archer paused for dramatic effect, secure in the belief that Mal was swallowing all of this. "Either you have to give her what she needs, or I'll make other arrangements for the Pixiedust." He smiled like a saint. "I have to put my wife's well-being ahead of business, old man. You understand."

Mal kept his gaze on the horizon, his mind working feverishly. Why would Archer be fixated on this, so much so that he was willing to risk his current deal? Of course he had other clients, but Archer should think twice about offending Mal's purported boss, one of the most powerful men in the world. It seemed that Archer was still dangerously obsessed with his treacherous wife and his need to punish her. If he weren't, he would have finished the job he'd started two years ago and had her killed. Keeping her alive was illogical—his need to torment her was a weakness Mal could exploit. Too bad that Sophie was a pawn between them, but she'd known what she signed up for when she'd first joined the Committee. That it was worse than she'd expected was no one's fault but her own.

"I understand," he said finally, not turning to look at Archer. "My employer is not the kind of man who accepts failure."

"Then you know what you have to do." Archer's voice was practically a purr of satisfaction, and Mal felt his stomach twist. Right then the last thing he wanted to do was put a hand on Sophie MacDonald, even as the possibility of her thrummed through his body. She'd bitch, she'd scream, she'd bite. And she wanted him, a fact that he knew filled her with disgust. He hadn't spent so long in the business without being able to read people, and he knew she was frustrated with her own mixed feelings.

His were mixed as well. She was a dangerous woman and he was far too susceptible to her. If he fucked her, he wouldn't be able to kill her, and that might just turn out to be a necessity. His hatred for Archer had reached immeasurable proportions. The fact that Archer had practically ordered him to screw his wife, something Mal wanted very much, only made it worse.

What if this was all a setup? What if Archer and his former-Committee wife were working together on a way to trap him? If his cover had been blown, why hadn't Archer had Mal killed?

He rose in one fluid motion. There was only one way to find out. "Lead the way."

She was sitting curled up on the sofa, exactly where Malcolm had first seen her, though without Archer draped all over her. The wheelchair was discreetly off to one side, and she looked at home as she smiled up at her husband, the bruise at the side of her face already fading. "Hello, darling," she said, and Mal had the oddest impression she was greeting him, not her husband. Not that she'd call him "darling." More likely "you son of a bitch."

"Baby!" Archer breathed, moving forward to kiss her cheek. Her bruised one, and he kissed it hard. Sophie didn't even blink. She reached up for him, but Archer deftly pulled away. "You look like a dream sitting there, my love, but I have a few things to check on. I had no idea you felt up to joining us for lunch."

"You won't sit with me?" She made a perfectly believable moue of disappointment.

"Can't do it. But Mal will join you—give you two time to get to know each other."

Mal could see her open her mouth to protest, but she saved her breath. He allowed Archer to maneuver him, push him down on the overstuffed sofa next to Sophie. The cushions were so soft she fell forward against him, and he could smell the faint gardenia scent of her skin, her hair.

"Be careful with the man, baby," Archer said with a hearty laugh that Mal wanted to cram down his throat. "He had a rough night, and he's got a gash on his arm from falling on a shard of glass. Don't be too energetic—we don't want it to start bleeding again."

She raised her eyebrows, looking at Mal. "You cut yourself?" It was a limpid question—she knew perfectly well she had bitten him like a rabid bitch, drawing blood.

He shrugged casually, leaning back into the octopus-like hold of the soft couch, feeling her settle against him. "Serves me right for drinking too much. Elena, the woman in the kitchen, stitched me up."

He could see the color bleach from her face, and he deliberately knocked one knee against hers in silent warning. She must have gotten the message, and she threw her head back and laughed. It was entirely feigned, of course, and he wondered what she'd look like if she really laughed. "You poor thing! It just goes to show how thick the walls are in this house, though. I never heard anything."

"Oh, I was crashing around like an elephant," he said easily, shifting a little, and he felt her body come to rest against his again, hip to hip. She couldn't push away—she wasn't supposed to have the strength, and he wasn't about to help her. "I ended up falling on a broken glass and slicing my arm open. Bled like a stuck pig."

She'd gotten over the shock, and she smiled brightly at him. "Well, I'm glad you learned your lesson. You need to be more careful."

"Being careful is for wimps."

Archer was beaming fondly at both of them, as if viewing a perfect arrangement of flowers. "You two are so cute together," he said. "I bet Sophie can give you a run for your money, Mal. She's a very bright girl." It would have been easy to miss the malice in his voice. "I'm heading out to the south end of the island—Joe told me there's been some erosion near the old sugar mill that I need to check on. You can carry her up to the bedroom if she gets tired, can't you, Mal? I'm afraid Joe and I won't be back for several hours."

Okay, if that's how you want to play it, Mal thought. "And where's your harem?"

If there was a slight annoyance in Archer's eyes, it passed quickly. "They're off-island on a shopping trip. I told them to pick up something for you, baby, but we couldn't decide what. You don't like jewelry and you hardly need shoes."

"I don't need anything, Archer," she said quietly, making no attempt to move away from Mal. "Just you." She looked up at her husband, practically batting her eyes, and for some reason it annoyed Mal.

Archer's solicitous smile irritated Mal even more. "We should be back in two or three hours. Remember your promise, Malcolm. I'm counting on you to entertain my wife. And Sophie, baby, don't do anything I wouldn't do. Of course, that's asking for trouble, isn't it?"

Archer didn't wait for a reply and headed out the door. Sophie sat in silence next to Mal, and Mal could feel the warmth of her body through his thin cotton shirt, could even sense her slightly elevated pulse. He said nothing either, waiting, until they heard the sound of the four-wheeler revving up and then fading into the distance as it moved up-island.

Sophie put her strong hands on him and shoved, hard, but the billowing sofa only made him fall back against her. "Would you mind sitting somewhere else?" she hissed in a low voice.

"Archer and company may be gone, but I doubt he's turned off the surveillance equipment," he said in an audible voice.

There was a faint stain of color across her cheeks, but she nodded. "I want you to know I love my husband, Mr. Gunnison," she said loudly, her eyes boring into his.

"Don't you think we've come far enough that you can call me Mal? And yes, I know you love your husband. He's a formidable man." It wouldn't do any harm to pass on a little flattery in the surveillance tapes. "But I'm getting the impression that he wouldn't mind."

"Wouldn't mind what?" she said, deliberately baiting him. They were playing a scene for the camera and they both knew it, but she seemed determined to throw him off his lines.

"Wouldn't mind if I fucked you," he said flatly.

She blinked, her only reaction to the word. "Don't I get a say in the matter?"

"I haven't made up my mind."

"My husband loves me." He could see the disgust in her eyes while she kept her voice soft.

"I'm sure he does. And he wants you to be happy. That's why he's offering me up on a silver platter."

"And you're the Thanksgiving turkey?" she snapped.

He couldn't help it—he laughed. "I think you're the one who's supposed to get stuffed."

She made a choking sound, which might even have been laughter. "You're a pig," she said.

"On occasion. Sometimes there's a lot to be said for getting down and dirty."

Her eyes widened, and this was no feigned reaction. He felt a little shiver run over her warm body, and it wasn't disgust. "I'm afraid that's something I don't have much interest in."

"Don't you, now?" His voice was a deliberate taunt, and he shifted slightly, just enough to bump softly against her body. He felt her shiver again, and her skin was warm. She smelled of body heat and gardenia-scented soap, and he wondered what would happen if he licked her exposed throat. Probably an elbow in the other kidney. He smiled at her benevolently. "You're in a bad mood, aren't you? I think you need your coffee. Should I summon Elena?"

"With a princely clap of your hands? I don't think so," she said. "Elena's busy enough."

"So you'd rather just sit here and cuddle?"

It was enough to get her moving. "If you'd be kind enough to get me my wheelchair, I can go get my own coffee."

He considered it. On the one hand, having the soft cushions imprison her against his body was definitely inspiring—he was half-tempted to see how far he could go with the cameras rolling. He knew women—even the toughest ones—changed once they'd screwed some-one, and he was very interested to see what Sophie would do once he'd gotten inside her. *All in the interests of the mission, you virtuous bastard,* he told himself. After all, what could Archer do to him if he refused? He was unlikely to jeopardize his relationship with a man like Mal's supposed employer. But the damned thing was, Mal wanted the excuse, wanted a reason to touch her, to take her, to fuck her.

That was probably part of the secret to Archer's unimpeded accu-mulation of wealth and power. He knew exactly what someone wanted, deep inside, and he got it for them, guilt-free. Which meant the very last thing Mal should do was touch Sophie.

With little effort he got to his feet, and she immediately fell over on the buoyant cushions, glaring at him as she pushed herself upright again. "In fact, I need a cup of coffee myself," he said.

He could absolutely see the wheels turning in her gorgeous, angry brown eyes. She wanted him to go away, but then she'd be trapped on the billowy sofa and he could come back at any time. He didn't wait for her to decide, he simply retrieved her wheelchair and brought it to her, setting the locks. He started to lean down to pick her up but she reared back.

"I can get out of this damned thing myself," she said in a steely voice.

"I have no doubt you can. From one damned thing to another." He scooped her up anyway, clamping her tight enough against him that he kept her elbow from slamming into his ribs, and deposited her in the chair. He knelt down in front of her, arranging her supposedly useless feet on the rests, and he knew how very much she wanted to kick him. He looked up at her from between her legs, and he didn't have to say a word, just simply put his hands on the armrests. She could read his thoughts, and she inadvertently tightened her thighs, a movement so subtle it wouldn't be picked up by the camera. He kept his Malcolm Gunnison face on, impas-sive. Rising, he leaned forward and unlatched the brakes, his head close to hers as he did so. He shouldn't. A smart man wouldn't. And he knew damned well he was going to.

"We need to talk," he said on a breath of sound.

She wanted to curse at him, he could feel it. She wanted to tell him to get the hell away from her. She even wanted him between her legs. Poor little girl, she'd landed herself in a big mess and she didn't know how to get out of it. And then she tilted her head back, so that their mouths were dangerously close, and smiled up at him, a steely challenge in her eyes. "Coffee is an excellent idea," she said. "You can push me."

Bastard, bastard, bastard, Sophie fumed as he rolled her into the kitchen. There was no longer any question in her mind—she was going to kill him too, once she'd finished with Archer. It didn't matter that he was Committee—he was probably just as much a danger to her as Archer was, and it would be self-defense. Justifiable homicide. A well-deserved execution.

The kitchen was deserted. "Penny for your thoughts," Malcolm said as he planted her in the middle of the big room, too far from any surface to find a weapon like a butcher knife or a heavy frying pan.

"I was thinking of ways to kill you," she said in a low voice.

He gave a surreptitious glance around him. "No surveillance in here?"

She wasn't going to help him. "You figure it out."

His half grin made her want to smack him. But, then, she already wanted to kill him—that was nothing new. "Two cameras, one trained on the door to the dining room, the other on the door to outside. Bugs in the same places—there'd be too much noise going on in here to have something ultrasensitive. So we're relatively unwatched. Where do you think Elena is?"

She stifled her irritation. Of course he would have checked the place out—he was Committee, after all. In another lifetime she might have admired how efficient he was. "She'll probably walk back in at any time."

"She's probably having a nice long siesta. Archer went to a lot of trouble to get rid of everybody—I'm sure he told her not to bother with lunch today."

"You willing to take a chance on that?" she challenged him.

"Yes." He took the kettle, poured out the water and refilled it, then set it on the stove to heat.

"There's a coffeemaker and an espresso machine."

"There's also a French press, and I'm a purist."

"Oh, God help me," she muttered.

"He hasn't so far." He reached for the tightly sealed container of oily black beans. "If you're in a hurry, I can make you one of those infernal pods."

She didn't want to accept anything from him, but the lure of French press coffee was irresistible. Too much about him was. She needed to learn how to resist. "I can wait," she said in a grumpy voice.

She could see the brief flash of amusement in his eyes. "I'm sure you can." He took out the coffee grinder, and she realized he'd already made a complete surveillance of the kitchen—he even knew where all the implements were. She unfastened the wheel locks and slid back, out of his way, farther out of the way of the cameras, and watched as he went about the ritual of coffee making in a charged silence. She needed to watch him, observe him, see if she could pick up anything about him that might help her, just as she'd been trained to do, but she wished she didn't have to. He moved so elegantly, with an economy of grace that belied the sheer power in his deceptively lean body. She'd felt that strength, the intractable nature of his hold, and the memory sent her stomach churning with mixed emotions. There was nothing wasted in his movements—it was all quick efficiency. She already knew he was too strong for her in straightforward combat, even with dirty infighting. Her only chance would be to take him by surprise.

"Stop thinking about it," he said as he poured the boiling water into the French press. "You aren't going to be able to get the better of me no matter how hard you try. Any devious, underhanded trick you can think of is something I've thought of already. I'm as ruthless as they come, and I've been honing my skills while you've been reading *War and Peace* and sitting on your backside."

"Sitting on my backside wasn't exactly my choice in the matter," she shot back.

He gave her a smile that was absolutely seraphic. "Poor little cripple," he said in a slightly raised voice. "Is that what your husband calls you?"

She shuddered. "Stop reminding me."

"Of what? The wheelchair? Or your husband?"

She just looked at him. The wheelchair wasn't real—the husband was. She didn't even like to think of Archer that way—he was the enemy, the one she had to destroy before he destroyed her.

But Mal was the enemy as well, a different kind of enemy. She'd been infatuated with Archer, charmed out of her once-formidable intellect, so in love, if she could call it that, that her brains had melted and her instincts had deserted her, at least in the beginning.

Mal was a different matter altogether. He wasn't trying to charm her—his enmity was up front and clear. She couldn't trust him any farther than she could throw him, and she'd learned the night before that she couldn't throw him at all. But she was becoming just as obsessed with him, in a different way. She could see something, feel something beneath that implacable exterior, something that drew her more powerfully than anything she could remember. It was nothing like what she'd felt for Archer, but she didn't trust herself any more than she trusted Mal. Whatever it was that called to her was probably nothing but her imagination, trying to justify her normal, sexual reaction to an undeniably hot male. Whether she liked it or not, she knew that her body reacted to his. To his words as well—taunting, tempting.

He moved over to her, holding out a cup of coffee, and she stared at it in surprise. He hadn't grabbed one of the hand-thrown pottery mugs—instead he'd taken an antique Limoges cup and saucer from the set she'd bought on eBay when she was first married. It had been obscenely expensive, and so delicate and beautiful that she'd loved it. She'd assumed that Archer had smashed every piece in a fit of pique, but he must have forgotten all about it.

There was one dark sugar cube on the saucer and a tiny silver spoon. She'd bought those spoons when she'd been in her early twenties, when she'd first moved to England. How the hell did he know she liked a small cube of turbinado sugar with really strong coffee?

She looked up at him without taking it, shaken. "How do you know so much?" she said in a hushed voice.

For a moment he said nothing, his eyes slowly running over her, from top to bottom, and it felt like a physical touch. Then he shrugged. "It's a combination of instinct and guesswork. I also picked what I would have chosen."

She glanced behind him, to the second cup on the wooden work top, the same china, the same tiny spoon. He'd added milk to his already, and the coffee was a dark, creamy color. "Why didn't you give me milk?" Her voice was uncomfortably breathless.

"You're lactose intolerant."

She wanted to give up in that moment. She had no idea how he knew, and she didn't care. In her entire life no one had ever remembered, no matter how many times she told them, that she couldn't touch milk. And now this man said it casually, as if it were simply a given.

She reached out and took the cup, her hand brushing his, but she kept hers steady, with not even a shimmer marring the serene surface of the inky black coffee. Persephone and Hades, she thought. She was about to eat six pomegranate seeds and be doomed to spend half her days with the Prince of Darkness. She dropped the cube of sugar into the brew and stirred it, the sound of the silver tapping against the fine bone china the only sound in the room.

"We're going to have to work together, you know," Malcolm said, moving back to collect his own coffee, the moment vanishing. "You may as well learn to trust me."

"Not in this lifetime."

He laughed, actually laughed, at her terse words. "You will," he said. "In the meantime, is there someplace nearby we can go that's out of range?"

She managed a noncommittal shrug, taking a sip of the coffee and then closing her eyes to savor it. This had to be the best cup of coffee she'd had in her entire life. A man who could make coffee like this couldn't be all bad. She said nothing, taking her time with it, stretching out the sensuous pleasure of it. He was leaning against the kitchen workbench, watching her as he drank his own, and it was a strange sort of communion, a silent time shared between the two of them. *Like some stupid commercial*, she thought in disgust, but she couldn't fight the betraying warmth that was low in her belly. When she reluctantly finished the last drop, she met his eyes, and the cup rattled in her hand.

She couldn't read his expression—there was something hidden, indecipherable in his green eyes. She pulled herself together. *The enemy*, she reminded herself. "And just what were *you* thinking?"

"Not about how I want to kill you," he said lightly, taking the cup from her and moving to the sink. To her surprise he washed everything, quickly and efficiently, and put things back where he found them. He turned back, and that hidden expression was gone. "Let's go." He scooped her up in his arms, leaving the wheelchair behind, and she wanted to scream in annoyance.

"Don't," she said in a tight voice as he carried her out the back door into the sun-warmed courtyard.

"Don't what? We're going to look for a private place to talk, and your chair isn't an all-terrain vehicle. If you don't like me touching you, you're going to have to put up with it. Just pretend I'm Joe."

"That's a little difficult," she muttered, then wanted to bite her tongue.

But he said nothing, moving down the carefully landscaped walkways. The small bungalows that housed the staff were on the right—he headed toward the left, down a narrower path. "You know there are cameras out here," she said.

"No shit. But the bugs are like those in the kitchen—they can function only when things are relatively quiet, and this island is filled with noise, from the birds to the wind to the sound of the waves. If they used regular bugs, everything would sound like a whooshing noise, and Archer isn't as cutting edge as he'd like to be. The Committee in New Orleans has developed the most amazing listening devices, ones that can be trained to pick up a specific voice even in a roomful of people. You have to have a sample of the voice first, but they're very effective."

For a moment she was distracted—she'd always had a techie streak that had gotten little liberation recently. "How did they do that?"

"If you get back to New Orleans, I'll have them show you," he said, moving farther into the shrubbery.

She tried to ignore the sudden longing inside her. She wanted to get back to New Orleans—she wanted to play with new inventions, live a sensible life, eat what she wanted, sleep when she wanted, fuck whom she wanted. Though at that point she didn't want to fuck anything, she reminded herself. *Danger, Will Robinson.*

"I'll hold you to it," she said, keeping her eyes trained on the path in front of them. It might have been her imagination, but it almost felt as if he tightened his arms around her for just a moment. If he had, the gesture would have been oddly comforting. But of course he hadn't. She had to stop looking for things that weren't there.

She should have known where they were going. The old boathouse loomed into sight, far enough away from the surveillance equipment that no one would hear her if she screamed. The ancient building perched out over the water, on the opposite side of the island from the brand-new building Archer had constructed to house his small armada.

This place had once sheltered small boats during the hurricane season or when the previous owner returned to the mainland for long months at a time back in the middle of the previous century. It was amazing it had stood up to so many storms—part of the roof had fallen in, though the walls were at least vertical, and the windows were long gone.

There was a heavy padlock keeping the wide doors closed, but she didn't expect Mal would have any trouble picking it. She just didn't expect him to do so while he was still carrying her, but he managed quite handily, nudging open the door with his foot and then kicking it closed behind them.

And then they were alone in the huge, cavernous interior, the sun blazing through the holes in the roof. It felt safe, quiet, when nothing had felt that way in longer than she could remember, and she couldn't rid herself of the feeling that this dangerous, dangerous man had the uncanny ability to make her feel protected. She cleared her throat. "What makes you think this place isn't bugged as well?"

"I went over everything a couple of days ago."

She controlled her instinctive doubt. "He could have had them done since you were here."

He shook his head. "I'm wearing something that alerts me to bugs."

She looked at him in surprise. "Really?"

"On my hip. If we run across something, trust me, you'll know."

She refused to think about his hips. "Great," she grumbled. "Are you just going to stand there holding me while we talk?"

"Nope." He released her suddenly, dropping her feet to the ground, and she was so startled she almost stumbled. He caught her upper arms to steady her, and they were too close, looking at each other, wary, suspicious, aroused.

"Oh, hell," he muttered, and before she realized what he was doing, he'd pulled her into his arms, placing his mouth on hers.

Chapter Thirteen

It had been a long time since kissing had been anything but a macabre form of punishment, and for a moment Sophie let herself dissolve into it, the heat and hunger of his mouth on hers, the raw desire that shot through her, unwanted, and she was sliding her arms around his neck, pulling him closer, when sanity reared its ugly head.

She shut off her brain and moved, and a moment later he was on the ground, the rotting floor cracking beneath his weight where he'd landed. She had only a moment to congratulate herself before he surged back to his feet, and she was poised, alert, ready for his attack.

Instead, he looked at her across the shadow-dappled boathouse with nothing more than amusement. "Not bad for someone who's been on her back for two years," he drawled. "You want to see if you can do it when I'm paying attention?"

She took a step back, even though he was making no move to approach her. "If I were you, I wouldn't drop my guard," she said, her heart hammering, though whether with adrenaline or in reaction to his kiss she wasn't quite sure. "I don't like you, and I'm going to take you down any chance I get." Why did that feel like a lie? It was exactly the way she *should* feel.

"So I gather," he said, unperturbed. "So why did you start to kiss me back if we're such dire enemies?"

"Why did you kiss me?"

"Because I wanted to see what you'd do," he said, moving toward the far wall and sliding down so that he was sitting on the dusty floor. "You've been cut off for years now—Archer assures me that he's no longer interested in his conjugal rights, and I wanted to see how desperate you are."

"You son of a bitch."

"Calm down," he said mildly. "You passed with flying colors."

"It was a test?" Her voice rose a little, and she bit her lips, ignoring the conflict inside her.

He shrugged. "If we're going to work together, I needed to test your reactions."

"We aren't going to work together," she said furiously. "When the Committee abandoned me here, they lost any claim to my loyalty . . ."

"Oh, come on! You surely didn't expect the Committee to bother with you after your betrayal? You know as well as I do that if I were abandoned here in the same situation, no one would come after me either. We had an operative spend three years as a prisoner in the South American jungles and no one bothered to rescue him. Once you start your mission, you're pretty much on your own. They'll help if they can, but in your circumstances no one was going to stick his or her neck out. You're an idiot if you ever thought someone would."

Why hadn't she brought the gun with her? She'd done a thorough breakdown and cleaning, making sure everything was intact, checked it and loaded it, but of course there'd been no chance to try it out. She could think of a perfect target to practice on at that moment, but the handgun was up in her room, hidden in the mattress with her stash of pills.

"I never thought anyone would," she said. "So it's a good thing I gave up on the Committee as well."

He shrugged again. "A good thing for you, maybe, but not so good for the rest of Archer's victims, and he's been amassing a lot of them in the past few years."

"So you've come here to save the world since I screwed it up," she said, ignoring her flash of guilt. She'd made peace with her mistake after all this time, or as much peace as she could. She didn't need to be reminded of the harm her foolishness had caused. "What a hero!"

He was unmoved by her sarcasm. "It's a tough job, but someone's got to do it," he drawled.

She dropped to the floor on the opposite side of the building, listening to the ominous creak. She could see the shimmer of the water beneath the floorboards, sending patterns up to what remained of the roof. "Did they tell you to kill me?" She managed to modulate her voice so that the question sounded like nothing more than idle curiosity.

"I told you last night, they don't care what I do with you. You're no longer a liability—enough time has passed, and it appears that Archer didn't get anything useful about the Committee structure from you."

"Not for want of trying," she said bitterly. "He may have never admitted knowing about me, but he made it clear he was wanting information. Information I wouldn't give no matter what he did to me."

She felt a sudden stillness in the room, but when she glanced across at him he was leaning back against the wall, looking up through the damaged roof to the overcast sky. Just as well—she didn't want to think about that time. Archer was undeniably brilliant and inventive, and when he put those qualities into finding ways to deliver pain, it was almost unbearable. But she'd borne it anyway. She'd gotten to the point where she could withstand anything.

Including the man who had lowered his head and was watching her again through the shifting light in the boathouse. "So why are we here?" she said.

"I have orders to have rampant sex with you."

For a moment she thought she misunderstood him. "Orders?"

"Archer informs me that you're suicidal and those impressive bruises are the result of self-harm."

"That fuckhead," she muttered, incensed.

"And furthermore he says that you need distraction and, presumably, physical release to come out of your desperate decline. If I don't do it, then it'll be up to someone else."

"Good. He can import stud service."

"If I don't do it, then he's hinted he'll find someone else to sell his fucking Pixiedust to."

She stared at him in disbelief. "That's ridiculous. Why would it matter to him who I end up screwing, as long as he can humiliate me into doing it? And why would he let it interfere with his business?"

"He believes you're attracted to me. And he's insisting because he likes power and he wants to make me follow orders so he can demonstrate he has the upper hand. He also seems obsessed with hurting you." He leaned his head back, at ease. "And since I'm not about to risk my mission over something we both want, I figured we could come down here and do the deed. There are too many cameras on this island—I'm not in the mood for witnesses."

She felt a tightness curl low in her stomach and her skin begin to tingle. "Something we both want? What planet are you from? I don't want you anywhere near me."

"That's too bad, because I'm going to be inside you," Mal said lazily, watching her out of those deceptive green eyes.

The tingle became electric on her warm skin. "It'll be a cold day in hell. You go away and I'll take care of Archer myself."

He shook his head, and his relaxed posture was even more of an affront to her. "Not going to happen."

"Well, then he'll just have to take your word for it that you debauched me."

"Debauched?" he echoed with a laugh. *How could he laugh at a time like this*, she thought. But then, Committee operatives were trained to do whatever they had to do to complete the mission, including having sex when required, regardless of gender. This was simply part of the job to Malcolm, and she wanted to hurt him, badly, though she didn't want to examine her reasons too closely. "What kind of romance novels have you been reading?"

"*War and Peace*," she said. "Sorry, your sacrifice is unnecessary. We'll just tell him we did it."

"He's not that gullible," Mal said.

"Convince him," she snapped.

He shook his head. "Never tell a lie when the truth will do—you must have learned that. Lying only complicates matters. Sorry, sweetheart. We don't have a choice."

Her breath hitched in her throat, then started again. She could feel her heart hammering—part of her training had involved controlling her heart rate, controlling all outward sign of panic, but too long had passed. Her heart was pounding so loudly he could probably hear it.

He looked far too comfortable, his long legs stretched out in front of him, seemingly at ease. But he wasn't—he was alert, like a snake ready to strike. "No," she said flatly. "Just lie a little harder."

"Well, I could," he said. "But I don't want to. I want you."

The words, casually spoken, were a shock. He rose to his feet, effortlessly, and she stared up at him, knowing he was coming for her. She was by the door—she could run, but there were too many security cameras. She could scream, but it wouldn't do any good—no one was around. She didn't move, like a rabbit caught in a snare, but she wasn't going to be a victim ever again.

"You touch me and I'll break your hand," she said steadily.

"You can try." His voice was calm, pleasant, as he came up to her. Huddled against the wall was no fighting position, and she pushed herself up so that she stood facing him, only a foot of space separating them. Too close. Too far. He reached out his hand for her, and she slapped him across the face as hard as she could, so hard that it jolted all the way up her arm. He didn't react.

"You have too many tells," he said in a conversational voice. He was wearing a gray button-down shirt, and he pulled it from his jeans, unbuttoning it while his eyes bore into hers. Deep, hypnotic eyes, and she wondered if she could fight him. Her whole body felt alive, tingling with sensation, and he hadn't even touched her. "I can see what you're going to do before you even realize it."

"Touch me and I'll kill you."

"You and what army?" Before she knew what was happening, he'd crossed that last bit of space, slid his arm around her back, and yanked her against his hard body. "Don't be a hypocrite. We both want it, and it helps the mission. Man up, Jordan."

It was a shock, hearing her maiden name for the first time in years. She could feel him, his hard cock unmistakable beneath his jeans, pressing against her stomach. "I don't think that's exactly what you're expecting me to do." He was right, damn him. It was taking everything she had to keep her body stiff against his, when she wanted to sink into his warmth. "We don't have to do this."

A slow smile crossed his face and he shook his head, his green eyes hot and slumberous. "Maybe not, but we want to." He put his other hand behind her neck, pulling her head up for his mouth, and she didn't move, letting him kiss her, letting the feeling flood through her body, heat and need, so long denied her. He was right. She'd wanted this from the moment she first saw him, whether she wanted to admit it or not, and his tongue in her mouth was the first claim—her response, the first acceptance.

His body pressed hers against the wall, and she felt him reach between them, unfastening his jeans, and she panicked for a moment, lashing out at him. He caught her wrists, holding them tightly together, and began to pull up her skirt. She wanted to shove him away, she wanted . . . she wanted . . .

She yanked her arms free and put them around his neck, slamming her mouth against his. She grabbed his shirt, trying to pull it away from him, wanting his skin against hers, and he'd managed to pull the top of her dress down, exposing her breasts. A moment later he'd hoisted her up in his strong, strong arms, and her legs wrapped around his narrow hips, and she was suddenly blind with hunger.

He shoved into her, and she gasped, shocked at the unexpected size of him, the thick cock deep inside her, so good . . . so good . . . and she tightened her arms and legs around him as spasms of pleasure washed over her. She couldn't speak, couldn't breathe, she just wanted to feel. She needed this to last forever, and she rode him, his hands on her hips, sliding her up and down on his cock. She threw her head back, wanting to scream, and he sank his head against her neck, his teeth against her shoulder, the sting of his bite sending her over the edge.

She had always been noisy during sex. But she came in powerful, urgent silence now, her entire body trembling, shaking, falling apart, as he thrust into her, over and over again, his hips sinuous, pinning her against the wall, until it was too much, and she tried to say something, but all she could do was push tighter against him, taking more, needing more.

Another wave hit her, and this time she did cry out, a wordless sound of rich pleasure, and he pulled away from the wall, turning around, still holding her as he moved, in and out, his thickness a wicked torment, harder, deeper, until he was suddenly rigid in her arms, in her body, his breath rasping as he poured himself into her, punctuated by each jerk of his hips, and she let go, let go of everything, drowning in sensation, in him, in Mal.

She lost all sense of time. Slowly, slowly, his arms loosened around her. Her heart was slamming against her chest, his own heart rate barely elevated, and when he pulled free from her, she wanted to cry out in anguish at the loss. There was no way that her legs could support her, and she dropped to the rough flooring at his feet, curling in on herself. She could feel the wetness of his semen between her legs. He hadn't used a condom—of course he hadn't.

She heard the creak of the wood, and looked up to see he'd collapsed against the wall, his eyes closed, his elegant face a sheen of sweat.

There was no way she could read his expression. She drew her knees up and buried her wet face against them, unable to look at him. Unable to look at him and not want him again.

She had no idea how long the silence lasted. How long it took her heartbeat to return to normal, for his ragged breath to calm. She just needed to be alone. "Go away," she said in a harsh whisper, her arms tight around her up-drawn knees, her face buried.

She didn't expect any mercy, any tenderness from him. She felt his hands on her arms, pulling them away, and she had no choice but to look up into his impassive face. At least there was no triumph in his green eyes. "You ready to go back to the house?" he asked in a perfectly calm voice.

She jerked her head up completely then, staring at him. He'd already fastened his jeans, though his shirt was still open, exposing his strong chest, and she could see his pulse at his throat. Clearly he was not as unmoved has he'd have her believe.

Her dress was down to her waist, still exposing her breasts, and she quickly yanked it up, covering herself, then used her arm to wipe the wetness away from her eyes. There could be no better way to punish her for her stupid treachery than making her want, need, ache for a man who had no use for her.

"I'm going to kill Archer," she said in a low voice, "and then I'm going to kill you."

His face creased in a faint smile. "Go ahead and try."

She shook her head, trying to dispel him from her mind, just as she needed to wash him from her body. She wanted to hate him, to blame him, but he'd been nothing but truthful. They'd both wanted it. She just wasn't going to let it happen again. "Take me back," she said. "I need a shower." Her voice was filled with honest disgust. Not with him. With herself. With her stupid, mindless desperation, with her orgasms, with her need to be back in his arms, her need for some small sign of tenderness, of sweetness.

Instead, he had the same enigmatic expression he usually wore. "All right," he said, pushing away from the wall. "But no shower until Archer comes back. We didn't go through this to have all evidence washed away."

Go through this? Like it was some form of torture? As it should have been for her? But he knew far too well it hadn't been torture for either of them—it had been a pleasure so exquisite that she wanted any witness, including both of them, dead.

He rose, towering over her, and she knew she should scramble to her feet, to lessen her feeling of weakness, but she still wasn't sure her legs would hold her. She was still trembling, so slightly he wouldn't see it, and her legs felt like rubber bands. It had been so long since she'd had sex with anyone that she couldn't remember what it had been like. Couldn't remember it ever feeling this powerful.

She looked up, way up, past his endless legs to his unreadable face. "I hate you," she said.

"You sound like a child," he said coolly.

"You fuck any children lately?"

"You've got a nasty tongue on you, don't you, sweetheart?" he said.

"Don't call me that!" She wasn't sure how much more of this she could take.

"What would you prefer? Baby? That's what Archer calls you."

She didn't say another word. It had happened, and there wasn't a damned thing she could do about it. She couldn't even blame him— it had only taken his strong hands on her and she'd gone willingly, eagerly.

She couldn't make herself move. He reached down and pulled her up, holding her for a moment, as if he guessed she wasn't too steady yet. "Don't worry, sweetheart." He used that hated term again, but it sounded oddly tender. "If you end up getting out of here, you can report me to the Committee for rape and see if it gets you anywhere."

"You didn't rape me and you know it," she said in a low voice.

"Depends on how you define rape," he said. "You said no, I said yes, then your body said yes. I don't think it'll make it to the Supreme Court, but it's an interesting distinction."

"You are such a fucking bastard," she said, and the last of her tremors vanished, leaving her suffused with anger, her misery dissolving. Had he done it on purpose? Of course not—he didn't give a damn how she felt.

"I never told you I was anything else." He picked her up, holding her high against him, and kicked open the boathouse door. In another moment they were heading back up the path.

She could still feel him inside her. Crying would be a waste of time, and besides, what was she crying for? Semantics aside, she had taken him into her body willingly, released him reluctantly. She had kissed him, and her mouth felt swollen and tender. She had had a rough reminder that she was still human, still female, prey to the usual biological hunger and needs most humans were. There was nothing to be ashamed about. It was part of the job, the job that she'd fucked up, and no one was hurt in the aftermath.

He was right—she needed to man up. She said nothing when they reached the house, Mal shoving open the kitchen door. Sophie had no choice but to sit in her chair when he placed her there, the dampness between her legs, until Mal accomplished whatever he'd set out to accomplish. Sooner or later she'd be alone, able to work through what had happened, able to rationalize and put it behind her. Right then she simply felt drained and empty.

Elena came in from the dining room, a laundry basket under her arm, and she greeted the two of them with a smile. "Did you have a good time, *señora* Sophie?"

A good time doing what? Sophie thought in a sudden panic. Did everyone know what she and Mal had been doing?

"We had a very nice walk," Mal said lightly. "Mrs. MacDonald showed me places on the island I hadn't realized existed."

Elena's face creased in a grin. "She knows this island very well. Back when . . . before . . . she hiked all over it. I don't think there was one place she didn't investigate."

"Really?" Mal said. "Then we'll definitely have to do this again, won't we, Sophie?" He leaned closer to her, and she could feel his warm breath on her skin. A final stray shiver danced across her skin.

She wanted to tell him to go to hell. She wanted to say, "I don't think so," in her iciest tones, but they had an audience, so she simply smiled with as much sincerity as she could manage. "You'd probably have a better time with Archer," she murmured, glancing up at him.

She sucked in her breath, because there was heat and laughter in his eyes as he looked down at her. "But he's not as pretty," he said, sounding perfectly sincere, as he picked up a strand of her hair and stroked it. The sight of his long, gorgeous fingers rubbing against the silken strands made her stomach clench once again.

"Can I get you both some lunch?" Elena asked, setting down her basket.

I want to press my head against his hand like a kitten looking for comfort, Sophie thought in disgust, about to shake her head, when she heard Mal's voice above her. "Sandwiches and coffee on the terrace would be very nice, Elena."

Elena gave them both a dazzling smile. "It will take only a moment."

Sophie waited until they were in the darkened kitchen. "I'm not hungry," she said in a small voice.

"I am." The house was cool and dark, with the curtains closed against the bright tropical sun. "And you don't eat enough."

That was enough to make her turn to stare at him. "I'm perfectly healthy."

"You are. But you're too thin."

Her laugh was brittle. "You certainly know the right words to a woman's heart."

He pushed her out into the bright sunshine again, on the veranda above the pool, the water blue and beautiful in the afternoon sun. "This isn't my first rodeo," he said as he placed her at the table, setting the brakes. "I know what to say to a woman to make her my slave for life."

The thought was so absurd she was almost speechless. Almost. "You must be out of your mind."

He shrugged, stretching out in the chair beside her. "Sanity is hardly the hallmark of a professional killer."

The thought startled her. *I just fucked a murderer*, she thought. She'd been so caught up in trying to blot it out that she'd forgotten who and what he was. Forgotten that he was just as likely to kill her as she was to kill him.

"Oh, I don't know," she said, making herself sound casual. "How long have you been getting away with it?"

"How long have I been a killer for the Committee? Eight years."

She stared at him. He'd said it casually, as if it were no big deal, but she thought she could see a bleakness to his eyes. "You were there when I was?" For some reason she had simply assumed he'd come in later.

"I was. I wasn't stationed in England at the time, but I heard all about you. Everyone did."

The familiar guilt swept over her, but she resolutely pushed it away. "That must have been entertaining for you . . ." Her voice trailed off as Elena came out on the veranda, a large tray in her capable hands. Sophie could smell the coffee, and she decided she might survive this day after all.

Elena set the food on the table—thick, crusty chicken sandwiches, mugs of steaming coffee, a plate of mangoes. There were also two pairs of Archer's unending supply of Ray-Bans. "The sun is too bright this time of day," Elena said.

Mal reached for the sunglasses, and for a moment Sophie was fixated on his hand. Had she ever looked at them before? He had long, elegant fingers and strong, beautiful hands. Damn it. He looked up at

Elena and smiled with such genuine sweetness that it felt like a punch in the stomach. "*Gracias*, Elena."

Elena was far from immune. Her cheeks flushed pink with pleasure. "*De nada, señor*. Can I get you anything else?"

"We're fine," Mal said, not bothering to check with Sophie.

She waited until Elena was gone. "Another member of your fan club?"

"Put on your sunglasses," he said, tossing them to her. She made no effort to catch them, and they landed in her lap. He reached for his mug of coffee. "Put them on or I'll put them on for you." It was gently spoken, but it was a threat, and she wasn't about to give him the excuse to touch her ever again.

She put them on, cutting the glare. They were some protection—not from the sun, but from him, and she preferred having his eyes covered as well. They were far too acute when they fell on her. "So what do you expect me to do when Archer comes home? Am I supposed to simper and fall all over you? Be rendered silent and in awe over your massive . . . skills?"

He actually laughed at that, setting off another inexplicable reaction inside her. "Do anything you fucking please. I have a little suggestion for you, though."

"I'm sure you do." She took a sip of her coffee and felt the warm caffeine slide down to her nerve endings. Not the liquid ambrosia of Mal's French press masterpiece, but close enough to renew her flagging will.

"You might try to remember this place is bugged just about everywhere."

She almost spat the coffee out before she stared at him, stricken. "You idiot! Why didn't you remind me?"

He was leaning back in his hair, surveying one sandwich with interest. "You were clearly too distracted by my massive . . . skills"—he echoed her suggestive pause—"to think about such things. Fortunately a good fuck doesn't turn me into a mindless idiot. I pulled the wire this morning."

Mindless idiot? She looked at him, deceptively calm. "You think you're improving matters by trying to drive me into a murderous rage?" She wasn't sure whether to be furious or flattered by the "good fuck."

"I'm not trying to improve matters."

"Good point." Elena had brought out a sharp knife for the mango slices, and Sophie wondered if she would have any chance of getting it and burying it in his thigh.

"Don't even think about it," Mal said, moving the knife out of her reach.

"Then stop pissing me off." It was a benevolent term for the anger that suffused her, but he didn't seem to care.

"You're better that way," he said. "More alert. As long as you're angry, you're more likely to stay alive."

"And exactly why do you care?"

He appeared struck by the thought. "Actually, I'm not sure. Maybe things *would* be easier if you were dead." He gave her a cynical version of the sweet smile he'd given Elena, his eyes unreadable behind the dark lenses. "Carry on."

She took a bite out of her sandwich, wishing she were biting his jugular. "Fuck you."

"You should have said that earlier—we could have stayed down at the boathouse. I don't suppose we have time to go back . . . ?" He looked at his watch suggestively.

"I . . ."

"Yes, I know, you hate me. Good for you. Now smile, my pretty little assassin. Your husband has returned."

She felt the color drain her face, and she set down the half-eaten sandwich, her bizarre appetite, which had unexpectedly returned, vanishing once more at the sound of Archer's loud laugh echoing from the living room. She barely had time to roll away from the table when the man who was technically her husband strode out onto the terrace, Rachel on his arm.

"I wondered where you two had gotten off to," he said cheerfully, his dark eyes glittering. "I was thinking . . . oh, my!" He stopped mid-sentence, staring at them. Sophie reached for her coffee again, not because she wanted any, but for something to do. Her hand shook slightly and Mal reached over and caught her other one. Archer would be sure to notice.

"Did you solve your problem up-island?" Mal asked lazily, leaning back in his chair, his long legs stretched out in front of him, his hand drifting over hers, his fingers touching, stroking, caressing. *Beautiful hands*, Sophie thought, closing her eyes behind the mirrored sunglasses.

Archer's eyes were bright with malicious delight. "Looks like all my problems were solved." He reached over Sophie's shoulder to take the untouched half of her sandwich, and he deliberately brushed his body against hers. She could smell his sweat, and her stomach roiled.

Archer moved around the table, watching them both closely, biting into the sandwich with his strong white teeth. "I can see you two have been busy," he said cheerfully. "Is that a love bite I see on your neck, Sophie, baby?"

Before she could stop herself, Sophie reached up to touch her neck, instinctively knowing just where the mark lay, where Mal's mouth had been, where she'd felt the sting of his teeth as he'd thrust into her. She couldn't help it—color flooded her face. "I'm feeling tired, Archer. I think I'd like to go back to my room."

Archer looked at her, then to Mal, then back to her again, and there was no wiping the self-satisfied smirk on his face. "I'll call Joe. It looks as if you've had quite the workout, my darling. Get some rest. I'll be up later to check on you."

At that point she almost threw up. She put the empty coffee mug down, careful not to look at Mal. "Don't worry about me, Archer. I'll be fine in time for dinner."

"Oh, I don't think so. You wouldn't want to wear yourself out with all this . . . socializing. You spend the evening in your room, having a quiet dinner, and don't let any of us bother you."

Don't let Archer bother her? That was an unlikely scenario—she couldn't fight back if she didn't want him to know that she wasn't crippled.

"I'll bring her back down if she wants to come," Mal said, essentially countermanding Archer's order. Sophie held her breath, waiting for the explosion, and Archer's eyes were suspiciously hard.

But Mal wasn't budging. She was a chew toy caught between two attack dogs, and neither of them really wanted her. They would simply rip her apart before they let the other one have her. She could already feel her insides begin to tear.

"Ready to go upstairs, Miss Sophie?" Joe said, appearing at her side.

Archer and Mal were watching her, and she had no idea what they expected her to say. The least she could do was confound them. "A nap is an excellent idea, Archer. Thank you. And there's no need for you to join me—Joe can bring me back down. Or Mal." She said his name deliberately, to gauge Archer's reaction.

"We'll see," Archer said pleasantly, but it didn't sound promising.

Chapter Fourteen

"So you fucked my wife," Archer said.

He'd waited until Sophie was gone—Mal could give him that much. Not that he'd done so out of regard for Sophie. There was little doubt he had plans for his wife, and they wouldn't be pleasant.

Mal shrugged, glancing out over the swimming pool to the sea beyond. He should leave well enough alone—he'd done what Archer had wanted. The episode should be over.

He heard the drag of the chair as Archer sat down across from him, the sound scraping across his nerves. "I'm glad you followed my suggestion," Archer said. "Now tell me all about it."

He could still feel her warm, supple skin, her arms around his neck, hear the quiet, choked sounds she made. He could still see the tears on her face. "I thought it was an order, not a suggestion."

"Oh, hell no! You mistook me—I wouldn't think of ordering a guest to do anything. I merely thought it might provide some distraction. From the look of that mark on her neck, it looks like it did the job."

"What can I say? She likes it rough." He was the world's biggest shit, worse than Archer MacDonald, because he liked thinking of his mark on her body. He wished she'd left her mark on him.

No, I'm not worse than Archer MacDonald, he thought, as Archer's face lit up in avid delight. *But I'm no fucking hero.*

"That's something new," Archer said cheerfully, finishing Sophie's sandwich with gusto. "It might almost make up for her lack of movement downstairs. Tell me, how did you handle it? Did you . . . ?"

"I think I'll go for a swim," Mal said calmly. Yes, he was supposed to kill Archer MacDonald, and he'd take untold pleasure in it, but he had to get to the source of RU48 first. Only then could he take his time. He'd never enjoyed killing—he'd simply done what he had to do without thinking about moral consequences. Everyone he'd killed had been some kind of monster, or the henchman of a monster, and there had been no room for emotion.

For the first time there was going to be emotion, a savage pleasure, in ending a man's life. He didn't like his sudden, furious need. It was a slippery slope, and he didn't want to go there, no matter how much he hated the man across from him.

It didn't matter, though—it was too late. He'd crossed a line somewhere, and Archer was no longer just a job. Mal was going to make it hurt.

"You disappoint me," Archer said petulantly. "I at least expected some juicy details, man to man."

What he'd expected was surveillance film, but he was going to be disappointed. "Sorry," Mal said, making it clear he wasn't feeling the slightest bit sorry. He rose, pulling off his shirt.

Archer laughed. "So you don't fuck and tell? I can respect that. I'll have a nice, quiet afternoon with my wife. I'm looking forward to seeing if Sophie learned any new tricks. I can just . . ."

"No."

Archer looked startled. "What do you mean, no? She's my wife. I loaned her to you, I didn't give her away. As a matter of fact, I look on this as a onetime deal, and I intend . . ."

"No," Mal said, his calm voice belying the rage that filled him. "You offered her to me and I took her. She's mine for as long as I'm here. I don't like sloppy seconds." He had no idea whether this was going to work or not, he just knew he wasn't going to take no for an answer. If he had to, he'd kill Archer there and then—to hell with the Pixiedust.

There was a long, tense silence. Archer was still seated, seemingly at ease, but Mal could sense the sudden strain of violence in the air, and he didn't give a shit. What the fuck was wrong with him?

Then he almost laughed. He was ready to do what Sophie had done three years ago—throw everything away because of Archer MacDonald. Granted, he was motivated by a primal hatred, but there was still an ugly similarity. Archer knew how to get to people in any way he could.

And Mal did laugh. "You wouldn't deny me, would you, Archer? You've been so intent on being the perfect host."

Archer's dangerously still face relaxed into an easy grin. "Of course. There'll be plenty of time once we've concluded our business and you're on your way."

"Plenty of time," Mal agreed companionably. "In the meantime, feel like a swim?"

"Certainly," Archer said promptly. "We needn't bother with suits. Tell me, did you use a condom? Surely that's a reasonable question from an anxious husband."

It was a challenge—the motive behind a sudden urge for nude bathing was obvious. Too bad Archer was going to feel inadequate. "Uncertainty makes life so much more interesting, don't you think?" Mal said, unzipping his jeans and dropping them on the terrace. "Coming?"

Archer surveyed him, not bothering to hide his curiosity, and his mouth tightened in annoyance. "My, my. It's probably a good thing my wife is numb from the waist down. I'm not sure she'd find that thing comfortable."

Typical of Archer to start a conversation about a man's dick. "Do you have a tape measure?" Mal drawled.

Archer laughed, all signs of irritation vanishing. "I wouldn't bother. I know when I'm outgunned, so to speak. It's just a good thing Sophie is so madly in love with me, or I might be jealous. I'm not worried—you're supposed to be a temporary distraction, something to break the tedium. She and I will have plenty of time to get reacquainted after you leave."

Archer wasn't happy, Mal thought. For some reason he wasn't going to push the issue, but Mal was going to have to watch his back. Not that there would be any change in how he handled things around Archer MacDonald. "A big dick never got in the way of true love," he said. Except Archer was the big dick, despite what he had between his legs. Mal didn't even glance at him when Archer dropped trou. There were a lot of ways to measure a man, and the size of his dick was one of the least reliable. Setting his sunglasses on the table, Mal started toward the surf, bypassing the warm pool. Wading out, he dove through the first big wave, slicing through the salt water with strong strokes. He needed to get clean, let the clear gulf water wash away his guilt. Wash away the dirty feeling Archer always left him with. He needed to rid himself of any trace of Sophie and what they'd done together in the boathouse. He just didn't want to.

By the time Archer joined him he had two naked women with him—Rachel of the plastic tits and someone Mal pretended not to remember, a wannabe actress with the name of Kirsty. He ignored them, even though he could see Archer giving Kirsty whispered instructions, and Mal could swim farther, longer, than any of them could. When Kirsty let the waves knock her lithe body against his, reaching between his legs, he simply swam out even farther. He'd been a competitive swimmer in college, he'd crossed the English Channel seven times in the dark as part of his training, he was strong enough to withstand riptides and deadly currents. In fact, he'd figured his best way off the island would probably be to swim—the coast of Mexico was only twenty-seven miles away, and remarkably free of dangerous tides except during hurricane season. He should have no problem.

He just hadn't counted on carrying a woman with him.

At least she could kick, he thought as he tread water out beyond the swells, his shin still aching a bit from one of Sophie's own kicks. His best bet would be to bring a tether with him when she got too exhausted to swim anymore. Whether he liked it or not, he wasn't going to leave her on this island, no matter what she'd done. He'd come to that conclusion an hour ago, a day ago, the first time he saw her. It didn't matter what the smart thing to do was, it didn't matter whether he could trust her. Hell, he didn't trust anyone.

But he'd bring her out with him. Because.

Archer and the women weren't making any attempt at joining him out in the deep, and he floated there, looking at the wide stone house in the distance. What was Sophie doing? Probably doing her best to scrub every trace of him from her skin, from inside her body. He remembered the look on her face when she came, the soft, hitching sound of her breath. She should know it wasn't going to do any good—she could never wash him away. This game was far from over.

He waited until Archer gave up and headed back to the terrace with his women, waited until the shadows grew deeper and lights began to come on. Sophie's windows didn't look out over the ocean—she'd have to be out on the terrace to see him, but he knew she was there, watching. What was she thinking about? Probably ways to dismember him. He'd have to watch her—her emotions were raw after their encounter in the boathouse. Someone had made a major mistake in recruiting her. She was strong, inventive, able to withstand years of abuse, but she was also too human, and it was too easy to prey on her emotions. Her misguided passion for a waste of oxygen like Archer MacDonald had put her into this mess, and her reactions to Mal were fucking her up even further. He'd recognized it and acted upon it, because *humanity* and *mercy* weren't in his vocabulary. And because he'd wanted her. He'd take her down if he had to, and he could do it without a qualm.

It remained to be seen how she reacted after she calmed down. So they fucked—it wasn't as if it was the first time for her, and she'd wanted it as much as he had. Scrap that—for some reason it had seemed as if he'd never wanted anyone as much in his entire life.

Rules didn't apply in this business. He wouldn't have raped her, but he knew he wouldn't have to. He still might have to kill her—would she prefer death before dishonor? He let out a humorless laugh, floating on the swells, feeling his body being drawn out deeper and deeper.

What if he just let go? Forget about Sophie, let the current take him, stop trying to control a hard, vicious life full of betrayal and murder and despair? He knew the currents in the area—he'd studied them during those weeks in New Orleans, just in case he had to make a swim for it. If he did, he'd need to leave from the west side of the island, near the old sugar mill, and head toward the mainland if he were to have any chance of making it. If he headed north toward the U.S., he'd run into the Coast Guard and drug runners. East was Europe, and that wasn't about to happen no matter how good a swimmer he was. And heading farther south, the way he was going, would get him into stronger riptides, ones he couldn't fight against.

He turned in the water, looking out over the endless horizon. Next stop would be the Yucatán Peninsula if he went straight—some six-hundred-plus miles. He'd never make it, and he wasn't sure he gave a damn. But he couldn't leave Sophie behind, even if it was the smart thing to do.

She'd probably laugh if he told her that. Those warm brown eyes would grow hard with distrust, and he wasn't in the mood to convince her when even he wasn't sure why he wasn't ready to ditch her. He just knew he couldn't.

He turned back, his gaze settling on the balcony terrace where he knew she was waiting, watching him, probably hoping Jaws would pop out of the water and eat him in one gulp. *Sorry, sweetheart*, he thought. *I'm not done yet.*

He started back toward the distant shore, his long arms slicing through the water. *Not done yet*, the words rattled in his brain. *Not done yet.*

Sophie rolled the wheelchair away from the railing. Once Mal got close enough, he'd know she was watching him, and she wasn't about to give him that satisfaction. She wasn't going to give him anything.

Something inside her had snapped this afternoon, and she had stopped caring, stopped planning, stopped waiting. She wasn't going to loll around in this fucking wheelchair, letting Archer hurt her in ways big and small, letting Mal get close to her again. He was here to kill her husband, to finish what she'd failed to accomplish. But Mal had a second agenda, to find and destroy Archer's latest pet project and bring that down too, and he couldn't kill Archer until he'd taken care of that little detail.

Sophie didn't give a flying fuck. Archer had his iron in a dozen fires, all of them disreputable, ranging from Ponzi schemes he was running for the hell of it, since he didn't need the money, to parts for nuclear warfare, to biological weapons. Wipe out one, and the others would just keep going under new management.

She wasn't going to wait any longer. She was going to put a bullet in her husband's brain, one long overdue, and it would be up to Mal to pick up the pieces. If that included killing her, then so be it. Anything was better than waiting.

She sat in hot water till the skin on her hands wrinkled. She washed and washed every trace of him away from her. She still couldn't get away from the phantom memory of him inside her, pumping into her, and each time she thought about it her stomach knotted with anger and confusion, and she refused to consider why. She had no concrete reason to hate Mal. In fact, she knew damned well she didn't hate him—she just wanted to cut his throat.

She laughed without humor. She was being emotional and ridiculous, the same flaws that had gotten her into this mess. What the fuck was wrong with her? You didn't hate a man for giving you the best orgasms of your life with just about zero effort. He was after the same thing she was—he'd even given her a gun. He was an ally, albeit an unwilling one.

She didn't want an ally. She'd been alone in this for too long, and she was afraid to trust anyone, even another Committee agent. Maybe especially another Committee agent—she knew as well as he did just how ruthless they were required to be. She was collateral damage and she accepted that fact. She just didn't want Mal to accept it.

She pulled her French doors closed. There was no way she could lock them, but she hoped Mal would get the message when he came back upstairs. She turned the air conditioner up high and levered herself onto her bed, using only her strong arms, then turned off the light, plunging the room into darkness. If she looked hard enough, she could find the pinprick of red light that gave away one of the surveillance cameras—whoever had installed them hadn't made much of an effort to hide them. For just this moment, for a short while, she was going to indulge herself. She was going to lie quiet and still in the darkness where no one could see her. She was going to stay very still and do something she hadn't done in almost four years.

She was going to cry. She had felt the tears on her face earlier, but she hadn't let go. Now she was going to release the tight hold she had on her emotions and sob.

Ever since she'd found out the truth about Archer, she hadn't dared give in to her emotions. Even when she was lying on the ground, a bullet in her back, vicious pain ripping through her, she hadn't shed one tear. She'd been afraid if she started crying, she might never stop, and she had to survive. She wasn't going to let Archer win.

Today she could cry. Today she could give in to all the disparate emotions that swirled around her and release some of the tension—she could cry for the lost years, for the stupid girl who'd been blinded by Archer's charm, for the stupid woman who'd fucked Malcolm Gunnison knowing he didn't care if she lived or died.

But she couldn't. She was wound so tightly with fear and tension that she couldn't let go. Tears would have broken through some of the stultifying despair. She felt like a kettle of water on a hot stove, the steam building up and no way to release it. She'd trained herself never to let go, and now when she needed to, for just a short, self-indulgent moment, she couldn't.

She'd cried when he'd fucked her. Because that was what that encounter in the boathouse was. He'd taken her, she'd been too needy to resist, and she thought she remembered that her face had been wet. She tried to bring that feeling back, to push herself into tears, but it was like trying to force an orgasm. She could get just as far as the despair but no further. She lay in the dark, dry-eyed, alone, and abandoned.

She was being ridiculous. She finally had someone she didn't have to lie to. They were hardly compatriots—in fact, he felt more like an enemy than Archer did at the moment, but the truth was, for the first time in two years she should have hope. After all, he was the one who'd brought the handguns onto the island, though he'd been stupid enough to let her get her hands on one.

Though that wasn't like Malcolm Gunnison. She told herself he was a dirty, treacherous snake, but he wasn't stupid. Unlike her, he didn't make mistakes. He would get the job done and get off the island, without letting any foolish weaknesses make him doubt his mission. He was a machine. She was human. It was no wonder they were mismatched.

But machines weren't subject to impulses, to emotions, to unexpected acts. And she knew what she was going to do.

Despite Mal's earlier words, he made no attempt to bring her down to dinner, proving once again that he was a smart man. If he didn't keep his distance, there was no telling what she might say or do that would incriminate him. He'd pushed her too far that afternoon, and he knew it. It would be one thing if they'd just gone through the motions of hasty sex. It had been more than that, though, and she hated it. There had been emotion flowing between them, feelings, ones she refused to admit to in the aftermath, ones he wouldn't notice in the first place. He just thought she was pissed.

He was giving her time to calm down, and she heard his and Archer's voices drift up from the veranda by the pool, the whisper of the waves from the ocean beyond coming and going, obliterating their words. It didn't matter. They would both be lying to each other—nothing they said would be important.

She lay still in the bed. Elena brought her a dinner tray, but Sophie sent it away, the thought of food making her stomach twist. Never eat before a job, Isobel Lambert, the Ice Queen, had told her. Tonight she had the biggest job of her life. She would do the one thing she could to break the bonds that tied her, the sticky spiderweb that trapped her with Archer and Mal. If she died doing it, so be it.

It was after midnight when she slipped out of her bed, reaching beneath her mattress for the handgun and taking it with her into the bathroom. She'd done a thorough cleaning when she'd first taken it, so she made do with a simple field cleaning now before reloading it. There were enough bullets—even if her aim was off it was more than sufficient to kill Archer and then run like hell. With luck, Joe's first instinct would be to go to his boss and try to stanch the blood, and if miracles happened, she could get back to her room before anyone noticed she was gone. After all, she was a cripple—how could she get up and down the stairs to shoot Archer?

She could try to ride that, or she could simply run like hell and hope Joe didn't find her. Elena had been right—there wasn't one inch of the island she didn't know, and with Archer dead, who'd be paying Joe's bills? She'd been in this world long enough to know that loyalty meant nothing—it was the bottom line that mattered. If there was no practical reason for Joe to find Archer's killer, then he'd simply leave, go somewhere else and find new employment.

And maybe pigs would fly. In the end she was willing to risk it. She couldn't wait any longer.

She climbed back into her wheelchair and headed out onto the balcony. The night was still and calm, and she could hear Archer quite clearly. He was fucking one of the women, encouraging her with particularly vicious threats, and she could tell by the sound in his voice he was close. Archer never minded having an audience—in fact, he preferred it, though she'd always refused that game when they were together. Where was Mal? Was he fucking someone else, side by side? Getting a blow job while he watched. Hell, was he the one being fucked by Archer?

She couldn't see that happening, though Archer would have loved it. So where the hell was Mal?

Joe would probably be in bed, though he was always on call when Archer wanted him. Mal could be anywhere—out swimming again, wandering around the island, asleep in the room next door. No, she would have heard him come in—she'd been paying careful attention. She looked out at the dark ocean, but there was no sign of him. She'd watched him earlier, slicing through the waves, his long, sleek body beautiful in the clear gulf waters. In fact, she couldn't look away, and when he finally gave in to the gathering dusk and waded in, she watched him until he disappeared from her sight. It wasn't until then she realized she'd been absurdly tense, barely breathing, her body growing warm.

She had to get the hell out of here, before she made another monumental mistake, and she was more than willing to risk her life to keep that from happening. She wasn't worried about reclaiming a normal life. She was hardly likely to lose her mind over some damned man when . . . *if* she got off the island. Clearly Archer and Mal were anomalies. Maybe she was attracted to danger. Except the classically handsome hit man from New York whom Archer had imported had left her cold.

In fact, she couldn't think of very many things Archer and Mal had in common. The dangerous world they lived in—but that was her world as well, and if anything she wanted to escape from that life. Archer was a sadist, Mal a straightforward bastard. All she could guess was that some strange trick of chemistry had opened her legs to Malcolm Gunnison, and the sooner she got away from him the better.

It was past two when she heard the footsteps on the stairs, the door next to her open and close. She held her breath, panicked that he'd decided a late-night visit would be a good idea, but within moments the lights went out, and everything next door was still.

She wasn't going to be fooled that easily, and she waited a full hour, sitting in her chair, alert, the gun tucked beside her. Even if Mal was trying to outwait her, see if she was truly asleep, he would have dropped off by now. Archer spent his nights plying his guests with alcohol, and even the most adept of men—and she did consider Mal very good at his job—would end up having to swallow a few. Mal would be sound asleep by now.

Besides, if he'd had any doubts about her, nothing would have stopped him from coming into her room and checking. Nothing would have stopped him from coming into her room, into her bed, into her body, if he'd had any interest in repeating this afternoon in a horizontal position. But he hadn't. He'd done what he had to do in the boathouse and it looked as if she wouldn't have to put up with it again, thank God. Because putting up with it wasn't really the right term for the most shattering sex of her life.

Looking back on it over the last years, she'd realized that Archer hadn't been that good a lover. He'd been more interested in being entertained than putting out himself, and she'd been happy to do it, besotted with him. Why?

She'd never know the answer, and she needed to stop looking for it. It wouldn't change the past, and she was never going to make that kind of mistake again. Archer would be dead, and the rest would fall into place as it would.

She locked the wheels of the chair and pushed herself up, moving silently toward the door. She opened it, just a crack, and peered into the darkness beyond. All was silent except for the ever-present sound of the ocean. Archer would be downstairs in that huge bed she'd once shared, a fitting place to kill him.

But would he be alone? He never liked to sleep with women—in fact, when they married he'd wanted them to have separate rooms, insisting he was a light sleeper. She hadn't paid attention to that, and he'd given in with sullen grace, but she thought he was unlikely to have changed in that regard. He wouldn't like having anyone around when he was asleep and vulnerable, and after discovering his wife had been sent to kill him, he'd be even more wary.

Not that she had any proof that he was behind the attempt on her life. She didn't need any. It didn't take a rocket scientist to see behind Archer's sadistic games, guess at the sudden turnaround in her previously adoring husband. As long as they never spoke of it out loud, they could continue this endless dance, and Archer seemed to have a boundless appetite for it. She had had enough.

If by any chance someone was in Archer's bed with him, she'd deal with it. She wasn't going to kill anyone else, even the wretched Rachel, tempting as it might be. The only person she really wanted to shoot, apart from Archer, was Mal, but that was irrational emotion, not common sense. With Archer it was cold, deadly determination.

She closed the door silently behind her—if Mal was listening, there was no way he could have heard it. She wished the damned man snored—it would give her some peace of mind. Then again, snoring would be an easy thing to fake, and someone as machinelike as Mal would be able to control even involuntary bodily functions like snoring. The man probably didn't even fart.

The living room was dark, but there was light coming from the terrace by the pool. The lower she crept on the stairs, the more she could see, and that was definitely Archer's silhouette on one of the chaises. He'd have a glass of whiskey in his hand—he'd always liked that moment of solitude. It was too nice a way for him to die, but she was past those kinds of considerations. She moved lower, down the stairs.

———————

Archer MacDonald looked out over the inky black sea. The sky was overcast—there were only a few bright stars visible through the clouds, but he liked it that way. There were times when he hated Isla Mordita, the bright, sunshiny smile of the place. There were times when only darkness would do.

He sipped at his scotch and watched the waves roll in, thinking about Malcolm Gunnison's dick and where it had been. The man was hung—he'd seen the evidence. He wondered whether Malcolm was interested in a little extracurricular activity. Archer had never had a man so well endowed, and the thought was enticing.

Enticing enough to make him forget how pissed off he was. He'd combed through all the surveillance footage and found nothing, just some silent footage of the two of them having coffee in the kitchen before disappearing outside. He couldn't believe Mal was going to fuck Sophie in the grass—not when he'd ripped out the cameras in his bedroom and was under the mistaken impression that he wasn't being watched. It had been child's play to replace the cameras with a newer, smaller, undetectable one, and there was no way Mal would find it. Not unless his employers had access to more advanced technology than Archer did, and that was simply impossible. The one camera, a prototype, gave up in sound quality what it gained in invisibility, and it covered only the bed. Last time he looked, Malcolm Gunnison was sound asleep, on his own, and as far as he could tell Sophie hadn't made a move in the darkness except for her peculiar bathroom habits. He needed to get some infrared in there—he had a scientist working on that down in Chile—though he sincerely doubted Sophie got up and walked when he wasn't looking. She wasn't that good an actress, and he knew the kind of pain she was in. If there was any way she could move, she'd be trying to win him back again.

He took another sip. He couldn't believe Mal had told him to keep his hands off his own wife. He admired his gall, enough so that he had agreed. Not that he had any intention of honoring that agreement—Sophie was his wife, his property, and no one was going to tell him what he could or could not do with her. With Mal being so tight-lipped Archer couldn't even find out how severe her limitations were, but he'd assumed he could check via the videos.

Mal had known he couldn't. The whole point of having him fuck Sophie was for Archer to gauge the extent of her damage, that and humiliating his darling wife. He'd wanted, expected, to watch, and Mal wasn't leaving this island until Archer had a good view.

He didn't stop to think about why it was so important to him—motivations didn't particularly interest him. He wanted what he wanted, and he set about getting it. It didn't matter why.

He'd been trying to watch Sophie in bed for two years now, and she'd shown no interest at all in the men he'd brought in. That was one reason he'd come to the conclusion that she really did love him, despite her treacherous lies. She wanted nothing more than to get back in his bed, and she wasn't about to do anything to jeopardize that possibility. Oh, she knew better than to make the first move—she realized that deformity and disability disgusted him, and she would know she'd be rebuffed.

Now he was thinking he just might try her out. Mal had certainly looked well served. Oh, it wouldn't be the way it used to be. For one thing she was a cripple, though he could always use her for blow jobs. He could even see if something could be done for her condition. He'd cut off all doctors, determined to make her suffer, but now that time had passed, there might be things they could do. It would be nice to have her wait on him, eager for his approval. He could get her to do all sorts of things she'd refused in the past.

Maybe he'd take Mal away for a while, give Sophie a chance to think about things. A little deprivation might do her some good. He'd abandoned her before, and Chekowsky's absence *was* growing tiresome. He could pack up the household and take them away, leaving her alone and helpless on Isla Mordita. After all, what could she do? They'd take the big motor yacht, though he'd never been able to manage a decent crew out of his various employees. Mal looked like someone who knew how to sail, and the *Sophia* was a responsive boat. He would have changed the name to *Traitor* if it weren't bad luck—Archer wasn't particularly superstitious, but he preferred not to tempt fate.

He'd even taken the boat out on his own for the sheer pleasure of it. This island was making him edgy; everything was getting on his nerves. Normally he wouldn't have visited Sophie as he had yesterday while they had a guest in residence. It could bring up too many questions, and he planned to have a great deal of fun with her once Mal concluded his business and disappeared.

But yesterday he hadn't been able to wait. It had been a need, driving him, and his pleasure had been so absolute that it had taken Kirsty only two good sucks to get him off later on. He hadn't decided if he wanted to hurt Sophie again, to punish her, or if he was in the mood to forgive her. He was feeling positively sentimental. It was probably Sophie's slightly dazed, "I've been royally fucked" look. Made him think of old times.

No, taking a break might be just what he needed, at least until he decided what he planned to do with Mal. He wanted to watch the man fuck his wife. He wanted to cut the man's throat.

There was no reason he couldn't do both. Clearly the two of them had enjoyed their little tryst in the forest—it shouldn't take much to get them to do it again in view of a camera. He'd always wanted to watch—now the promise of violence between the two of them was even more enticing.

He just had to decide exactly what it was he wanted. And then it would be his for the taking.

———————

Sophie checked the gun before she reached the bottom step. Her bare feet were cold on the stone floor, but she didn't mind. It reminded her she was alive, that her body worked, and that she could do this. She edged toward the doors that were open onto the terrace, very, very slowly, following the circumference of the room to avoid casting any telltale shadows. Archer was alone out there, nursing his drink just as she'd suspected. A creature of habit was always easier to take down, Isobel, the woman who had trained her, once had told her. Someone who thought he was invulnerable made it close to child's play. This was going to be a piece of cake.

The only thing that would make it better was if she'd had a silencer. She halted for a moment, considering. There was such a thing as a poor man's silencer—she could filch a potato from the kitchen and cram that onto the barrel of the gun. That, or take one of the pillows from the curving sofa in the middle of the room, but that might ruin her aim. She needed to be precise, deadly, if she had a chance in hell of getting away with it, and she definitely preferred it that way. She'd already spent enough of her life as a martyr.

Three of the four doors facing the pool and ocean were open— Archer was by the farthest one. She stopped at the edge of the first and checked her sites. His head was just above the edge of the chaise, and it would be an easy shot from that relatively close range. She could even get off a couple of rounds, just to be sure, before throwing the gun away and racing back upstairs. She wasn't worried about fingerprints or gunpowder residue. As long as she didn't have the gun in her possession, no one would really give a damn.

She raised the gun, slowly, silently, taking in a deep, steadying breath, and aimed it at Archer's head, carefully cocked it, and pulled the trigger.

The only sound was a very audible click.

The arm that shot around her was so fast and strong she couldn't fight back. Her hand went numb, she was slammed back against a hard body, and then a hand covered her mouth, silencing any noise she might be fool enough to make. She didn't resist. The Beretta had been sabotaged, and there was only man who could have done it. The man who had given it to her, the man who held her.

Malcolm Gunnison.

Chapter Fifteen

At least Sophie had the good sense to stop struggling, to remain absolutely still in his arms, Malcolm thought, and he slowly moved his hand from her mouth. She knew better than to make a sound, particularly when the scrape of the iron furniture against the stone patio screamed in the night.

He shifted his hold, gripping her wrists together in one hand while he tucked the handgun in the back of his jeans. At least now he knew that she wasn't playing him—she had been more than ready to shatter Archer's skull, and a part of him was sorry he couldn't let her do just that. But his temporary fury with Archer had faded—too much was riding on this mission, more than simple revenge.

He crowded her into the corner of the nearest door, one that was still closed to the warm night air, and pulled them behind the floor-length drapes. If Archer had heard that quiet click, if he decided to turn on the lights and search the room, then their hiding place wouldn't last, and Mal might have no choice but to terminate his host, leaving the job half-finished. But he wasn't ready to give up yet.

Sophie was scarcely breathing, unmoving in his arms. Unmoving except for the occasional stray shudder that vibrated through her. If they got away with this tonight, they were going to have to have a long conversation when they found a place without surveillance. Archer had planted a new bug in his room, one Mal had decided to leave in place.

He was better off with Archer thinking he knew what was going on. Besides, the Committee had had that technology for a couple of years now, and he knew there was no microphone. He could say any damned thing he wanted, as long as things looked right.

Archer came into the large living room, his sandaled feet shuffling. He had a drink in one hand, and he appeared to be half in the bag. Archer could hold his liquor better than anyone Mal had ever met, but right now he didn't know he had an audience. There was no need for him to act sober if, in fact, he wasn't.

Except they'd made enough noise to rouse him from his position on the chaise, exactly where Mal had left him two hours earlier, though he'd had Kirsty servicing him noisily. Mal had never been into voyeurism, and the sex going on in front of him simply reminded him of Sophie— Sophie, whom he wasn't going to touch again if he could help it.

And yet here he was, wrapped around her like a fur coat, his dick hard, pressing into her. She was probably too freaked to notice, which was just as well. He had every intention of keeping it in his pants unless he had a damned good reason not to.

Archer turned on the table lamp next to the suffocating sofa, humming to himself, and Mal cursed inwardly. If Archer suspected something, it wouldn't take him long to find them. Or he might be smart and call for reinforcements. Either way, they could be royally screwed.

Which brought him back to Sophie again, breathless against his body. If they got out of this current mess, maybe he *would* screw her again. The problem was that then they couldn't pretend they didn't want to do it. Sophie had come twice and hated him. If they didn't have an excuse she might not be able to take what she wanted. What he wanted. What they needed.

Her skin was warm in the night air. She wasn't wearing much—the same sort of outfit she'd worn when she'd crept into his room the previous night, thinking she'd managed to drug him into a stupor. She was far too naïve, but then, she'd been thrown in the deep end before she'd been ready. If she had a few successful missions under her belt, she'd be more careful about rushing into things.

He pulled her tighter against him. He needed to be ready to shove her behind him if Archer had a gun, but as far as he could tell, Archer hadn't been carrying the entire time he was here. He relied on others to do his dirty work.

So far Archer hadn't summoned Joe. Mal could see him through a crack in the curtains, and his host was simply standing there, weaving slightly, as he turned his head and looked up at the stairs.

He was considering paying his wife a visit, Mal thought with a controlled, deadly fury. He must be jonesing for her pretty bad if he was going to risk offending his guest. Mal had insisted he wouldn't share Sophie with her husband, and he'd said it more to annoy Archer than anything else, but the moment the words left his mouth, he knew he meant them. Archer wasn't going to touch Sophie, not now or ever again.

To his relief Archer turned away, wandering toward the kitchen, and a moment later he was out of sight. Sophie wriggled slightly in Mal's arms, assuming they were home free, but he simply tightened his grip, keeping her still.

With good reason. Archer reemerged from the kitchen, a plate of food in one hand. He sank down on the enveloping couch and began to eat a sloppy, overstuffed sandwich, and Mal sighed inwardly. Sophie had gone from feeling warm to being cold all over, her body vibrating, and he needed to get her away from here before she lost it. She'd psyched herself up to kill Archer, and the sudden letdown was making her woozy. He really didn't want her collapsing in his arms.

Then again, that would be the smartest thing to do. If Archer found them, he could say he'd been carrying her downstairs for a little sex in unexpected places.

Archer leaned back in the sofa, sinking into it, leaving half his sandwich on the plate. If he fell asleep there, it was going to be tricky to get back upstairs. Mal could do it with no problem, but not lugging Sophie. She'd gone from occasional tremors to shaking, and he knew the signs of someone going into shock. He was going to have to cover her mouth again if her teeth started chattering. He couldn't even whisper calming words—Archer was too close, and stroking her might get the opposite reaction. He had no choice but to hold her in the iron circle of his arms and hope to Christ that Archer decided to go to bed.

It was another five minutes before his patience was rewarded. Archer rose, his gaze sweeping around the shadowed room, then fixating once more on the graceful staircase. Then, to Mal's relief, he turned and headed for his bedroom.

Mal waited another five minutes. If it had been him alone, he would have stayed for an hour, but Sophie was leaning against him, letting him support her, and he needed to get her out of there as soon as he could. With a silent profanity that was half curse, half prayer, he picked her up in his arms and moved to the stairs.

No one popped out from behind a door, no lights flooded the place. He took the steps three at a time, easy enough with his long legs despite the weight in his arms, and a moment later they were on the landing, and he had to decide on the safest place to take her. Her own room was still bugged, and that one camera in his place was focused on the bed. He pushed his own door open, silently, easing her through it, prepared to subdue her if she realized where he was taking her and decided to fight him.

Either she didn't notice or she didn't care. She was trying to catch her breath—difficult when she didn't want to make a sound—and he carried her straight through his bedroom, skirting the range of the camera and taking her out into the night air on the balcony. Not the best choice for someone nearing shock conditions, but he'd have to find other ways to make her warm.

He sank down in one corner in the darkness, well out of range of the cameras, still holding her. She immediately tried to scramble away from him, but he had no intention of letting her go, and his hold tightened to just this side of painful. Maybe it went over a bit, because her soft mouth tightened in a grim line.

"Stay still," he breathed, hardly any sound on the night air. "You almost fucked everything up royally tonight, you idiot. I need a moment to get my breath and my temper back under control."

She stopped struggling, probably not because of his words, but because it was useless. He could feel when her body calmed, when the heat began to return to her skin. He could have released her then, but he didn't want to.

"You fucked with the gun," she said finally in a low voice that only held a faint tremor. "I know it worked before—I broke it down and checked it. What did you do, take the firing pin?"

"The classics are the still the best," he said. "I couldn't risk having you kill Archer before I'd finished my mission, and I wasn't going to give you the chance to put a bullet in me."

She had to be feeling better—her eyes were filled with fury. "Then why give me the gun in the first place? I know you did—you're too good to leave weapons so easily available. You also know that you never point a gun unless you intend to use it, and having one that was tampered with could have gotten me killed. Maybe you enjoy games the way Archer does."

He told himself that particular jab didn't sting. "I don't need to explain myself to you."

"You do if you don't want another enemy to deal with."

He cocked his head, looking down in her face in the murky light. She felt good in his arms, draped across his lap, and he knew he was still hard with her sweet butt riding him. He wondered if she knew. "We were already enemies."

She didn't deny it. "Not mortal ones."

He sighed, and she managed to scramble off him. He made no effort to hold her there—he could bring her back at any time, and for now he was better off without her body pressed against his. It distracted him when he couldn't afford to be distracted. "I left the gun because I thought you could do with some form of protection besides your body. It was only later that I realized you were too hotheaded to make sensible decisions. After our time in the boathouse I was afraid you'd put one of those .22s in my brain, and I thought I'd better hedge my bets. If I'd known you were going to go after Archer that fast, I would have done something about it."

"You did."

"I almost didn't make it. You're just lucky he didn't hear the click of the gun."

"I don't know if I believe in luck. He came inside immediately afterward—he must have heard something," she said stubbornly.

"But he didn't call for reinforcements and he didn't go looking for anyone."

"I told you, Archer likes to play games. This island is his own private fiefdom. He has complete control over everything, and if he did hear the click, he would have known exactly what it was. Meaning the gun didn't work and he was safe. If I were you I'd be extra careful about the rest of your arsenal."

"The only reason you found the guns was that I wanted you to. Trust me, Archer's not going to find them now."

"Don't underestimate Archer. He can find anything he wants."

"Then you'd better do something about that stash of pills in your bed."

She glared at him, but didn't respond. "Are you going to give me the firing pin?"

"Are you going to promise not to shoot Archer until it's time?"

"You mean you'll let me do it?" she said skeptically.

He shrugged. "I figured you earned the right. But I need to make sure RU48 is dealt with first. Promise?"

Her face was cool, impassive, but he could feel the anger and heat boiling beneath the surface. "And you'd trust me?"

"No."

"Then why bother asking?"

"In fact, I don't feel like asking." He could move fast, and she wasn't at the top of her game. He'd hauled her back into his arms before she could react, so that she straddled him, and he was ready to restrain her flailing body with one arm as he cupped her chin with his hand.

She didn't fight, and he didn't kiss her. They stayed that way, looking at each other for a long moment. He couldn't read her thoughts, and he knew damned well she couldn't read his. But there would be no question she could feel his hard cock beneath her. It was up to her what she wanted to do about it.

She pulled her arms free from his grasp, and he let her go, leaning back against the wall, waiting. If she tried to get away he could stop her, but wouldn't. This was up to her to take what she wanted.

She was statue still, looking at him, her teeth sunk in her lower lip, and he felt an odd little hitch in the area of what might be called his heart. She reminded him of a defiant child, determined not to react, terrified and brave as hell at the same time, and for the first time since he could remember, he felt like a bully. She was vulnerable, whether she wanted to admit it or not, and she was trying desperately not to show it.

She also wanted him. He knew that too. If he let her go, she would scramble away from him, probably try to kill him the first chance she got. He watched her warily, not touching her. He would let her go. He could be a decent human being for a change.

"You're such a bastard," she said with barely a trace of sound, but they were close enough that he heard her anyway.

"I know." There was no shame or regret in his response, no guilt for all the things he had done. He simply was who he was, and he'd learned long ago the futility of trying to be someone else.

She didn't climb off him. She simply stared at him, and the heat moved between them like a living thing, slow and sensuous. She was no longer fighting it. She shook her head, though he had no idea whether it was disappointment in him or disgust at her own reaction. And then she reached down for the hem of her T-shirt and pulled it over her head, leaving her half-naked in the dark, astride him, only the skimpy boxers covering her.

He didn't move, didn't breathe, for fear he'd spook her. Her breasts were perfect, he thought. Not quite a handful, with taut nipples from the night air. Or maybe something else.

She put her hands on him, reaching for his shirt, and he let her, watching her as she pulled it off, throwing it onto the balcony. "Well?" she said.

He could have taken over then. He might have, but this was up to her. "Well?" he echoed, his hands beside him.

Her soft mouth twisted in annoyance, and he was ready for her to climb off, determined not to catch her and pull her back no matter how much it killed him, when her hands dropped down to the waistband of his jeans, flicking open the button. The zipper was beginning to part with the thrust of his erection pressing against it, and she didn't hesitate, pulling it down all the way, exposing the soft gray cotton of his boxers. Then she reached for his hips, and he lifted up, enough for her to shove everything down his thighs, and his cock throbbed between them. She shifted a bit, down and back, straddling his thighs, and he could feel she was wet through the last bit of clothes she was wearing. If anything it made him even harder, and he wanted to get his mouth on her nipples, he wanted to suck at them, pull at them, bite them.

"Move back," he said hoarsely. "Please."

Her face was very still. She hadn't touched him yet, but he could feel her long, cool fingers so close to him that he wanted to groan. "Why?"

"I want to suck your breasts."

"It doesn't turn me on," she said in her cold little voice.

"Maybe you haven't had the right person do it." He didn't wait for her reply, pulling her closer, so that her center rested against his solid cock, nestling there. She frowned, but he couldn't give her complete control, and he leaned over and licked one taut nipple.

She had small breasts, nothing like Rachel's monumental constructions, and he didn't care. He let his teeth graze her, and he felt a shiver rip through her body, clearly surprising her. "I told you I didn't like it," she said, a little strangled, and he smiled against her.

He let his teeth surround her, softly, enough to imprison but not enough to hurt, and he let his tongue tease the little nub, flicking back and forth until she began squirming, rubbing against him almost involuntarily. He took her other breast in his strong hand, squeezing her just to the point of pain but no further, and she bucked again, letting out a tiny moan.

He lifted his head. "In case you ever find yourself in a position to make love to a woman," he murmured, "you need to remember that breasts are different with everyone. A lot of women need gentle coaxing, almost worshipful attention. But more women than you'd imagine need a little roughness." He pinched her breast, and he saw the reaction in her face, the dazed expression in her brown eyes. They'd been soft before, except when she was staring at him in rage, but now they were positively unfocused in reaction to what he was doing. "You're one of the ones who need a little roughness." Leaning forward, he took her breast into his mouth, stroking, soothing with his tongue, and when she rubbed against him in sudden need, he bit down.

The sound she made was a little bit louder then, dangerous under the circumstances, but he fed on it anyway. He didn't care if she had the noisiest orgasm in the history of the world—he wanted it from her. He wanted her to take it from him, to drain him dry and then suck him off. He wanted sex—sex with *this* woman—and he wanted it all night long and the next day besides. In fact, he couldn't imagine ever getting sick of her, but he knew that was a fantasy. He wasn't a man for relationships, for monogamy, for long-term flings. He was a night or two at a time, energetic, healthy fun for both with no strings attached. Sophie came with so many strings she might just as well have been a marionette.

Except she was pulling her own strings. No one was making her do anything she didn't want to do, and she squirmed against him, pushed against him, wanting more.

It was going to make things worse, he thought dazedly, holding still while she pressed against his erection. They'd done it once, in anger and reluctant need, something that simply needed to be done.

It should have meant nothing. Instead, it had been a taste of something very sweet, dangerously so, and he wanted it again. He could feel her hands on his chest, sliding down, and then they were on his cock—cool, clever fingers—tugging at him, and he let out a small huff of air, trying to control his reaction. She was wet, she was willing, and he wanted nothing more than to flip her over on her back and slam into her. He didn't move, leaning back and closing his eyes. That afternoon had been too close to force. This time she wasn't going to be able to hide behind blaming him. This time she was going to take what she wanted.

To his shock, she did just that, sliding down his legs so that her mouth was just above his straining dick. He could feel her warm, soft breath on him, and he wanted to moan out loud, but he didn't move, his arms rigid as he held himself under tight control.

She glanced up at him from beneath her tangled hair, and there was a slightly wicked expression in her eyes. For the first time he caught a glimpse of who she had been, before she'd run afoul of the Committee and Archer MacDonald. He thought he'd known her, understood her, the victim who was still fighting back.

He was wrong. She was nobody's victim, and the Sophie he thought he knew was the last person to be half-naked astride her avowed enemy's body, ready to take his cock into her mouth.

She started with her tongue, gently licking the crown, and this time his groan was audible. And then she explored him, her tongue dancing around his shaft, tracing the thick veins, then putting her mouth over him and taking him into her until he was rubbing at the back of her throat, and his fingers tried to dig into the floor beneath him as he forced himself to keep still.

She was taking her time, learning him, driving him to levels of insanity with her curiosity, her obvious pleasure in the act. She closed her lips around him, increasing the pressure, and he didn't want to come that way, not in her mouth, not this time. He wanted to be tight inside her, so deep he wouldn't know where he ended and she began. She was no innocent—she knew what she was doing, and she liked what she was doing. This was no great gift for him, as he'd first assumed. This was Sophie, taking what she wanted.

He was getting close, dangerously close, and cautiously, carefully, he lifted one hand to thread his fingers through her hair, not guiding her or forcing her, just caressing her as she sucked on him, and he knew he wouldn't last much longer. She slid her hands under his balls, squeezing lightly, and lifted her head for a brief moment.

"Come in my mouth," she whispered.

He no longer had a choice. His body bucked, and she held onto his hips, taking him in, everything, her fingernails digging into his skin, and as he exploded he thought he felt an answering orgasm ripple through her body as she straddled him.

She drew back, away from him, sprawling on the floor in what should have been graceless exhaustion but instead looked like pure sexual abandon. He'd climaxed, come hard in her mouth, but he wanted more from her, he wanted her every way he could have her, and this time it was for nobody's pleasure but theirs.

It took him a moment to get his breath back. She moved, starting to crawl away from him, but he somehow found the speed and strength to stop her, catch her, his body covering hers from behind. He tore away her skimpy boxers and slid his hands between her legs. She was wet and swollen and ready, he was still hard, and he pulled her hips up, pushing into her.

She was tight, despite the wetness, and he tried to slow down, to make it easier for her, but when he was halfway in she suddenly shoved back, taking all of him with a small cry of pain and triumph. He held her like that, his hands on her hips, staring down at her elegant, narrow back, at the unmistakable scar of a bullet dangerously close to her spine. He wanted to give her time to get used to him, to stretch it out as long as he could, the sleek grasp of her cunt driving him to the point of madness. He wanted to slam in and out of her, but he knew he could hurt her, so he stayed very still, feeling her body relax around him, then tightening again, as her body recognized what it wanted, needed.

He didn't know whether her brain was in agreement, and at that point he was past caring. He just needed to lose himself inside her. He could be slower now, take his time, stoking into her. It was too damned dark on the balcony—he wanted to see her—but he wasn't taking the chance on Archer listening in. Slow and hard, and she was silent beneath him, only her body signaling her agreement, her pleasure. She came, too quickly, the walls of her sex clamping down on him, and he held still, letting her ride it, before he moved again.

She began to shiver, and he thought that if she dared to make any sound, she would have told him she couldn't take any more, but he knew she could. That ripple of reaction was hardly strong enough to take her over the edge, give her the release she needed, and he kept up his steady pace, into her, deep, so deep, and he heard an almost imperceptible sound from the back of her throat. It made his cock swell even more inside her, and he slid his hand under them, finding her slick clitoris, circling it. She was shaking so hard he felt the need to hold her together, keep her safe, pushing, pushing, until she froze, a low, keening sound coming so quietly from within her, a sound more powerful than a full-throated scream, and he went over the edge with her.

He couldn't hold himself up anymore—he was shaking as hard as she had been, and he fell onto the balcony, taking her with him, protecting her from the hard floor, still deep within her. His heart was racing—that never happened to him—and he pulled her deeper into him, holding her tight when he should have been withdrawing, moving away. It was over, and he couldn't let her go.

She lay very still in his arms, still wracked by shudders, tiny orgasms shimmering through her body. He'd thought of her as the enemy, but right now she needed protection, and he held her, stroking her hair away from her damp face. This wasn't the sex he was used to—the pleasurable buildup and satisfying release. This was something much more complicated, something he should have had the sense to avoid. His instincts had told him she was trouble, but he hadn't imagined the half of it. He couldn't let her go.

He had no condom to get rid of. Damn it—that was the second time he'd come inside her with no protection. He doubted she was on any kind of protection, given Archer's control over her body. He didn't even want to think about what diseases she could have contracted from Archer, though he knew he himself was clean. That was the least of his worries—Archer MacDonald had a strong OCD streak that would make him fastidious when it came to sex. Mal just had to hope this wasn't the wrong time of the month.

He'd always planned to get a vasectomy, but the time had never worked out. It wasn't that he didn't want children, but his lifestyle made it far too dangerous. How people like Peter Madsen in England and James Bishop in New Orleans managed was beyond him—if he had to worry about a wife and babies, he'd never be able to do his best work, and anything but his best could get him killed.

Whether he wanted to pull out or not, his cock was finally softening, though he suspected not for long. He still held her, not wanting to let go. He had no idea what she was thinking, what she was feeling, only that she'd had at least three orgasms, one of them so powerful it had almost knocked her flat. But beyond that he couldn't even guess.

The stone floor was cold and hard beneath them, and he wanted to carry her back to his bed, pull the covers around them, sleep with her in his arms, but Archer had put that fucking camera in. Her room wouldn't do either—even if the place was too dark to film, the microphones were supersensitive, and he could just picture Archer sitting in the dark, listening to them and jacking off.

She was beginning to stir, getting restless, and he knew she was going to pull away, and he wouldn't be able to stop her, not without drawing attention to them. With strong but gentle hands he turned her in her arms, pushing her hair back off her face, and put his mouth on hers, kissing her with extraordinary sweetness. He swallowed her strangled sob, and she kissed him back, sliding her arms around him and pulling him close, so close, their sweat-slick bodies growing chill in the night air, and he wanted to say something, tell her something, but he couldn't imagine what. So he simply kissed her, until she pulled away from him, disappearing silently into the darkness.

Chapter Sixteen

Sophie sat in her bathtub, shivering, as the hot water showered down on her. She'd left her clothes on the balcony—would Mal find them and dispose of them? Or would the cameras pick up on them when it grew light? She had her knees drawn up, and she put her head down against them, wishing she could somehow disappear. How had life managed to get twisted into such a sick fuck-all? She'd been doing fine, managing despite the situation. Married to a sadistic madman, trapped by her feigned condition, she'd been busy planning escape and revenge, her hatred keeping her going, not letting her collapse when she came so close.

And then *he* had arrived, and everything had gone to hell. He'd touched her, kissed her, fucked her, and when she'd spread her legs for him, she'd opened herself to a world of hurt.

This time she couldn't blame him, or the circumstances. There was no need to convince Archer they were sleeping together—he'd already accepted that and congratulated himself on his manipulations. She could have gone to her own room—how had she ended up in his? And then it came back to her.

She'd been certain she would finally kill Archer tonight, and she hadn't cared one way or another if she went down with him. Instead, Mal had tampered with the Beretta he'd so generously left for her, putting her in the worst danger of her life with no chance of defending herself. That was unforgiveable. It had taken so much to psych herself up into shooting Archer in cold blood, and the letdown when the gun didn't fire had almost made her pass out. He'd stopped her, caught her, held her when she wanted to run. He'd hidden her, protected her, carried her out of there when she probably couldn't have made it on her own. He was a monster. He had almost gotten her killed. He had saved her life.

Why hadn't she just left him? She was the one who'd initiated the sex, not Mal. In fact, for a brief moment she'd wondered whether he even wanted her. He'd acted as if the sex in the boathouse was simply part of the job. So why was he hard when he held her?

Hell, men would take anything that was offered, wouldn't they? So why had she offered? Was she wanting to make things more difficult?

She raised her head, letting the water sluice down over her face. She could think of one very good reason. She'd wanted to feel alive. She'd almost killed a man in cold blood, and she needed to feel human. It didn't matter that Archer deserved to die ten times over for what he'd done, not just to her, but to so many people. That guilt that Mal had thrown in her face was inescapable—it was the only reason she could bring herself to commit cold-blooded murder.

No, it was an execution, she reminded herself. One that was long overdue. She pushed herself up to stand in the shower, taking the soap and scrubbing herself ruthlessly, washing between her legs, trying to wash him away. She was still sensitive there, and the more she washed, the more she thought of Mal, so she gave up and staggered out of the tub, wrapping a towel around her.

There was a bench in front of the mirror, an inconvenient intrusion for someone who really had to get around in a wheelchair, but at the moment she was grateful, and she sank down on it, staring at her reflection in the mirror. She didn't recognize herself. Her brown eyes were huge, her mouth swollen, her entire reflection looking . . .

Looking well-fucked. And she had been—there was no denying it. Mal knew what to do with a woman's body—she didn't think she'd ever come so much or so quickly. That it made things that much more complicated didn't seem to bother Mal at all. It bothered the hell out of her.

But then, Mal hadn't been celibate for the last two years. He'd probably traveled all over the world, a fuck buddy in every port, while she'd been moldering in her bed. It wasn't that surprising that her emotional reaction practically equaled her physical reaction. It might even trump it. After all, physically it had felt nothing but good, so fucking good, and nothing she did could make her convince herself otherwise. Emotionally it had felt like suicide, like complete surrender, like death.

She looked at her stony face. She could see the bite mark that Mal had left on her neck from last time quite clearly. She had red patches from the roughness of his beard. No matter how fierce an image she was trying to project, there was still a slightly hazy, out-of-focus look to her. She'd never seen that look on her own face before, not even when she'd first been with Archer, but she knew it. It was the look of a woman in love.

She almost threw something at the mirror when that absurd thought came into her mind. She didn't even believe in love anymore, except for a few rare, special couples. It must simply be the look of satisfying sex—she could deny almost anything else but not that.

Staring at herself wasn't going to change anything. She brushed her teeth, then pushed back from the low-slung sink. She needed to sleep. Tomorrow she would have to face Malcolm Gunnison, tomorrow she would have to look at Archer and think about putting a bullet in his brain. Accept the reality of it—because sooner or later it was going to happen.

Her wheelchair was folded up behind the bathroom door. She climbed into it, switched off the light and rolled out into the darkened room. She needed to sleep, to block out all the mental and physical images that were assaulting her. She'd been doing that for that last few years—dismissing the mess she was in. Tonight it wasn't going to be that easy.

———✂———

It was a good thing Mal slept lightly. He'd just drifted off when he heard the sound on the stairs, and his hearing was acute enough to know it wasn't Sophie making another crazy attempt to kill Archer, but Archer himself mounting the stairs. Tension ratcheted through him, but he lay very still in the bed, waiting. If Archer went to Sophie's door, Mal was going to stop him, by any means necessary. He'd already made it clear that Sophie was his exclusive property for as long as he was on the island, but Archer hadn't liked it, and he wasn't a man to agree to anything he didn't want to. Archer would have picked up on the tension and raw sexuality that pulsed between his wife and his guest, and it would be hard for a psychopath like Archer to resist tasting some of it himself, but Mal wasn't letting it happen. He'd kill him if he had to.

Which was insane—he'd just stopped Sophie from doing that very thing. The mission mattered a hell of a lot more than one treacherous former agent.

Except that it hadn't been entirely her fault. She'd been dropped off in the deep end when she had barely learned to dog-paddle, and she'd faced a barracuda. All the excuses in the world didn't matter. He couldn't throw away an important mission like this one for personal reasons.

But he wasn't going to let Archer touch Sophie again.

To his mingled annoyance and relief his own door opened, and he felt Archer approach him. He hoped to God Archer wasn't going to make a pass at him. He was usually willing to take one for the team—sex was a tool, and it didn't much matter to him who he had to fuck in the line of business. He wasn't so sure he could carry it off with Archer.

Fortunately that didn't seem to be what Archer wanted from him. "Hey, Mal," he said in a stage whisper, leaning over him. Would Sophie be able to hear him? What would she think? She'd probably just distrust him all the more, but there wasn't much he could do about it.

He opened his eyes, blinking as if roused from a deep sleep, and pushed himself up in the bed. "What's up?" he said sleepily.

"Shhh. We don't want to wake Sophie up. I've decided it's time to get out of Dodge."

"Say what?" Mal said in a slow voice, his mind working feverishly.

"I think we need to pay a little visit to my laboratories. There's a late-season storm brewing, and if we hesitate, we'll be stuck here. If you're worried about Sophie, don't. This place is perfectly safe in the worst of storms, and Sophie's fine on her own. I go off all the time," Archer assured him. "There'll be enough people left behind to look after her, and she enjoys the time alone. You want to get your business dealt with, don't you?"

Mal said nothing, considering things. He wasn't in the mood to abandon Sophie, though as long as Archer was with him she was probably better off. The question was, why was Archer suddenly determined to leave the island? Who was in the most danger, him or Sophie? Maybe both of them. Archer had thrown them together, but he clearly hadn't liked the results. He'd be even more pissed by what they'd done tonight. Mal didn't think there was any way Archer could have seen or heard anything, but it wasn't wise to underestimate someone like Archer MacDonald.

"I would have thought this whole business deal would be over and done with by now anyway," Mal growled, deciding slightly sullen would work well.

"Don't say you haven't enjoyed yourself, Mal, old man," Archer chided him. "And I'm hoping once we find out what the holdup is with Chekowsky, you might come back. You seem to have enjoyed my wife yesterday, which I admit surprises me. She was never that good in bed."

Mal refused to rise to the provocation. He shrugged. "Maybe she needed someone else to inspire her."

Archer's conspiratorial grin froze for a moment. "She was in love with me."

Past tense, Mal thought. "I'm sure she still is," he said, sounding bored. "If we find your man and conclude the deal, why would I bother to come back?" He damned well had every intention of coming back, but it wouldn't be wise to seem too amenable.

Archer made a face. "Haven't I been a good host? I've offered you anything you could want, including exclusive rights to my own wife. Consider it a vacation."

Why the hell would Archer want him back? More of his game playing? Or maybe he'd decided he really didn't like bartering his wife after all. If Archer was planning to kill him, then it wouldn't make sense for them to go away, any more than it would for him to return. Archer could get one of his men to put a gun to Mal's head no matter where they were. "I don't take vacations." His voice was neutral.

"Well, you should," Archer said cheerfully. "Life's too short not to be enjoyed, and I expect you work very hard for the no doubt impressive amounts of money you get paid."

Malcolm said nothing, just watched him.

"Besides, just because we're checking in on Chekowsky doesn't mean he'll be ready to part with his project. He's a perfectionist and a pain in my ass, but in the end I find it better not to rush him. If there's a time limit on your offer, then perhaps we ought to just forget about it—as you can imagine, I have a great many other people interested in Pixiedust . . ."

So it's a game of bluff, is it? Malcolm thought, trying not to react to Archer's obnoxious name for the deadly poison. He had no doubt at all that there were any number of offers on the table, nor did he think it likely that Archer would sell such a powerful weapon to only one plutocrat or dictator. Archer would do his best to sell it to everyone he could, all the time swearing it was exclusive.

"There's no time limit," Mal said. "I don't have anywhere else I need to be right now." He paused. "And I enjoyed fucking your wife."

Archer beamed at him, but the smile didn't reach his eyes. He had something planned, though Mal couldn't begin to know what. He only knew that it would be extremely unpleasant and most likely involve Sophie as well. At that point there was nothing Mal could do but go along with things and watch very closely.

"Good enough!" Archer said. "The boat should be ready by now. Grab a few things and we'll go."

He had to see Sophie before they left. "It'll take me a few minutes . . ."

"No, it won't. Rachel's here to take care of things—all we need to do is head down and get settled and the others will follow. Nothing to worry about," Archer assured him.

Mal looked Archer squarely in his guileless eyes. He didn't want to go, which was crazy. He needed to stick to Archer MacDonald, and leaving Sophie behind was probably the best thing he could do for her. So why the hell was he so reluctant? Why was he determined to make his way back here, even if Archer and his fucking Pixiedust were terminated?

There was no way he could justify it. Even if he finished Archer and managed to either turn or kill the scientist, then he needed to get back to New Orleans and make his report. Sophie had made her own bed—she'd probably already had a plan to get off the island on her own. If he and Archer were gone, she'd have an easier time of it, and he wouldn't have to deal with her getting in his way while he tried to take care of business. She would have fucked everything if he hadn't tampered with the Beretta. Once they were off the island, he probably wouldn't have to see her again.

Wouldn't have to worry about her either, though there was no earthly reason why he should. Peter Madsen or Matthew Ryder in the

New Orleans branch would want to make sure the island was cleared and secure, and they would see to getting Sophie off there if she hadn't already found her own way.

It had nothing to do with him. She was a distraction, a dangerous one. In the end, she wasn't any of his business, and the brutal truth was that he was a killer, not a rescuer. He couldn't afford to feel anything for anybody, and Sophie was acceptable collateral damage, given her fuck-up three years ago. He really didn't give a shit, he told himself, ignoring the faint queasiness in his stomach.

He gave Archer his cynical half smile. "I wasn't worried," he said, pushing back the covers and climbing out of bed. He always slept naked, but he was already used to Malcolm's interested gaze, and he quickly pulled on his clothes, ignoring him. "What are we waiting for?"

Archer grinned widely. "Excellent!" he said, slinging his free arm around Mal's shoulders. They were about the same height, six foot two, but Archer was bulkier, seemingly stronger, and for a moment Mal considered twisting around, wrapping his own arm around Archer and snapping his neck. Stupid idea—there were too many people in the house who'd put a bullet in him before he heard more than the satisfying crunch.

Malcolm managed a cool smile. "Whatever," he said, and allowed Archer to pull him out toward the stairs, bypassing Sophie's door. She was probably listening to every word, doing a little dance of excitement at getting rid of both of them. She was probably ready to celebrate never seeing him again, ready to forget all about the time in the boathouse, the time on the balcony.

She could think whatever she wanted. Right now he had to get down to business, get the mission finished, and then he could decide what he wanted to do with her.

For now he had to stick to business.

Chapter Seventeen

Sophie woke up with the feeling that something was desperately wrong. It was six, too early, and she lay still, trying to remember why everything felt so messed up. Life had been a shitstorm for three years—why would today be any more complicated? And then she remembered.

She sat up, checking out her room in the murky light. The door to the terrace was closed, blocking out the sunshine, and the air-conditioning was on high, chilling her skin. She felt a strange combination of exhilaration and exhaustion, of fury and something that was dangerously close to happiness. She knew her body still bore the marks of Mal's hands on her, despite all her ruthless scrubbing. She could still feel him inside her—why did that sensation last, taunting her?

She lay back down again, listening carefully for sounds from the room next to her. She couldn't hear a thing, but then, she wouldn't. Mal knew how to be silent—he was the epitome of the perfect Committee agent. Ruthless, cold-blooded, impossible to catch. He had no emotions, no weaknesses as far as she could tell—except, perhaps, for lust. There was no other reason last night would have happened, at least the part he had initiated. Mostly he'd been intent on getting in her way while he pursued his own agenda. Maybe last night had simply been part of a plan to keep her off balance and out of his business.

She could have died last night because of that stupid gun, and he hadn't cared. He'd rescued her, but it probably had more to do with keeping his cover than any concern for her. He was a merciless, heartless bastard.

And yet . . . he'd shoved her behind him when he thought Archer was going to find them, and he'd carried her into his room, not hers, held her when he should have set her down and sent her on her way.

Most of the operatives she'd known would have simply gotten rid of her by now. The Committee had been a tight ship when she'd gone through her abbreviated training, and she'd learned enough to know that no one risked a mission over collateral damage. If someone or something posed any threat to the successful completion of your job, you got rid of it. It was that simple, that necessary, and that brutal.

The room looked just as she had left it. The door to the balcony was still locked, her wheelchair by the side of her bed. It seemed as if it were about a foot farther away from her than usual, but she could chalk that up to the semi-dazed state she'd been in, awash in sensation and guilt and fury, and a powerful, physical satisfaction, whether she wanted to admit it or not.

Rachel would appear by eight, bringing fresh fruit and some repulsive oatmeal that she conscientiously ate every morning. *Pancakes*, she promised herself. *With real Vermont maple syrup.* Assuming they had the real thing in Mexico or Louisiana or wherever she ended up once she got off this island. *And bacon.* She could smell it cooking sometimes, wafting up from the kitchens, but none had ever appeared on her breakfast tray. Archer had never particularly liked bacon—that should have tipped her off to what a bastard he really was. He probably had Elena cook bacon just to torment her.

Maybe she'd cook bacon sometime for Mal. Maybe she could sneak into his room . . . no! She closed her eyes in disgust. She'd truly lost her mind. She needed to get the hell out of here. If she went back into his room, it wouldn't be bacon she was looking for, and it would have nothing to do with what she'd end up doing again. Unless she ate bacon off his hard, flat stomach and . . .

She flopped back down on the bed, covering her flushed face with a pillow. Maybe she could just smother herself—it would be a kinder, gentler death. She even allowed herself a quiet groan, muffled by the pillow. If the microphones picked it up, Archer could make of it what he wanted. She was too tired, too screwed up, to worry about it.

When she woke again it was past eleven, and even in the cold room she was sweating. She knew why, but she refused to think about it. Erotic dreams were not her responsibility, and there was nothing she could do about them but stay awake, and that would wreak havoc on her training. His mouth hadn't tasted of bacon. It had tasted of sin, of darkness, of pure delight.

Something she was never going to taste again. She shoved her hair back, then levered herself into the wheelchair, ignoring the odd shakiness that her too-vivid memories had left her with. Her skin prickled, and she knew she was flushed.

She needed a cold shower. Picking up the telephone, she was shocked to hear nothing but silence. Someone had turned off the on-island phone network. It wasn't the electricity—the air conditioner was still humming away. She rolled herself over to the door and opened it, coming out onto the upper hallway overlooking the main floor.

"Hello?" she called. "Elena? Joe?"

There was no answer. She could see outside now, through the tall windows of the main floor, and it was unnaturally dark, stormy, wind lashing at the trees. Maybe the weather had taken out the phone system—the infrastructure on Isla Mordita was the best money could buy, but under such primitive, private circumstances, money couldn't buy much.

She glanced back at Malcolm's room. The door was open, and he had to be gone as well—otherwise he'd probably be out there, taunting her. At least he wouldn't have any idea what she'd been thinking about—small blessing.

There was no way she was going to find out what was going on in the suddenly silent house without getting her body downstairs, and there was only one way to do it.

She'd discovered a great trick early on—she'd picture herself a Disneyfied mermaid, her legs encased in an immovable tail whenever she had to do things that might be observed. Locking the wheelchair, she carefully picked up one foot and then another before flipping up the footrests, then sliding out of the thing and onto the floor. Chances were Archer was somewhere watching this whole production, delighting in her awkwardness. He probably had Malcolm with him, and when she got to the bottom of the wide, winding stairs he'd appear, applauding.

There was always the possibility Archer had abandoned her. He'd done it before, always without warning, but people had been left behind. She had the curious feeling that the island was completely deserted, but she knew how unlikely that was. After all, she was Archer's toy, like a catnip mouse for him to bat around and then ignore when he wasn't interested. Archer never gave up anything willingly, and he certainly was never going to let her go. Sooner or later he planned to kill her, and even though a few long years had passed, nothing had softened him, nothing had changed him. He was still the sadistic megalomaniac he'd always been, back when she'd been too stupid to recognize it.

She never did anything that would give away her condition except in total darkness, and despite the strong winds and cloudy skies it was still bright enough for Archer's myriad cameras to catch her in the act. Scooting on her butt, she slid down to the first step, dragging her legs with her as she leaned back against the balustrade.

By the time she reached the ground floor she was covered with sweat. And then she remembered she'd left the fucking wheelchair at the top of the landing. *Shit!* She should have pushed it down the stairs and hoped for the best. The damned thing was made of titanium, and it probably would have been fine. Now she was stuck at the bottom with no way to get around but dragging her virtual mermaid's tail with her.

She tried calling out. She tried screaming. No one answered, though the sound of the wind through the trees probably drowned out her voice. She heard a sudden great crack of thunder, so loud that it shook the house, and she screamed like a baby, immediately ashamed of herself, as the lights flickered and went off.

She sat back against the bottom stair, taking a deep breath. It was November—the hurricane season should be just about over. They'd only been hit once, when she and Archer had been newly married, and everyone had left the island for safety, coming back to find almost the entire place flooded except for the old sugar mill at the top of the hill.

Was that it? Had there been hurricane warnings and Archer had left her here alone to drown? If so, it was a piss-poor method of murder, she thought, irritated. The water had covered the island, all right, but it hadn't reached the second floor of the old house. It would take a category 5 to do that, and those were few and far between, and certainly not at the tail end of the season—that or a tsunami.

Of course, with this brewing storm, now was the perfect time to abandon her. No one with any sense would set out in a boat until this thing passed—she didn't need guards to keep her here. She was well and truly trapped.

With a sigh she leaned forward, dragging herself toward the kitchen. The servants' sleeping quarters were on that side of the house, as well as Archer's private little cadre of bodyguards. If there was anyone left on the island, they'd be back there.

I never would have made it as an actress, she thought as she reached the end of the massive dining room. No doubt she would have been very good—she could lie with the best of them—but the physical demands were a pain in the butt. Once she got off this island, she never intended to sit down again.

Once I get off this island, once I get off this island. As a mantra it wasn't as calming as it usually was. The food, the sex, the myriad wonders a free life presented her—all were seeming more and more distant.

Maybe, given her track record, she should just give up sex entirely. She seemed to have very bad taste in men, if she'd been besotted with one psychopath and was currently tormented by sexual longings for a ruthless operative.

Of course, that was ignoring the fact that she'd intended to be the same kind of operative, though she'd had delusions of helping the world, not just getting the job done. And she wasn't lusting after Malcolm. So they'd had sex, twice. The first time he'd initiated it, the second time she'd taken back the power and gone down on him. She wanted to do it again, when it was something she'd always done out of duty, never desire. She was vulnerable, no matter how hard she tried not to be, and it was no surprise she was feeling totally fucked, physically, mentally, and emotionally.

Simple hormones, long denied, that's what it was, she decided, yanking her body over the threshold into the large kitchen. It was just her body's way of proving that she was still alive.

She had to stop thinking about it! He was nowhere around, at least for now, and she needed to concentrate on finding out exactly what was going on.

The kitchen was dark, and she heard the rain start, hard, tiny pellets lashing against the windows. She called out again, to nothingness, the only response the rumble in her empty stomach. The house was empty, the power was off, which would render the cameras and listening devices useless, and she'd dragged herself across this honking big house like something out of Wyeth painting.

"Fuck it," she said out loud, and stood up. If anyone was still on the island, she could immediately cling to something and announce there'd been a miracle, and she was regaining her strength. At that point she didn't give a rat's ass.

She went straight for the huge refrigerator, poking her face inside to peer into the darkness. She found a wedge of cheese, half a chicken, butter, and several underripe mangoes. She dumped them on the wide kitchen island, managed to locate some of Elena's homemade bread, and made herself the best sandwich in the history of sandwich making. And then she made another.

Heading back to the fridge, she grabbed a Corona, popped off the cap, and took her feast into the living room, setting it on the low-slung coffee table that still held a copy of *Time* magazine from three years ago with Archer on the cover. For the first time in her memory she seemed to be completely alone on Isla Mordita, though *seemed* was the operative word. In the shadowy darkness she was relatively safe, as long as the power was off. At one point Archer had equipped the cameras with battery power, but storms kept shorting them out, much to his frustration, and he'd settled on old-fashioned personal surveillance when technology failed him. Problem was, there didn't seem to be any humans left on the island except for her.

She stretched out on the overstuffed sofa, devouring her sandwiches and savoring the beer. When Archer left he was usually gone for at least a week—that would give her more than enough time to leave the place. She couldn't go anywhere in this storm, not unless she wanted to end up on the bottom of the ocean floor, but she could plan, and the moment the weather calmed, she could take off in Marco's little skiff.

Leaving Archer to Mal's tender mercies. She should be grateful—she'd learned last night that killing someone was a lot harder than she'd thought, no matter what she'd gone through. She wasn't letting Archer get away with the years of torment, the horrendous things he'd done, the horrifying things he'd still do. Malcolm would take care of it, and she'd never have to see either of them again.

Only problem was she wasn't sure she could just turn her back on everything. She wasn't sure she could ever feel whole again until she faced her tormentor, the stupid man who'd fooled her so badly when she'd been young and vulnerable. She'd earned the right to kill him—she wanted to kill him. She just had to accept what it would cost her soul.

She'd learned one other thing during her Committee training, and that was to trust her instincts. After her monumental mistake with Archer she hadn't trusted anything, but she knew that Mal hadn't gone for good. He was coming back. She wasn't sure whether that ache inside her was hope or despair.

She'd had plenty of time to learn how to fill the empty hours, and she was perfectly content to curl up on the sofa, nursing her beer and watching the storm lash the island. It suited her mood—her emotions were storming around inside her, her defenses were bending like trees in the wind, and the intermittent cracks of lightning were like a slap, reminding her she was an idiot.

If she'd had any electrical power, she would have been tempted to blast Archer's custom stereo and dance around the empty house in her underwear. As it was, she simply enjoyed the freedom to take the stairs two at a time when she went up to take a shower and bring the damned wheelchair back down, and contented herself with singing loudly to scare away the ghosts.

She stood naked in her room for the first time in two years, staring into her closet. All those enveloping dresses depressed her—just for a short time she didn't want to be swathed in fabric, mummified in her charade. She would have thought they'd tossed out everything from before the shooting, but there was a box on the top closet shelf, and when she pulled it out she found a pair of khaki shorts, clean and pressed. She stared at them for a long moment, then turned them over. The stain on the waistband had been impossible to get out, though she didn't know if anyone had tried. Of course Archer had made certain these were kept—the clothes she was wearing when she'd been shot and supposedly crippled. The shirt was there too.

It had been one of those unending sunny days, a stark contrast to her mood at the time. For two months she had known just how wrong she had been about Archer, and she had yet to figure out what she could do about it. She couldn't finish her mission and kill him—she had no access to any weapons, and the thought of breaking his neck made her ill. He couldn't suspect anything—he still had sex with her every night, though his recent gentleness felt absolutely creepy. At least she'd had enough training to be able to put up a good show, and she was excellent at faking orgasms. Make enough noise, squeeze your vaginal walls, and any man would be convinced.

They were going on a picnic at the old sugar mill that day, something that filled Sophie with trepidation. The last time they'd been up there she'd still been hoping for the best with Archer, even though she'd begun having doubts within a week of their wedding, and their al fresco sex had been inventive and stimulating. That morning she'd wanted to vomit at the memories.

She'd ending up wearing one of Archer's oversized, custom-tailored Oxford shirts, rolling the sleeves up, the hem almost reaching the bottom of her shorts. She planned on telling him she had her period—Archer was fastidious about such things, and he probably wouldn't even touch her hand if he could get away with it.

It hadn't gotten that far. She still remembered it clearly—if felt as if someone had driven a fist into her back, throwing her forward onto the ground, and a second later there'd been an explosion of sound. She hadn't moved, hadn't been able to move, but she could see Archer on the ground as well, covered by Joe's protective body, as bullets flew overhead. Archer was smiling.

She pulled the pale blue shirt out of the box and held it up. The bullet hole was surprisingly small in the back of the shirt, and the blood had washed out of it, probably to Archer's disappointment. "Fuck it," she said out loud. She still had no choice apart from her uncomfortable, lacy underwear, but she didn't need a bra, and she pulled on the shorts and the shirt, rolling up the sleeves and tying the long tails around her waist so that the hole was lost in the bunched fabric. It should have felt morbid, but instead it made her defiant. She was just about to head back downstairs in the gathering dusk when she noticed something on her dressing table.

It was the Beretta. *Big help*, she thought cynically, until she saw the firing pin lying beside it. So the asshole was feeling regrets, was he? She wasn't in the mood to forgive anyone.

She scooped it up—she'd need more light to break it down and reinsert the pin, and this time she could make sure the thing worked. When had he come into her room? He definitely wasn't on the island right now—no one was—so he must have done it before Archer took him off. Sometime between having sex on the floor of the balcony and dawn he'd come into her room and left her the gun. Had he looked down at her while she slept? And why the hell hadn't she woken up— her reflexes were excellent and she slept lightly. She was always alert when someone even neared her room.

Some deluded part of her conscience must have felt he was no threat to her, or she never would have slept on, even if she'd been awake for days. It was appearing as if she was still the idiot she'd been so long ago, falling in . . . trusting the wrong man.

Once downstairs she broke the gun down, cleaned it, and reassembled and loaded it. It looked right, felt right, but she couldn't be certain until she tested it. She glanced around her, then saw the *Time* magazine with Archer's charming smile shining in the dim light.

Scooping it up, she headed for one of the side doors. There were waves in the pool, but at least someone had stowed the outdoor furniture. The wind was high, but not bad enough that she had trouble standing. She stepped out into the warm rain, moved to one of the sculptured bushes some two hundred yards away, and propped the magazine in the shaking branches. This would be a true test of her previously excellent marksmanship. If she could hit a moving target from that distance, she'd count herself lucky. Any corner of the magazine would do.

In the murky distance she could just make out Archer's smug eyes from the black and white cover, and she trained the gun directly between them and pulled the trigger.

The magazine exploded in a flurry of wet paper, and she ran down to get it, her feet light on the soaked grass. She had to chase it for a moment as it was tossed in the wind, but when she reached it she saw the bullet hole, and it took her only a moment to find the cover. Two inches off—in the middle of his forehead, not between the eyes. It would do. She ripped the cover off, letting the wind take the rest of the ruined magazine, folded it, and slipped it in her pocket. It would be her talisman.

She found candles and matches before the night closed in, then opened one of Archer's most treasured bottles of red wine and let it breathe. The flashlights and battery-powered lanterns were all in working condition, which made sense with the unreliable power, and she turned one on and set it on the coffee table. It had been so long since she hadn't been watched that she was happy enough just to stretch out on the sofa and drink. She probably had a few days to decide what to do. For now, she was simply going to lie there and finish the best wine she'd ever tasted and regard her wineglass as half-full.

The night was filled with noise. There were hurricane shutters on the building, but no one had bothered to close them before they left, and half of them had come loose and were banging against the house in the stiff breeze. The thunder and lightning were intermittent, coming just when she'd decided it had finished for the night, and occasionally she heard a great cracking noise as a tree broke beneath the force of the wind. It was too dark to see anything—she could hear the roar of the waves, but she had no idea whether the water was coming closer or not. She didn't care. If it came into the house and reached the sofa, she'd still be able to climb to the second floor, and that would be safe enough.

The crash of broken glass awoke her, and she struggled to sit up on the overstuffed sofa. The lamp had burned out and the cavernous downstairs was filled with an eerie darkness. After all that noise there was silence, an ominous sense of waiting. The constant wind had stopped for the moment, though she could still hear the angry surf in the distance. Or maybe it was closer than she thought, the rising tide edging toward the house and the first floor.

After a couple of failed attempts she managed to push herself up in the smothering sofa, and then she froze. She was no longer alone on the island.

She stayed exactly where she was. There was only one person in the world who knew she could walk, and there was no guarantee it was that man. She could hear shuffling footsteps, and for a moment the image of zombies came to mind, and she wanted to laugh. In this mess she'd made of her life, zombies would be the least of her worries.

She saw his silhouette from her spot on the couch, and she held very still. It was definitely someone she'd never seen before, not one of the usual inhabitants of the island. Presumably male, he was short, squat, and out of breath. That didn't mean he wasn't dangerous—when Archer left the island he might have made arrangements for a professional to finish the job on her that Emilio had flubbed.

And then he spoke, his voice high-pitched and slightly fretful. "Hello? Anyone home? Don't tell me I almost died getting here for no reason."

Sophie lit a match, setting it to one of the collection of candles on the coffee table, knowing the flare of light would illuminate her. "Who are you?" she called out.

He moved toward her, but she kept lighting candles against the darkness, so that by the time he came around the sofa she could see him fairly well. He was balding, with a fringe of white hair surrounding his skull, late middle-aged and looking irritated. He was wearing a white suit that must have once been immaculate but now looked as if it had been tossed around in the ocean, and what were once spotless white tennis shoes were now covered with mud. Clearly he was a man who was fussy about his clothing, which meant at the very least he was vain. She could work with that.

"Who are you?" she said again.

"Dr. Benjamin Chekowsky," he said in an affronted voice, clearly believing she should have known who he was. "And who, may I ask, are you, and where the hell is Archer MacDonald?"

In fact, she knew exactly who Dr. Benjamin Chekowsky was, even if she'd never seen him before. Archer's pet scientist, he was the man responsible for the biological weapon that had been Archer's obsession for the past few years.

He didn't look like a man who spent his time and his considerable intellect trying to devise ways to kill as many people as he could in as short a time as possible. In fact, he looked a little like a cross between Alfred Hitchcock and Truman Capote, a thought that should have amused her, but there was nothing funny about Dr. Death.

"You're the man who designed Pixiedust," she said slowly.

"Don't call it that stupid name," he snapped. "I've told Archer it needs to be treated with proper respect."

"What do you call it?" she asked, thinking perhaps "genocide" and "mass murder" while she kept her face still. Not that he could see her that clearly in the candlelight, but it wouldn't do to underestimate this little man.

"It's RU48 at this point," he said in a voice that sounded like he should have added "you idiot" at the end. "I'm thinking the Chekowsky Solution might be a more dignified name for it."

She stared at him, momentarily speechless. This was all she needed—another demented egomaniac. "So your name will go down in history?" she said. "That is, if there is any history after you set that stuff off."

He puffed up a little bit, like an outraged pigeon. "What's Archer doing with a naïve little bleeding heart like you? You're not pretty enough to be one of his bimbos."

"He married me."

Chekowsky's beady little eyes immediately went to her motionless legs, and Sophie silently cursed. He knew about her, and she was really loath to give up walking. "I've heard about you," he said slowly.

She gave him a flinty smile. "I expect you have. I'm afraid that there's absolutely no one else on the island. How did you manage to get here in this storm?"

"Wasn't easy," he said, giving nothing away, and Sophie's annoyance built.

"Are you alone?" she asked. That seemed highly unlikely—Chekowsky didn't look like the kind of man to brave the elements or thrive on adversity. In fact, he looked a little like a fat, drowned rat. A white one.

"I'm the only one who made it." He glanced around him. "I don't suppose there's anything to eat? I've been through quite an ordeal."

Oh, her heart was breaking for him. He'd probably drowned the sailors who'd brought him this far. "There's plenty of food in the kitchen, though I'm afraid all the servants have left the island. You'll have to get your own. Obviously I'm in no shape to help you." She added that just to rule out all possibility of him thinking she could walk.

"Obviously," he said in a dismissive voice. Her annoyance spilled over into a cool, quiet rage. "Where's the kitchen?" he asked.

She gestured, and he turned and disappeared, without asking the poor crippled woman if he could get her anything. She sat very still, contemplating dark deeds. And then she called out, "Bring yourself a wineglass. I've opened one of Archer's best bottles of cabernet." She gave her legs one last, luxuriant stretch before tucking them up on the sofa, then leaned forward to pour herself a final glass of wine. By the time he returned, his plate piled high and one of Archer's best Waterford crystal wineglasses in his hand, she was lazily sipping at her own glass, watching him over the rim.

Chekowsky heaved his bulk into one of the chairs opposite and reached for the wine bottle. "I don't usually indulge," he said with a belated attempt at affability, "but this is a special occasion." He filled the wineglass to the top, leaving no room for the bouquet, and took a hefty gulp. Archer would have been horrified, Sophie thought happily.

"Is it?" she said, taking another sip. "What are we celebrating?"

Chekowsky hesitated, but she could sense that his need to brag exceeded his natural caution. "I've finally perfected the Chekowsky Solution. That's what I was coming to tell your husband. I told him to be patient," he added with the trace of a whine. "He should have called me to tell me he was coming—it would have kept me from risking my life like this."

"I think his trip was spur of the moment. But my husband told me RU48"—she decided not to call it by the silly name of Pixiedust or the egocentric Chekowsky Solution—"was already developed." In fact, he hadn't said anything about it, but she was adept at listening to even the slightest bit of information, and RU48 had already been tested several times in the Middle East and Ukraine.

Chekowsky drained his wine in the second gulp, then poured himself another too-full glass before diving into his food. "Anyone can make a biological weapon," he said in dismissive tones as crumbs littered his crushed white suit. "It requires a singular genius to devise one that can be used for extortion and civil unrest."

She raised her eyebrows. "Oh, really? And how is that? I can imagine its uses for civil unrest—you simply wipe out those who disagree with you. But how can you extort money . . . ?"

He sighed, washing down a huge mouthful of food. She couldn't believe anyone that short could put away so much food, but he was making an impressive effort. "It's the vaccine, you see," he said in a condescending tone. "And the antidote."

She stared at him. "I would think a biological weapon with a vaccine and an antidote would be less valuable, not more."

"One would think that," he agreed, pouring the very last of the wine into his glass. He paused a moment, remembering his nonexistent manners. "Did you want any more of this?"

She shook her head. "So why is RU48 more valuable?"

"The vaccine is prohibitively expensive to make, and the drug is cheap. Only the very few with power and money can get their hands on the vaccine, the same ones who can afford to buy the weapon in the first place," he said smugly.

"And the antidote?"

"Also very expensive, though not as bad as the vaccine or the drug itself. All someone has to do is release the toxin and hundreds of thousands, even more, will fall victim to it. And it spreads from person to person, by touch, or even, if we're extremely lucky and the batch is particularly potent, it can be airborne."

"If you're extremely lucky," she echoed, smiling sweetly, wanting to throw up.

"The only problem was that people needed to get the antidote within twelve hours of being exposed, or it would be too late, and that doesn't allow enough time to negotiate. I've been working on extending the window of opportunity to thirty hours, and I've finally succeeded." He looked so pleased with himself Sophie considered shooting him with the gun she had tucked beneath the cushion. He yawned. "Good grief, I'm exhausted!" His small, slightly bulbous eyes blinked at her from behind his glasses. It wouldn't be long now.

"Would you answer me one fucking question?" she said, unable to control herself.

The man frowned. "I don't like your language, young woman. Or your tone."

For a moment Sophie wanted to laugh hysterically. This monster was lecturing her on manners. She managed a tight smile. "You're a brilliant scientist. A genius."

He nodded, taking the words as his due.

"So why didn't you take your remarkable intellect and put it toward something positive, like . . . like helping people like me to walk. Is it the money?"

He waved a hand, airily dismissing such a notion. "Of course I can understand your obsession with such paltry matters, but the fact is I have no wish to dedicate my life to the few people who've managed to cripple themselves riding motorcycles or driving too fast. Where's the glory in that?"

She was calm now. His words were slurring just slightly as exhaustion set in. "So it's glory you're after?" she said.

"Certainly not! But it's glory I deserve. I want to make a difference in this world. The Chekowsky Solution will stop people from their petty squabbles . . ." He yawned again, the muscles in his face growing slack. "And keeping . . . and keeping revolutions and wars . . . wars . . ." His head nodded, then drooped on his chest, and the room was silent.

Sophie didn't move. What had she expected him to say? Most evil people thought they were the good guys. "Dr. Chekowsky?" she said in a loud voice.

He didn't move. She stretched across the sofa, ending up flopping on her stomach, and tapped him on the leg. "Dr. Chekowsky? Are you awake?"

No response. She leaned back, glancing at his empty wineglass. The dregs of her crushed Vicodin lay in the bottom—it served the old glutton right for gulping his wine like that, she thought. He'd been much too trusting—in his line of work he needed to be more suspicious, like Mal had been. Instead, he'd gulped down what she'd handed him without a second thought.

She pulled her stash of pills from beneath the cushion and set it on the table. It had been a last-minute impulse that had made her grab the medicine along with the gun when she came back downstairs, and for once, just this once, things were going her way. Just to be on the safe side she waited another five minutes, sipping her undoctored wine, occasionally poking at the comatose man, before she rose to her feet, satisfied. If she remembered her training he should be out for a good six hours, maybe longer given his difficulty in getting to the island. Now the question was, where to stash him?

The obvious choice was the wine cellar, which was actually little more than a mud-packed cavern beneath the kitchen. The man probably weighed over two hundred pounds, and only that little because he was short. She was strong, but maneuvering him there was going to be difficult. And then she remembered her titanium wheelchair.

It was lying on its side by the foot of the stairs where she'd sent it tumbling, and when she set it upright it was, of course, undamaged. Archer never stinted in his loving care of his wife, she thought bitterly. After rolling it over beside Chekowsky's chair, she set the brakes and turned to look at him.

It wasn't the most graceful transition—he felt twice as heavy when he was a dead weight, and his arms and legs flopped everywhere as she tried to haul him into the chair. He kept sliding off it, and she pulled off his jacket and tied it around him, the sleeves around the back of the chair to keep him in place. He was so large the wheels rubbed against his body as she rolled him into the kitchen, but she persevered, determined.

There was a combination lock on the cellar door, but she already knew from her previous excursion that Archer hadn't changed it—it was still his birthday. *Idiot*, she thought, spinning the dials and opening the door into the dankness. There was no light down there—Archer usually used a lantern when he went in search of wine—and there wasn't much room. Dr. Chekowsky wasn't going to notice these little inconveniences, and the glorified hole was on the far side away from the living room. If he woke up before she got out of there and started making a fuss, there was a good chance she wouldn't even have to hear him.

She brought the wheelchair to the edge of the short, steep flight of stairs, untied his jacket, and tipped him forward. It sounded as if he hit every single step as he went down, ending with the crash of broken glass as he landed up against the wine bottles. Another crash, which sounded as if one of the fully loaded sets of shelves had collapsed on top of him. No, he wouldn't be bothering anyone for a long time.

She threw his coat after him, closed the door and locked it again, then examined her conscience. He could die—from injuries, from exposure . . . hell, from an overdose of the acetaminophen in Vicodin. Did she feel guilty?

Nope.

She went back into the living room, stretched out on the sofa, and finished her glass of wine.

Chapter Eighteen

Mal dragged the boat as high onto the sand as he could make it before he collapsed, coughing up water. The rain had stopped, but the wind had picked up again, fierce in its determination to wipe him off the face of the earth, and he'd barely managed to reach shore. There had been the broken pieces of other small boats and even the occasional body floating in the raging waters, and it had taken all his skill and more to avoid them. His skill, and Archer's.

Archer was sitting in the sand on the other side of the wrecked boat, a little winded but not even coughing. Somehow he'd managed not to swallow any water, and they'd made it back to Isla Mordita just as the first fitful rays of dawn were appearing on the horizon.

Mal rolled over on his back, looking up. The sky was still dark and angry, despite the early light, and the storm was far from over. He'd thought he was never coming back here—he had every intention of finishing with Archer and his scientist while they were gone and sending someone else in to rescue Sophie. It would be so much simpler if he never had to see her again.

He couldn't stop thinking about her, and that was far too dangerous in his line of work. She was a distraction, she made him vulnerable, and therefore he had to get rid of her. He'd make the Committee treat her well—it hadn't been her fault that she'd been flung into such a tough situation before she was ready—but he still had no intention of ever going near her again. She was like a drug, ~

of her. The only thing to do was never have an~

"You all right, Gunnison?" Archer called over ~

"Just peachy," he growled. He'd had no choice. ~

had foundered off the gulf coast, Archer had abandoned th~

survived, stolen the first boat he could find, and headed bac~

Mordita, and he'd turned the gun he'd used to kill the older c~

who'd owned the boat on Mal.

"Afraid I'm going to need you, old man," he'd said affably. "None of my men are any good on a boat, and you know what you're doing. Besides, I think you're far too interested in getting back to my wife, aren't you? Get on board. Now."

Mal lost his own gun when the boat had broken up, and killing Archer while they were out on the rough ocean would have been too fucking dangerous. He wouldn't have made it without Archer, though he hated like hell to admit it. Then again, Archer had needed him to survive, so that wiped out the debt.

Mal pushed himself into a sitting position. The remains of a small cabin cruiser were smashed against the rocks at the bottom of the cliff, and there was a dead body lying on the sand. It was hard to be certain, but he didn't recognize the man or the boat. "Who's that?" he said, tipping his chin in the direction of the corpse.

"Beats me," Archer said, bored. "Someone who got caught in the storm and didn't have our expertise, I'd guess. That, or you've got some competition when it comes to my little Sophie."

"Your little Sophie is about five foot eight," he snapped. He couldn't wait to kill the bastard.

"How would you know? Did you measure her lying down?" Archer said lazily, and Mal, already cold from his plunge into the gulf, froze.

How could he have made such a mistake? He knew Sophie's height because he knew where she came up against his own six foot two when she'd pressed up against him in the boathouse.

e recovered quickly. "I'm an observant man," he drawled, "and I
igure things out. She's got long legs."

"So she has," Archer said pleasantly. "Too bad they don't work. You
ady to tackle the cliff?"

They'd landed on the western beach, just under the bluff of land
that held the old sugar mill. A rickety set of stairs, so many flights he
didn't want to count them, led up to the promontory, and that was the
only way they would get back to the house. The steps were so flimsy
they didn't look like they could hold a butterfly, and they were going
to have to hold both his and Archer's bulk. There was no way Archer
would wait until Mal reached the top to head up there, no way Mal
would let Archer have a chance to reach Sophie before he did.

He shrugged. "Now's as good a time as any." If the steps collapsed,
then so be it—at least Archer would be wiped out. Mal rose to his feet,
steady despite the last few harrowing hours. His jeans and shirt were
soaked with salt water, and he felt bone weary. He was going to have
to make this up as he went along. One thing he knew for sure: Archer
wasn't going to make it back to the house alive.

The stairs were in worse shape than he'd suspected, cracking beneath
Archer's heavy, muscular weight. He'd gone first, of course, leaving Mal
no choice but to follow, and he kept pace, even as the wood creaked
and splintered beneath his soaked deck shoes, watching every move
Archer made above him. Archer was talking, of course—he never shut
his fucking yap. How he managed to bound up the wooden steps and
still talk was beyond Mal's comprehension, but then Archer wasn't your
normal, everyday megalomaniac billionaire. He always seemed to be on
some form of speed, though Mal suspected it was just his own hyper
nature that drove him. In years and years of intel, there'd never been a
hint of drug use—Archer was just high on himself.

The sky was growing a little lighter, and the cold breeze biting through
his wet clothes seemed to grow a little softer. He wasn't shivering—that
was easy enough to control, but he was so damned cold he probably had

icicles coming off his dick. He needed to break Archer's neck and get someplace warm.

The bird came from out of nowhere, a gull, shrieking, startling him for one impossible moment, long enough for Archer to kick downward with his foot, knocking Mal off the stairs.

Mal grabbed at him, catching his ankle, as the wooden structure collapsed beneath them, with only the final flight clinging to the top of the cliff. Beneath them he heard the wood shatter on the rocks below, and he looked up at Archer grinning down at him.

"Might as well let go, old man," Archer said jovially. "I don't need you—I've got plenty of customers for Pixiedust, and I think my wife likes you a little too much."

Mal was swinging loose over the sand, only his iron grip on Archer's ankle keeping him from falling to his death. "After all we've been to each other, Archer?" Mal called up. "I saved your life out there."

"And I saved yours. Which makes us even, don't you think? I like you, Mal, I really do, but you've outworn your usefulness. I can sell the stuff directly to your boss and cut out the middleman." He shook his leg, trying to break free of Mal's hold, but it did no good—Mal had no intention of letting go. "You're annoying me," Archer shouted over the increasing wind. "I'm cold and tired and I want to get back to my wife. Just let go, won't you? You're never going to make it up here, and I haven't got all day."

Mal laughed breathlessly. "Why don't you pull me up, and we can talk about it man to man?" He was strong, but he'd used up a lot of his strength in their battle against the sea, and he wasn't certain how long he could last. Long enough, he told himself, his fingers digging into Archer's leg as he slid his other hand inside his pants. The custom sleeve that rested beside his junk had kept the knife in place despite all the tossing of the boat, and he pulled at it, careful not to let Archer see what he was doing.

"I'd love to, but you disapprove of the way I handle my marriage, I know you do, and I really dislike disapproval. Besides, my wife was supposed to feel degraded by your attentions—she wasn't supposed to actually like it. I'm afraid you've worn out your welcome . . ."

Mal swung himself upward with a huge lunge, stabbing the knife into Archer's foot as he grabbed for the bottom step of the stairs.

Archer's scream howled through the night. He kicked wildly, trying to free himself, when his hold on the stairs broke and a moment later he was gone, falling head over heels down the cliff to disappear into the darkness below.

Mal stayed where he was for a moment, clinging to the broken step. Beneath him, there was no scream, only the sound of the surf. Not even Archer MacDonald could survive a fall like that. He was dead, gone, that quickly, after such an interminable time. So why didn't Mal believe it?

He took a deep breath and began to pull himself up onto the remaining flight of stairs. It shook beneath him, and it wasn't going to last long. With his final ounce of strength he surged upward as the rest of the wooden structure let go and crashed down on top of where Archer MacDonald would be lying, and Mal landed on the crumbling cliff just as the lightning split the sky once more, and the rain poured down on his weary body.

———

Sophie thought she heard a scream. She'd fallen asleep on the sofa again, a little creeped out by the darkness overhead, and she woke up with a start. She could hear nothing but the wind, which had picked up once more, and then, a few sleepy moments later, a huge clap of thunder followed by another deluge. She sighed. She'd known the storm wasn't over yet, but she'd hoped.

It was marginally lighter outside, but with the storm she had no idea whether it was dusk or dawn or even high noon. She'd left her watch upstairs. Time had been so meaningless over the past few years, and keeping track of it only made things worse—she'd stopped thinking about it, structuring her solitary days on her own terms. There was no clock in the vast living room, or if Archer had added one it was lost in the shadows. She was exhausted—and until the power came on there was nothing she could do but think about the man she'd tossed into the cellar and wait to hear whether he survived, whether he made enough noise . . .

It was driving her crazy. She was going back to bed. The short-lived calm of the storm disappeared, and it was raging with a vengeance, and even if the mad scientist in the cellar had managed to get here in one piece, she had very strong doubts she'd be able to leave—at least, not quite yet.

She headed up the stairs, leaving the remains of her picnic dinner and Chekowsky's drugging on the glass coffee table. The sofa, for all its enveloping, even smothering comfort, provided very little support, and she was used to sleeping on her hard-as-nails mattress. She got to the top of the landing and hesitated.

Goldilocks had rejected too soft in the living room, and now the thought of her own hard bed was less than appealing. Hell, she could make all the excuses she wanted, but she was going to sleep in his bed, in his sheets, and she'd always planned to.

The door to the balcony had blown open in the storm, leaving the floor of Mal's room wet, the room filled with the fresh ozone of a tropical storm. Leaves and flowers scattered the room, blown in by the wind, and she wanted to laugh. The bed itself was unmade—Archer must have sent the servants off-island before they finished their morning routine. Of course he had—he'd clearly wanted everyone gone before she woke up.

After setting the gun down on the bedside table, she shoved her shorts and underwear down her legs, then untied the dress shirt and pulled it over her head. It had felt good wearing those clothes today. It had been a spit in the eye of an undiscriminating fate, a way to take back what had been stolen from her. She slid into bed, pulling the bamboo sheets around her body.

It had been so long since she had slept naked, and the feeling was heavenly as she stretched between the soft sheets. She closed her eyes in the semidarkness, and Mal was all around her, the feel of him imprinted in the bed, the sheets wrapping around her like strong arms.

She'd had too much wine, too much stimulation. She was half drunk and well past making any sensible decisions. When she woke up she'd shower if the gravity-fed water still allowed her to, dress, and head down to the beach to find a way off this place. No matter how violent, storms couldn't last that long, and it should start to clear before much longer. The seas would be choppy for a while, and she'd put it off as long as she dared, but in the end, what better reason was there to risk her life but for freedom?

She rubbed her face against the pillow like a kitten rubbing against a stroking hand. She could smell his skin, she thought, not sure how she recognized it. Not sweat or cologne, just something indefinable that made him there with her, and she knew she should get up and go to her own room, knew this was dangerous in her current condition, but she couldn't bring herself to move.

She sighed, settling in more deeply, but the exhaustion that had been chasing her downstairs seemed to have traded itself for unruly thoughts. She had every right to luxuriate in this bed. In *his* bed. She'd spent enough time in her own narrow bed to last her a lifetime, and where else was she going to go, Archer's vast bedroom? Not if she wanted to keep from throwing up.

There was just one problem, she thought, opening her eyes to the murky darkness. Lying naked in his sheets effectively stripped away whatever defenses she had left. She was the very essence of vulnerability where she lay, and her choice was simple. Leave his bed, and all uncomfortable thoughts of him, or stay where she was and accept things.

She wasn't moving.

All right, she thought. *Let's look at this from a practical standpoint.* Her reaction to him was completely logical—it would have been odd if she hadn't responded. A, he was gorgeous in his lean-hipped, clever kind of way. B, even if he hadn't actually offered her a way out of this mess, his appearance on the island had been a catalyst for change, and it was normal to feel grateful. C, he was . . . sexually capable. He had aroused and then satisfied her more than anyone she'd ever been with, but she could blame her long abstinence for that. Besides, wasn't danger an aphrodisiac?

E . . . or was she on D? Anyway, he was the first and only person who knew the truth about her, that she could walk, that she was filled with fury, not forlorn love for Archer. The very thought of that made her ill, but she'd been playing her part so well for the past few years that a lesser woman might even start to believe it.

So why else was she so infatuated with the man? He'd given her a gun, then taken it away from her, putting her in danger, but then returned it, and it had to qualify as the best present, under the circumstances, in the history of present giving. His light mockery annoyed and aroused her. He was a smart man, and not a sociopath, and she'd always had a weakness for smart. He'd stood up to Archer for her, the first person ever to do so, and he'd succeeded. He'd kissed her when she thought she'd never be kissed again. He'd held her when she shook and wept. He had wickedly clever hands, and she wanted . . .

Damn. Erotic fantasies had no place in this bed, she thought, moving beneath the sheets. She had to stop thinking about him, about his body, the smoothness of his skin over taut muscles, the taste of him in her mouth, the warmth of his body against hers, the . . .

"Oh, fucking hell!" she said out loud in total disgust. The more she fought it, the more power it had over her. She might as well accept the fact that she had a . . . a crush on him. Like a lovesick teenager.

She tried that notion on for size, but it didn't feel right. There was no fluttering in her heart when she saw him, no worrying about what he thought of her. He probably disliked her as much as she disliked him. Which was monumental, of near-nemesis proportions, and . . .

There's a thin line between love and hate. Where did that come from? And how stupid was that—if you loved someone, you cared about him, worried about him, wanted to do things for him . . . you loved him. If you hated them, you wanted them dead. Very simple and mathematical.

There was an easy way to put it in perspective, she told herself, rolling over in the bed. The mattress was perfect, neither too hard nor too soft, the sheets were like smooth silk, and she couldn't get comfortable.

Love was sacrificing your own good for others. It was about compromise, about letting go. If someone wasn't getting off this island alive, and it was up to her to choose, would she choose Mal or herself?

On the face the answer was easy. She'd fought long and hard to survive—there was no way she was giving up now. She hadn't killed anyone just yet—unless she'd accidentally offed Dr. Chekowsky— but Malcolm had. She was basically a good person, determined to do the moral thing within the ruthless confines of the Committee. She doubted the same thing could be said of Malcolm. He wasn't evil, but he certainly wasn't good.

She'd been a complete idiot, surprising considering the time she'd spent in the State Department. The Committee was responsible for some very bad things. Collateral damage kind of things. Innocents killed. Stable governments destroyed. Bad people getting their way. If Mal were to die, his death wouldn't have any impact on her life. Once she got off this island, she was never going to see him again anyway.

If she ever had to make some kind of Sophie's choice and decide whether she or Mal survived, there was no question. She closed her eyes, picturing a firing squad aimed at the two of them, and only one of them going down, riddled with bullets. No, her choice of who would live was simple.

Malcolm Gunnison.

"Stupid bitch," she said out loud, disgusted with herself. But the bottom line was that it mattered. Whether she ever saw him again or not, she needed to know he was still alive, was still being a pain in someone's ass. She tried to talk herself out of it—picturing him in bed with all the other women who would follow, picturing his snark and mockery. He was the one who should get the bullets, not her.

But she couldn't. She couldn't imagine living when he was dead—it was that simple. She couldn't even blame Stockholm syndrome—he wasn't the one who imprisoned her. If she were the fool she'd once been, she'd say she'd fallen in love with the bastard. But of course she hadn't—you don't fall in love that quickly, that easily, especially with an SOB like Mal. There was no such thing as soul mates, and just because her entirely fucked-up instincts told her he was the one was . . . was . . . insanity. Once she got away from here, she'd be much more sensible.

But right then she lay in his bed and touched herself beneath the sheets and longed for him with every bit of her being. Maybe, just for tonight, she could be in love with him. There was no one to know, no one to witness, no one to pass judgment. She could allow herself that much.

Tomorrow she'd be sensible. And if he ended up in front of a firing squad, she would give the order to fire.

<hr/>

It took him longer to cross the island than Mal expected. Trees were down everywhere, some uprooted, some snapped in half, and he tried to remember if there were any large ones near the house. Had Sophie stayed in her room like a sensible human being, or had she tried to take off the first chance she got? He hoped to hell not. If she had, she might have been one of those unrecognizable bodies bobbing in the waves. Archer MacDonald had already miscalculated, leaving too late, and they'd been hours ahead of any possible time Sophie could have set out. If she'd gone, she was dead, and the sooner he accepted that fact the better.

But he didn't have to accept any facts until they were staring him in the face. He moved as fast as he could through the debris, but the heavy rain and wind kept his pace to not much more than a crawl, and the meager daylight beyond the clouds didn't help. She was not going to be dead. He was sure of it. He'd know if she'd been an idiot and taken a boat out and drowned. Well, of course she was an idiot, absolutely fearless when she should be hiding in a closet, but she wasn't stupid.

The house was at a much lower point on the island than the sugar mill, which was still standing tall. How high had the waves risen? Were they going to get any higher? He couldn't imagine them reaching the second floor of the house, but if everyone else had left the island, Sophie was unlikely to stay in her room, and storm-driven waves could rise fast.

No, she'd be fine. He had good instincts—he had to—but he never treated them like gospel. And in fact, it wasn't his instincts that told him she wasn't dead. It was something else, something indefinable, as if there'd be a hollow place somewhere inside him if she were gone.

Ridiculous, he thought, wiping the rain out of his eyes and plowing onward, shoving branches out of his way. And why the fuck did he care? He'd been ready to leave her on the island and let the Committee sort her out. He was going to put in a good word for her, despite the fact that she'd done everything she could to get in his way. He didn't know whether it would be up to Madsen or James Bishop to decide what to do with her, but both were reasonable. He had little doubt they'd bring her back to the States and resettle her. In the end it hadn't really been her fault that the mission had become such a clusterfuck.

For some goddamned reason he was worried about her. Again, that was the problem—he couldn't afford to think about anyone but the mission and his own safety, and his safety came second. At least he'd accomplished the first half of the job. Archer MacDonald lay crumpled at the bottom of a cliff, though at this point the rising tide could have very easily carried his body out to sea. He still had to find Chekowsky and deal with him—at least he'd gotten a name out of Archer during the rough trip back to the island—but that didn't give him much of an advantage. As soon as he was sure Sophie was safe and taken care of, he could cut her out of his life.

He looked up, squinting through the pounding rain, and saw the great bulk of the old plantation house ahead of him in the distance. It was still in one piece, and there was no water surrounding it, though the rising tide might make it there soon. There were no lights on, but that was to be expected. He doubled his efforts, sprinting across the field, deftly avoiding the mess of tree limbs and branches that the storm had brought down.

He didn't bother trying to be quiet as he climbed onto the wide veranda, and he half-expected the front doors to be locked, but they opened easily, and he stepped in out of the downpour, leaning against them.

It was warm and dry in there, though his wet, clammy clothes were making him want to shudder. There were candles on the coffee table in front of the smothering sofa of doom—most of them had burned out but two were still glowing. He pushed away and moved over to the couch, thinking he'd find Sophie asleep on the treacherous piece of furniture.

She wasn't there. He glanced at the table—it looked as if she'd done nothing more than gone to the kitchen and brought food back. There were three different plates with nothing but crumbs left on them, two wineglasses, two empty glass Coke bottles, and an empty bottle of a really wonderful cabernet. If she'd downed all that she must be upstairs, sound asleep.

With a sigh he piled up the plates and glasses and carried them out to the kitchen. There was no second bottle of wine, so he made do with a Corona—Archer wouldn't be needing them anymore. He knew he should eat something, but he was too damned tired to feel any interest in food. He drank down the beer in four gulps, set the bottle down, and reached for his belt, dumping his wet clothes on the slate floor in the kitchen.

He'd hoped that the soaking rain would wash the salt spray off his nude body, but he still felt sticky. The power was off, and he had no idea whether the water depended on electricity. He wasn't in the mood to experiment, so he simply went out into the tiny kitchen courtyard to stand there and let Mother Nature wash him down. The hard pellets of rain slammed against his body, and for a moment he shivered, then controlled it. He needed a nice warm bed. He wanted a nice warm body, Sophie's body, to wrap around, but that was a very bad idea.

He tripped on Sophie's wheelchair on his way back in, and he shoved it out of the way, then paused. What the hell was that doing there? Was there someone else on the island? It had looked as if Archer had sent everyone away, but maybe he'd left someone behind.

He froze, as the unacceptable flooded into his mind, and once there, he couldn't get it out. Had Archer left someone behind to kill her? Anything was possible. Otherwise what the hell was her wheelchair doing in the kitchen? In front of the door to the wine cellar, he realized, and if anything he felt even colder than before.

If someone was going to hide a body, the wine cellar would be the perfect place. Getting rid of a corpse in what amounted to a hurricane was problematic, to say the least, but leaving it around tended to get unpleasant. The cellar would be naturally cool, keeping decomposition to a minimum. He kept his thoughts businesslike, straightforward. If she was down there, it was too late to do anything about it. No one would dare make a mistake a second time.

He knew he ought to go down there and look. There was a combination lock on the door, and he needed to find something to cut through it. Whether or not he wanted to see Sophie's body, he had to find out.

Corpse, he reminded himself, using the word deliberately. If, despite his instinct and ridiculously romantic imaginings, she was dead, then the sooner he accepted it, the better. People died all the time. Sophie Jordan had no family left, no one who cared about her. No one to mourn her.

He realized he was shivering again, and he broke out of his momentary trance. He needed to search the rest of the house to make certain she wasn't hiding somewhere, and then he'd need the proper tools to break in. He was going to need some clothes on first—he never would have imagined feeling so cold on a tropical island. So cold it felt as if he'd never get warm again.

He moved through the living room, pinching out the last two candles. Her killer would still be around—there was no way to get off the island in this weather, and whoever had been here wouldn't have been gone long. He didn't feel like facing the man he would torture and kill, very slowly, before he got clothes on.

He looked up, and the door to her room was closed. A faint spark of hope went through him, and he went up the marble steps three at a time, pushing open her door, ready to annoy her.

The bed was empty. He sagged against the doorjamb, unmoving for a moment, as that hollow feeling he'd imagined started growing inside him. There was nowhere else she would be on the island—the only place she would have gone was high ground near the sugar mill, and he'd seen no sign of her. He was going to have to go down into that claustrophobic wine cellar that Archer had showed off earlier in the week and find her lifeless body.

He shook himself. It wasn't like him to jump to conclusions, but he was cold, exhausted, and his emotions had been haywire from the moment he looked into Sophie's huge brown eyes. And he'd been fool enough to think he no longer had any emotions.

Feeling numb, he moved away from the bedroom, pushing open his own door in search of clothes and calm.

There she was, her hair spread on his pillow, sleeping peacefully. He stayed very still, watching until he could see the rise and fall of her breathing. She was fine.

There were leaves and flowers on the wet floor—either she had opened the door or it had blown open. It didn't matter. He could smell the scent of gardenias and could even pick up the soft sound of her breathing, despite the noise of the wind and rain overhead. He glanced down at his hardening cock, and he wanted to laugh. Five minutes ago he was in the depths of despair and now he was back to being a horny bastard.

Well, "depths of despair" is a little too dramatic, he reminded himself. He might be a little conflicted when it came to her, but he was hardly in . . . well, he was hardly . . . he couldn't think of an acceptable phrase. He simply hadn't wanted her to be dead—for some reason that had been extremely important.

So she was back to being a pain in his ass and almost irresistible. Archer was dead—Mal no longer had any excuse to touch her, other than the strongest one: he wanted to. If he had any sense, he'd close the door and head back to her room, sleep in her bed.

If he had any sense, he'd never have touched her in the first place. *Face it*, he told himself. *You've got a thing for the girl. The more you fight it the worse it'll be. Get in there and fuck the shit out of her and you'll be able to walk away.*

Silently he moved into the room, coming around to the far side of the bed, staring down at her. A good operative would have known he was there, he thought, and a moment later her eyes opened, those warm brown eyes that were the best thing in the world.

She just looked at him, not moving. "You're back," she said in a low, sleep-husky voice, stating the obvious.

"I'm back," he agreed, being just as predictable. "Why are you in my bed? Something wrong with yours?" It wasn't the most welcoming of statements, but his natural wariness had kicked in.

She opened that gorgeous mouth of hers to say something, then seemed to think better of it, as tension stiffened her body. "Is Archer with you?"

Just to be an asshole he gave an exaggerated look around him. "I don't see him anywhere, do you?"

Her shoulders didn't relax. Bare shoulders, which meant she was probably naked between his sheets. His cock got even harder at the thought, but he didn't change his expression.

"Is he on the island?"

He should take pity on the edge of fear in her voice. "Nope," he said. By now Archer's body would be washed out to sea for the fish to nibble away at, but he wasn't ready to offer that information.

"Is he coming back soon?" Her voice was marginally less nervous.

He glanced toward the French doors and the storm raging outside. "Not likely." Years of training were hard to break, and he couldn't bring himself to tell her the truth, not when he was still unsure of her.

Then again, he'd learned not to trust anyone, and life had born his skepticism out. The woman in front of him could be a treacherous snake or an unwitting temptress. He had his own opinion, but that wasn't enough to go on. Not yet.

"Okay," she said, and for some reason the nervousness hadn't left her. "I'm sorry I usurped your territory. I should be in my own bed."

He didn't respond to that one—she was just asking for flattery. She had to know he found her almost irresistible. "You still haven't told me why you're here. Is your bed made of nails or something? I wouldn't put it past Archer."

"It's a hospital bed—they're made to be uncomfortable," she said with a grimace.

"So like Goldilocks you decided to check out the competition and this one was just right?" He was mocking her again—trying to keep her at arm's length when he wanted nothing more than to pull her into them.

She just looked at him, and he wondered what kind of lie she was working up to. It would be a complicated, fully believable one, if he were even the slightest bit gullible.

Her big brown eyes were deceptively vulnerable, and she licked her lips nervously. Taking in a deep breath, she blurted, "It felt safe."

"Why?"

"It felt like you."

Chapter Nineteen

Sophie had no idea why she'd said such a stupid thing. Maybe because she was tired of lying. Maybe because he was standing there stark nude and obviously aroused and it was all wrong. Men usually looked silly without their clothes on. There was nothing the slightest bit silly about Mal.

And then, when she'd essentially laid her heart and her vulnerability on the line, he said absolutely nothing. He looked at her as she huddled naked beneath his sheets, as if trying to read her thoughts, and she realized he still didn't trust her. Not on any level.

When she'd first heard him come in, she kept her eyes closed, pretending to be asleep in case it wasn't Malcolm. It wasn't until he moved close, silent as a cat, that she was certain, and a slow joy had filled her.

That joy had vanished now in shame and uncertainty. There wasn't any way she could salvage her pride, but then, that had been MIA for years. Dignity was overrated as well. She plastered on one of her fake smiles, the one she perfected for Archer, as she tried to figure out her easiest way to exit.

"You must be exhausted," she said in her best garden-party, social hostess voice. "I should let you get some sleep." She started to sit up, clutching the sheets to her chest. Why the fuck hadn't she put on some clothes before she'd gotten in his bed? She knew the truth, though. She'd wanted to feel Mal's sheets all around her body, and she didn't want to put on any of the whore's lingerie that Archer kept her supplied with.

He still said nothing, not moving. She could ask him to turn around, she could wrap the loose sheet around her like a toga, but she wasn't going to bother. She'd lost her dignity when she'd told him she was there for him and he hadn't responded. She wasn't going to show an ounce more vulnerability.

She sat up, pushing the covers away, and climbed out of the bed, not giving a damn about her own nudity. She was still slightly tipsy from the wine, she realized. Just enough that she didn't give a shit. She shook her tangled hair out of her face, squared her shoulders, and started toward the door as he stood there, making no move to stop her. It wasn't until she put her hand on the doorknob that he spoke, his voice low and rumbling.

"Where do you think you're going?"

She could stalk naked from the room in dignified outrage—she couldn't stand around having a civil conversation. She doubted she could do anything civil with this man.

You can do anything you have to, she reminded herself, and turned, her social smile in place. "Leaving you to get some well-deserved rest," she said lightly.

"You're not going anywhere."

She stared at him like an idiot, and then her temper reasserted itself. "I'll go anywhere I damned please," she snapped.

"Tomorrow," he said.

"It already is tomorrow."

"Don't be technical. After we get some sleep. And we won't be sleeping for a while."

She was still so fixated on his seeming rejection of her that she didn't understand. "What are we going to be doing?"

He tilted his head, giving her a pitying, you must be kidding look, and realization flooded her. She didn't know whether she was relieved or furious at the game he was playing. Probably both. "But Archer's not here. We don't have to convince him."

"Archer wasn't out on the balcony when you went down on me either," he pointed out lazily.

It was a good thing the power was out, she thought, as heat flooded her cheeks. She wasn't nearly as good at hiding her reactions from this man as she was from Archer and his henchmen.

"Get back in my bed, Sophie," he said, his soft voice not belying the steel beneath it.

She was starting to feel cold while at the same time heat was building inside her. "Do I have any choice in the matter?"

"You always have a choice. But you want it and I want it, and it would be a waste of time to pretend otherwise. Life is short, and the good things are few and far between. You don't get too many chances at them, and you'd be a fool to ignore it when it may not come again."

Cryptic and to the point, she thought, discomfited. "That's quite a seduction technique," she said caustically. "You get a lot of girls with that line, do you?"

"I'm not seducing you. We're well past that point. Get in my bed before I put you there."

So much for free will, she thought. It didn't matter that that was exactly where she wanted to be. She'd been Archer's victim—she wouldn't be his.

"Make me," she said, defiant. The moment the words were out of her mouth she wanted to groan.

"Glad to oblige," he said, stalking toward her.

She was just deciding whether to run when she found herself scooped into his arms and then tossed back on the bed, and he was on top of her, pinning her down. She didn't struggle, didn't argue. She simply looked into his face, his clear green eyes, waiting.

He didn't move either. A sudden hush had come over the room, despite the storms raging outside. They simply looked at each other, and Sophie could feel her body soften beneath his, welcoming his touch, reveling in the feel of his smooth, sleek skin touching almost every part of hers, and she wanted to melt into him, and then a shiver ran across her body, followed by another.

"Jesus Christ!" she said. "You're freezing." Without thinking she pushed at him, and he landed on his back beside her in the bed as she started pulling the covers around him, up to his neck. "What did you do, pour ice cubes over your body?" His skin was cold to the touch, when she was used to heat pouring from him. She tried to tuck the covers around him, to warm him up, but he simply batted them away and pulled her body against his.

"The ocean's a cold place tonight," he said. "And you'll warm me up faster than anything else."

She was too caught up in worry to respond to that. "Why the hell were you walking around the house naked if you were so cold? I realize there's no chance of a hot shower, but you should have at least . . ."

He reached behind her neck and pulled her down to his mouth, stopping her spate of words. His mouth was cool and delicious, tasting of the ocean, and she sank into his kiss, her body warming, heating his. She tried to rub his muscled arms to get the circulation going, but he caught her wrists in his hands and pulled them away. "That's not the way to warm me up, sweetheart," he growled against her mouth. He rolled her beneath him again, and she could feel the heat coming back to him. His cock was still iron hard, pressed against her stomach, and she frowned.

"How can you have an erection when you're so cold?" she said, distracted. "I thought being cold disabled men."

He laughed, and there was no darkness in it this time. "Sweetheart, if you're around I could have a boner in Antarctica," he said.

She looked at him in surprise. "Is that a compliment?"

"Take it as you want."

"Because if it is, it's the first nice thing you've ever said to me," she went on, trying to ignore the treacherous need that was building inside her. She wanted, needed the words, but in a few more moments she wouldn't care what he said to her, as long as he kept touching her.

He moved his mouth down to the side of her neck, his teeth against her smooth skin. "I've said other nice things to you," he said absently, clearly not caring.

"Name one."

He laughed again. "You are such a woman," he said.

"Were you confused about that fact?" she countered, and then she felt his cool hand slip down her stomach, between her legs. "I guess not."

"I guess not," he echoed wryly. "And I have a very good idea." He was barely touching her, and she was ready to leap out of her skin with need.

"You do?"

"I've been wanting to taste you for days," he said softly, moving down her body.

Oh, God. She'd never cared much for this part of things, particularly when the men always seemed so pleased with themselves about it. They probably wouldn't do it at all if they didn't think it guaranteed them a blow job.

But she'd already gone down on Mal. In fact, she wanted to again. The crazy thing about that was she'd liked it. More than liked it. "I don't think . . ." she began to protest.

"That's for the best," he said, sliding his palms along her inner thighs, pulling them apart. "Thinking is highly overrated."

Oh, God. She could feel his breath warm between her legs, his fingers sliding in the dampness that seemed to have come out of nowhere, and then she felt his tongue against her clit, nothing more than a light, teasing touch, and she stiffened. "You don't have to do this," she said somewhat desperately.

"Oh, yes I do. Try and stop me." He did it again, and a ripple of pleasure went through her body. She hadn't felt *that* before—and it had been a long, long time. Archer had never . . .

He lifted his head, looking at her. "What are you thinking about? You suddenly stiffened."

"Archer," she confessed.

His response was impressively obscene, and he surged up her body, pinning her there, cupping her face with both hands and holding her still while he stared down into her eyes. "Archer doesn't exist," he said with grim certainty. "There's just you and me in this bed. Do you need me to prove it to you?"

"I think you are," she said in a small voice.

"Then stop remembering Archer. Lie back and think of England, Sophie," he said, sliding down again, and when he put his mouth on her this time she arched up in the bed in surprise. It wasn't supposed to feel *that* good. She knew from using her own hands that a tongue wouldn't have enough strength or friction, but she felt the first stirrings of reaction, and she pushed into him.

She knew he smiled against her. He slid a finger inside her, then two, and she almost jumped off the bed. She put her hands down to clutch his shoulders, and he was warm now, blazingly warm, as he licked her, everywhere, using his mouth, his lips, his teeth. And his tongue . . . *Oh my God, his tongue.* His fingers were pumping in and out, and she knew she couldn't come this way, but damn, it felt good, it felt wonderful, it felt like . . .

With no warning at all the orgasm slammed into her, and she clutched at his shoulders, digging in, a low, keening wail coming from the back of her throat as wave after wave of reaction flowed through her. She started to shove one hand against her mouth to silence herself, but he must have had some preternatural sense of what she was doing, because he reached up and yanked her hand away, putting it back on his shoulder. "I want to hear you scream," he said in a low, tantalizing whisper. "I want you to scream so loud they hear you all the way down to the Caribbean."

Oh, God, he had slid three fingers into her now, and she was inco-
herent as she shuddered against him, drowning in sensation. It lasted
forever; each time the waves slowed he did something with his mouth or
his fingers that would make it start again, and she was sobbing, begging
him, not knowing if she wanted more or needed him to stop.

But he knew. He pulled away from her, surging up her sweat-slick
body, and he was hot too, his damp skin sliding against hers, as he
kissed her, deep and hard. She tasted herself on his mouth, she tasted
the ocean, she tasted Mal, and God, if he kept kissing her like that she
was going to come again, and she wasn't sure her body could handle it.

His hard, hard hands were gentle on her as he pushed her legs apart,
and she felt him there—big, strong. He was taking the tip of his cock
and rubbing it against her, around her, spreading all the endless mois-
ture, and she lifted her hips, waiting for him, breathless, needing him.

He dropped his head to look down at her, but he said nothing as
he began to push, slowly, filling her, their eyes locked in silent commu-
nication. He stilled, giving her a moment to get used to him, but she
ignored his steadiness, needing him, now, and he pulled out, pushing
into her again, slow and hard, filling her. She wanted to weep. She'd
been empty for so long, all her life, it seemed, and now she was whole.

She wrapped her legs around his slim hips, her fingers tight on his
shoulders as he moved inside her, steady, deep, and she wanted more,
needed more. This was like nothing she'd ever felt before, it was sex, it
was fucking, it was making love. Her heart seemed to flow through her
body, into his, a total joining that beckoned her, frightened her, almost
destroyed her. He was so big it hurt, a sweet pleasure-pain that simply
moved her deeper into this dark, magic, scary place where there was
no Sophie, no Mal, just them, sliding together in the murky light, and
she felt another orgasm building inside her, deep and powerful, and
she knew if she climaxed her heart would explode, and she didn't care,
didn't care at all.

Conscious thought had disappeared. This was a simple animal need brought to a different level, something almost surreal, and her body convulsed. She felt like she was floating, awash in endless sensations, with nothing to tether her to safety. All she could do was cling to him, eyes closed, waiting, until he shoved in deep, so hard she cried out, and she could feel him pulsing inside her, life inside her, and she was gone, into the night and the darkness and the magic, into Malcolm, part of him forever.

Damn, she was crying, she realized some endless time later. She rarely cried, no matter how bad the pain, how cruel the treatment, how much she'd screwed up, how empty and lonely she felt. For the first time in memory she was no longer alone, and now she finally cried. It was ridiculous, she thought, fighting it. She wasn't going to cry over some damned man.

A little sob broke through, and she tried to cover it with a cough. Mal had pulled out, collapsing beside her, and she hoped to God he was asleep. If she just managed to stop crying, he'd stay that way, and she dug her fingernails into her palms, remembering that someone had told her it was a way to stop unwanted tears.

That person had lied.

She tried to think of happy things, like the fields outside in bright sunlight, the color of the sea, the music that she missed so much. It was making things worse, so she quickly started envisioning depressing things, like Archer and the possible corpse in the basement. It didn't work. Shoving her fist into her mouth, she tried to stifle it, but it was already too late, Mal had reached out for her and while she tried to bat him away he wasn't having any of it. He simply tucked her against him, stroking her hair away from her face, his lips against her ear, murmuring soft, comforting things that made no sense.

She wanted to let go completely, to sob in his arms, weep until she was too tired to move, to speak, cry herself out and then sleep for days. But she didn't, couldn't, trust him. Somehow she managed to swallow her tears, letting him hold her, comfort her, concentrating on the sensations of his skin, his touch, his smell. And she was the one who fell asleep.

Mal lay still in the shadowed room, holding Sophie. He should slip away, he thought. Use the shower, head downstairs, and catch a few *z*'s on that quicksand of a couch. The longer he stayed in bed with her the harder it was to leave.

He should never have fucked her again. The other times had been hot, fast, random. This had been something else, something almost otherworldly, and it scared the hell out of him. He couldn't shake the feeling that this woman, what happened in this bed, was a potential life changer, and he liked his life just fine. He wasn't going to put himself in anyone's hands, particularly not a woman who'd betrayed the Committee and had been fool enough to fall in love with a monster like Archer MacDonald.

There were a million excuses. She'd been too young, untrained, Archer was notoriously charming—it should have been little wonder that she'd been compromised.

But she wasn't just anyone they'd picked up from a temp agency. She'd worked for the State Department, the CIA. She had a formidable intellect and an instinct for the business, plus an innate gift for the physical demands. She'd been sensible and low-key with her emotional involvements—there'd been nothing to hint that she might suddenly lose the brain she'd been given and drink Archer's Kool-Aid.

He didn't trust her. Didn't want to trust her. So why was he lying curled around her, skin to skin? And why did that feel so right?

Feelings weren't worth pig shit. He was tired; he'd killed a man tonight, which always made him feel . . . off. Sex was the best way to lose that feeling, and sex with Sophie was, for whatever reason, the best sex he could remember having. Not with tricks or acrobatics or tantric positions. There was something between them, something that so far had been impossible to define. Once he figured it out he could let go, but he hadn't made much progress in that direction.

She smelled like flowers and sex, and he realized with disgust he was hard again. He wasn't going to do anything about it—she needed her sleep. He needed some too—he had to rest before he could figure out how to deal with the rest of his problem. Chekowsky was out there somewhere, still in possession of the chemical weapon. Archer had found out the man had decamped with all his research records, possibly in search of the highest bidder himself, which left Mal's job only half finished. He didn't have time to think about pussy.

But as much as he'd like to define Sophie as simply that, he knew that was much too disingenuous. If she were simply a good fuck he wouldn't feel so twisted up inside over her. He wasn't used to fussing over women—he steered clear of the complicated ones.

Get up, you stupid bastard, he told himself, not moving. He heard the change in her breathing, the slight hitch, and he knew he should slide out of the bed. He also knew he wasn't going anywhere.

She turned in his arms, when he'd expected, half-hoped she'd leap out of the bed. She slid her hands up his chest, putting her arms around his neck. There were the salt tracks of dried tears mixing with the faint freckles on her cheeks, but she looked at him, and smiled. It was small, soft, tentative, and he felt something crack inside him.

He brought his head down and kissed her, slow, nibbling kisses, the seduction she'd complained about before. He did nothing with his hands, simply used his mouth, kissing her eyelids, the sides of her mouth, the freckle-splashed cheekbones, her lips—God, her lips— and she was growing hot, restless beneath him. He kissed the side of her neck, her earlobe, and then he used his teeth on that soft flesh. Her shiver of reaction made him even harder. He was losing his mind, and he couldn't afford to, not when he had so many things left to do.

He pushed her onto her back, planning to shove inside her, take her quickly and get it over with, but as he moved above her he stopped, looking down into her eyes. And then she said the worst thing she could possibly say.

"I love you."

He froze.

She looked almost as horrified as he was at her words, and she quickly scrambled to explain. "I mean, I don't really. Of course not, you're a cold-blooded bastard. It's just that I've been alone so long, and there's no denying you're really, really, really good in bed, and it's no wonder that I've gotten a little confused. As soon as I get out of here and away from you, I'll come to my senses and you don't need to worry, but in the meantime"—she was running out of breath—"I love you."

"Oh, Christ," he muttered weakly. He didn't need this. "I'm supposed to take Archer's place as your lord and protector? Let me tell you one thing, sweetheart. Between him and me there isn't much difference. I may work for the good guys, he's one of the bad ones, but we're both just as cold-blooded and ruthless."

"I know."

"So you get off on being treated like shit?" he said, unaccountably disappointed in her. "They should have figured that out before they even brought you into the program."

"I don't. Archer was a mistake, made when I was a vulnerable girl."

"And what am I—the best thing since sliced toast?" he shot back. *Why am I still hard?* he thought. Those three words were better than saltpeter at deflating a libido, yet he was still going strong. "I'm not better than your husband. Don't look at me like some starry-eyed twit—I'm a rat bastard."

The soft smile that curved her mouth drove him crazy with the need to wipe it off her face, kiss it off her face. "I know you are," she said, agreeing far too readily. "I have lousy taste in men—at least we agree on that one. Don't worry—I'll get over it."

"I'm not going to worry about it," he said in a rough voice, his insides roiling. "I don't give a shit."

He expected her to shrink back, pull away from him, hell, burst into the tears that had startled him a short while ago. She didn't strike him as the kind of woman who cried, but then, he'd never pegged her as the kind of idiot to fall in love with a man like him. She didn't even blink at his harsh words.

He started to pull away from her. "I've got things to do," he said.

She slid her hand down his chest, lower, to wrap around his rigid dick, and it took everything he had to still a moan of sheer animal pleasure. "I know," she said, sliding her hand down with just the perfect pressure.

He felt a slow-burning rage fill him. She'd screwed up everything. She was supposed to be an easy shag, deserving anything he tossed her way, and she was forcing herself into his life, into his thoughts, into his heart . . . Screw that, he didn't have a heart. Hadn't since he'd started to work for the Committee.

He reached down, caught her hand, and pulled it away from him, shoving her onto her back. He was going to leave her there, wet and wanting, he was going to turn his back on her and walk away . . .

The hell he was. He shoved her legs apart, moving between them, and thrust his cock into her so hard she cried out, not in pain but in fierce satisfaction. She was everything he wanted—she was nothing but trouble. He reached up and pulled her hands from his shoulders, slamming them into the mattress and holding them there as he surged into her, deeper and deeper. He was rough, but she met him, thrust for thrust, moving with him, taking him deep inside, the walls of her sex milking him as the first orgasm hit her, and then the second, and then she was lost in one endless convulsion as he shoved into her, over and over and over again, their slick bodies sliding against each other, her teeth on his neck, biting down hard, and then he was coming, losing it all inside her, caught in the tight grasp of her cunt.

He was still hard when he pulled out of her, rolled out of bed, and headed for the bathroom, and he knew if she joined him in the shower, he'd take her again. He couldn't be around her and not want her, no matter what she said or did. He had to get rid of her, now, before any more damage was done.

The water was cold, of course. He'd forgotten about the power, but the shower seemed to work anyway, and he figured it must be some kind of gravity-fed system. He didn't mind the cold anymore—he wanted to be icy, frigid, distant. He rubbed soap over his body, trying to ignore his prick, and rinsed clean, waiting for Sophie, knowing she'd follow him, knowing she couldn't resist any more than he could.

But the door never opened. He turned off the water, listening, but there was no sound from the room beyond. Grabbing a towel, he dried off, then wrapped it around his waist. Not that he was trying to preserve Sophie's modesty, but he was better off without his erection waving in the wind.

The bed was empty. The door to the balcony was open, and he realized the rain had stopped. It looked like late afternoon, a reason-able-enough guess, and he wondered where the hell Sophie had run to. Was she sulking in her room? He should go check on her . . . no, he should not. He needed to go downstairs and try to get word to the Committee that he needed a pickup. He was going to have to start all over again with Chekowsky, and time was of the essence. At least Archer was gone—no matter how bad Chekowsky was, he couldn't be as irritat-ing as Archer's cheerful malice.

He dressed quickly, not bothering with the formal wear that was such a part of Malcolm Gunnison, making do with jeans and a loose shirt. There was no sound from the other side of the wall—maybe she'd fallen asleep. It was more than likely—he'd done his best to wear her out in his bed, and when he left her sitting there, she had a slightly fragile look to her.

Sophie Jordan isn't the slightest bit fragile, he reminded himself. She could fend for herself—he didn't have to worry about her. She'd be fine. Just fine.

He unearthed his hidden PDA and messaged headquarters for a pickup, then headed downstairs, and he was almost at the bottom when the lights came on again, the fans starting up, machinery from the kitchen and outside providing a soft hum. To his surprise Sophie was already down there, dressed in jeans herself, no longer those flowing dresses to hide her supposedly useless legs. She was looking at him, a still, quiet expression on her face, and after a moment's hesitation he walked into the living room.

He went straight to the small bar Archer had set up, pouring himself a scotch, neat. It kept him from having to look at her while he spoke, and he needed a drink. "I'm making arrangements to get you off the island," he said, turning.

She'd skipped the sofa, taking the chair opposite, her long legs dangling over the side. She'd taken a shower herself—her hair was wet around her well-scrubbed face, and she looked like a child. But she wasn't, he reminded himself. She was an operative, a failed one, to be sure, but dangerous nonetheless.

"That's very kind of you," she said with exquisite courtesy. "What are you going to be doing?"

"I've got more work to do. Just because Archer's dead doesn't mean my job is done."

"What?" Her voice was a rough whisper, and he fought off his guilt. He should have told her sooner, but he'd been too busy losing himself between her legs.

"I forgot to tell you," he said, taking a sip of the whiskey while he waited to see whether she believed him. He couldn't tell. "We landed together on the island. We had a disagreement on the old wooden steps up from the beach by the sugar mill."

"Those steps are dangerous," she said, still staring at him in shock. "They're about ready to fall into the ocean."

"They *have* fallen into the ocean," he corrected her. "With your late husband."

"He fell?"

"With a little help from me," Mal said.

For a moment she said nothing, as if considering his words. She looked more dazed than relieved. "You're certain he's dead?" she said. "You saw his body?"

"It was pitch black with heavy rain and I was clinging to the very top of the stairs. I wasn't in a position to go down and check for a pulse. Trust me, he wouldn't have survived a fall like that."

"You don't know Archer," she said glumly.

"You don't know me."

She reacted like he'd hit her, but a second later her face was calm. "No, I suppose I don't," she said quietly. "How long will it be before you never have to see me again?"

He didn't bother to correct her. She needed to get away from him if she was going to have any kind of life at all. She'd already given up too many years to the Committee, just as he had. She needed to get away from all of them, but most of all him. He was pretty sure he'd managed to convince her of that.

"As soon as they can get here. It looks like the storm has passed, so it shouldn't take too long."

"Lovely," she said. "So if he's dead, what else do you have to do?"

"Find the man who designed RU48. Problem is, I have no fucking clue where he is, and I don't know how long it's going to take me to find him."

She was giving him an odd look. "What's his name?"

"Chekowsky. I'm sure you heard Archer talking about him."

"And if you found Chekowsky you'd leave when I did? With me?" Her voice was wary, and he had absolutely no idea what she was getting at.

He shook his head. "We're going different places."

She nodded. "In that case," she said, "try the wine cellar."

Chapter Twenty

The self-proclaimed rat bastard was looking at her like she'd lost her mind, Sophie thought with a wistful trace of triumph. She wasn't the complete loser he thought she was.

"What?" he thundered.

"Did you need him alive? Because I can't guarantee that. I drugged him with Vicodin—he was more gullible than you. He was unconscious in less than ten minutes. He was too heavy for me to drag, so I put him in the wheelchair and dropped him down into the wine cellar. There was a lot of breaking glass, so if the Vicodin didn't kill him, the broken wine bottles might have."

He was still staring at her in disbelief. "He can be dead," he said after a moment. "Just so long as no one else has him."

She shrugged. "If he survived he ought to be awake by now. Do you want to go see?"

"Do you know the combination?"

"How do you think I got him in there in the first place?" She headed into the kitchen, not waiting for him to follow her. She put her ear to the door, but there was no sound from the cellar. Maybe he really was dead. At that point she couldn't bring herself to care.

She was a fool, an idiot, even worse—she could have just kept her mouth shut and never embarrassed herself. What had she expected, protestations of undying love in return from the rat bastard? He didn't have it in him. She was an idiot to love someone like that, and she had the sincere hope that any irrational and inconvenient feeling she might have would disappear when she didn't have to look at him. It might take a while, but sooner or later she'd stop thinking about him. About the way his hands felt on her body. About the taste of him.

She slammed her fist against the door in sudden fury. "You alive down there, Dr. Chekowsky?"

No answer, but Mal was beside her, towering over her. She forgot how tall he was—she hadn't been used to standing beside anyone at all. "Turn on the light," she snapped, and bent down to the combination lock, twirling the dial expertly before slipping it free and opening the door.

There was no light down there, of course, but a quiet groan wafted up. She turned to Mal. "I guess he survived."

She couldn't read the look he gave her, and she didn't care. "We better bring him up," he said.

"What's this *we*?" she said caustically. "There's barely room for one person down there, much less three. And Dr. Chekowsky is no sylph."

Mal gave her a look of exasperation mixed with a grudging respect. "Okay, hold the door open so I don't get locked in."

She considered it for a moment. "Don't tempt me."

A moment later he scrambled down the stairs, and she could hear more moaning and the sound of broken glass. She stuck her head down into the darkness, unable to make out a thing. "Is he still in one piece?"

"Barely," Mal said, unmoved. "I'm going to get him to his feet and help him up the steps. You be there to catch him."

"Have you taken a good look at him?" she shot back.

"You put him down here, so you'll have to help get him out."

She pulled her head back out of the open doorway, frowning. For a moment she thought she'd heard something from the living room, but the wind had been making a racket for days. She turned back to the cellar. "Okay, push him up. But I can't promise I won't let him fall back on top of you, and you wouldn't like that one bit."

"Don't." The one word was warning enough, and she sighed. A moment later Dr. Chekowsky's head and shoulders appeared at the top of the stairs. He had a cut on his head, one that had bled liberally, and his beady little eyes managed to be unfocused and glaring at the same time.

"You bitch," he spat.

"Play nice, Dr. Chekowsky, or I won't help you out of there." It was an empty threat. In fact, she was relieved he was in relatively good shape. She reached down for him, braced herself, and hauled him up into the kitchen, dumping him in the wheelchair as Mal leapt up behind him. He looked at the man in the chair.

"You can't walk?" he said skeptically, and Sophie took the faint comfort that at least he was as abrupt with everyone, not just stupid women who said "I love you."

Chekowsky fumed, pushing his little body out of the chair. "I can walk," he said furiously, starting toward the door to the living room. "That terrible woman drugged me and then dumped me in that cellar," he announced, heading through the door with Mal by his side, Sophie taking up the tail end of their little procession. "And she's not even crippled."

"No, she isn't, is she?" said a smooth voice, and Sophie froze. Standing a few feet away from them was the ghost of her husband.

Chekowsky and Mal had halted as well, blocking her view, and she had a hard time looking around them. Archer was leaning against the sofa, looking like death warmed over. He was soaking wet, bruised and bloody, with the same insanely affable smile on his face, a gun in his hand. He was no longer so aristocratic looking—the storm had taken its toll on his patrician good looks. He was missing one of his impressive front teeth, and a trail of bloody footprints led from a set of French doors. She looked down and saw that one of his feet was soaked in red.

Archer pushed away from the sofa, moving across the room with a painful limp. Casually he put the gun under one arm as he poured himself a drink, much as Mal had done just a few minutes earlier. He took a sip, then beamed at them, repositioning the gun.

She was holding her breath, Sophie realized absently, and released it silently. She felt numb with shock, and she wanted to pinch herself to make certain she was awake, but she couldn't move. Of course he wasn't dead—hadn't she known it, deep inside? It was never going to be that easy. He was still alive, and if she were extremely lucky, he would kill her instead of inflicting more psychological and physical torture.

But he'd kill Mal as well, and suddenly her frozen muscles moved, and she edged into the room. She wasn't giving up.

"It takes a lot to kill me, baby," Archer said. "Do any of you have weapons on you, hmm? I really don't think we want a firefight in the living room, now do we? I'm already going to have to spend a fortune cleaning this place up from the storm damage. No? Excellent."

Sophie glanced over at the sofa, just out of reach. Her gun was still tucked in the cushions, and she wondered whether she'd have a chance in hell of getting to it before Archer put a bullet between her eyes. Who would he try to kill first, her or Mal? Probably whichever would cause the most pain, but she couldn't begin to guess at the way Archer's mind worked.

"What are you doing back there, Sophie?" her husband crooned, trying to peer behind the two men. "Come on out and let me see you. I hadn't realized there'd been a miraculous recovery."

Maybe it was going to be her. She started to move, but Mal immediately blocked her way. "I don't think you can kill us all, Archer," he said in a cold voice. "Not before one of us gets to you."

Archer laughed softly. "I must say, Malcolm, you did have me fooled, old man. I really believed your story—I'm impressed. I haven't been particularly trusting since my sweet wife betrayed me. But right now I'm more interested in what my esteemed colleague is doing here. I told you that we were coming to you, Dr. Chekowsky. Did you have a reason for disobeying my instructions?"

"I'm not your servant!" the man snapped. "The Chekowsky Solution was finished and ready to go, and I got tired of waiting for you. Don't worry, I brought everything with me."

"The Chekowsky Solution?" Archer echoed. "Oh, dear me, no." Before Sophie could realize what he was doing, he'd raised the gun and pulled the trigger. The doctor's head exploded, splattering her as the man went down, twitching in an ever-widening pool of blood until he finally went still. Part of his skull had been blown away, and Sophie's nausea increased. She jerked her eyes upward.

"Get back in the kitchen," Mal murmured beneath his breath. "Go out the back and run like hell."

"Oh, I really don't think so." Archer limped forward, coming closer to inspect the dead body. He looked back at her. "I suppose I shouldn't have killed the man—he still could have been of use, but I've had a trying day. As for you, baby, you lied to me, many times over. You don't think I'm going to let you get away with that, now do you?"

"You can't kill us both," Mal said, moving into the room. One hand was behind his back, signaling her to run, but that was the last thing she was going to do. Perhaps literally. She wasn't going to escape while Archer shot Malcolm.

She stayed with him, trying to move in front of him, but Mal simply caught her arm and shoved her behind him. "Stay put, damn you," he muttered.

"Oh, she never does what she's told—hadn't you realized that by now?" Archer said, having lost interest in the doctor's corpse. "And while she deserves to be punished for her duplicity, I'm thinking there are sides to her I have yet to explore. I might bring her back into the fold—Rachel didn't survive our unfortunate trip to the mainland, and I do like variety."

"You're not touching her," Mal said.

Archer was surveying the gun in his hand like it was a new toy, sniffing at the barrel, checking it from every angle. And then he turned his beatific smile on both of them. "What's it to you, old man? She's just part of the job. I'm still willing to discuss business with you, despite our little setback on the sea stairs, but we certainly can't let Sophie come between us."

"You're a sick fuck."

"Yes, I am," he said cheerfully. "I'm giving you a choice. I've got to kill one of you if I'm to keep my self-respect, but I'm perfectly willing to keep one of you alive. You for business, Sophie for pleasure, but I can't have it both ways. You decide."

Sophie stared at her husband from behind Mal's back. She needed to get to the sofa, find the Beretta. No one had to die but Archer, and damn did he have to die!

"You're not touching her," Mal said again.

"Well, there's our problem. If you're dead, you can't protect her from my villainous clutches. If she's dead, there's nothing to protect. I think you've solved the conundrum for me. Step out from behind him, Sophie. I'm afraid you drew the short straw. Move, or I'll shoot you through him. You saw what one of those bullets did to the good doctor's substantial brain—it won't have any problem going through his body to get to yours."

"Don't move," Mal said furiously, but Sophie was no longer listening. If she could buy them a few more moments, then Mal could take him, even without a gun. She didn't doubt for one moment that Archer would do exactly as he threatened, and he could make his move at any moment. Before Mal could stop her she darted out from behind him, moving toward the sofa on the off chance that Archer would miss.

For a nanosecond all was still. Archer was smiling at her, his mad, bulbous eyes red-rimmed and gleeful, and he brought the gun up, pointing it straight at her chest. She heard the click as he cocked it, and she couldn't move, frozen like a deer in the headlights.

"Sophie!" Mal screamed, throwing himself in front of her just as the gun went off.

She went down hard beneath his body, and she wondered whether he'd knocked her down or if Archer had done as he promised and shot them both with one bullet. She could feel the hot wetness pouring over her, and she realized Mal had been hit. He was so heavy she couldn't budge him, couldn't even move.

She could hear Archer's laugh. "What a hero!" he said in a mocking voice. "That poor fool must have really loved you." He was coming toward them—she could see his bloody foot dragging along the floor. "I'm afraid I did mislead him. There's no way I could allow either of you to live."

She was helpless, frozen, and too numb to care. His blood was wet and sticky, soaking into her clothes. He was dying, because of her.

Closer, closer. Step, drag . . . the smear of blood making a path across the room. "Maybe I'll blow off his skull too, and let you watch, before I finish with you," he said cheerfully. "I wouldn't want to do a job half-assed."

Half-assed. Maybe Mal wasn't dead yet. But if she didn't move he would be. With an inhuman effort she shoved, and Mal rolled off her, a dead weight, as Sophie leapt for the sofa. Bullets whined over her head, but she was able to duck behind the sofa in time. For a second she thought the gun was gone, but then her fingers closed around the butt, and she cocked it as she pulled it out from the cushions, aimed it, and fired, over and over and over again.

Each bullet hit Archer. He recoiled as they struck him, his chest, his neck, his face, the force of the last one spinning him around until he fell on the floor, his gun skittering far out of reach. A smart operative would wait where she was to make certain the danger was passed, but she wasn't smart and she wasn't an operative. She didn't even look at what remained of her husband; she went straight to Mal's body, turning him over.

Archer had shot him in the chest, and blood was pouring from the wound. He was unconscious, his color was pale, and when she fumbled for a pulse it was thin and thready.

"Don't you dare fucking die on me!" she screamed at him, ripping off her shirt and pressing it against the wound. "You goddamned noble idiot, you don't even like me. Why the fuck would you die to save me?"

His eyes fluttered open for a moment, focusing on her. "Who says I don't like you?" he whispered, and closed them again.

She cried then. Loud, miserable howls as she pressed the shirt against his wound. He didn't open his eyes again, the shirt was soaked with blood, and she was making so much noise she didn't hear the helicopter land, or the pounding of booted feet, until someone reached for her and tried to pull her away.

She fought them, screaming that she wouldn't leave Mal, but they were stronger, and people were bending over Mal, and she quieted. Whoever was holding her released her, and she fell back on the blood-streaked floor, numb.

To her left lay Archer's body, his long limbs splayed out, his mouth and eyes open in shock. On her right medics were working on Mal, at least she assumed that's what they were. They'd gotten a breathing tube in and someone was working a bag over his mouth, forcing air into his lungs. His shirt had been cut off, the gaping wound exposed, and it was even worse than she thought. She felt dizzy, sick, staring at him as they tried to jolt his heart into working again.

A hand touched her arm, and she yanked it away, but he was inexorable. She looked up to see a tall man with dark blond hair, a cane over one arm, and then she remembered who he was. She'd met him years ago when she'd trained with the Committee. His name was Madsen, Peter Madsen.

"Come with me, Miss Jordan," he said in crisp British accent. "There's nothing we can do for him now. They'll do everything possible."

"I'm not leaving him," she said fiercely.

"Yes," he said gently, "you are."

Everything went black.

Chapter Twenty-One

Sophie moved through the French Quarter in the rain, head down, newspapers clutched in her arms. Malcolm Gunnison had been dead for three months and Sophie was still in denial. Her therapist had warned her about it—the longer she refused to accept his death, the harder the eventual grieving would be, and Sophie had dutifully said yes, she knew, and she would work on it.

In fact, there wasn't any particular advantage in denial. Even if she couldn't believe he'd really died on that island, she was still grieving, alternating between anger and feeling numb. Pictures kept playing in her mind, Mal looking at her with that half smile, Mal on the floor, bleeding out. Her heart was twisting inside her, but damn it, he wasn't dead.

The trolley cars were packed in the rain. It was tourist season, close to Mardi Gras, and everyone in the city seemed amped up. Everyone except her.

Even the businesslike operatives in the house in the Garden District had lightened up, just a bit, but the mood wasn't catching. Sophie knew that sooner or later she was going to have to accept the truth, but until then she was just putting one foot in front of the other.

She got off at her stop and walked up Magazine Street to the old mansion that housed the new American branch of the Committee. The plaque outside said American Committee for the Preservation of

Democracy, but she doubted anyone was fooled. Apart from the occasional ballsy tourist who showed up requesting a tour, no one came around, no solicitors or religious fanatics, and those who did show up came in the back way.

She was one of the few people who used the front door, but then, she was part of the decoration. She'd been working in the front office, a supposed receptionist, for the past two months, with James Bishop and Matthew Ryder looking out for her. She knew she had Peter Madsen to thank for it, and she didn't give a fuck, but she knew she'd better do something with her time.

Her apartment in the French Quarter had seemed perfect until Mardi Gras started approaching, and each night the noise got worse. She had the firm conviction that by the weekend there'd be no sleeping at all.

"Morning, Sophie, darling," Remy Vartain said as he scooped the newspapers out of her arms. "Still raining out there?"

"Don't I look like a drowned rat?" she countered. She liked Remy, despite his charm and exceptional good looks. She wasn't in the mood to be charmed, but with Remy she couldn't help it. He made her laugh. The others, Bishop and Ryder, treated her a little like glass, as if she'd shatter with one nudge. They hadn't seen what she'd done to Archer MacDonald without blinking.

But no one was offering her a job as an operative, despite her training, and she didn't want one. She was just biding her time.

She had no family left—her elderly aunt had died the year she graduated from Sarah Lawrence. When she'd gone to work for the Committee, she'd severed any close friendships, and now she had nothing. Scratch that. She had a bank account so hefty that she always thought the number was a mistake.

Peter Madsen was now head of the Committee, and he had determined that she was still under its employment during her time with Archer, despite her rejecting her mission and their support. That entitled her to almost three years of hazard pay, and the Committee paid very well indeed.

She had a tentative plan. She was going to buy a house in the country, though for the life of her she couldn't decide where. She rejected the South—she'd had enough of warm sunshine to last her for a good many years. She wanted seasons again, blinding winter snowstorms and green hills and crystal blue lakes. She wanted to be miles away from civilization—she could make do with going out once a week for groceries. Sooner or later she was going to have to accept the truth about Malcolm, and she needed to be alone to do that. Someplace where she could go outside and scream and no one would come running. Someplace with water, so she could go kayaking in the early morning and then drink her coffee on a covered porch. Someplace to open the wound, let it bleed, and heal, if such a thing were possible.

She headed into the front office, pushing open the pocket doors that slid like silk on their tracks. Her ridiculously thin computer monitor awaited her, with its innocuous screensaver of alpine peaks and its magic button that accessed the closed-circuit cameras. She could lock this place down with one stroke of a key, something that astonished her. Archer hadn't let her near a computer, and with no commercial TV, no magazines, she had no idea how technology had changed in a few short years. She remembered the iPhone she had when she'd first been in London—it was a far cry from the skinny little sliver that rested in her purse.

She dumped her umbrella in the eighteenth-century umbrella stand, shook the excess water from her hair, and took her seat behind the computer. A moment later she was busy at her day's occupation, killing everything she came across in *Dark Souls Three*, the most brutal video game she could find. The body count rose, and Sophie smiled grimly.

"You about ready to get to work?" Madsen said as he slid behind the table at Malcolm Gunnison's favorite pub near the Committee's offices in London.

Mal shrugged, then cursed at the dull pain slicing through his shoulder. Archer's bullet had made a mess of it, and three surgeries later it was as close to normal as it was going to be. He was never going to enjoy a pickup game of basketball again, but all things considered, it could have been a lot worse. "I told you, I'm quitting."

"Yes, you told me. I didn't believe you."

Mal reached for his beer. "Why not? Don't you think someone can get burned out by all this? I want to quit before I lose my soul and become nothing more than a ghost wandering through life. Like you," he added with deceptive humor. In fact, the hardest decision in his life had ended up being a no-brainer. Something was dead inside him, and had been since they'd flown him off that fucking island, and nothing seemed to matter anymore. Staying in the business with an attitude like that was a short trip to failure and death. Not that he currently gave a shit about his own life, but he wasn't going to let his mistakes take down anyone else.

Madsen laughed. "My kids would disagree with you. They'd like it a hell of a lot better if I were a little less involved with them."

"Your fault for having so many goddamned children. You need to stop picking up strays wherever you go."

Madsen shrugged. "What can I say? Genny and I like our brood." He took a sip of his scotch. "So what can I do to talk you into staying? A raise?"

"I've got more money than I need and you know it," Mal said. "I need a break. I was thinking of going to the States for a while."

He didn't like Madsen's smug smile. "Heading down to New Orleans, are you?"

"Of course not," he said stiffly. "Sophie thinks I'm dead, and that's the best way to leave it. She's building herself a new life—she doesn't need reminders of the past." It had been another easy decision, he thought, showing nothing on his face. He was no good for her—he was well past the time that he could let himself care for anyone else, and Sophie needed someone to love her as she needed to be loved. Deserved to be loved. When he looked back at his life, he knew he didn't deserve shit.

Madsen laughed. "You're such a pathetic bastard. Sophie's wandering around like a lost soul, and you're moping over here. Why don't you grow a pair and admit it?"

"Admit what?" he said icily.

But Madsen wasn't about to come right out and say it. "If you haven't figured it out yet, then far be it from me to tell you. Next thing you know we'll be having sleepovers and you'll be fixing my hair."

Mal gave an unexpected bark of laughter. "I don't think so. Besides, I was thinking of heading up north. Maybe Montana."

"Full of survivalists and wackos. You could find plenty to do there."

Mal growled. "I've quit, remember. Starting today."

"I took you off the payroll last week," Madsen admitted. "I never really thought you'd change your mind, but I figured it was worth a try, and I promised Genny that I would."

Mal drained his beer. "Give her my love. She deserves better than a mangy old bastard like you."

Madsen grinned. "So she does. And give Sophie my best. She didn't think very highly of me when she woke up back in New Orleans and I told her you were dead, but I imagine she'll figure out where the blame falls."

"I'm not going to New Orleans."

"Have some crawfish étouffée for me."

Malcolm growled.

"This is the wrong city to live in if you don't like parades, *cher*," Remy said, leaning against the kitchen counter.

Sophie made a noncommittal noise as she waited for her coffee to squirt through the complicated machine. She couldn't believe all the changes in technology in such a short time, but this coffee machine was a definite improvement over the old way. "I'm just not in a festive mood."

"Nobody who lives in New Orleans can stay gloomy during Mardi Gras," Remy protested.

She gave him a withering glance. Remy was born and bred in New Orleans, full of sly charm and devilish wit, and he was so insanely gorgeous that any normal, red-blooded female would respond with a little mild flirtation. She couldn't even manage that much. "I'm not going to be in New Orleans for much longer," she said. "I'm moving to Oregon."

"I thought it was going to be Montana?"

"Bishop told me it was full of survivalists," she said gloomily.

"Well, shoot, honey, Oregon's full of aging hippies," Remy said cheerfully. "Not to mention that it rains all the time. How are you going to feel if you never see the sun?"

"The same," she said. "I probably won't even notice."

Remy sighed. "I consider you my greatest failure. I'm usually an expert at fixing broken hearts, but you just don't want to be fixed."

"He died, Remy," she said stonily, trying to get used to the words. "He didn't just walk out on me. That's a little harder to bounce back from."

Remy immediately looked contrite, which only made him more luscious. It really was a shame she couldn't appreciate him, Sophie thought wearily. "I'm sorry, darlin'. Of course you're right. I keep forgetting he's dead. But you have to know that Committee operatives make terrible partners. You're better off without him."

She gave him an outraged expression, and he held up his hands as if warding off an attack. "All right, *cher*, I know you loved him. But Malcolm Gunnison didn't look like a man who would ever settle down—he'd been in the life too long."

Sophie stared at him in shock. "Did you know him?"

"Why, sure. He stayed with us for two months before he headed out for Isla Mordita to go after MacDonald. Bishop was overseeing the operation with the London office. In fact, Gunnison was going to be assigned to this office when he got back. Too bad he changed his mind."

Sophie set her coffee down. "He didn't change his mind, Remy. He died." Damn, she hated those words. No matter how many times she tried to convince herself they were true, she never could feel it in her heart.

"Sorry," he said again. "So what are you going to do in Oregon? You've got so much money you probably don't ever have to work again. Wouldn't last me more than a couple of years, but then, I like my creature comforts. You're more on the penitential side."

"Remy . . ." she said in a dangerous voice.

"I know, I know," he said, sounding not the least bit sorry.

"I have to get back to my office."

"Why? You don't have any real work to do."

"I have bosses to kill in *Dark Souls Three*," she said grimly.

"You and your computer games. I can't get anywhere with that one—I think I'm more of a zombie guy. If you're going to pick a game, why don't you go for something a little less gruesome? Like *World of Warcraft*?"

"I like gruesome," she said, shoving her hair back from her face. "And I'm about to go get me some."

Remy moved fast, stationing himself by the door. "You still haven't told me what you're going to do in Oregon."

"Watch the storms over the Pacific Ocean, drink craft beer, and read anything I damned well please, as long as it's not written by a Russian." Remy would have no idea what she was talking about, but she didn't care. And then she softened. "You can come and visit me if you ever get tired of all this sunshine."

"It rains here plenty. Don't you remember a little storm named Katrina that did a number on this town?"

"I do," she said, feeling unaccountably guilty. She'd been in such a cesspool of misery that she'd stopped considering all the shit other people had gone through. Lots of people lose the one they love. And it wasn't as if he had given a flying fuck about her.

Who says I don't like you? Those had been his dying words, and for a declaration of true love, they left a lot to be desired. It didn't matter. She treasured those words like they were a Shakespearean sonnet.

"And frankly, I think you're a fool to refuse your husband's money. He didn't leave a will, and apart from his father you're his only heir. His father won't touch that money, and there's no reason you shouldn't enjoy it."

"It's blood money, Remy. And I don't need it, remember? I've got plenty."

"There's no such thing as too much money, darlin'," he said with the solemnity such a statement deserved.

She sighed. "We'll argue about it later. I'm going back to my office . . ." She was moving past him when he jumped in her way, startling her so much she sloshed hot coffee on both of them.

"Not quite yet, sugar buns."

She halted, staring up at him, a stern expression on her face. "What's going on, Remy?"

"Someone's coming from the London office," he said after a moment's hesitation.

"So?" she said. "Why does it matter to me? They've had almost a complete turnover since I trained there. The only one still there is . . . Peter Madsen," she ended on a depressed note. "Why is he here?"

"Above my pay grade, sugar. I just do what I'm told, and I was told to keep you busy this morning."

"Jesus Christ!" she exploded. "Why didn't someone just call me and tell me not to come in? Besides, why would Madsen be here? We don't have anything going on as far as I can tell. And what's it got to do with me?"

"Oh, there's always stuff beneath the surface. And I'm afraid Madsen's here to see you. He wants to talk to you about Gunnison's death."

"Absolutely not!" Her voice was rising, bordering on incipient hysteria, and she didn't care. "I know all I need to know. Archer shot him and he died. Case closed, story ended."

"Well, he must have some reason for coming all this way to talk to you. Maybe Malcolm left you money like everyone else has. You know operatives—they pick those of us without family or close friends." He sounded a little gloomy at the thought, and for a brief moment Sophie's dried and withered heart offered up a random beat.

"I'll be your friend, Remy," she said.

"Damn straight," he said. "And you can start by seeing Madsen. He's a stubborn sum'bitch and he won't leave until he does what he came for. And Bishop wants him gone. Can't have two chiefs in the same tribe, not with wild Indians like the rest of us.

"Your racial sensitivity is impressive," she said in a caustic voice. "But this little Indian is going back to her office and locking the pocket doors so no one can bother me."

"You think there's a creature in this house that can't pick any lock made? Even the cat could probably figure it out," Remy scoffed.

"Then I'll barricade it," she shot back. "And don't forget I've still got a gun. I've killed before and I can do it again."

"You're going to shoot Peter Madsen?" Remy emitted a hoot of laughter. "I'd like to see you try."

She shook her head. "I might shoot you instead."

For a moment he looked uncertain, and then he pushed his gorgeous curly hair away from his classical face, laughing. "I know you're a crack shot, darlin'."

"I didn't say it would be an accident," she said demurely. "My coffee's getting cold and I have creatures to kill. Are you going to let me go back to my office or am I going to have to get dangerous with you?"

His grin was charming, she acknowledged that. Just as she acknowledged that it didn't work on her. He glanced down at his watch, an impressive Rolex that looked almost real. "I give up. Don't say I didn't warn you, though."

"What were you supposed to do, keep me here until Peter Madsen was ready to see me?"

Remy shrugged. "Not exactly, *cher*." He moved out of the way, bowing extravagantly. "Enjoy yourself, sugar."

She made a derisive noise, stopped as she passed him to give him a kiss on his cheek, and headed out the door, her heart hammering. It wasn't Peter Madsen's fault that he had to be the one to tell her Malcolm was gone, but he'd been responsible for taking her last few minutes with him away from her, and she'd never forgive him for that. If he thought she was willing to see him, then he was in for a major disappointment.

But the hall was empty except for one of the guards standing between the front door and the closed pocket doors to her office. "Hey, Alphonse," she said. "Have you seen Peter Madsen around? I don't want to run into him."

"Madsen, Miss Jordan? He's not here. At least, not that I know of."

Sophie frowned. Alphonse would never lie to her, but if Madsen was in town, he would most certainly know it. This odd day was getting even odder, and she didn't like it. "I must have misunderstood," she said, sliding one of the pocket doors open. "I'm going to lock the doors, just in case. I've got a lot of work and I don't want anyone disturbing me."

Alphonse grinned. "I don't know how you can play that game. I couldn't get past the first level, and I've been gaming most of my life. You haven't been near a machine in years."

"Ah, but I've got a lot of rage to get rid of," she said. "Thanks, Alphonse." She stepped into the room and slid the doors shut again, turning the lock. She looked to either side of her, wondering if there was anything she could use to block the entrance, when the unmistakable sound of her game came to her ears. It was muffled, as if coming through someone's earphones, and she turned around slowly.

Malcolm sat in her chair, his gorgeous green eyes trained on the screen, his hands busy with her controller, not even bothering to glance up at her. He was dressed casually in a loose shirt and presumably jeans, and his left arm was in a sling. It didn't even seem to be slowing him down.

She couldn't move, couldn't breathe. It shouldn't have come as a surprise—she'd known deep down somewhere he wasn't dead. But for some reason a wave of dizziness had washed over her, and she swayed slightly, putting a surreptitious hand behind her to steady herself against the locked doors, as she tried to gather her shocked senses.

She could hear the muffled music that signaled the end of one stage and the death of one more evil boss, and then he deigned to look up. He'd known she was there all along, of course. He would have known she was there if he'd been comatose. Committee agents were just that good.

She considered her options. Her favorite, bursting into noisy sobs of relief, was rejected immediately. Dropping to the floor in a dead faint would give her a little time to get used to this miraculous return from the dead and decide how to respond, but she was already past the first rush of shock and joy and well into rage at grieving for him, aching for him. If she had her gun with her she could shoot him, but that was back at her apartment in the French Quarter.

She couldn't think of anything to say that didn't involve screaming rage and wild tears, so she said nothing, simply leaned back against the door. She'd set the three locks—she wouldn't be able to make a fast escape, and she suspected he wasn't about to let her walk out.

He took off the headphones and set them on the desk, and his eyes met hers, and she had no idea what he was thinking. Nothing had changed. "I would have thought you'd be on level four by now," he said.

Okay. "I only started it on Monday. I had to get through *Dark Souls One* and *Dark Souls Two* first." Her voice was the tiniest bit shaky, but most people would never notice. Malcolm would.

"I finished it in two days."

"Of course you did. Did you rise from the grave just to tell me how good you are at video games?"

He had the fucking gall to look faintly amused. "Madsen said you didn't believe him."

She realized with sudden shock that deep down inside she really *had* believed him, and she'd spent untold reserves of energy to keep her state of denial. Suddenly she no longer needed to do so—he was really there, and she felt weak.

Yes, and she was going to pass out in front of him? Not in this lifetime or any other. "It seemed too good to be true," she said calmly.

He laughed. "That's pretty harsh for the woman who loves me."

Shit, he remembers. Of course he does—he probably never forgets a thing. "I was drunk," she said.

"No you weren't. And you almost got killed trying to save my ass."

"Then we're even. You took a bullet for me."

He shrugged, and then winced. He looked thinner, a little older, and she remembered the gaping wound in his chest. It would have taken time for him to recover from something like that, and he looked like he wasn't quite there yet.

"Well, if you came by to tell me you're alive, then thank you very much and you can go." She took a sip of the coffee in her hand. It was cool by now, but she could hardly taste it. At least she looked nonchalant.

He pushed the chair back from the desk and rose, and she'd forgotten how tall and lean he was. How he moved with such feline grace. How he stalked toward her, but she wasn't going to back away from him, wasn't going to show any reaction at all. In fact, she took a couple of steps away from the door. She didn't need it to hold her up—she could do this, she knew she could. She'd been living a lie for the past three months, ever since she'd left the island, and she should have no problem keeping it up.

He came right up to her, so close she could feel the heat from his body. His shirt was open at the neck, and she could see the fine-grained skin, the place where she'd bit him when he'd been driving into her, both of them covered with sweat and shaking with love and lust. At least on her part. It had just been temporary lust on his. Too bad neither of her emotions had proved temporary.

"Is Peter Madsen really here?" she asked after a long silence while he just stood there, looking at her.

"In New Orleans? Hell, no. He's afraid of you. Besides, he didn't have anything to do here."

She almost wanted to smile, but there was nothing to smile about. She'd been tricked, her stupid emotions mocked. "He has good reason to be afraid. What about you?"

He considered for a long moment, then shook his head. "No, you don't scare me."

Annoyance was building inside her, something she welcomed, something that would drive out her desperate need to throw herself into his arms and weep on his chest. "No, I mean do you have anything to do here, or is this merely a social visit? Your way of gloating."

"What would I be gloating about?"

Over the fact that she loved him and he didn't care. She remembered those words too. "Cheating death one more time. Though I imagine that's old hat for you by now. You probably don't even think you're mortal."

"I'm mortal," he said. "I figure most of my nine lives have run out. Better to pack it in than to tempt fate."

"So you've come by to announce your retirement? Lovely. I'll get you a gold watch. I can afford one—Peter Madsen decided to give me back pay."

"I know."

They were two simple words, but just like that she knew the truth. "It was your idea, wasn't it?" she said in an accusing voice, like he'd committed a heinous crime.

"It might have been."

More sympathy from the devil. She blew it off. "Then I'll definitely get you that gold watch. Anything else? I have work to do." *Monsters to kill*, she thought. She was going to make the "Big Bad" in the video game Malcolm.

"No, I think that's it," he said, moving past her and heading toward the door without even touching her. She watched him go, her mouth agape in astonishment.

"You came all the way from England just to tell me that?" she demanded.

He turned to look at her. "Yup. How long will it take you to get packed?"

She just stared at him like an idiot. "I beg your pardon?"

"I said, how long will it take you to get packed? I bought a midsized SUV this morning and it's already loaded. I hope you pack light—there's not much space left."

She felt fury and confusion bubble up. "And why should I be packing at all? Where do you think I'd want to go?"

"I figured we'd check out Oregon first—Remy said you had an interest in seeing it. If that doesn't work, we'll try other places until we find something that feels right."

She felt dizzy, like Alice down the rabbit hole. "Why in God's name do you think I would go anywhere with you?" Her voice had risen just a bit, and she wondered how many people were out there with their ears to the door. Probably none—the entire house had a better surveillance system than Archer's, and they were probably all upstairs watching on the closed-circuit TV.

"Because you love me," he said impatiently. "Remember?"

"I remember. I got over it." She was cold, shaking, but she wasn't going to let him see it.

His smile was absolutely dazzling, a smile she'd never seen from him before. "No, you didn't. But I got over my severe case of head up my ass and came back to get you because whether I like it or not, I love you too. Now get packed. I want to get out of town before they start another damned parade."

For a moment she didn't move. He didn't mean it, he couldn't. This was just a game, a way to toy with her . . . But he wasn't Archer. He was Mal, and he was absolutely serious, despite the unexpected, lighthearted expression in his face. "And you expect me to come with you, just like that?" she said in a dangerous voice, afraid to believe him, afraid to love him, suddenly afraid of everything when she'd always been fearless.

"Just like that," he agreed in a soft voice.

Now he was showing her sweetness. Now he was opening up when she had to go through his death for that dubious pleasure. Where was her gun when she needed it? she thought, trying to summon her rage. She'd been so miserable, for so long, and none of it had been necessary if he actually loved her.

The gun was where it belonged, locked up and out of the way. She looked at the man she loved. "You're a rat bastard," she said in a shaky voice that sounded suspiciously like love.

"I'm the one who told you that."

"So you did." She took a step, coming right up to him, then reached up and grabbed his long hair in her fist, yanking his head down so that she could put her mouth against his in a rough, claiming kiss. He kissed her back, and her entire body was humming with it, with love and lust and joy and fear. She could do this. She could love him. She didn't have to be afraid.

When she finally pulled back he was grinning at her. "Running out of time here, sweetheart," he said.

"It'll take me five minutes," she said, knowing she had stupid tears in her eyes. "Don't leave without me."

"Never," he said. And she believed him.